W9-BTS-722

DALE BROWN

PLAN OF ATTACK

A Novel

AVON BOOKS
An Imprint of HarperCollins*Publishers*

AVON BOOKS
An Imprint of HarperCollins*Publishers*
10 East 53rd Street
New York, New York 10022-5299

Copyright © 2004 by Air Battle Force Inc.
Author photo by Robert Love
ISBN: 0-06-050292-4
www.avonbooks.com

First Avon Books paperback printing: January 2005
First William Morrow hardcover printing: June 2004

Avon Trademark Reg. U.S. Pat. Off. and in Other Countries, Marca Registrada, Hecho en U.S.A.
HarperCollins® is a registered trademark of HarperCollins Publishers Inc.

Printed in the U.S.A.

10 9 8 7 6 5 4 3 2 1

This novel is dedicated to the men and women serving as part of Operation Enduring Freedom and Operation Iraqi Freedom, and to their families and loved ones. Thank you all for your service and sacrifice.

This is also dedicated to the peacemakers of all nations who are still wise and bold enough to know that free nations must still keep their swords sharp, their eyes open, and their resolve strong in order to be prepared to combat the evil in the world.

ACKNOWLEDGMENTS

Thanks to Gene and Alison Pretti, Steve and Chris Johnson, and Dave and Cheryl Duffield for their generosity.

Special thanks to William Dunsmore, Major, U.S. Air Force (retired), for his invaluable insights and experiences.

AUTHOR'S NOTE

CAST OF CHARACTERS

Brigadier General Patrick McLanahan, commander, 966th Information Warfare Wing; plans intelligence operations; 4 ops groups, 1 intel group

Major General Gary Houser, commander, Air Intelligence Agency

Colonel Trevor Griffin, deputy commander, 966th Information Warfare Wing, Lackland AFB

Command CMSgt Harold Bayless, Command NCOIC

Chief Master Sergeant Donald Saks, NCOIC, National Air Intelligence Center, WPAFB; produces foreign aerospace intel for DoD

Brigadier General David Luger, commander, First Air Battle Force

Brigadier General Rebecca Furness, commander, 111th Attack Wing; commander, 1 ABF/Air Operations

Colonel Hal Briggs, commander, 1 ABF/Ground Operations

Sergeant Major Chris Wohl, NCOIC, 1 ABF/GO

First Lieutenant Mark Bastian, Ground Ops squad leader

Staff Sergeant Emily Angel, ABF Ground Ops

Tech Sergeant James "JD" Daniels

Lance Corporal Johnny "Hulk" Morris

Colonel Daren Mace, Ops Group commander, 111th Attack Wing

Lieutenant Colonel Samantha Hellion, Fifty-first Bomb
    Squadron (EB-1C)

Colonel Nancy Cheshire, commander, Fifty-second Bomb
    Squadron (EB-52 and AL-52)
Colonel Kelvin Carter, operations officer, Fifty-second
    Bomb Squadron, AL-52 AC
Lieutenant Colonel Summer O'Dea, EB-52 AC
Major Matthew Whitley, EB-52 remote-control technician
Major Frankie "Zipper" Tarantino, AL-52 MC
Captain Johnny "Soccer" Sammis, EB-52 MC

U.S. Marine Corps Captain Ted Merritt, Marine Special
    Purpose Forces platoon leader

Lieutenant General Terrill Samson, commander, Eighth Air
    Force
Brigadier General Charles C. Zoltrane, acting deputy
    commander and operations officer, Eighth Air
    Force

General Charles F. "Cuz" Kuzner, chief of staff, USAF

General Thomas "Turbo" Muskoka, commander, Air
    Combat Command
Lieutenant General Leah "Skyy" Fortuna, deputy
    commander, Air Combat Command

Admiral Charles Andover, chief of Naval Operations
General Walter Wollensky, commander, U.S. Space
    Command
General Randall Shepard, commander, North American
    Aerospace Defense Command; also commander of U.S.
    Northern Command
Colonel Joanna Kearsage, C-crew command director,
    Cheyenne Mountain Operations Center, Cheyenne
    Mountain Air Force Station

Lieutenant Colonel Susan Paige, C-crew commander, Air Warning Center, NORAD, Cheyenne Mountain Air Force Base, Colorado

Brigadier General Jerrod Richland, E-4 AOC battle staff commander

Thomas Nathaniel Thorn, president of the United States
Robert Goff, secretary of defense
Richard W. Venti, USAF general, chairman of Joint Chiefs of Staff
Admiral Charles Andover, chief of Naval Operations
Douglas R. Morgan, director of Central Intelligence
Maureen Hershel, secretary of state
Darrow Horton, attorney general

RUSSIANS
General Anatoliy Gryzlov, president of the Russian Federation
Army General Nikolai Stepashin, chief of staff of the Russian military and commander, ministry of state security (chief of all intelligence bureaus)

Aviatskiy Kapitan Leytenant Josef Leborov, Tu-95MS-16 pilot
Aviatskiy Starshij Leytenant Yuri Bodorev, his copilot

TURKMEN STARSHIY LEYTENANT
General Jalaluddin Turabi, interim commander of Turkmen armed forces
Abdul Dendara, his aide

AIRCRAFT AND WEAPONS
MV-32 PAVE DASHER tilt-jet special-operations transport, cruise speed 320 KIAS, endurance 5 hours (conventional

takeoff/vertical landing/vertical takeoff/vertical landing), carries 18 combat-ready troops plus crew of three; cargo ramp allows Humvee-size vehicles to fit inside; 2 retractable weapons pods for defensive or attack missiles; 1 20-millimeter Gatling gun in steerable chin turret; satellite and inertial navigation plus imaging-infrared sensor and millimeter-wave radar allows global terrain-following flight

MQ-35 CONDOR air-launched special-operations transport, cruise speed 300 KIAS, endurance 3 hours (glide insertion/ conventional takeoff from rough field/conventional landing on rough field); carries 4 combat-ready troops plus up to 260 pounds of cargo; remotely piloted; mission-adaptive skin and lifting-body technology allows aircraft to be controlled without wings or flight-control surfaces; small turbojet engine and tricycle landing gear allows aircraft to take off from unimproved fields

RAQ-15 StealthHawk long-range reconnaissance and attack cruise missile; turbojet engine, 600 KIAS max cruise speed, max range 2,000 miles; lifting-body design, mission-adaptive flight controls; carries 6 AGM-211 mini-Maverick guided attack missiles; 2 can be carried by EB-52 Megafortress bombers on wing pylons or 2 in center bomb bay of EB-1C Vampire bomber; reloadable and refuelable by EB-1C bombers; launch weight 3,500 pounds

AGM-211 mini-Maverick, small TV-guided attack missile, 28-pound thermium nitrate (TN) warhead, glide- and rocket-boosted, 6-mile range

AGM-165 Longhorn TV- and IIR-guided attack missile, 200-pound TN warhead, MMW radar guidance, 60-mile range, 2,000 pounds each

AIM-120 Scorpion AMRAAM air-to-air missile, 50-pound warhead, 35 miles max range, triple-mode active radar, passive radar, or infrared, max speed Mach 3, 350 pounds each

AIM-154 Anaconda long-range radar-guided air-to-air missile, 50-pound TN warhead, 150-mile max range, ramjet engine, active-passive radar/IR guidance, max speed Mach 5, weight 6,000 pounds

AGM-177 Wolverine cruise missile, turbojet powered, max 50-mile range, 3 weapon bays, IIR or MMW radar terminal guidance, 2,000 pounds

AGM-154 Joint Standoff Weapon (JSOW), range 15 to 40 miles depending on release altitude, 1,500 pounds, unpowered glide weapon, carries 200 antipersonnel/ antivehicle bomblets, 10 BLU-108/B antiarmor submunitions, or 500-pound high explosive; EB-52, B-2, or EB-1C can carry 8 on rotary launcher

ABM-3 Lancelot air-launched anti-ballistic-missile weapon, 200-mile range, plasma-yield or conventional warheads, 3,000-pound launch weight

Russian:
AS-17 "Krypton" (Kh-31P) medium-range air-launched antiradar missile, max 120-mile range, speed in excess of Mach 3, 225-pound blast/fragmentation warhead; carried by Tu-22M Backfire bombers

AS-X-19 "Koala" (Kh-90) long-range air-launched attack missile, ramjet powered, max range 1,800 miles, speed in excess of Mach 8, 1-kiloton nuclear warhead with delayed trigger fuze and armored nose cap, designed for destroying deep underground or armored facilities; two carried by Tu-95 Bear bombers

AS-16 "Kickback" (Kh-15) inertially guided supersonic
attack missile, 90-mile range, max speed Mach 2, 300-pound
high-explosive warhead or 1-kiloton nuclear warhead;
Tu-160 bomber can carry 24 internally on rotary launcher

PLAN OF
ATTACK

PROLOGUE

BATTLE MOUNTAIN AIR RESERVE BASE, NEVADA
June 2004

"SA-17 target-detection radar, twelve o'clock, fifty miles, no problem, well below detection threshold . . . oh, wow, a newcomer, SA-12 surveillance radar, one o'clock, eighty-five miles," the reconnaissance technician reported. The guy looked all of nineteen years old and sounded even younger. He could've been commenting on the appearance of aliens in a video game—he was neither excited nor surprised, just gleefully energized. "SA-12 datalink signals being transmitted . . . still not locked on, but he knows we're out here. He— Wait, radar's down. He shut it off in a big hurry."

"Well, well—the Russkies sneaked an SA-12 into the theater," Major General Patrick McLanahan remarked. He was well accustomed to the youthful expressions and seemingly laid-back style of his soldiers, and he tried not to impart his own "red alert" mentality on them. The forty-seven-year-old two-star Air Force general typed in commands on his computer terminal, calling up any additional information on this new contact. "Possibly a full SA-12 battery—six transporter-erector-launchers plus five loader-launchers tied into a surveillance radar vehicle, sector-scanning radar vehicle, and command post. He's pretty far outside Ashkhabad—it's obviously not intended to protect Russian forces in the capital. It's a clear violation."

"They're moving the heavy guns a little farther east every day," Air Force Colonel Daren Mace remarked. The fifty-one-year-old Air Force veteran watched as the large, full-color tactical display updated itself with the location and identification of the new Russian surface-to-air missile unit. The SA-12, similar in performance to the American Patriot antiaircraft system, was one of the Russian Federation's most advanced surface-to-air missile systems, capable of destroying large aircraft out as far as sixty miles. "You'd think they didn't want us out there watching them or something." He made a few inputs on his own keyboard. "The task force has been updated with the new intel, and we've sent warnings to all the United Nations participants," he went on. "The Russians are threatening past the sixtieth meridian now with the SA-12, sir. If they keep this up, they'll have surface-to-air missile coverage over Mary itself in just a few days."

Patrick nodded. The Republic of Turkmenistan had been cut in half since the Taliban invasion last year, with the Turkmen government and military virtually exiled to the city of Mary in the east and the Army of the Russian Federation in control of the capital city of Ashkhabad in the west. The United Nations Security Council had ordered all parties to stand fast until peacekeeping forces could be moved into the country to try to sort everything out, and to everyone's surprise the resolution passed without a veto from Russia. Now it appeared that the Russians were violating the order and moving steadily eastward, taking steps to control the skies first and then slowly taking more and more of the countryside. "I'll go to Eighth Air Force *again* and make sure they know that the Russians haven't stopped pushing east."

"Think that'll do any good, sir?" Daren asked. "We've painted a pretty clear picture of the Russians moving east across Turkmenistan, in violation of the Security Council's resolution. The SA-12 is a lot more than a tactical defensive weapon—one battery can shut off two hundred thousand cubic miles of airspace."

"Our job is to surveille, monitor, analyze, and report—not attack," Patrick said with a hint of weariness in his voice as he keyed in commands to submit a report to Eighth Air Force's senior duty controller. Eighth Air Force, located in Shreveport, Louisiana, was the Air Force major command in charge of all of America's heavy bomber forces. "I'm taking it upon myself to have the assets in place in case we're asked to respond. I have a feeling I'm lucky to continue to be doing *that*." Daren Mace said nothing—he knew that the general was *definitely* correct.

Patrick, Daren, and their technical crew were conducting an aerial surveillance and reconnaissance mission over central Turkmenistan, a former Soviet Central Asian republic—but they were safe and secure in the BATMAN, or Battle Management Center, at Battle Mountain Air Reserve Base in north-central Nevada. The aircraft flying over Turkmenistan was a QB-1C Vampire III, a highly modified unmanned B-1 bomber loaded with electronic surveillance and monitoring equipment. Eavesdropping equipment allowed Patrick to intercept signals from a wide variety of sources, and the bomber's laser radar, or LADAR, allowed them to take incredibly detailed images of ground and air targets from long range.

Along with defensive weapons—six AIM-120 Advanced Medium Range Air-to-Air Missiles (AMRAAMs) on external fuselage hardpoints—the Vampire bomber carried two StealthHawk UCAVs (Unmanned Combat Air Vehicles) on a special rotary launcher in its center bomb bay. Resembling wide, fat, winged surfboards, the StealthHawk drones carried small but powerful precision-guided missiles and cluster munitions to attack hostile ground targets. The StealthHawks could be retrieved, refueled, and rearmed inside the Vampire, allowing each drone to attack dozens of targets while the mother ship stayed well out of range of antiaircraft threats.

Patrick punched the radio channel command, entered a password, waited a few moments until the secure channels synchronized, then spoke, "Fortress, this is Avenger, secure."

"Avenger, Fortress is secure," the Eighth Air Force senior controller on duty responded.

"How are you tonight, Taylor?"

"Just fine, General," Air Force Lieutenant Colonel Taylor Viner replied. Taylor Rose Viner was a young and talented aerospace engineer and command pilot that Patrick had tried for years to recruit to Dreamland, the top-secret weapon center in Nevada, but the mother of twin boys had opted for a halfway normal family life as one of the shift commanders in charge of Eighth Air Force's command center. "Go ahead, sir."

"We've detected a new SAM site in central Turkmenistan, an SA-12 less than forty miles outside the city of Mary," Patrick said. "It's not a threat to task-force aircraft right now, but that's only because we're stealthier than the average bear. If we put up any standard reconnaissance aircraft, they'd be dead meat."

"The Security Council resolution prohibits Russian forces from approaching closer than fifty kilometers from Mary—that's thirty miles," Viner said. "He's legal."

"But an SA-12 is a threat to large aircraft out to forty miles, and that means over the city of Mary," Patrick said.

"I understand, sir," Viner said. "I'm not arguing, only playing devil's advocate." She was also gently reminding Patrick of the first likely question the Eighth Air Force commanders would ask if she woke them up with this information. "What do you want to do, sir?"

"I'm requesting permission to launch a StealthHawk UCAV over the city in an effort to ascertain the Russians' intent."

"UCAV? You've got UCAVs on board the task-force aircraft, sir?" Taylor asked with surprise. She paused for a moment as she typed on her own computer terminal, then added, "Sir, there's nothing on the frag order about UCAVs. Are they armed, sir?" Patrick hesitated—and that's all Viner needed to know. "General, my recommendation to you would be to launch another aircraft immediately that is armed exactly per the frag order to replace the one you have on station."

"The frag order doesn't prohibit us from carrying UCAVs, and it does permit us to carry defensive weapons."

"Yes, sir," Viner replied, in a tone of voice that clearly said, The bosses aren't going to like that argument one bit. "Shall I upchannel your observations and request, sir, or would you like to continue monitoring the situation?"

Taylor was making one last attempt to dissuade Patrick from taking any action, and Patrick decided she was right. "We'll continue monitoring the situation, Colonel," Patrick said. "You can put in your report that we have StealthHawk UCAVs on board the Bobcat patrol aircraft and that we are ready to respond immediately if necessary. Please mark the SA-12 battery-contact report 'urgent' and let them know we're standing by."

"Yes, sir," Viner responded. "Anything else to report, sir?"

"No, Taylor. Ops normal otherwise. We're standing by to respond."

"Roger that, sir. Fortress clear."

"Avenger standing by." Patrick sat back in his seat and studied the displays in front of him. "Well, Daren," he said to Mace beside him, "I sure hope I didn't piss off the brass—any more than I already have."

"If you'll pardon an unsolicited observation, sir, I think they're probably going to be perpetually pissed at you, whether or not you launched the Vampires with UCAVs," Daren observed. Patrick nodded in agreement. He was right: This whole mission was a no-win situation from day one, and Patrick was the center of the shit storm.

The United Nations Security Council resolution ordered aerial observation of Turkmenistan only. President Thomas Thorn, in a surprise move, pledged support, and the council accepted. The secretary of defense ordered U.S. Central Command, the major command in charge of military operations in Central Asia, to set up round-the-clock reconnaissance; Central Command in turn tapped the U.S. Air Force to perform the reconnaissance task.

At first the Air Force tasked Twelfth Air Force, the Air Combat Command headquarters that owned long-range reconnaissance aircraft, to plan a reconnaissance schedule. Twelfth Air Force built a plan to deploy its conventional reconnaissance aircraft—the unmanned RQ-4A Global Hawk, the U-2 "Dragon Lady" spy plane, the RC-135 RIVET JOINT electronic reconnaissance plane, and the E-8 Joint STARS (Surveillance and Targeting Radar System) ground-reconnaissance aircraft. With a combination of these aircraft over Turkmenistan, augmented with satellite reconnaissance, they'd have a complete, 24/7 real-time picture of the situation there.

But the 111th Bomb Wing's aircraft, already deployed to Diego Garcia during the initial conflict in Turkmenistan, offered so much more than just simple surveillance. An unmanned QAL-52 Dragon airborne-laser aircraft could protect as much as 20 *million* cubic miles of airspace from ballistic missiles, cruise missiles, aircraft, and even some ground targets; the unmanned QB-1C and QB-52 "flying battleships" each provided as much offensive and defensive firepower as a flight of tactical fighters. At Patrick McLanahan's urging, Central Command vetoed Twelfth Air Force's plans and ordered Eighth Air Force, in charge of the Air Force's long-range bombers, to deploy McLanahan's Air Battle Force to patrol Turkmenistan. The high-tech bombers of the 111th Bomb Wing had acquitted themselves well in the opening conflict with the Russians, and this was seen as a reward for their efforts; besides, they were already in place and knew the tactical situation thoroughly.

This decision managed to upset both Eighth and Twelfth Air Force commanders, although they had no choice but to accept it. Eighth Air Force had its own fleet of strike aircraft, of course—160 long-range B-1B, B-52, and B-2 bombers and several hundred aerial-refueling tankers, along with a dazzling array of cruise missiles and precision-guided munitions. But they were all back in the States or providing long-range patrol duties with U.S. Navy Surface Action Groups around the world.

Although administratively part of the Air Reserve Forces—most of the men and women in the Wing were part of the Nevada Air National Guard—the 111th Bomb Wing operationally belonged to Eighth Air Force. But when it came down to it, no one at Eighth Air Force knew how to deploy or fight with the high-tech gadgets at Battle Mountain Air Reserve Base. They had no choice but to place Major General Patrick McLanahan in charge of the operation, reporting directly to Eighth Air Force headquarters.

The decision to let Patrick's Air Battle Force patrol Turkmenistan created a much more effective presence there for far less cost than Twelfth Air Force's planned operation, but the decision did not sit well with many Air Force general officers. No doubt they were all waiting for Patrick and his fleet of robot planes to fail.

Daren Mace let Patrick stew in silence for several long moments. Daren was a bit older than Patrick, but his Air Force career had not been nearly as successful or dynamic—until he met up with the young two-star general. Now, as operations officer of the 111th Bomb Wing, Daren Mace commanded a growing fleet of the most high-tech warplanes on the planet, the majority of which were created by Patrick McLanahan in the supersecret desert research center at Elliott Air Force Base in Groom Lake, Nevada, commonly known as Dreamland. A few years ago, aerial-warfare expert Mace had made his living flipping slides and making coffee for generals and administrators in the Pentagon. Now those same generals and bean-counting bureaucrats were coming to him asking for answers to America's tough defense problems.

"Want to bring that Vampire home," Daren asked, "and replace it with one without StealthHawks aboard?"

Patrick looked as if he didn't hear Mace. He was staring intently at the large, full-color tactical situation display, with the new SA-12 battery in the center. Finally he pointed at the screen on the wall before him. "You see anything wrong with how that SA-12 is deployed, Daren?" he asked.

Daren studied the display. Something had been nagging at him ever since the surface-to-air missile battery had been detected. The SA-12's precise position was plotted on the screen, along with a circle representing the maximum effective range of the two-stage solid-propellant Russian 9M82 antiaircraft missile, a larger but almost direct copy of the American Patriot missile. "Well, I wouldn't have put it there myself," Daren said a few moments later.

"Why?"

"It's too far south," Daren replied. "If we were going to fly a strike mission against Russian forces coming from Ashkhabad, we could easily circumnavigate that SA-12."

"Which tells you . . . ?"

"That . . . maybe the Russians have another SA-12 battery farther north?"

"Exactly," Patrick said. "How many batteries can a single SA-12 command post control?"

"Up to four—almost a hundred missiles total."

"We might have two or three more batteries sneaking their way east as we speak." Patrick pointed at several laser-radar returns well north of the SA-12 battery. "There's a bunch of newcomers up there, but we haven't identified them yet—"

"Because they haven't broadcast any radar or radio

datalink signals," Daren said. "They could be anything—
tanks, SCUDs, SAMs, camels—but if they didn't flash a
radar or broadcast what we think might be a fire-control
datalink signal, we left it alone until we had time to give it a
closer look."

"But the SA-12 could use a hardwired cable datalink,
which we couldn't detect. They could be ready to fire within
seconds," Patrick said. He pointed at the screen on his console. "I count ten vehicles in this area and twelve in this general area here. They could be SA-12 batteries, sitting silent.
I wish we had authorization to send some Tin Man recon
units into the area." But that was not going to happen. Part of
Patrick's Air Battle Force, the Tin Men were small commando teams outfitted with electronic battle armor, sophisticated sensor systems, and high-tech infantry weapons. They
could move quietly, survive in extremely hostile situations,
and reconnoiter large areas far behind enemy lines very
quickly. Naturally, the Russians didn't want them anywhere
near their troops. They convinced the United Nations Security Council that the Tin Men were nothing but search-and-
destroy squads, not a monitoring team, and so were
forbidden to enter the theater of operations at all.

"I think it might be time to take a look," Daren said.
"Eighth Air Force might squawk if we launch a Stealth-
Hawk, but if we move the Vampire bomber in for a closer
look . . ."

"Do it," Patrick said.

Daren smiled and pulled his headset microphone closer to
his lips, issuing orders to the technicians in the "virtual
cockpit" behind him in the Battle Mountain Battle Management Center. The QB-1C Vampire III bomber normally
operated under a preprogrammed flight plan written and
uploaded on the ground, which commanded the bomber to
patrol a certain area for a certain amount of time, then return
for refueling or landing. But it took only moments for the
technicians in the ground-based "cockpit" of the big bomber

to change the flight plan and radio it to the bomber via secure satellite transmission.

Moments later Patrick and Daren watched as the unmanned Vampire bomber began moving farther and farther north. It took almost thirty minutes to change the patrol orbit a hundred miles north. "Laser radar transmitting . . . LADAR identifies the vehicles as transports. No SA-12s."

"Get it in closer," Patrick said. "I want a detailed identification."

"Roger." Daren issued more orders, and they watched as the Vampire bomber moved even closer to the suspect vehicles—now within twenty miles of the unidentified "transports." "LADAR now classifying some of the vehicles as transporter-erector-launchers," Daren reported. "We might have something here. What next, General? You want one of the StealthHawks to make a pass now?"

"Not quite yet," Patrick responded. He thought for a moment, then, "Open the bomb doors."

"That should get their attention," Daren said. Into his microphone he ordered, "Send to Bobcat Zero-seven: open center bomb-bay doors. Do not launch UCAVs. Repeat, do not launch UCAVs."

The QB-1C Vampire III bomber had the radar cross-section smaller than a bird—until one of its three sets of bomb-bay doors were opened. Once that happened, its radar size increased a thousandfold. Radar energy bounced and reflected inside the bomb bay, making the bomber's apparent size on radar jump exponentially. Seconds after Daren issued the order, they heard a computer voice in their headsets: *"Warning, threat radar, SA-12, eleven o'clock, twenty-two miles, surveillance scan . . . warning, datalink active, SA-12, eleven o'clock, twenty-one miles."*

"There it is," Daren remarked. "You were right, sir—they

have another SA-12 system farther north. And it's a lot closer to Mary. They have full radar and antiaircraft-missile coverage of the city now." He hit his intercom button. "Bobcat Zero-seven, close bomb doors, activate all defensive countermeasures, and get out of there *fast*." He knew that the flight-control techs would simply take manual control of the Vampire and fly it directly away from the SA-12, while at the same time reprogramming the flight plan for a low-level evasive dash. "What do you want to do with the SA-12 batteries, General?"

"Kill them, Colonel," Patrick said simply, punching up the datalink code for Eighth Air Force headquarters again. "It's an unidentified hostile threat that is not authorized by United Nations resolution. Destroy it. Command vehicle first, then the radars, and then the missiles. I'll notify Eighth Air Force of our actions."

"Yes, *sir*," Daren responded enthusiastically. On the secure command link, he ordered, "Bobcat Zero-seven, this is Bobcat. Designate the SA-12 contacts as hostiles and attack. Repeat, designate all SA-12 contacts as hostile and attack. We think they rolled an entire brigade into the area. If they did, I want them all found, and I want them to die soonest. Order of target priority: command-post vehicle, missile-control radars, scanning radars, and launchers." The Vampire flight technicians acknowledged the order and hurriedly reprogrammed both the Vampire and its StealthHawks for the attack.

The Vampire began a fast turn to the east and a rapid descent. The tactical display showed the lethal-range ring of the SA-12 system—as the Vampire descended, the ring was getting smaller, but the bomber was still well within kill range. The display suddenly showed the Vampire's rate of descent slowing dramatically. Daren was about to ask why when he realized that Bobcat Zero-seven had to almost level off to launch its StealthHawks—the UCAVs could not safely leave the center bomb bay with the bomber in a steep descent. "First StealthHawk away . . ."

"Hurry, damn it, *hurry,*" Patrick breathed.

"Warning, SA-12 missile guidance radar, six o'clock, thirty miles," the computer blared. *"Warning, missile launch . . . warning, second missile launch!"*

"Second StealthHawk away . . ." Moments later the icon representing Bobcat Zero-seven disappeared. "Lost contact with Bobcat Zero-seven," the flight-control tech reported. "Looks like both SA-12 missiles hit dead on."

Daren Mace slammed a fist into a palm and swore loudly. "I don't want to see anything but smoking holes in the ground where those SA-12s are!" he shouted.

"Take it easy, Colonel," Patrick said. On his secure datalink, he spoke, "Fortress, this is Avenger, secure. Priority-alert notification."

"Go ahead with your priority-alert notification, Avenger, Fortress is secure." Patrick could hear the warning tones being sounded in the Eighth Air Force command center as Taylor Viner hit the ALERT button on her console, which sounded a tone in the entire room and would page each of the headquarters' staff officers.

"Bobcat Zero-seven has just been shot down by a Russian SA-12 surface-to-air missile. Request permission to return fire with ground-attack UCAVs."

"Copy your request, Avenger. Stand by."

"General . . . ?" Daren asked. The StealthHawks were beginning their attack runs.

"Continue," Patrick said without hesitation. "Nail 'em."

Each of the StealthHawk UCAVs carried millimeter-wave radar and infrared sensors that could precisely locate and identify the enemy targets. They received initial target-area instructions from the Vampire bomber, but, once released, they searched for targets on their own. A screen on the "big board" showed the decision-making matrix each Stealth-Hawk employed. It was extraordinary to watch: The BAT-

MAN staff saw the image the StealthHawk was looking at, saw it compare the image to its stored catalog of vehicles and come up with several possibilities. A few seconds later, the StealthHawk would take another "snapshot" of the target and refine its guess until it came up with only one possibility. Then it selected a weapon that would be most effective in destroying the target: an AGM-211 mini-Maverick missile for the armored SA-12 command vehicle, and CBU-87/103 Combined Effects Munitions mines against the radar arrays and transporter-erector-launchers.

Two more SA-12 missiles launched moments after they picked up a sector-scan warning, followed by two more from a different set of launchers, but it was obvious the radar didn't have a solid lock-on. *"Four SA-12s in flight . . . missiles are deviating, the missile-tracking radar has lost contact . . . back to surveillance-scan mode only . . . clean misses."* The radar cross-section of each StealthHawk was one one-thousandth the size of the already-stealthy Vampire bomber—the Russian radar had no chance at all of tracking it except at very close range.

Both StealthHawks bypassed the second SA-12 battery and instead rushed the first group of vehicles detected—the one with the command-post vehicle, the nerve center of the SA-12 system. The Ural-4320 six-by-six was the smallest vehicle in the group, but that didn't matter to the UCAVs—both launched a single mini-Maverick missile at the correct vehicle. Patrick and Daren watched the attack unfold as the area images from the StealthHawk's sensors, and then the target images from the mini-Mav's imaging infrared sensor, showed the missiles closing in. The mission commander had the option of designating another target or correcting the aimpoint, but it wasn't necessary—the StealthHawks were perfectly accurate. Both missiles plowed dead-center into the command-post vehicle, transforming it into a cloud of fire in seconds.

Like meat-eating bees buzzing around a picnic table, the

StealthHawks continued their work. The first UCAV sent its second mini-Maverick into the nearby 9S15MV surveillance-radar vehicle, which consisted of a large tracked vehicle carrying a massive billboardlike long-range radar. The second UCAV rolled in on another large radar array not far from the command-post vehicle, but Patrick hit his intercom button. "Negative on that target, Zero-seven," he said. "That's the sector-scanning radar—it's only effective against ballistic-missile attack. Put another mini-Mav into that 'billboard' radar." The remote mission commander overrode the StealthHawk's target choice and instead guided it against the same long-range radar attacked by the first UCAV. Without the command-post vehicle, the SA-12 was lobotomized. Now, without the surveillance radar, it lost its long-range vision.

The StealthHawks continued their attack by orbiting the two SA-12 batteries, searching for targets for their second weapon—two canisters, each filled with thirty BLU-97 Combined Effects Munitions bomblets that were scattered in a wide oval pattern above a target cluster. Each bomblet was a two-pound high-explosive fragmenting case with an inflatable Ballute parachute tail and a tiny radio altimeter that measured how far aboveground the canister was and set off the explosive at precisely the correct instant. When detonated, each canister shot several thousand steel fragments in all directions out to fifty to sixty feet, strong enough to penetrate automotive steel and light armor. At the same time, a mixture of zirconium in the Cyclotol explosive ignited, creating a fireball hot enough to set off unprotected fuel tanks, detonate ammunition—or kill a human being—for thirty to forty feet away.

The two StealthHawks could not hope to destroy all of the over 180 remaining SA-12 missiles in the brigade, but their final attacks were still devastating. Each StealthHawk automatically adjusted its altitude and track so as to maximize the kill pattern of its Combined Effects canisters, dropping the canisters so that the scatter pattern of the BLU-97 bomblets hit as many targets as possible. Each run managed to hit at least two SA-12 transporter-erector-launchers or reload-launcher trailers, which created spectacular secondary explosions as the shrapnel ripped open missile casings and fuel tanks and the incendiary fireballs ignited the fuel or explosives within.

As the StealthHawks continued to orbit the area, they sent back images and radar maps of their handiwork. "Command vehicle, surveillance radar, and most of two entire SA-12 batteries destroyed or heavily damaged, sir," the Stealth-Hawk flight-control officer reported. "No radar or datalink transmissions detected."

"Over thirty missiles destroyed and several more damaged," Daren said. "Friggin' unbelievable. We pretty much pulled the plug on this entire brigade." Left unsaid was the casualty count—each SA-12 battery was manned by almost fifty soldiers, and the command vehicle alone had twelve officers and technicians on board.

But even after all of their weapons were expended, the StealthHawks were not finished. Because they knew that their Vampire mother ship had been destroyed and they did not have enough fuel to reach friendly territory or rendezvous with another mother ship, they located one last target—both of the UCAVs selected a surviving launcher filled with SA-12 missiles—and dove in on it. Their small, thirty-pound "suicide" warheads ensured that both the target and the UCAVs themselves were destroyed in their final kamikaze attack runs.

"Direct impacts on two more transporter-erector-launchers," Daren reported. Patrick was still listening for word from Eighth Air Force headquarters. "Almost two entire SA-12 batteries destroyed, including their command-and-surveillance center."

"Pass along to your Bobcat crews, 'Well done, good shooting,' Daren," Patrick said. It was over in less than ten minutes—one QB-1C Vampire bomber and two Stealth-Hawk UCAVs destroyed with no casualties, versus half of a Russian SA-12 brigade with possibly dozens of casualties. Even Patrick was astounded by the power and efficiency of his unmanned aerial-combat warplanes. "Let's get another Vampire airborne and on patrol, and let's pinpoint the rest of that SA-12 brigade."

"Roger that, sir," Daren responded eagerly. He left his station beside Patrick to go up the theaterlike Battle Management Center to the Bobcat flight-control center to pass along the general's congratulations. At the same time, Patrick heard a chime in his headset. He entered his passcode and waited for the secure linkup. "Fortress, Avenger is up and secure."

"What's your report, General?" Patrick recognized the groggy, gruff voice as Major General Charles Zoltrane, the deputy commander of Eighth Air Force. Well, he thought ruefully, the brass was awake now. He was probably speaking from a secure phone in his quarters, and he definitely did not sound happy about being awakened at this hour.

"One of my unmanned Vampire bombers was shot down by a Russian SA-12 surface-to-air missile battery just outside Mary, sir," Patrick replied. Patrick had known Zoltrane for many years, and they were of equal rank. But when Zoltrane used "General" instead of "Patrick," McLanahan knew to keep this conversation formal and carefully observe their chain of command.

"Shit," Zoltrane murmured. "How in hell did you manage that, General?"

"We were investigating some unidentified ground returns just twenty miles outside Mary, well within the prohibited area, when it popped on and nailed us. We detected two SA-12 batteries and their command-and-control units."

"Transmit the site's coordinates and electromagnetic signals to headquarters, and let's have a look." But Zoltrane detected the hesitation in Patrick's response and said, "What else do you have to report, McLanahan?"

"The SA-12 batteries have been neutralized, sir," Patrick said. "The command-and-control unit, surveillance radar, and a total of ten transporter-erector-launchers have been destroyed."

"*Destroyed? Destroyed with what?*"

"StealthHawk UCAVs, sir, launched from our Vampire just before it was shot down."

"StealthHawks? *You had Stealthhawks on board your reconnaissance aircraft? How many?*"

"Two."

"Where are they now?"

"They were both completely destroyed when they kamikazied into SA-12 transporter-erector-launchers."

"Who gave the order to attack those SA-12 batteries, General?"

"I did, sir, as soon as my Vampire bomber was attacked and destroyed by hostile ground fire from within the prohibited area around Mary."

"You received no guidance from General Samson or from CENTCOM?" Zoltrane asked. Lieutenant General Terrill Samson was the commander of Eighth Air Force and the immediate task-force commander. Although anyone up the chain of command could have issued attack orders to Patrick—even the president of the United States himself—most if not all commands would have gone through General Samson at Eighth Air Force except in the direst of emergencies.

"No, sir."

"I see." There was silence for several long moments, during which Patrick could tell that Zoltrane was still on the line. Then, abruptly, he said, "Stand by," and the connection was broken. That was not a good sign, Patrick thought.

Daren Mace returned a few minutes later. "Bobcat Zero-four is inbound inside the ingress corridor over western Pakistan and should be on station in less than an hour," he reported. "He does not have any StealthHawks on board. Bobcat Zero-two will be ready to launch from Diego Garcia in about thirty minutes, and he's loaded with two UCAVs. We can only load fifty percent of our Vampires with UCAVs for now, but we expect to get a few more ready to upload within twenty-four hours. Within forty-eight hours, all Vampires will have UCAVs on board."

"Very good," Patrick said. "Get Zero-two airborne as soon as possible, with StealthHawks and full defensive armament. All Vampires that launch from now on will have StealthHawks on board unless further advised. The Russians might have many more SA-12s waiting for us out there."

"Yes, sir."

Patrick glanced up and saw Brigadier General David Luger, his second in command, trotting down the stairs toward the command console, apparently in a very big hurry, looking worriedly at Patrick. "Put Zero-four on patrol, and have him identify each and every laser-radar return within fifty miles of Mary," he went on. "If the Russians have a portable latrine out there, I want to know about it."

"You got it, sir," Daren said enthusiastically. He started to put on his headset to talk with the flight-control crew in the BATMAN and his ground crews on Diego Garcia, but David Luger came over to him, bent down, and whispered something to him. Daren Mace looked quizzically at Luger and shook his head, but Luger grasped Mace by his right upper arm, and Mace stood up and retreated up the stairs toward the flight-control crews.

Patrick watched this interchange with a slight feeling of dread that he tried not to make evident in his voice as he asked, "What's going on, Dave?"

"I received a call from Eighth Air Force headquarters, Patrick," Luger replied. Patrick noticed that David was in a flight suit but was unshaven and had barely taken the time to lace up his flying boots. At that moment a tech from the communications center trotted down the steps carrying a message. He handed it to Luger, who read it quickly. Patrick saw his face turn ashen. "Oh, shit . . ."

"What in hell's going on, Texas?" Patrick asked.

"You . . . you've been relieved of duty, Patrick," Luger responded, his voice shaking with disbelief and shock. He handed the message to Patrick. "I've been ordered to take command of the Air Battle Force and to confine you to quarters until you can be reassigned. All of our planes are being recalled. You . . . Christ, Patrick, you've been demoted to brigadier general."

Patrick read the message, shrugged, and simply nodded. "Guess they didn't appreciate me blowing up a Russian SAM site without letting them know first," he said simply.

"Patrick . . . Muck, this is not right," David stammered. "Eighth Air Force can't take away your command just like *that*—we don't belong to *them*. And only the president, the SECDEF, or the chief of staff can take away your stars."

"This message is not from Eighth Air Force," Patrick said, holding up the note and tapping the relevant line. "It came from the Pentagon, transmitted in response to a request from General Samson," Patrick said. He crumpled the paper in his hands. "You have command of the Air Battle Force, Dave. I've been ordered to go home." He looked at his friend, clasped him on the shoulder, then took off his headset and dropped it on the command console. "I'll be with my son in quarters. If they want me, they can reach me there. I'll have my earset on—don't ring my home phone. It might wake Bradley."

David Luger was just too stunned to move. "Muck . . ."

"Don't let them take away your ability to fight, Dave," Patrick said, looking at his longtime friend and partner with a defeated expression Luger had never seen before. "The staff weenies at Barksdale don't have a clue. Don't let them take away your strength." And with that, Patrick McLanahan marched up the steps and out of the Battle Management Center.

In the blink of an eye, a general reduced to nothing.

MINISTRY OF DEFENSE OF THE REPUBLIC OF TURKMENISTAN, ASHKHABAD, TURKMENISTAN
That same time

"Yes, sir, I know what my orders were," Colonel General Boris Kasimov, commander of Turkmenistan Defensive Alliance forces, forcibly responded on the secure telephone line. "The order was 'all weapons tight.' But we were under attack, damn it. The Americans had an *armed* B-1 bomber up there over Mary, and it rolled in on my brigade and attacked without any warning."

"Take it easy, Boris, take it easy," General Anatoliy Gryzlov, president of the Russian Federation, replied in a soft, understanding tone. Short, slender, with thin brown hair and bright blue eyes, the former cosmonaut, test pilot, and, until recently, chief of staff of the Russian military, usually appeared as if he would very much like to beat up everyone to whom he spoke. But when he was speaking to his generals, Gryzlov's entire demeanor was different; he treated them all, from the most senior commanders to the lowliest conscripts, with fatherly attention.

"Sir, I take full responsibility for this incident. I—"

"Boris, hold it," Gryzlov implored. "It's me, Anatoliy, your classmate at the academy, your squadron leader, your poker buddy. We've served too long together, fought too many battles, for you to talk to me like an altar boy caught yanking his wanker in the confessional. Just speak to me, all right? What happened?"

Gryzlov could hear Kasimov take a deep, relieved breath and a hard swallow. "General, we came under attack, and the air-defense brigade reacted, plain and simple," he said wearily. "All of a sudden that damned American bomber appeared out of nowhere and headed right for the number-one battery, and it had its bomb doors open. The crews saw it on the optronic sights, and everyone panicked. They lit it up and fired on it without requesting permission."

"For Christ's sake, Boris, I know your crews have more discipline than that," Gryzlov said. "That's the reason we picked that brigade to deploy on this mission—they knew how to preserve operational security. My orders were specific: Weapons stayed tight unless I personally, verbally gave the order to attack. And that was only going to happen after we started moving the armored divisions eastward—not for another six months at least. I was hoping by then that the world would have forgotten about that stinking rathole called Turkmenistan and leave us alone to do our business, just like Chechnya. This incident puts the conflict right back on the world media's hot sheet."

"General, blame it on the Americans," Kasimov said angrily. "They weren't permitted to bring armed attack aircraft into Turkmenistan, just unarmed reconnaissance planes and other aircraft armed with defensive systems only."

"I know that, Boris," Gryzlov said. "What I'm asking you is, what were your orders to the brigade? Exactly." There was a long pause. "Boris, let's not play games here. Talk to me."

"I told my brigade commanders that the order from you was 'weapons tight,' but I made it clear to them that I did not want to lose the brigade to attackers, especially Americans or Turkmenis," Kasimov said finally. "I told the colonel that they were not to initiate an attack, but they were not to lose the brigade under any circumstances." He quickly added, "Surely, General, you did not expect me to just allow that S-300 brigade to be attacked from the air without fighting back? I know that your orders didn't mean we should just let the entire brigade be wiped out. . . ."

"Boris . . ."

"The Americans had a B-1 bomber that launched *two*

unmanned attack aircraft," Kasimov said, his voice pleading now. "Each one of those things employed at least two guided missiles and two cluster munitions before flying themselves into another target. They took out nearly the entire antiair-craft brigade! At least we got the fucking bomber—and if you ask me, we should follow it up by attacking their forward base in Diego Garcia. We can't let the Americans get away with this!"

Gryzlov winced when Kasimov reminded him of that fact. The Antey S-300V-series surface-to-air missile system—what the West called the SA-12 "Gladiator"—was the best long-range, high-altitude antiaircraft weapon system in the Russian Federation, and probably the best in the world; it was also the world's first workable mobile antiballistic-missile system. Despite its effectiveness, however, Russia's outmoded and inadequate industrial and technical develop-ment centers and its rapidly shrinking defense budget couldn't produce enough spare parts and reloads for its own training and operational needs, let alone fully support its export customers. Just a single pair of missiles expended in a rare live-fire training exercise took weeks, sometimes months to replace—losing *two entire missile batteries,* not to mention the command-and-surveillance radar vehicles, would be devastating.

And the men that were lost . . . five officers and thirteen technicians killed, including the brigade commander and his deputy; three officers and thirty techs injured, some criti-cally. It was a devastating loss. It didn't matter that the United States was technically in violation of the UN Secu-rity Council's peacekeeping agreement: Russia had suffered a tremendous loss, in a country where it had almost total control.

The plan to move the S-300 brigade secretly into central Turkmenistan was Gryzlov's, but it could be accomplished only with perfect and careful security. All of the components of the S-300 could easily be disguised while on the march, and it could stay well disguised and hidden even when fully set up and operational—it could go from completely closed up and camouflaged to ready to fire in just five minutes. The key was simple: Keep the radars off the air and the datalink transmissions between radar and fire-control centers limited to fiber-optic landline cables. The orders were not followed—or were never properly issued—and the brigade was discovered. No one in Moscow thought the Americans would immediately open fire on the brigade with precision-guided and cluster munitions, but they did, and the cost in human life and loss of equipment was high indeed.

And someone was going to have to pay it.

"Damn it, Boris, I'm sorry it happened," Gryzlov said. "I wish your boys had kept their fingers off the COMMIT buttons."

"I apologize for that, General," Kasimov said. "I take full responsibility. But the fact remains: The Americans killed almost two dozen men and injured many more. The Americans provoked a response by their actions, and they employed offensive weapons in violation of the peacekeeping agreement."

"I know, and I will hold them fully responsible for the deaths they caused," Gryzlov said. "I'm sorry, Boris, but I have to bring you back to Moscow. You did not pull the trigger, but you *are* responsible for what happened out there and for the actions of your men."

"Yes, sir. I understand."

"Don't worry, Boris, I'm not going to make you the whipping boy—you know more about Central Asia than almost any other general officer, and you've done a commendable job commanding our forces in Turkmenistan all these years. You'll still be involved in everything that goes on in Central Asia. Turn your staff operations over to General Bilatov, hop a flight back, and report to General Stepashin. After you two have a chance to talk, we'll meet and discuss our next moves, once the furor over this incident dies down."

"Yes, sir," Kasimov replied. "I'll depart within the hour."

"Good. That will be all. I'll see you in a day or two."

Colonel General Kasimov felt somewhat relieved as he called for his staff transport jet, a Yakovlev-40, to be made ready for departure and his staff car brought around to take him home so he could pack. He was going to be roasted over the coals by Nikolai Stepashin, the new chief of staff and the commander of the Ministry of State Security, perhaps even demoted. But Gryzlov needed experienced, well-educated officers for his Central Asian campaign, and Kasimov felt confident that his talents were not going to be wasted commanding some frozen remote radar site in Siberia for the next ten years just because one of his lieutenants had an itchy trigger finger.

Kasimov briefed his deputy commander while he loaded files into his briefcase, then shook hands with his office staff members and strode out to his waiting car. The plane would not be ready for at least another hour, so he had time to relax and have a few drinks in his quarters, an unassuming concrete-block building on the northeast side of Ashkhabad International Airport. He told his aide and driver to stay in the car—he could pack easier and faster himself, and he wanted to be alone. He would be done as soon as the plane was fueled and ready for takeoff.

He was sure as hell not going to miss this shitty little house, he thought as he fixed a stiff drink, retrieved his A-3 kit bag from under his bed, zipped it open, and started throwing clothing into it. Duty in Turkmenistan was great until this whole incident had blown up in their faces—the Taliban invasion of eastern Turkmenistan, the threat to Russian interests, the mobilization of troops, the American involvement, the battle for the cities of Mary and Chärjew, and the Americans' preemptive strike inside Russia to cut off their counterattack. Since then all officers who had formerly lived in nice apartments in the capital had to move to these little houses at the airport, where it was a bit more secure. Inadequate heat and light, terrible water, leaking plumbing, drafty doors and windows, cold in the winter and hot in the summer—he now lived only slightly better than his troops in their tents or out in the field camping beside their armored vehicles.

Satisfied that the rest of his packing could be finished in a few minutes, Kasimov kicked off his boots, stretched out on his bed, and took a deep sip of his vodka on ice. Still at least a half hour to wait. He thought he should call his wife but decided instead to call her from base operations right before departure. He took another sip, then closed his eyes for a short catnap.

Kasimov never heard the gunman enter through the back door, step silently into the bedroom, place a pistol muzzle under the general's chin, and fire a single sound-suppressed round into his brain. In seconds the gunman retrieved the spent shell casing and replaced it with one from a small plastic bag, left some hair and fabric samples near the body so they could be easily found by forensic investigators, and departed.

THE KREMLIN, MOSCOW, RUSSIAN FEDERATION
A few minutes later

Russian president Anatoliy Gryzlov replaced the telephone receiver on its cradle. "Something terrible has happened— General Kasimov has been murdered in his quarters," he said tonelessly, matter-of-factly.

Minister of State Security and Chief of the General Staff Nikolai Stepashin nodded. "A horrible tragedy. I shall commence an immediate investigation. No doubt anti-Russian Turkmen assassins or Muslim terrorists were involved. They will be hunted down and summarily executed." He could have been reading from a long-ago-prepared script—which, in fact, he was.

"Now that we have the unpleasantries out of the way," Gryzlov said, "these are my orders: I want Turkmenistan in complete Russian control in thirty days. I want every Taliban fighter and sympathizer dead and buried, and I want every American aircraft blown out of the sky. That idiot Kasimov tipped our hand and gave away the element of surprise, but it doesn't matter. I don't care what it takes, I don't care what forces you need to mobilize—just *do it*. I want every oil and natural-gas field in that entire fucking country with a Russian infantry battalion on it."

Stepashin nodded—he dared not voice any of the dozens of concerns he had—and picked up the telephone to issue the orders that would send a hundred thousand more Russian soldiers into Turkmenistan.

1

Weeks later

"Where is he, Chief?" Colonel Trevor Griffin, operations officer and acting commander of the 996th Information Warfare Wing of the Air Force Air Intelligence Agency, asked as he hurried through the doors. His excitement was obvious as he waited at the verge of impatience exchanging security badges with the guard, facing a sensor for a biometric face-identification scan, and entering a security code into a keypad to open the outer door. Griffin was a sort of caricature, like a kid wearing his dad's military uniform—short in stature, bean-faced, with slightly protruding ears and narrow, dancing blue eyes. But the broad shoulders, thick neck, and massive forearms under his overcoat only hinted at the soldier hidden behind those giddy eyes.

"In the boss's office, sir," the command's Chief Master Sergeant Harold Bayless responded as he met the colonel on the other side of the security barrier. "I came in early to get caught up on some paperwork, and he was already here. I buzzed you and the boss as soon as I found out."

"Let me know when the boss gets in," Griffin said as he removed his Air Force blue overcoat and handed it to the chief master sergeant. "Make sure he has an office, a car, and billeting set up."

"Yes, sir," Bayless said. Physically, the two men could not have been more different: Bayless was husky and tall, with lots of thick, dark hair and humorless, penetrating dark eyes. Despite their height difference, Bayless had trouble keeping up with the quick full bird—Bayless finally had to let Griffin hurry off ahead of him, and he retreated to his own office to make all the appropriate notifications on behalf of this most unexpected distinguished visitor.

Despite his fast pace, Griffin wasn't even breathing hard as he hurried past the stunned noncommissioned officer in charge and into his office. There, sitting on the sofa in the little casual seating area, was their unexpected visitor. "General McLanahan!" Griffin exclaimed. He stood at attention and saluted. "I'm sorry, sir, but I didn't know you'd be here so soon. I'm Trevor Griffin. Good to meet you, sir."

Patrick McLanahan got to his feet, stood at attention, and returned the colonel's salute. Griffin came over to him and extended his hand, and Patrick shook it. "Good to meet you, too, Colonel Griffin," Patrick McLanahan responded.

"For Christ's sake, General, please, sit down," Griffin said, a little confused at McLanahan's formal bearing. "It's a pleasure to have you here, sir. Can I get you anything? Coffee?"

"Coffee is good, thank you. Black," Patrick said.

"Me, too—commando style." Griffin buzzed his clerk, and moments later the man came in with two mugs of coffee. Griffin introduced his NCOIC, then dismissed him. "I apologize, sir, but I didn't expect you for quite some time—in fact, I was only just recently notified that you'd be joining us," Griffin said. He stood aside so Patrick could take the commander's seat, but Patrick reseated himself on the sofa, so Griffin, a little confused, took his armchair at the head of the table. "We're thrilled to have you take command of the unit."

"Thank you."

Griffin waited until Patrick took a sip of coffee, then said with a smile, "I'm Trevor—or 'Tagger' to my friends, sir."

"Sure," Patrick said. "I'm Patrick." Griffin nodded happily and took a sip of coffee, still acting as excited as a kid about to go through the turnstiles at Disneyland. "I guess it's been a while since I've reported in to a new unit. I'm a little nervous."

"And I'm not used to two-star generals showing up without a lot of fanfare."

"I'm no longer a two-star, Tagger."

"It was either a mistake, or a temporary budgetary/billeting/allotment thing, or somebody's sending you a pretty strong message, Patrick," Griffin said, "because the Air Force doesn't take away a general's stars, like you're some young captain that just got a DUI. If they did, guys like MacArthur and LeMay would've been buck sergeants in no time. General officers either get promoted or they retire, either voluntarily or involuntarily—they don't get demoted." He couldn't help but stare, bug-eyed, at the ribbons on Patrick's chest, especially the Air Force Cross—the highest award given to an Air Force officer besides the Medal of Honor—and the Silver Star. "But whoever's testing you or pushing on you," he went on, dragging his attention back to his new commanding officer, "it's their loss and my gain. But we didn't expect you for another month at least."

"I decided to show up early and meet everyone," Patrick said. "My son is with his aunt in Sacramento."

"And your wife?"

"I'm a widower, Trevor."

Griffin's face fell. "Oh, shit . . . I'm sorry, sir," he said sincerely. He averted his eyes apologetically, embarrassed that he hadn't known this extremely important piece of information. "I received your personnel file, but I only glossed over it—as I said, I didn't expect you for a few weeks."

This uncomfortable pause gave Patrick a chance to look Trevor Griffin over. His compact frame only served to accentuate his powerful physique—he looked as if he had been power-lifting most of his life, and perhaps still did. Griffin's short-sleeved casual uniform had few accoutrements—command jump wings under a senior weapons director's badge—but Patrick saw his Class A uniform hanging on a coatrack behind the door, and it appeared as if Griffin had every ribbon and award an Air Force officer could have—and then some: Patrick noticed a Combat Infantry Badge and even a yellow-and-black RANGER tab.

"That's okay, Trevor," Patrick said. "I guess I've thrown a monkey wrench into your office by coming here early like this. I'm sorry."

"We both have to stop saying 'sorry' to each other."

Patrick smiled and nodded. Wishing to quickly change the subject, he nodded toward Griffin's uniform blouse hanging behind the door. "I know of only one other Air Force officer that wears a Ranger tab."

"I think there *is* only one other: Hal Briggs. I convinced him to go to Ranger school as a brand-new second lieutenant fresh out of Security Police school—he had so much energy I thought he'd drive us all crazy. I lost track of him over the years."

"He's a full bird colonel at my previous base in Battle Mountain, Nevada."

"What's he doing at Battle Mountain?"

"Hal commands a unit of high-tech, highly mobile ground forces that direct unmanned close-air-support and reconnaissance aircraft."

"It must be under some very tight wraps for us here at AIA not to hear about it," Griffin said. His eyes sparkled in excitement even more. "Sounds very cool, Patrick. I want to learn more about it."

"Sure. You'd fit right in, I think—you look like you're

either an Olympic gymnast or you're from the special-ops community."

"I was in special ops before the Air Force really had them," Griffin said. "I was an Army Ranger and fought in Grenada, then decided I wanted to join the Air Force and be an officer—I thought I was done crawling and bleeding in the mud. I was in Security Police for a while—that's where I met Hal Briggs—but I couldn't leave the special-ops career field and became a combat air controller.

"I directed a combat-controller wing in Desert Storm— my guys set up a half-dozen forward-resupply points and landing strips inside Iraq, including three that we set up in the western side of the country weeks before the air war started. I had one squad that actually put a laser beam on Saddam Hussein's getaway vehicle—he was hightailing it to Jordan—but we couldn't get a shooter in to launch on him fast enough.

"After Desert Storm I attended Air War College, was assigned to U.S. Special Operations Command headquarters at MacDill, then married a great woman that had two small kids; I adopted hers, and we had one of our own. It was then, after realizing I was almost forty with three young kids, that I decided to settle down. I joined the intelligence career track, and except for service schools and one year at the Pentagon, I've been either at Kelly Field or here at Lackland. I like to think I contribute the ground-pounder's perspective to the high-tech Air Force."

"The Air Battle Force is designed to have shooters deploy with ground forces at all times," Patrick said. "We use unmanned long-range bombers to launch unmanned armed attack vehicles that can be directed via datalink by the ground forces."

"We *definitely* need to talk and compare notes, sir," Griffin said enthusiastically. "If you can forgive all my ignorance-based faux pas until I'm up to speed, I assure you

again that I'm thrilled that you're coming here and working
with our wing."

"Thanks."

Griffin looked at McLanahan carefully for a moment,
then said, "If you'd allow me to make an observation, sir?"

"Go for it."

Griffin's smile dimmed a bit. "I'd say you're here early to
check out this agency . . . to decide whether you want to stay
in the Air Force or not."

Patrick looked at Griffin sternly, as if he were ready to
challenge him on his observation—but moments later he
glanced away, then nodded. "I hoped it wouldn't be that
obvious," he said.

"Like I said, very few general officers get demoted," Griffin said. "Maybe they want to see what you're made of, what
your real goals are. The rumors are still hot and heavy that
you're being considered for the post of national security
adviser if the president wins reelection—or maybe even to
help Thorn win reelection. If you got kicked out of the Air
Force, or were even forced to resign, it might look bad for
the president to consider bringing you on. Maybe they want
to see whether you'd stick it out or not, show some loyalty."

"Trevor, I assure you, I'm not going to be national security adviser," Patrick said.

"Hey, I didn't make up the rumors—I'm just helping
propagate them," Griffin said, his energetic and engaging
smile returning. "Do you have any intel background?"

"No," Patrick replied. "Bombers, engineering, research
and development. The units I flew with had their own
organic intel capabilities—we rarely called on outside intel
sources."

Griffin grinned again, getting more and more intrigued by
the minute. "The Air Battle Force operated with its own intel
sources? Sounds cooler all the time, Patrick." Griffin looked
at Patrick carefully. "Hold on . . . that attack on the Russians
in Turkmenistan a few weeks ago. The Russians claim an

American B-1 bomber attacked an unarmed observer team being sent into Mary."

"It wasn't an 'unarmed observer team'—it was a mobile SA-12 site, a full brigade, sitting twenty miles inside the cease-fire zone."

"I knew it," Griffin said. "We caught a glimpse of it here, requested some ground support—send some special-ops guys to go in and take a look—but that was vetoed by General Houser. Your own intel sources identified it as an SA-12?"

"We were lucky and caught one squeak from its search radar," Patrick explained. "We couldn't get it to turn the radar back on—until we made like we were going to attack it."

"Well, we certainly didn't think of using our air-intel assets as decoys to incite the Russians to attack us," Griffin admitted, "but if it worked, I won't knock it. The SA-12 attacked?"

"Shot down an unmanned B-1 bomber."

"*An unmanned B-1 bomber?* We have them?" Patrick nodded. "Cool!" breathed Griffin. "Now I understand why you'd use your own plane as a decoy. I assume your unmanned bomber launched a few of those armed drones and made mincemeat of that SA-12 site just before it got shot down, huh?"

"Exactly."

"Shit-hot!" Griffin exclaimed. "Everyone was starting to believe what the world press and the Russians were saying—that one of our guys attacked without provocation—and then when we heard that an Air Force general got canned for the attack, we thought maybe it was the truth. I knew the Russians were lying through their teeth. No surprise there, huh?" The pride was evident in Griffin's face—he was beside himself with awe that Patrick McLanahan was sitting in front of him. "But I thought we were only supposed to be surveilling Turkmenistan, not patrolling with attack drones."

"My rules of engagement were unclear on that point,"

Patrick said uneasily, "so I erred on the side of caution and loaded my bombers up with SEAD weapons."

"Good thing you did," Griffin said. "So let me guess— your orders to Lackland were being cut the next day."

"It didn't take even that long," Patrick admitted. "I was relieved of command before the last bomb fragments hit the ground."

"All for doing what you were supposed to be doing— making sure the Russians weren't trying to move against Turkmenistan's new military forces before they could organize," Griffin said disgustedly. "Now look at what's happening out there: Russia is claiming that Turkmeni guerrillas are attacking their observer forces, and they're flying so-called defensive-counterinsurgency missions against Turkmeni military forces. They've violated the United Nations cease-fire dozens of times in just the past few weeks, but no one is saying squat about it. Things are too hot for us to send recon aircraft like Rivet Joint and Joint STARS in to monitor their movements, so the Russians now have free rein."

"I would like to keep a careful eye on the Russians and continue to report their movements to the Pentagon," Patrick said.

"You've come to the right place, Patrick," Griffin said proudly. "That's what we do best. I believe we have the best and possibly the only remaining true brain trust in the intelligence field: Our guys stay here longer than in any other career field, and we maintain the only seriously long-term database of enemy threats in the world. Let's talk about this unit, and maybe I'll help talk you into staying—or it may convince you to take whatever might be waiting for you on the other side."

"Fair enough."

"The unit you'll take command of, the Nine-sixty-sixth Information Warfare Wing, is one of several wings and centers managed by the commander of the Air Intelligence

Agency, who as you know is Major General Gary Houser."
He noticed Patrick's suddenly stony face. "You know him?"

"He was my first B-52G aircraft commander, almost
twenty years ago."

Griffin chuckled at that. "That's funny. To listen to him,
you'd think he was *always* an intel weenie—in fact, he trash-
talks fliers, especially bomber guys, all the time. I knew he
was a pilot, of course, but I didn't know he flew B-52s. He
sees the BUFF as another Cold War relic sucking money
away from information warfare." He looked carefully at
Patrick again, then added, "So . . . maybe you're here to
check out General Houser and not just the Nine-sixty-
sixth—decide whether you're cut out to work for your old
aircraft commander again?"

"Let's not try to psychoanalyze this thing too much, okay,
Tagger?"

"Yes, sir," Griffin said, his eyes falling apologetically
again. Patrick couldn't help but like the colonel: He wasn't
afraid to express his feelings and thoughts, which made
him a trustworthy person. Patrick felt very comfortable
around him.

"Anyway, the Nine-sixty-sixth is probably the last vestige
of the old Mighty Eighth—which, now that I think about it,
might be another reason why you're here: This is a good
place to hide someone nowadays," Griffin went on. "Like
most of the Air Intelligence Agency, we're a combination of
many Air Force agencies. We were known as the Strike
Information Center not long ago, and the Air Force Strategic
Planning Agency before that, and we absorbed the Sixty-
sixth Combat Support Group last year. When General
Houser changed everything over to an 'information warfare'
theme, the combined group became the Nine-sixty-sixth
Information Warfare Wing. Our primary mission is to gather
information vital to planning and directing strike missions
by Eighth Air Force aircraft. Any country, any objective, any

target, any weapon, any threat condition—the Nine-sixty-sixth's job is to find a way to attack it.

"We can tap in to any intelligence or imagery source in the world, but primarily we use overhead imagery produced by Air Force assets, combined with domestic satellite assets and augmented by HUMINT field reports," Griffin went on. "We still do a fair amount of covert ops ourselves, but General Houser thinks that's unnecessarily dangerous and doesn't yield proportionally higher-quality data."

"What do you think about that?" Patrick asked.

"Well, as a former ground-pounder, I believe you always need boots on the ground to do the job right—but I'll also admit that I'm pretty old-school," Griffin replied. "Give me a few good trained operatives, a parachute, and a pair of binoculars and drop me anywhere on the planet, and I'll bring back information that no satellite can get you—and if you need the target blown up, I can pull that off, too. Ask your typical satellite to do that." He looked at Patrick, then smiled. "And if you give me Hal Briggs and a few of his shooters that you spoke about a minute ago, I can probably blow up a lot more—like what went down in Libya recently? Or inside Turkmenistan . . . ?"

Griffin punched in further instructions, and the satellite imagery shifted to a more desolate landscape. "I might as well tell you now, Patrick—the Nine-sixty-sixth had an ongoing covert reconnaissance operation against the Russians in Turkmenistan. Your . . . incident . . . near Mary forced us to pull out."

"I don't suppose anyone will ever blame the Russian army for causing the problems over there in Turkmenistan, will they?" Patrick asked sarcastically.

"Sorry, sir, I didn't mean it was your *fault* . . ." Griffin said. "Anyway, we were running covert ops out of a small air base in Bukhara, Uzbekistan. We made contact with some members of the Turkmen army, made some payoffs, traded weapons and ammo for information, that sort of thing. We left several of our Turkmeni contacts behind, and we'd sure like to pull them out.

"The border crossing and highway into Mary is sealed up tight now, and the Russians have a pretty solid air-defense setup out there now—too hot even for normal Air Force special-ops planes or helos, let alone the normal modes of transportation the Nine-sixty-sixth uses. What might the Air Battle Force have that we could use?"

"Dave Luger can insert a Battle Force team in about thirty-six hours and get one, maybe two of your guys out," Patrick said.

"Thirty-six-hours? That's impossible."

"But neither the Pentagon nor Central Intelligence would ever approve it. It would have to be someone pretty damned important."

"Ever heard of General Jalaluddin Turabi?"

"Turabi?" Patrick exclaimed. "Chief of the Turkmen army? *He's* your contact?"

"You tangled with him?"

"He saved our team in the first battle against the Russians in Turkmenistan. He's a hero."

"He's a better spy and guerrilla than he ever was a general," Griffin said. "He's been out collecting information and harassing the Russians, and at the same time recruiting soldiers for his army, using Air Intelligence Agency dollars. But when you hit the Russian SA-12 site, he scattered. We gave him up for dead. He resurfaced recently, one or two steps ahead of the Russians. We'd sure love to yank him out."

"Then let's do it."

"It won't do us any good to go into Bukhara, Patrick. We still need to go another two hundred and fifty miles to—"

"I'm not talking about Bukhara, Tagger—I'm talking about Mary."

"Mary?" Griffin exclaimed. "How can you do that? We can't overfly Turkmenistan. . . ."

"We're prohibited from overflying Turkmenistan with

combat aircraft," Patrick corrected him. "Transport aircraft are still allowed by peacekeeping and observer forces."

"The Russians will spot a transport plane anywhere within two hundred miles of Mary."

"Not our transport plane, they won't."

Griffin opened his mouth as if he were going to say something, then stopped and smiled. "Okay, Patrick. What is it? What do you guys have that I don't know about?"

"A little toy we've been working on for a few years—an old idea we've just modernized. We—" Patrick stopped himself. He still couldn't stop thinking about the Air Battle Force as "his." "I mean, the Air Battle Force can get you in anywhere you want to go."

"I'll start working on getting authorizations right away."

"Dave Luger at Battle Mountain is in charge of surveillance and observer air operations over Turkmenistan—he'll give you permission," Patrick said.

"I'd have to join the team, of course," Griffin added with a sly smile.

Patrick smiled and nodded. Yep, he thought, he definitely liked this guy. "*That* you'll have to take up with General Houser," Patrick said. "But I'm sure Dave Luger can put in a by-name request for you to be part of the team. You'll have to undergo a few days of training with the Air Battle Force ground-operations team and their equipment. But I don't think you'll have any problem keeping up with the team—in fact, you might be teaching them a thing or two. And you'll be working with Hal Briggs again."

"*Outstanding*. I like going to school, especially for new stuff." Griffin was so excited that he was literally stepping from foot to foot—the man could hardly wait to get started.

"Anyway, let me continue with my orientation before the boss shows up," Griffin went on. "Our work product is called the Strike Assessment Catalog, or what we call 'The List.'" Griffin went to his desk, punched in a few commands on a computer keyboard, and a blank line on a large plasma wall display appeared. "The List used to be just that—a list, a paper catalog—but of course we've computerized it. Pick a target. Any target."

Patrick thought for a moment. "Pro Player Stadium—I hate the Miami Dolphins."

Griffin shook his head and smiled. "Good thing you didn't say the Dallas Cowboys or Houston Texans, or you'd have a fight on your hands. Unfortunately, we haven't done any U.S. targets—and you're the first guy to ever ask to see the lineup for a U.S. target. How about we take a look at the latest on what the Russians are doing in Turkmenistan?"

Griffin punched instructions into the computer, and soon some satellite photos appeared.

"The western outskirts of the city of Mary," Patrick said. "I recognize that area well."

"We have pretty decent coverage of this area right now, maybe one photo every couple hours, so we have a good database going," Griffin said. He entered more instructions into the computer, and several blinking yellow circles appeared. "We can overlay synthetic-aperture radar images in with the visuals, and we see several newcomers to the area. We can digitally enhance and enlarge the picture"—the photo distorted for a moment, then sharpened to show an individual vehicle—"and here we have what looks like a Russian BTR scout vehicle, with a couple dismounts standing nearby. The other targets we identified are also scouts."

"Driving right to the outskirts of Mary," Patrick remarked. "They're not even bothering to hide anymore."

"We can have the computer select the best weapon to take them out, or we can select the weapon system and the computer will recommend the best plan of attack," Griffin went on. "But the real value in our system is not picking targets but in identifying and risk-assessing the threats. Here, I'll ask to overlay the most recent threat depictions for the area." A few moments later, several large red circles appeared, along with lists of weapons on the side of the image. "The number-one threat in this particular area is from mobile antiaircraft systems—in this case it's from known twenty-three-millimeter optronically guided weapons on the scouts themselves. But this outer dashed circle represents the threat from SA-14 man-portable antiaircraft missiles that are known to be carried aboard Russian scout platoons."

"So a planner or even a politician can ask for information on a particular target," Patrick said. "You start feeding all this information to the brass, and they decide if the cost, risk, and complexity are worth the desired result."

"Exactly," Griffin said. It was unusual, Griffin thought, to hear an Air Force general thinking of political realities when planning strike missions. This could be why, he thought, the guy was still being considered to be President Thorn's first national security adviser. "Ninety-nine percent of the time, we don't even get past the threat analysis—some assistant deputy secretary of one of the services wants to know how we can blow up a breeder reactor in China, and we just pull up the threat analysis. He's all hot to trot when it comes to contemplating an attack, but they go away very quickly when they learn how many assets it takes to do it. Diplomatic initiatives start to look a whole lot more appealing."

"Tell me more about the Air Intelligence Agency and Gary Houser," Patrick said.

"Getting right down to the meat of the matter, eh?" Griffin asked, his ever-present smile and twinkling blue eyes reappearing. "Okay, here goes:

"Quite simply, the Air Intelligence Agency is one of the most far-reaching and, in my opinion, powerful commands in the entire American military. General Houser has his fingertips on every piece of intelligence data generated in the free world. He personally directs the activities of a score of satellites, dozens of aircraft, and thousands of analysts and operatives around the world. He is also the American military's one and only 'quintuple hat,' at least as a deputy: As commander of AIA, he's also a deputy commander of intelligence for Air Combat Command, Eighth Air Force, and U.S. Strategic Command, as well as a deputy director of the National Security Agency and Defense Intelligence Agency. He is definitely Mr. Intel in the Pentagon.

"Over the years various intelligence and electronic-warfare units were shut down or consolidated, mostly because of budget cuts but also to minimize redundancy and enhance security, and Air Intelligence Agency—when it was known as the Air Force Electronic Security Agency—gained most of them. AIA controls almost all of the Air Force's intelligence-gathering operations, but it also controls areas such as MIJI—meaconing, interception, jamming, and intrusion of enemy electronic signals—electronic counterintelligence, decoy deployment, and spycraft. Now, instead of just intercepting enemy transmissions, AIA has the capability to *manipulate* transmissions—change them, scramble them, or move them, in order to confuse the enemy. When computers came to the forefront, AIA began doing to computer data what we did with the electromagnetic spectrum—intercept and analyze, then manipulate and distort, while protecting and securing our own data. Other units and services started doing the same thing, but AIA had been doing it for a decade before anyone else.

"At first AIA's work product was so timely and valuable that it began serving customers in other numbered air forces, not just the Mighty Eighth. Then it eventually replaced Air Combat Command's intelligence stuff, and finally its information was being shared with planners in other commands. AIA has become so powerful and far-reaching that its mission has even supplanted Eighth Air Force's mission, and it gets a lot of funding that normally goes to many other branches, command, and agencies.

"My predictions are that General Houser will easily win his third star, become commander of Eighth Air Force, and begin the transformation to an intelligence-gathering combat command. General Houser insists that Eighth Air Force will eventually *become* the information-warfare command and that bombers will be all but obsolete."

"Not in my lifetime, I hope," Patrick said.

"It's already happening, Patrick," Griffin said. "It won't be long before the number of LDHDs—low-density, high-demand aircraft like spy planes, radar planes, jammers, dedicated anti-air-defense attack weapons, and data-manipulation platforms—will exceed the number of strike aircraft in the inventory.

"But I think General Houser is shooting higher: If General Samson gets selected as the Air Force chief of staff, he'll see to it that Gary Houser gets his fourth star and becomes the first commander of the new U.S. Information Warfare Command, a major unified command on a par or maybe even surpassing the theater commands in importance, tasking, and funding. It will probably combine all the intelligence-gathering assets of Strategic Command, the Air Force, the Navy, and perhaps even the National Security Agency and Strategic Reconnaissance Office into one supercommand.

"That could change the entire face of warfare as we know it. General Houser says that it takes the Air Force twenty-four hours to blow up an intercontinental-ballistic-missile launch site or a bomber base in Russia—but soon his information warriors can put that same site out of commission in twenty-four *minutes* by jamming, spoofing, interfering, reprogramming it, giving it a computer virus, or shutting down its power by computer command."

"I don't know *how* it's done," Patrick said, "but if you guys have progressed to the point where you can hack into a computer that controls a power grid or networks air-defense sites together and shuts them down with the push of a button, it would be an incredibly powerful weapon. Maybe it will replace bombers someday—but I wouldn't recommend replacing the bomber fleet with computers or aircrews with hackers."

"This is the new Eighth Air Force, Patrick," Griffin said. "The bombers in Eighth Air Force are still dedicated to the nuclear mission, but I think they'll soon shift to Twelfth Air Force along with all the other nonnuclear attack units.

"Even Strategic Command is supporting planning and targeting for nonnuclear conflicts, using all their staff and computers that were originally dedicated to planning World War III against Russia and China to plan missions in every area in the world where any level of conflict could break out. Nuclear warfighting is all but dead. You have to speak in terms of 'network-centric warfare' and 'low-density conflict.' Your Air Battle Force sounds like the kind of thing Houser wants to transform Eighth Air Force into, but he wants the shooters to support intel, not the other way around."

"Then I'd better get up to speed as soon as possible," Patrick said.

"That sounds pretty positive to me, General," Griffin said. "I take it you'll stay on with us for a while?"

"Tagger, to be honest, there wasn't really that much chance I'd just get up and leave," Patrick admitted. "I'm not the kind of guy who gets out because I don't like the working conditions. I'm an Air Force officer, and I go where I'm assigned. If they asked me to get out, I'd be out of here—but they didn't. Now they have to contend with me."

"Contend with *us*," Trevor Griffin said. He extended his hand, and Patrick shook it enthusiastically. "Welcome to the Nine-sixty-sixth, sir. I think we'll set this command on its ear—and have some fun doing it." Patrick was about to say something, but Griffin interrupted him with an upraised hand. "And I truly believe they'll eventually give you your stars back."

"I wouldn't count on it," they heard a voice behind them say.

They turned and found two men standing in the doorway—the command's chief master sergeant, Harold Bayless, and the commander of the Air Intelligence Agency, Major General Gary Houser. Griffin glanced accusingly at Bayless, and the chief returned his look with a smug smile—they both knew that Griffin had asked the chief to notify him when the commander arrived in the headquarters, but instead Bayless had facilitated this little surprise arrival and eavesdropping opportunity.

"Room, ten-*hut*," Patrick said, and both he and Griffin stood quickly and snapped to attention.

Gary Houser stepped over to Trevor and Patrick, keeping his head up to emphasize his height advantage over the two. Gary Houser was at least seven inches taller than Patrick, with a beefy frame, big hands, a square face, dark eyes, and closely cut hair to deemphasize his baldness. After he moved close to both officers in the room, he tried to look into their eyes to read their expressions, but of course he towered over both of them, especially Griffin. Both Griffin and McLanahan stayed at attention, eyes caged.

"So," Houser asked in a low voice, "which one of you clowns do I have to contend with?" Neither one replied. Houser gave Griffin a warning glare, put his hands behind his back, and went closer to Patrick. "Patrick McLanahan. Long time no see. My long-lost crew navigator who supposedly goes TDY to Fairchild but who mysteriously disappears off the face of the earth and ends up getting involved with cockamamie ideas such as the Border Security Force and . . . what was that other group? The Night Riders? Night Invaders?"

"Night Stalkers, sir," Patrick replied.

"Right . . . the Night Stalkers. Big, bad, vigilante assassination squad. Are you a big, bad assassin now, Patrick?"

"No, sir," Patrick replied, still standing at attention.

"You a close and personal friend of that big shot Kevin Martindale?"

"No, sir."

"Are you going to be national security adviser, secretary of defense, or maybe even the fucking president now?"

"No, sir."

"So you just screwed the pooch too many times at this new super-duper bomber attack base up in Nevada, and you got your ass kicked all the way down to me by SECDEF, is that it?"

"No, sir."

"Then why are you here, Patrick McLanahan?"

"Reporting as ordered, sir."

"Why did you lose a star, ex–Major General Patrick McLanahan? Why am I getting a disgraced and demoted general officer who has no intelligence experience, no prospects for promotion, and no future in the United States Air Force?"

Looking straight ahead, standing stiffly at attention, Patrick replied, "Because you're one lucky son of a bitch, sir."

Houser's face puffed, his eyes bugged out, and for a moment it appeared as if he'd explode with rage. Then he laughed out loud, guffawing directly—and purposely—into Patrick's face. "Good one, nav!" he barked. "Sounds like you finally got yourself a sense of humor. About fucking time." He glanced at Griffin and shook his head. "Look at you two, standing at attention like academy plebes! Stand at ease, stand at ease. I don't want you jokers to pass out on me from the strain." Griffin relaxed enough to go to parade rest.

Houser stuck out his hand, and Patrick shook it. "How the hell are you, Patrick? Good to see you." To Griffin he said, "This guy was on my BUFF crew for three damned years. He went from a know-nothing, pud-pounding kid to the best bombardier in SAC, and that's no shit. We won the Fairchild and LeMay trophies two years in a row and won a shitload of other awards, too. During a competition run, he dropped a *shack* bomb with a completely failed bomb-nav system and helped the crew shoot down an F-15 fighter. No lie." He slapped Patrick on the shoulder and added, "All under my outstanding leadership and tutelage, of course." Both Griffin and McLanahan were careful not to forget to smile and nod in agreement. "You done with him, Tagger?"

"Yes, sir."

"Good. Follow me, Patrick." Griffin called the room to attention as Houser strode out.

Patrick turned and extended his hand. "Good to meet you, Tagger. We'll talk after I meet my troops."

"Good to meet you, too, Patrick," Griffin replied as he shook McLanahan's hand. He gave Patrick a warning glance, and Patrick nodded that he received it.

Patrick had to take giant steps to keep up with the Air Intelligence Agency commander as he made his way downstairs to his office on the first floor. Houser neither acknowledged nor greeted anyone, and most everyone they passed in the corridors, Patrick noticed, chose not to make eye contact with the general. They reached a set of oak double doors flanked by an Air Intelligence Agency flag and a two-star general's flag, guarded by a lone Security Force armed guard in blue Class A's with white web belt, pistol holster, shoulder braids, ascot, and spats. The guard snapped to attention and pressed a button to unlock the door.

Houser quickly walked through the outer office, without bothering to order those in the room as they were, and stepped through another set of double doors into his aide's office. "Coffee, Major," he said to the officer at the desk.

"On the way, sir," the aide responded immediately.

Inside his office Houser jabbed a finger at the sofa, and he took the large leather wing chair at the head of the coffee table. He withdrew a cigar from a humidor on the table. "You don't smoke, as I recall," he said by way of explaining why he wasn't going to offer one to Patrick. Patrick didn't bother to correct him. "So how the hell have you been, Pat?" he asked as he stoked the cigar to life.

"Not bad, sir."

"Can the 'sir' shit, okay, nav?"

"Okay . . . Gary," Patrick said. Houser took a deep pull on the cigar, and the silent message conveyed by his rattlesnake-like warning gaze through the cloud of smoke, despite the amused smile, was unmistakable: It's "General" to you, mister, now and forever.

After the aide brought coffee in for both general officers, Houser sat back in his big chair, took a sip, and puffed away on his cigar. "So, nav, you've had one train wreck of a career since you left Ford Air Force Base—when you got shanghaied by Brad Elliott," Houser began. "Man, you had it made in the shade before you took up with that nutcase. Despite your less-than-firewalled effectiveness reports, me and the wing king had been discussing when to send you to Air Command and Staff College in residence and what your next assignment was going to be—the Pentagon or SAC Headquarters. You were on the fast track to a senior staff job or even a command of your own.

"But then you got recruited by Brad Elliott to join him at Dreamland," Houser went on. "You bombed the hell out of the Kavaznya laser site in eastern Siberia, taking out a half-dozen Soviet fighters and a dozen SAM sites plus their big-ass antisatellite laser. Then you—"

"That's classified, General," Patrick said sternly, "and I *know* you aren't cleared for that information."

"Shit, Patrick, I and ten other guys here at AIA know everything you've done over the past fifteen years—I found out about it a month after I first arrived here," Houser said. "That mission was the beginning of the end of the Soviet Union—and the beginning of this agency. Intelligence became the name of the game starting the day after you dropped that bomb on that laser. Everyone was shocked that we underestimated the laser's capability, and everyone wanted to be the one to discover the next Kavaznya site."

"With all due respect, General, I advise you to drop that

topic," Patrick said seriously. "You may think you know everything and that you have the right clearances, but you don't."

"Come off it, Pat," Houser said with a chuckle. "You Dreamland guys—rather, you *ex*–Dreamland guys—think you're so special. Remember who I work for: Terrill Samson used to run Dreamland. The place was blown wide open after the Kenneth Francis James spy incident. 'Dog' Bastian barely had it under control: General Samson had to clean house to make the place right." Patrick laughed inwardly: He knew that Colonel Tecumseh "Dog" Bastian had been firmly in control of the High Technology Aerospace Weapons Center—in fact, he created the kind of unit that the Air Battle Force had been patterned upon.

It was Terrill Samson, the black man who rose through the ranks after enlisting in the Air Force to avoid being drafted into the infantry during the Vietnam War and who made it all the way to three-star general, who'd never had control. Samson wanted nothing more than to get promoted, to be the newest and greatest black man to reach the highest echelons of power and leadership in the American military.

But in his quest to become a symbol, he found that the harder he tried to control the men and women at Dreamland, the more he lost control. Samson got his wish: He got himself promoted to lieutenant general and commander of Eighth Air Force, in line to become commander of Air Combat Command, maybe even chief of staff of the Air Force. He left Dreamland without giving it any purpose or direction. The world's most high-tech laboratory-turned-combat-unit had become little more than a high-tech aircraft boneyard during his leadership, but it had served its purpose—it was the footstool Terrill Samson needed to step up to the next level.

"I'm just giving you my recommendation here, Gary," Patrick said. "Don't talk about Dreamland. Let's change the subject."

That was three times in a row McLanahan tried to tell a superior officer what to do, Houser steamed, and that was three times too many. "Pat, I know all about the activities there, why you got canned, why you were called back, what you did," Houser said. "I know Dreamland's budgets, its projects, personnel, and progress. Same with Battle Mountain, the Air Battle Force, and the One-eleventh Wing—"

"Those units are different, General," Patrick said. "They're part of the Air Reserve Forces Command, and their budgets and missions are mostly classified 'confidential.' HAWC is still classified 'Top Secret—ESI' Level Three, which means nothing gets discussed outside the facility, not even in passing. Let's drop it before I'm forced to make a report." He had *already* decided to make a report—he was just trying to limit the length and detail at this point.

"Nav, don't lecture me about security procedures, all right?" Houser retorted. "I'm commander of AIA. I live and breathe secrecy and security. You're the one that needs to be reminded of his duties and responsibilities here, I think."

Patrick's mouth literally dropped open from astonishment. *"Sir?"*

"The way I see it, McLanahan, you've been marching roughshod through the Air Force, pulling shit that should have landed you in prison for a hundred years, and somehow you've not only gotten away with it but you've been rewarded and promoted for it. Only one man, Terrill Samson, had the guts to say, 'Enough is enough,' and he pulled the plug on you and your wild-ass excursions into personal aggrandizement. Your buddy President Martindale overruled him and gave you your stars back. I can't figure out why. But what I do know is this: You screwed up again, your buddy Martindale couldn't save you, Thorn and Goff *wouldn't* help you, and so you got dumped on my doorstep."

Houser took another deep drag on his cigar. "Maybe the Chief wanted to stick you with me to keep you out of sight, or force you to resign. I don't know, and I don't give a shit. But you're here, and now you're my problem.

"So here are the rules, and they're simple: You do as you're told, you keep your nose to the grindstone, and I'll help you dig your way out of this shithole mess you've gotten yourself into," Houser said. "You can finish out your twenty right here in San Antonio, maybe get your second star back—maybe—and when you retire, the private consulting firms and security agencies will be throwing plenty of six- and seven-figure offers your way. If the rumors of you going to Washington are true, you can do that, too. You probably won't be national security adviser, but you can snag some high-ranking post in the White House National Security Council staff—"

"I'm not looking for a government or a private consulting job."

"I don't care what you are or are not looking for, General," Houser said. "I'm just telling you that I don't like my agency being used as a detention facility for out-of-control disciplinary hard-cases. You were a loner with a give-a-shit attitude when I first pulled a crew with you back at Ford, and you're the exact same guy now. You may have been able to get away with being like that because of a combination of luck and skill as a bombardier, but that *won't* cut it here.

"If you try to pull just one-tenth of the shit you pulled on General Samson, my friend, I guarantee I'll make your life a living hell," Houser went on, jabbing his cigar at Patrick. "You're with the Nine-sixty-sixth now, which doesn't deploy and gets pretty good face time with the brass and politicos in Washington, Offutt, and Barksdale. That's a plum job for you. Keep your nose clean, and you can stay there, studying satellite photos and HUMINT contact narratives, then briefing the four-stars on enemy activity, and you might just improve your reputation after a couple years.

"Here it is in black and white, Pat: You were sent here to cool your heels, and I don't like it," Houser went on bitterly.

"I don't like you being dumped in my lap, and I don't like golden boys who think they know it all and can tell their superior officers off. I want you out of my face and out of the limelight. I want you as quiet as I can make you without cutting out your fucking tongue myself with a pair of rusty scissors. Maybe we'll both get lucky and Thorn will give you a job in his new administration, and then you'll be out of here soonest. Otherwise you have two years and nine months before you can retire: I would advise you to keep your yap shut and put in your time in the Nine-sixty-sixth, and then you can go out on the lecture circuit at ten thousand a pop or be a talking head on Fox News Channel at five hundred dollars a day.

"The Nine-sixty-sixth commander is a two-star billet, so maybe you'll get your second star back and regain a little bit of the decorum and pride you've squandered over the past few years," Houser said. "If you play ball, I'll help you ease on out of here so you can take care of your son, get your cushy government position, or maybe go back to Sky Masters Inc. and rip off the government with those hyperinflated defense contracts your friend Jon Masters is so fond of negotiating. I don't give a shit what you do after you get out. But while you're in my unit, under my command, you will shut your mouth and do what you're told. Am I making myself perfectly clear, Pat?"

Patrick looked at Houser for a long moment, never breaking eye contact, long enough for Houser to feel the anger start to rise in his temples. But finally Patrick responded. "Yes, sir. Perfectly clear."

Houser couldn't find any hint of rebellion or defiance in that simple answer, which made him all the more angry. "Good to see you again, Pat," he snapped. He jabbed the cigar toward his office door. "Now get the hell out."

OVER CENTRAL UZBEKISTAN, CENTRAL ASIA
Days later

"Thirty minutes to go, sir," Hal Briggs said gently. "Time to get moving."

Trevor Griffin was instantly awake and alert, but he didn't know where he was. The place was dark, smelled like old oil and even older body odor, and was as noisy as hell—he felt as if he were trapped in a garbage truck roaring down a freeway at ninety miles an hour. Then he remembered where he was, and what he was about to do.

And he thought that this wasn't a bad place after all, compared to what he was about to step into. Not bad at all. Pretty darn nice, in fact.

Griffin unfastened his safety harness and swung out of the bunk he'd been napping in for the past few hours. He was on the upper deck of a QB-52 Megafortress bomber, a highly modified B-52H Stratofortress bomber. The QB-52 Megafortress was a "flying battleship," capable of delivering up to sixty thousand pounds of the world's most advanced weapons, from ultraprecise cruise missiles to antisatellite weapons. Except for a pod on each wing that carried radar- and heat-seeking air-to-air defensive missiles, however, the QB-52 carried no ordnance on this mission.

In fact, as Griffin looked forward toward the cockpit, he reminded himself that this B-52 didn't carry something else either that he *used* to think was important: a *crew*. This B-52 bomber was *unmanned*—it had flown halfway around the world without anyone's even setting foot in the cockpit. They received constant messages and updates from the folks back at Battle Mountain Air Reserve Base in northern Nevada, but the plane flew and even aerial-refueled all by itself.

The other unusual thing about this flight was that this B-52 carried something it rarely ever took along on its missions: passengers. Trevor Griffin was one of them.

But not for long.

Hal Briggs, who occupied the bolt-in bunk on the left side of the aircraft, was already climbing down the ladder to the lower deck. Griffin followed, moving carefully, still getting accustomed to the strange suit he was wearing. The Air Battle Force guys unflatteringly called it BERP—Ballistic Electro-Reactive Process—but Trevor called it simply "un-fucking-believable." It was a full-body coverall design, made of material that felt like stiff fabric, such as the kind that knife-proof bank deposit bags were made of. But once connected to a power unit worn like a thin backpack, the material electronically, instantly became as hard as an inch of titanium when struck. Griffin had watched a demonstration during his daylong training course and couldn't believe what he saw: The wearer was protected from thirty-millimeter Gatling-gun fire, explosions, fire, and even a fall from a twenty-five-story parachute-training drop tower.

That wasn't all. The boots had a jet-propulsion system built into them that compressed and stored a large air charge that allowed wearers to jump several dozen meters in height and distance—they no longer had to run or even drive into combat. The battle armor had two electrodes on the shoulders that could send a lightning bolt of electricity in any direction out to a range of about thirty feet, powerful enough to render a man unconscious. In addition, Briggs wore an exotic-looking exoskeleton device that enhanced their bodies' strength by automatically stiffening sections of the BERP electronic body armor, then using microhydraulic actuators to amplify muscular strength. Griffin saw BERP-outfitted commandos tossing engine blocks around the training course like pebbles, hefting and firing thirty-millimeter cannons as if they were handguns, and demolishing small buildings like bulldozers.

His new helmet was something out of a science-fiction movie, too: It had sensors that gave him "eyes" in the back of his head, superhearing, night vision, and allowed him to talk to practically anyone on planet Earth with a radio. Even the color of the gear was high-tech: It was some sort of computerized multicolored pixelated design that allowed the wearer to blend into any background, from broad daylight in the desert to night against snow.

Trevor climbed down the ladder and met up with Briggs. On a signal from Hal, Griffin donned helmet and gloves and powered on his battle armor, as he was taught to do back at Battle Mountain days ago. Hal glanced at his old commanding officer with a hint of humor in his eyes occasionally as he checked Griffin's battle-armor systems. "How do you feel, sir?" he asked.

"Like I gotta pee," Griffin responded. "I'm finding it hard to consciously pee in this thing." Like some sort of Frank Herbert sci-fi invention, the BERP gear collected urine and sweat from its wearer and circulated it through small tubules in the suit, which provided incredibly effective temperature control. The suit also had small filters built into the fluid-circulation system that removed bacteria and other contaminants from the collected fluid and allowed the wearer to drink the fluid from a tube—it tasted terrible, but it would save you in an emergency.

"That's standard for everyone wearing battle armor for the first time," Hal said. "But the more you pee in it, the better you'll feel—and I guarantee if you're thirsty enough, you'll want it. Any questions for me, sir?"

"How many times have you used this aircraft before?"

"On an actual mission?" Briggs asked. Griffin nodded. "Never."

"*Never?*" Trevor remarked. "How about test flights?"

"This *particular* aircraft? Never. How many total test flights . . . ?"

"Don't tell me, let me guess: never, right?"

"We have very good computers that model and simulate the flights for every possible loading and flight condition," Hal said. "It's been tested a hundred times—just not with any live human beings on board. I think we made one test flight with instrumented dummies a while back."

"And?"

Hal smiled, shrugged, and said, "You know, sir, instrumented test dummies make terrible pilots."

"Great."

"And the best part, sir—you *volunteered* for this," Hal said. "We're happy to have you along." He turned away and spoke, "Bobcat Control, Tin Man One. How do you copy?"

"One, this is Control, we read you five-by," Brigadier General David Luger responded from his Battle Management Center, or BATMAN, at Battle Mountain Air Reserve Base. With him was Colonel Daren Mace, the operations officer for the 111th Wing; Colonel Nancy Cheshire, commander of the Fifty-second Bomb Squadron, the unit in charge of all the Megafortresses, who was "piloting" this unmanned Megafortress; Marine Corps Sergeant Major Chris Wohl, noncommissioned officer in charge of the Air Battle Force's ground forces; and Colonel Kelvin Carter, the Fifty-second Bomb Squadron's operations officer and the man in charge of the special mission that was about to begin in a few minutes. They were supported by intelligence, weapons, surveillance, and maintenance technicians seated with them in the Aircraft Control Group of the BATMAN.

"We're ready to board Condor."

"We're ready here."

"Let's mount up." Hal hit a switch and watched a cabin-pressurization gauge, which showed the cabin altitude slowly increase until it equaled thirty-two thousand feet, the same as the aircraft altitude. Their oxygen system was already built into their BERP suits, so they didn't need oxygen masks. Griffin tried and failed to control his belches and other bodily outgassing as the lower outside pressure allowed trapped gases in his body to escape. When the pressure was equalized, Briggs undogged the aft bulkhead door and stepped aft. Griffin followed. A short walk later, they were in the QB-52's bomb bay. Briggs flipped on the lights—and there it was.

They called it the MQ-35 "Condor," but it had no official

designation because it was as experimental as anything ever before fielded by any Air Force unit. The Condor was designed as a stealthy long-range special-operations forces insertion transport aircraft, using a long-range bomber to get it close to its target, then using its onboard propulsion system to fly the team out at the end of the mission. It resembled a giant stealthy air-launched cruise missile, with a smoothly blended triangular lifting-body fuselage, a long flat nose, and a gently sloping aft section culminating in a small-diameter engine-exhaust nozzle. Thirty-six feet long, nine feet high and wide, it took up almost the entire bomb bay, leaving a very narrow catwalk around it. Briggs opened the entry door on the side of the craft, and Griffin clambered inside and began strapping in. Hal performed a brief walk-around inspection using a flashlight, climbed into the front seat, closed and latched the entry door, and strapped himself in.

The interior was tight and cramped. The team members sat in heavy-gauge steel seats, not quite side by side and not in tandem, but slightly staggered so they had a bit more shoulder space. The only windows were the forward cockpit windows. There were two more seats behind Griffin, plus a small cargo area behind the rear seats for their weapons and gear. They all were quiet as they tightened shoulder and lap restraints and readied themselves for their mission. Hal flipped some switches and powered up the tiny ship's internal power and instrumentation. "Control, Condor, power on, ready for systems check."

"Systems check in progress, Condor," Kelvin Carter responded from Battle Mountain. Hal Briggs could manually operate and control Condor, but, like the QB-52 Megafortresses, it was designed to be controlled, monitored, and flown via satellite from Battle Mountain. A few moments later: "Condor, systems check is complete, aircraft is ready for flight. I've been informed that we're sending updated intel info to you now. We might have to make a change in the landing zone. Stand by."

"Select the tactical area chart, sir," Hal told Griffin.

Inside his helmet Griffin glanced at the electronic display, which was a very wide field-of-view visor, similar to the view from a quality full-face motorcycle helmet. At the extreme upper left side of the display was a small yellow bar. When Griffin looked at it, a menu similar to a Windows or Macintosh computer popped up. He scanned down the menu until he came to the "Charts" selection, then glanced at the star icon to the left. Another menu popped up, displaying a set of charts. Griffin selected the proper one. The entire chart appeared to be floating in front of him. By glancing at navigation icons on his display, he was able to display changes to the chart from the last briefed information.

"Looks like Russian troops have moved even farther east than we anticipated, sir," Hal said after studying the symbology on the new chart. "I'd say they've completely taken Tedzhen. A few patrols have moved almost all the way to the Sakar Reservoir. Colonel?"

"Our contact point is on the north side of the reservoir," Griffin said. "Our landing zone is between them and the Russians' new position. It's close, but I don't think it's been compromised—yet."

"Top? What do you think?"

"The data is over thirty minutes old, sir—they may have compromised your landing zone already," Chris Wohl responded by the secure satellite link. "But there's only one way to find out."

"I agree," Hal said. "Colonel? Your thoughts?"

"This is your show, Hal," Griffin said. "But going in at night, in this contraption—I'd say we go for it. No way in hell they'd ever expect us."

"That's the spirit, sir," Hal said happily. "Control, recommendations?"

"This is Intel, Condor," the intelligence officer responded. "We have a few other alternate infiltration spots, but it'll extend your ground-travel time past your reserve power limit." The BERP electronic battle armor ran off very high-tech fuel cells that supplied an enormous amount of power but for relatively short periods of time, depending on usage. In a simple "sneak and peek" operation, their power might last hours—but if they had to fight their way out of a battle, the power could last only minutes.

"The last two fuel cells are emergency-only, Control. We never plan to use them," Briggs said. Each team member carried extra fuel cells—they were even more important than ammunition on this mission. "If we can't do this mission without using the emergency fuel cells, we don't go. We'll do the approach to the planned landing zone, and if it's hot, we'll bug out."

"Sounds good to me, Condor," David Luger said. "We're good to go."

"Roger that," Carter acknowledged. "Five minutes to release, Condor."

It was the longest five-minute wait in Trevor Griffin's life. All the techniques he had learned over the years to calm himself—controlled breathing, consciously unclenching muscles, Transcendental Meditation—refused to work this time. But soon he wished he'd had to wait a little while longer. It seemed only a few seconds when Carter gave a one-minute warning.

The bomb doors below them slid open. The rumbling sound reverberating in their helmets quadrupled in intensity, and the little craft shook violently in the disrupted airflow, as if it were a young stallion trying to break the wrangler's grasp on the rope to free himself.

But the worst part was when they dropped free of the Megafortress's bomb bay and fell out into space. Griffin felt as if his stomach had flown up into his throat. Blood rushed to his head, causing his vision to "red out," and he thought for sure he was going to lose his lunch. The Condor's sudden deceleration caused his body to mash up against his shoulder harness, which dug mercilessly into his body, so hard he could feel it pinch even through the thick BERP body armor.

The Condor's nose pitched over, and for a very long, uncomfortable moment, he thought he was heading straight down, ready to slam into the earth facefirst.

"Good separation, Condor," Carter's voice said. "How are you feeling, Colonel?" Undoubtedly the BERP rig had some sort of telemetry device that was sending body-function readouts back to Battle Mountain. "You can breathe anytime now, sir." Griffin found he was holding his breath, and he let it out with a gush and found that the pressure on his chest had already greatly subsided.

"I'm okay," Griffin said, willing his breathing to quickly return to normal.

"That first step is *definitely* an eye-opener," Briggs exclaimed. Griffin silently cursed his desk-bound stomach and vowed to stay in better shape.

If he made it through this mission in one piece.

"MA flight controls responding normally," Carter reported. "Coming up to best glide speed . . . now." The Condor's nose pitched up greatly, assuming a much more normal, albeit slightly unsettling, nose-down attitude. Underneath Condor's skin were thousands of tiny computer-controlled hydraulic actuators that twisted and manipulated most of the outer fuselage—in effect, the entire body was a wing, with an almost infinitely controllable amount of lift or drag. The craft could glide as slowly as a feather one moment, sink as fast as a fifteen-thousand-pound rock the next moment, and then float like a cloud the next, all without deploying one aileron or flap. "Looking good, Condor. Sit back and relax, folks. We're on glide path to target."

MARY, REPUBLIC OF TURKMENISTAN
That same time

Although it was at the crossroads of travel and commerce in Central Asia, and had been for centuries, Mary was definitely a very lonely and desolate place now.

Mary once was the second-largest city in Turkmenistan and the nexus of the railways, highways, and petroleum pipelines that transported Turkmenistan's immense oil and natural-gas wealth to other parts of Central Asia and as far east as the Indian subcontinent. It was also now the eastern-most stronghold of the Army of the Russian Federation, which was trying to wrest control of Turkmenistan away from its interim Muslim government and replace it with a pro-Russian government again. Most of the Muslim popula-tion had fled north toward Chärjew, ready to cross the border into Uzbekistan if necessary; a few hardier souls had decided to make the perilous journey across the burning sands of the Kara-Kum Desert toward Kerki, ready to escape to Uzbekistan or Afghanistan if the Russians dared pursue them this far.

Mary was Podpolkovnik Artyom Vorobev's first field command. He was in charge of the 117th Rifles, a motorized rifle regiment with about three thousand troops carried aboard a conglomeration of vehicles, everything from cargo trucks to BTR-60 armored personnel carriers and BRDM scouts. Vorobev, however, was lucky enough to have a battal-ion of T-72 light tanks augmenting his force, which he deployed right up front on the Ashkhabad-Mary highway. He also had almost a full air-defense battalion, including four ZSU-23 mobile antiaircraft artillery vehicles and three 9K35 Strela-10 mobile surface-to-air missile units, along with a command-post vehicle, radar vehicle, and reloads.

He *used* to have an S-300 brigade up front, but of course the damned Americans and their unmanned stealth bombers had taken care of that unit. The furor regarding his decision to deploy the S-300 air-defense brigade so far ahead of his regiment had thankfully quieted down in the wake of the United Nations' decision to exclude all foreign military combat aircraft from Turkmenistan. He was still in com-mand, and he was determined not to screw up again.

The Strela-10 heat-seeking antiaircraft missile system was much more capable than the ancient ZSU-23 against high-performance aircraft, such as the American bomber that was shot down a few weeks earlier. But as commander of the point scout unit, Vorobev's objective wasn't to take on a massed air or ground assault but simply to make contact with any enemy forces out there, report their strength and position, disengage, and maintain contact until heavier reinforcements arrived. The main force was many kilometers away, but it was two full reinforced brigades spread out along the fifty kilometers between Mary and Tedzen, supported by several aviation, air-defense, engineer, and special-operations companies.

Vorobev's command vehicle was located near the rear of his regiment, about ten kilometers southwest of the main airport at Mary and four kilometers behind the lead scout formation to the east. He was proud of this force, and he told his battalion and company commanders that every day. Vorobev had been deployed all over the Russian Federation in various units throughout his eighteen-year-long army career, but mostly as a staff officer, never as a field commander. He had worked hard and used his contacts to go to the best schools and training centers so he could fill out his résumé with plenty of academic experience, but despite top marks and glowing endorsements from many high-ranking generals and even a few vice marshals in Moscow, he had always lacked the one thing he needed to compete for flag rank: actual experience commanding a combat unit in the field.

When he got his orders to go to Turkmenistan, he thought his career was over—an assignment to Central Asia was worse than one to Siberia. But it turned out that one of his many patrons did him a favor: He would be taking command of a full regiment, which looked good on any subcolonel's record, but his first command was in a relatively quiet and safe location—Ashkhabad, Turkmenistan. Nothing ever happened there.

That is, until about two months after he took command of his unit. Then, as his grandfather always used to say, *"On idyot pyerdyachim parom,"* or "He was going to the top propelled by fart steam." The Taliban had invaded Turkmenistan, one of the other Russian army regiments in his division assigned to defend the city of Mary had been crushed, and now he was suddenly thrust to the forefront with strict orders from Moscow not to underestimate the Taliban-led forces and let the same happen to him. Vorobev's regiment was now expected to blunt any advances by any hostile forces, whether they be Turkmenis, Taliban—or American B-1 bombers. Mary was the "line of death" here in the wastelands of Turkmenistan. If he held fast, Vorobev would get his long-awaited promotion, perhaps back to a staff job as *polkovnik* or maybe even a general major. If he failed, the best he could hope for was an honorable retirement with his *podpolkovnik* stars still on his shoulders.

If he survived.

It was nearing 9:00 P.M., which was patrol shift-change time for most of the regiment. Because so many of his men would be out and about at this hour, Vorobev made it a habit to stop by at least one security-sector company to watch the changeover before heading to his tent to start reviewing reports, making notes, and issuing orders to his battalion commanders. His driver was waiting for him as he put on his helmet and pulled the chin strap tight. One of his young lieutenants, a mortar-company commander named Novikov, and a battalion commander named Kuzmin were accompanying him on this evening inspection. These ninety-minute-long tours gave his junior officers a chance to have a look at the rest of the regiment, ask questions, and get some face time with the boss.

It was a rather pleasant night so far, but Vorobev knew that the weather in southern Turkmenistan in late spring was unpredictable and sometimes harsh. "Let's go, *serzhant,*" he said. He returned the salutes from his two junior officers, then shook hands. He chatted with them idly as they headed to the first security checkpoint, about twenty minutes away.

"Looks like we came a long way for nothing," Hal Briggs said. The inside of the little Condor was eerily quiet, with just the faintest whisper of airflow audible through their helmets. But it wasn't the ride that was bothering everyone.

It was the landing area. It appeared as if several Russian patrols were moving directly toward the landing site itself.

"We've been working with Turabi and these Turkmen guerrillas ever since the peacekeeping force was established," Griffin went on. "They risked their lives to pass on valuable intelligence information to us."

"Well, it appears the Russians are about to nab them," Briggs said, studying the latest satellite-imagery download. "One Russian patrol looks like they've got them right now, and two others seem to be on their way."

"The landing site is compromised," the intel officer back at Battle Mountain radioed. "I recommend you abort. From your altitude you can make it back to Bukhara with plenty of fuel left."

"Colonel Griffin? Speak to me. I'm considering getting the heck out of here."

"We can't let those Turkmen forces get captured if we want any chance of keeping Turkmenistan out of Russian hands, Hal."

Hal paused. Then, "Top? Comments?"

Chris Wohl had encountered Jalaluddin Turabi before on two occasions—the last time, Turabi's former Taliban fighters helped the Battle Force commandos escape a Russian attack in Turkmenistan. "It's hard to tell, sir," Wohl responded, "but I don't see much more than a squad out there near the landing zone, and maybe a platoon within ten miles. You can take those guys easily. All you have to do is make sure you're in the air before more troops show up."

Briggs thought about it for a few moments. "Roger that. Control, Condor is proceeding as planned."

"Are you sure, Hal?" Dave Luger asked. "It's looking pretty hairy."

"Not as hairy as it is for Turabi," Hal said. "Put us down, sir."

There was a pause, this time from Battle Mountain—Carter was obviously inquiring as to the wisdom of this decision. But soon he said, "Here we go, Condor. Everyone, prelanding checklists. Hold on tight."

They were just a few miles from the planned landing zone, still gliding to the southwest at seventeen thousand feet. Just as Griffin thought there was no way they could make that landing zone from this altitude, the nose came up and his body was shoved forward on his shoulder straps as the Condor decelerated. His stomach again churned up into his throat as they careened earthward. Then, through the sudden wind-blast noise and intense buffeting, he thought he heard and felt the landing gear pop out, and moments later they hit the ground.

The noise level suddenly increased a hundredfold as the mission-adaptive fuselage went into maximum-drag configuration, and Griffin's body dug into the shoulder harnesses again for what seemed like five minutes but was only a few seconds. The moment the pressure released, Hal Briggs had his restraints off and his door unlatched, and Griffin had to hurry to keep up with him. As they briefed, Griffin kept watch using the battle armor's sensors while Hal pushed the Condor off the highway and spread a camouflaged antiradiation net over it—it would be easily discovered in daytime, but at night it looked like a pile of sand, and the net would keep it from being spotted by infrared sensors.

Griffin had his weapon ready—a big, heavy rifle that no commando would ever carry but was the perfect weapon for the Tin Men and their powered exoskeletons. The rifle was an electromagnetic rail gun that propelled a large titanium sabot projectile several thousand feet per second with amazing accuracy. Coupled with the battle armor's sensors and steered with the exoskeleton, the weapon was devastating to any war machine, from a tank to a bomber, out to a range of over three miles.

"You okay, sir?" Hal asked.

"Yes. All clear," Griffin said.

"Then let's go find your boy, Colonel," Briggs said. He checked his electronic charts, stepped in the proper direction, then fired the thrusters in his boots—and, in a *whoosh!* of compressed air, he was gone.

Here we go, Griffin said silently. He pointed himself in the right direction, braced himself, and gave the electronic command—what he called during training "clicking the ruby slippers together." He felt the push of the thrusters, but for all he knew he was still standing upright—there was no sense of flying or falling at all. The battle armor's stabilization system made the jump so smooth that he had to check his sensors to be sure that he was moving at all. But moments later he felt the thrusters fire again to slow his fall, and he knew enough to bend his knees slightly in order to help take the landing impact.

Hal was about five yards away. "Good jump, sir. Follow me." And he was gone again.

Very cool, Griffin thought as he waited for the thrusters to recharge before he made his next jump. Very, very cool . . .

The security patrol had a group of three men on their knees in the sand, hands atop their heads, when the second patrol team, driving a wheeled BTR armored personnel carrier, arrived. An officer got out of the BTR and approached the group. "What do you have here tonight, Sergeant?" he asked.

"They were out here in shallow spider holes, sir," the sergeant replied. "They seemed to be taking a lot of notes. And look at this." The officer looked at the object in his flashlight. "It's a pair of high-powered binoculars, sir. But there's something else. . . ."

"A camera—it's a digital camera, designed to take digital pictures through the binoculars," the officer said, examining the binoculars carefully. "And this port on the side . . . looks like it hooks into a transmitter, perhaps a satellite transmitter, *da?* Get someone out here with a metal detector—I bet we'll locate the transmitter nearby." He motioned to the captives. "You find out which is the leader yet?"

"They don't appear to understand Russian, sir," the sergeant said. "But I think that one is the leader." He pointed to a very tall Turkmeni soldier with an empty shoulder holster. "He was the only one with a sidearm. It was Russian, in very good condition, and it looks like he knew how to wear it."

The officer approached the man and shone his flashlight on him. Moments later, after grasping the man's face, he broke out into a wide grin. "Well, well. Sergeant, don't you see who we have here? This is General Jalaluddin Turabi himself, the new commander of the so-called Turkmen armed forces." He bent down. "Am I not correct, General? And this is your aide, Abdul Dendara, no? Speak up so all your men can hear you." The man remained silent, shaking his head that he did not understand. "Still playing dumb, General?" The officer withdrew a pistol, aimed it at the head of the younger man beside him, and fired. The headless body of the young recruit toppled over almost into Turabi's lap. "How is your Russian now, General? Coming back to you?"

"Yob tvoyu mat' khuyesas!" Turabi swore in Russian.

"There, you see, Sergeant? General Turabi knows Russian very well. We must take him with us back to the capital, and be very careful not to hurt him—at least for now. As for the other—execute him. We don't have enough supplies to feed the entire damned Turkmen army."

"Bastards! You can't just slaughter us like this! We are prisoners of war!" Turabi shouted. As Turabi was dragged away, the patrol sergeant barked an order. One of his troops clicked the safety off his weapon. . . .

But at that second they heard a loud *banngg!* The lights

from the patrol vehicles that were illuminating the area snapped off, steam and diesel fuel gushing from a completely ruptured engine and fuel tank. The soldiers, Russians and Turkmen alike, dropped to the desert floor.

The security officer saw several bright flashes nearby that he assumed were gunshots, all coming from near his men. "Sergeant!" he shouted. "Where are the attackers?" No response. "Sergeant! Answer me!"

"I'm afraid he can't answer you right now, sir," came a strange, synthetic, computer-like voice. Suddenly the Russian felt himself hauled up by his jacket. He found himself dangling in the air—being held aloft by an alien-looking figure straight out of a science-fiction magazine.

"Vyyabat!" he shouted. "Who the hell are you?"

"Turn off his lights, and let's get out of here, sir," Hal Briggs said.

"Americans? You are Americans?" the officer shouted. "What are you doing here? I will—" But Griffin silenced him with a quick bolt of energy from his shoulder electrodes, then dropped the unconscious officer to the sand.

Trevor Griffin went over to Jalaluddin Turabi and helped him to his feet. "Are you all right?" he asked in Russian via the battle armor's electronic interpreter.

"You . . . you are the American robot warriors," Turabi gasped. "Why have you come here?"

"I'm from the Air Intelligence Agency, General Turabi," Griffin said. Turabi still looked puzzled. "From Texas, General, remember? You've been sending us pictures of the Russians for weeks now. We're here to get you and your man to safety. Let's go. We've got to get out of here."

They returned to where the Condor aircraft was hidden, took the camouflage netting off, and pulled it out onto the highway. Turabi and his sergeant, Abdul Dendara, climbed in the back and strapped in, followed by Griffin and then Briggs. He had the power on immediately. "Bobcat Control, Condor, we're up."

"Good to hear it, guys," Dave Luger said.

"We're running a systems check now, Condor. Stand by for engine start." A few moments later: "Systems check okay. Hydraulic fluid is a little low—we may have a leak somewhere. Engine-start sequence in progress." On the back of the Condor, a small retractable air inlet deployed, and moments later they heard the high-pitched whine of a turbojet engine. "Engine start complete, running another systems check . . . Hydraulic pressure is low, almost to the red line. Let's see if we can get airborne before we lose the whole system. Hal, use the tiller and keep her straight on the highway. Ready?"

"Let's do it."

But it wasn't going to happen. As soon as the Condor started moving forward, the nose slipped sideways, and they could feel a severe shuddering under their feet. "Control, I can't steer it," Hal said, "and I feel a really bad vibration in the nose."

"Hydraulic pressure is down to zero," Kelvin Carter reported. "The nosewheel will just free-caster without hydraulic power. Hal, you'll have to lock the nosewheel in place with the locking switch on the tiller. You won't have any steering, so you'll have to manually line the Condor up on the highway. Use differential braking until you get enough airspeed to steer it aerodynamically. Careful on the brakes—you'll flip yourself over if you have takeoff power in and you hit the brakes too hard."

"I'll get out and line it up," Griffin said, and before Hal could protest, he had undogged his hatch and was scrambling out. It was no problem for him to lift up the nose of the aircraft and reposition it on the highway centerline.

But just as he did, a warning beeped in his helmet. "I'm picking up an aircraft coming our way." He raised his rail gun and followed the prompts in his helmet until he could see the threat symbol in his electronic visor. "Got him! Got him!" he said excitedly. "Low, six miles, speed one-ten. Probably a damned helicopter gunship or attack plane."

"Easy, sir. Wait for him to come into range," Hal said.

With the powered exoskeleton, Griffin tracked the incoming aircraft easily. "Should be any second now. Don't lead him—the projectile will move a hell of a lot faster than—"

Suddenly Griffin heard in his helmet, *"Warning, laser detected. Warning, laser detected."*

"Laser!" he shouted. "He's laying a laser designator on us!" He didn't wait any longer—he fired the rail gun at the incoming aircraft, even without a lock-on, hoping that the shot would make the pilot veer away or the gunner break his lock-on or concentration.

It did neither. As Griffin watched, his electronic visor showed another target—this one moving much faster than the helicopter.

He didn't hesitate. He jumped atop the Condor aircraft and watched as the laser-guided missile streaked in. Like a hockey goalie, he crouched down, keeping the missile centered in his sights while balancing. He raised the rail gun and tried to line up on the incoming missile.

But before he could get a shot off, it hit. The missile deflected off the barrel of the rail gun, off Griffin's right arm, veered away from Condor, hit the ground, and exploded. The rail gun shattered in his hands, and he was blown backward off of the Condor and several yards through the air onto the hard-baked desert floor.

He was still alive. He heard warning buzzers, his electronic visor was cracked, and his body felt as if he were being turned on a rotisserie over a blazing bonfire—but he was still alive.

"Colonel Griffin!" he heard Hal Briggs shout. Briggs was kneeling beside him, putting out an electrical fire from his backpack and belt and removing his helmet. "Holy shit . . ."

"Where . . . where's that gunship, Hal . . . ?" Griffin breathed. "Get him, damn it!"

Hal turned and raised his rail gun—but before he could line up on the aircraft, another explosion erupted a short distance away. The Russian gunship had shot a second laser-guided missile into the Condor, blowing it to pieces. "Oh, my God!" Griffin shouted. "Turabi and his sergeant . . ."

"They're clear," Hal said. "They're trying to find a place to hide." Just as he was about to fire on the aircraft, he received warning in his helmet. "Oh, shit, another aircraft inbound."

He turned to take a shot at the second aircraft, then slung his rail gun over his shoulder, picked up Griffin, and leaped away—just as another laser-guided missile exploded in the exact spot where they'd been a fraction of a second earlier. Hal landed from his jump and had barely enough time to cover Griffin with his body when the second aircraft, a Russian Mi-24 Hind-D attack helicopter, peppered him with thirty-millimeter cannon fire. The shock of the heavy-caliber shells hitting Briggs was so fierce that, even protected by Briggs's armored body, Griffin felt his breath being knocked out of his lungs by the impact. As soon as the cannon fire stopped, Briggs scooped up Griffin and made another thruster jump in a different direction, away from Turabi and Dendara.

But the explosion, the gunship attack, and that last leap substantially depleted his power—warning tones were popping up the moment he landed from his jump. Griffin obviously saw them, too, because he held out his spare power pack. "Turn around—I'll swap power packs."

"Not this one, you won't," Hal said, examining the pack— it had shattered along with the rest of Trevor's backpack. He quickly ejected his nearly spent power pack and replaced it with his emergency one, then made another leap when he noticed the first gunship lining up for a cannon or missile attack.

But it was soon obvious that the Russian helicopter pilots had set up their attack-orbit plan well. Hal couldn't jump in any direction without a gunship able to bear down on him quickly with only minor corrections. As soon as he landed from his last jump, cannon shells were raining down on him, while the other gunship was circling to begin his attack.

Hal found that he was a few yards away from a shallow

wash, and while he waited for his thrusters to recharge, he carried Griffin to it. "You gotta stay here, sir," Hal said. "If we're going to stop these bastards, I need to get some room to fight. Burrow down as deep as you can and hide under the sand—your suit will help screen your heat signature from their IR sensors."

"Hal . . ." But he was gone seconds later.

As soon as Briggs landed, he hefted his rail gun, took aim on the closest gunship, and fired. Nothing happened—he saw the bluish yellow streak of vapor hit the helicopter, but it kept on barreling toward him. Hal leveled the gun again and prepared to fire another round.

But he realized moments later that the big helicopter was no longer flying toward him but *crashing* toward him. The main rotor had sheared off milliseconds after the large titanium projectile shattered one engine and the transmission, and seconds after being hit the gunship was nothing more than a man-made meteorite. The crew compartment and cockpit were filled with burning fuel and transmission fluid, and almost instantly ordnance started to cook off out on the pylons and stub wings from the intense fuselage fire. Hal jet-jumped away from the impact point seconds before the copter crashed into the desert right in front of him.

"Got the bastard, sir," Hal radioed, before realizing that Griffin's equipment was destroyed and he couldn't hear. He activated his sensors to locate Griffin.

And realized with horror that the second Russian gunship had zeroed in on Trevor Griffin and was about to attack! He raised his rail gun just as the gunner started walking thirty-millimeter rounds onto Griffin's hiding spot.

But at that very moment, two missiles streaked out of the night sky and rammed into the Hind's engine exhausts. The gunship immediately exploded, and the flaming fireball buried itself in the desert a few hundred yards away from the Air Force colonel.

Just as he was wondering who'd shot those missiles, Hal

heard, "Sorry we're so late, Tin Man." It was Kelvin Carter. "Got here as quick as I could." Soon the unmistakable roar of their QB-52 Megafortress could be heard, less than five hundred feet overhead.

"You were right on time," Hal said. "Three more seconds and the colonel would've been turned into Swiss cheese."

"Roger that," Carter said. "Glad we could help. We're going to pay a visit on a couple other Russki aircraft heading your way. The closest ground troops are about eight miles southwest. We don't have any air-to-ground weapons on board the Megafortress, but we can create some confusion for you. Watch the skies."

"Thanks, Bobcat." Briggs jet-jumped over to Griffin. "You okay, sir?"

"I'm here to tell you, Hal," Griffin said weakly, "that it *is* possible to see your life flash in front of your eyes *twice* in one night. I sure as hell did."

"You saved our bacon, Colonel," Hal said, helping Griffin strip off the useless battle armor. "You've earned the right to join our exclusive club if you so choose."

"I've got a desk back in San Antonio waiting for me, along with a wife and kids—I think that's where I'll stay for a while," Griffin responded honestly. "That is, if we can get out of here without Condor."

At that moment Hal turned. He'd received another warning tone in his helmet. "A vehicle heading toward us—I thought Carter said it was clear?" Hal raised his rail gun, preparing to engage.

Then he saw Jalaluddin Turabi frantically waving from his perch atop the Russian armored personnel carrier. He and Dendara had returned to the place where they'd been captured and absconded with the APC and weapons.

"It's a piece of crap! Don't these Russians believe in cleaning their vehicles?" Turabi asked. "But it should get us to Repetek, where my men will be waiting. Shall we go?"

CIA AIR-OPERATIONS BASE, NEAR BUKHARA, REPUBLIC OF UZBEKISTAN
Later that day

"Confirmed, sir," the unit intelligence officer said, handing his commanding officer a report. "The damned Air Force again."

"I thought so," the commander said angrily. He read the report, shaking his head, then crumpled up the paper and banged a fist on his desk. "A commando operation *supported by a damned B-52 bomber*—and they don't say one *friggin'* word about it to us or to anyone at Langley. Where was Turabi taken?"

"Chärjew, then by air to the USS *Lincoln* in the Arabian Sea," the intelligence officer replied. "Bob, we've got to pull all our assets in *right now*. The Russians are going to sweep east, take Mary, then sweep north and bomb the living daylights out of us at any time. We've got to exfil our guys and get out of here."

"I know, damn it, I know. A year of work down the tubes—not just in Turkmenistan but all the way to Iran and all over Central Asia. The Air Force really screwed us last night."

The commander looked up from his desk at the hangar where his office was located. He had a U.S. Air Force MH-53M Pave Low IV special-ops helicopter and crew standing by ready to go, along with its crew of six and a team of twelve commandos—and there was no doubt that he could get volunteers to fill up the chopper if he asked. He had a large contingent of operatives and valuable informants on the streets of Ashkhabad, the capital of Turkmenistan, and also down inside Iran, throughout Afghanistan and Pakistan, and as far away as Krasnovodsk, the big Russian port on the Caspian Sea—all turning up information on enemy activity in Central Asia. He had guys deep inside Al Qaeda, the Russian military, Afghani drug cartels, and terrorist groups for thousands of miles around.

All compromised because of some half-assed Air Force operation near Mary.

It was too risky to stay in Uzbekistan now. The Russians were going to be like a large hive of angry bees—stirred up, swarming, and mad as hell, ready to lash out at anything that wasn't 100 percent verified Russian. The whole Central Asia operation was in danger. A lot of Russians had been killed by the Americans as they fought their way out of Turkmenistan—no doubt the Russians wanted payback.

"We got no choice," he said finally. "Send messages via secure microburst transmissions and radio interference, telling our guys to hightail it out into the back country and start monitoring the pickup points." The CIA operatives used their own secret microburst transceivers—coded messages sent and received by devices that compressed messages into microsecond-long bursts, thereby reducing the chances of their being detected or used to backtrace their location. The CIA headquarters also sent messages by broadcasting interference signals overlaid on regular radio and TV broadcasts—sometimes as simple as bursts of static, other times images that could be seen only with special lenses or by slowing down videotapes of certain shows—to relay messages to their informants or agents in deep cover.

Over time all the field operatives and informants who wished to leave would get the message, and they would execute their escape plan. The actual procedure differed widely for individual agents, but the objective was for each agent to report to one of several exfiltration points near where he or she lived or worked and wait for a sign or message that the agent was going to get picked up. It could take days, sometimes weeks—patience and trust were the key words here. Sometimes agents would be on the run, hiding out in the wilderness. If they were lucky, they could maintain their covers while checking the spots daily for a sign that their rescuers were nearby.

"Roger that," the intel officer said. "Everyone's been in fairly close contact. We should have no trouble rounding them all up."

"That's because the Air Force stirred up the Russians *before,* too," the commander said bitterly. "I am going to make sure that Langley chews some butt at the Pentagon this time. Someone's got to lose his stars over this. They just can't—"

The unit commander was nearly knocked off his chair by the first massive explosion, but by the time he leaped to his feet and began running for the exit, the second bomb crashed through the ceiling of the hangar and exploded. He never heard or felt anything after that. . . .

The CIA air base in Uzbekistan was certainly no secret to anyone—especially not the Russians. Since Russia was a full partner in the defense of Uzbekistan, and Russia was mostly responsible for Uzbekistan's border security and defense, the Russians had plenty of information on anyone moving across the frontier—including the CIA agents and their most trusted informants.

But instead of simply raiding the CIA field headquarters, Russia had other plans for them.

A lone Tupolev-22M Backfire bomber swept in over the desert plains of eastern Uzbekistan. It had been cleared into Kazakhstan by Russian air-traffic controllers based at Alma-Ata and monitored by other Russian air-traffic controllers in Bishkek, the capital of Kyrgyzstan, who watched the speedy bomber as it descended rapidly from high altitude down to just a few hundred meters from the surface. There were actually three Backfires that had launched from their secret Siberian base, but after their last aerial refueling, the crews chose the best-operating aircraft to complete the mission.

Skirting the Bishkek radars, the Backfire bomber proceeded at low altitude across the vast southern Kazakh plains, staying below the coverage of air-defense radars in

Tashkent, Uzbekistan. Minutes later the bomber started a slight wings-level climb. At an altitude of one thousand meters, it began its attack.

The Tu-22M carried three large air-launched missiles called the Kh-31, one in the bomb bay and one on external hardpoints on the nonmoving portion of each wing. Each six-hundred-kilogram missile had a ninety-kilogram high-explosive fragmentary warhead designed to blast apart lightweight structures like radar arrays and antennas with ease. After release, the missile shot ahead of the bomber using its small first-stage solid-rocket motor, then climbed rapidly through fifteen thousand meters' altitude using its big second-stage motor. When the second-stage motor burned out, the motor casing became a ramjet combustion chamber, which automatically fired and quickly accelerated the missile through Mach 3. The Kh-31 initially used its inertial navigation system to steer toward its target, but it received position and velocity updates through its GLONASS satellite-navigation system, which greatly improved its accuracy to near-precision quality. It needed less than four minutes to fly the two hundred kilometers to its target. Once within thirty seconds of its target, it switched to a passive radar detector and homed directly in on a specific radar frequency.

One Kh-31 missile lost contact with its carrier aircraft and hit harmlessly somewhere in the central Uzbek deserts—but the other missiles continued their flight with devastating accuracy, destroying the air-defense radar sites at Tashkent and at Samarkand, a large city in southeastern Uzbekistan. With the Uzbek radars shut down, the Tu-22M proceeded south into Uzbekistan and set up an orbit, blanketing the area with electronic jamming signals and also monitoring the activities about to begin.

The second part of the operation had actually taken place nearly a half hour earlier. Orbiting over southern Siberia at fifteen thousand meters, a Tupolev-95MS "Bear" bomber, a long-range turboprop aircraft first designed in the 1940s, had released two eleven-meter-long missiles from wing pylons about twenty seconds apart. Code-named the Kh-90 "Karonka," or "Crown," it was one of the world's most advanced land-attack missiles. The missiles' first stage was a solid rocket motor, which accelerated the missile to almost Mach 2. As in the Kh-31s launched by the Backfire bomber, when the first-stage motor burned out, the rocket chamber became a ramjet engine. Air was compressed and accelerated inside the ramjet, and liquid rocket fuel was injected and burned. As the missile gained speed, air and fuel were squeezed and accelerated even more, until the missile soon was cruising at over *eight times* the speed of sound.

The missiles streaked across Siberia and Kazakhstan, climbing to twenty-five thousand meters' altitude, then started a steep dive toward their target. Steered by signals from the Russian GLONASS, their accuracy was superb. At an altitude of ten thousand meters, each missile ejected two independently targeted 150-kilogram high-explosive warheads.

The CIA operations base next to the abandoned airfield outside Bukhara, Uzbekistan, consisted of only four buildings inside a ten-acre fenced compound—two aircraft hangars, each of which doubled as a storage facility, ammo dump, and training center; a natural-gas-fired power generator and well pumphouse; and a headquarters building, which doubled as a barracks. The warheads hit each structure dead on. The explosions were so powerful that the fuel and munitions inside the hangars did not even have a chance to explode.

They simply disappeared in a cloud of superheated gas.

2

BARKSDALE AIR FORCE BASE, BOSSIER CITY, LOUISIANA
Days later

"What in hell do you mean, *you don't know where it came from?*" Lieutenant General Terrill Samson, commander of Eighth Air Force, thundered. Terrill Samson was a truly imposing man, even when seated, and a few of the staff members arrayed around him in the headquarters battle-staff area jumped when he shouted, even though they were accustomed to his loud, frequent outbursts. "A Russian bomber completely wipes out a CIA field-operations base in Uzbekistan, and you're telling me we *still* don't know where it came from or what weapon it used, General McLanahan? It didn't just pop up out of nowhere!"

"Sir, we're working on it," Patrick McLanahan said. He was speaking via secure videoconference from the Command and Operations Center of the Air Intelligence Agency at its headquarters in San Antonio, Texas. "The Nine-sixty-sixth should have that information shortly. We have almost constant surveillance on every Russian bomber base west of the Urals. So far every one of those bases' normal inventory has been accounted for—"

"What about Engels's bombers, General?" Major General Gary Houser asked.

"Sir, we still have no firm estimates on how many planes survived, how many damaged planes were reconstituted, or where any survivors were relocated," Patrick responded. Engels Air Base in southwestern Russia was the largest bomber base in Russia and the headquarters of Aviatsiya Voyska Strategischeskovo Naznacheniya (A-VSN), or Strategic Aviation Force, Russia's intercontinental-bomber command, composed of subsonic Tupolev-95 Bear bombers, supersonic Tupolev-160 "Blackjack" bombers, Ilyushin-78 "Midas" aerial-refueling tankers, and Tupolev-16 "Badger" tankers and electronic-warfare aircraft. "Our poststrike intelligence after the raid reported twelve possible Backfire survivors, plus another ten with only minor damage. The base itself is still not operational, but it may be usable, so it's likely that any surviving bombers could have made it out."

"Engels's bombers, eh?" Samson muttered, shaking his head. "I should have known." It was well known throughout the command—and most of the world—that Patrick McLanahan's former unit, the Air Battle Force, had conducted a surprise bombing raid on Engels Air Base. During the conflict with Turkmenistan, Russia was about to initiate a massive bomber raid from Engels against government and Taliban troops threatening Russian bases and interests in that oil-rich country. Using his fleet of unmanned long-range bombers launched from Diego Garcia in the Indian Ocean, Patrick had destroyed several Russian bombers on the ground at Engels, damaged several more, and severely damaged the base itself.

Although Patrick's raid had halted the conflict in Turkmenistan and allowed United Nations peacekeepers to enter that country safely and establish a cease-fire, most of the U.S. government, the Pentagon, and the world had blamed Patrick McLanahan for the rising tensions between Russia and the United States. No one expected him still to be wearing an American military uniform, let alone a general's star.

Least of all Lieutenant General Terrill Samson, Patrick's new boss.

"We've tried to account for the survivors, through surveillance as well as through diplomatic channels, but have not been successful," Patrick went on. "We should have an answer shortly as to where they came from. The Russians are bound by the Conventional Forces in Europe Treaty and the Strategic Arms Limitation Treaty to state exactly how many long-range bombers they have and their precise location; under the Open Skies Treaty, we have a right to verify that information ourselves. Russia can't legally withhold that information. We will—"

"General McLanahan, thanks to your unsanctioned, wasteful, and wholly unnecessary attack on Engels, we will be lucky to get any cooperation from Russia on any aspect of the CFE or SALT agreements," Samson interrupted. "You will make it your top priority to find out exactly where those bombers came from and what Russia's current long- and medium-range strike capability is. I want that info on my desk in twenty-four—no, I want it in *eight* hours, in time for the next scheduled battle-staff meeting. Is that understood?"

"Perfectly, sir." Patrick knew that was all his staff had been working on ever since U.S. Strategic Command alerted them of the attack—they would have the info ready by then.

"What *do* you know about the attack?" Samson asked heatedly.

"Reports from Uzbek air-traffic-control authorities in Tashkent have confirmed that the aircraft that crossed over from Russia was a Tupolev-22M bomber, call sign Mirny-203," Patrick said. "Air-traffic controllers from Alma-Ata, Kazakhstan, reported the bomber to Tashkent but did not provide any flight-plan information. The aircraft was spotted about one hundred and seventy-five miles north of the Uzbek border by radar operators at Tashkent before the radars were knocked off the air and communications were disrupted.

"The Russians have one missile with that kind of range: the AS-17, code name 'Krypton,' " Patrick went on. "The AS-17 is an antiradar weapon designed to exceed the range and performance numbers of the Patriot antiaircraft missile. However, the AS-17 was not originally designed to be fired from the Tupolev-22M. One AS-17 apparently malfunctioned and crashed in the desert in Kazakhstan."

"CIA will undoubtedly send out teams to recover data on that lost missile," Houser said. "I'll have the info as soon as they get it."

"Sir, we've heard from CIA, and because of the strike against their base, they're not prepared to mount a covert mission into Kazakhstan to retrieve the missile," Patrick said. "Colonel Griffin has put together a mission plan for your approval. He can deploy with a team, or we can brief a team based in—"

"So Griffin wants to lead another covert-ops team into Central Asia, eh?" Houser asked derisively. "He obviously thinks he's the newest action hero now."

"Sir, no other agencies have offered to get that data for us," Patrick said, daring to show his exasperation at Houser's remark, "and if I may remind you, we have very few military or intelligence assets in place in that region since the United Nations Security Council ordered us to leave so they could install peacekeeping forces. If we want a chance to get that data, Colonel Griffin needs an execution order immediately. We can have him and his team deploy immediately to—"

"I think Colonel Griffin has stirred up enough shit in Central Asia for the time being," Houser interjected. "Although we certainly applaud him for successfully retrieving General Turabi of Turkmenistan, who has proved to be an extremely valuable source of information on the Russians' advance into Mary, it is clear now that the Russians felt threatened and retaliated against what they thought was a CIA operation. In addition, I personally feel that I was led astray by General Luger at Battle Mountain. Colonel Griffin took an awful risk by going on this mission, an especially unnecessary risk considering all the forces Battle Mountain had available."

"Sir, Colonel Griffin's plan utilizes forces based in—"

"General Houser said he'd discuss this with you later, General McLanahan," Samson cut in irritably. "Can we get on with the briefing, please?"

"Yes, sir," Patrick said. "The antiradar missiles flew for approximately one hundred and thirty miles. Speed of each missile was in excess of Mach three. They were on a ballistic flight path at first, but during descent the radar operators said the missiles made minute course changes that placed them precisely on target, indicating that perhaps the missiles were operator- or GPS-guided, not just inertially guided. This matches the AS-17's flight profile. They scored direct hits on the Uzbek radar sites.

"As far as the attack on Bukhara itself—it's still a mystery, sir," Patrick admitted. "Observers near the impact points there, including a couple surviving CIA operatives, reported the explosions were tremendous, perhaps five-hundred-pound high-explosive warheads."

"You have *nothing?*" Samson asked. "No leads at all?"

"We're investigating a few uncorrelated bits of data, sir," Patrick replied. "Greatly increased air traffic in eastern Siberia and a few rocket launches from test-launch sites in Siberia detected by DSP satellites apparently shot into the Kazakh missile-test ranges. So far nothing that could give us any clues on the attack all the way west in Uzbekistan."

"Then maybe you shouldn't be wasting your time on these other 'uncorrelated bits of data,' as you call them," Samson said. "Any conclusions at all to report to us?"

"Sir, it appears that the missiles shot from the Backfire were intended to screen the real attack on the CIA headquarters in Uzbekistan," Patrick went on. "The AS-17 is designed to be launched from tactical fighter-bombers, so the existence of these weapons on large bombers is a new development for the Russians: using tactical precision-guided weapons on strategic bombers instead of just long-range subsonic cruise missiles. It appears that the Russians had excellent intel and acted on it remarkably quickly. They knew exactly when and where to hit. They probably loaded those bombers within hours of the mission to exfiltrate Turabi and launched the attack immediately.

"I feel that this indicates a substantial increase in the capabilities and effectiveness of the Russian heavy-bomber forces. Wherever these bombers came from, they were highly modified and their crews trained to levels of proficiency and tactical coordination that rival our own. They obviously used sophisticated covert bases, perhaps underground or well-camouflaged facilities, and a supply system that is many times faster and more efficient than—"

"General McLanahan, I know you're new to the Air Intelligence Agency and the Nine-sixty-sixth Wing, so I'll give you a pass on this one," Gary Houser said. "But in the future when you brief the command or battle staffs, we expect facts, not interpretation. And the facts are that you still don't know where those bombers came from or where they went. That's what we need to know. Is that clear, General?"

"Yes, sir," Patrick responded. Houser looked at the darkened glassed-in booth where the communications officers sat and drew a finger across his throat. Moments later the link between Barksdale and Lackland was terminated.

"Let's go on with the status of forces," Samson said, giving the screen on which McLanahan had appeared one last disgusted glance that was very apparent, even across the secure videoconference network. "General?"

Conducting his briefing from his seat, in Samson's preferred style, the Eighth Air Force deputy commander for operations and the acting vice commander, Brigadier General Charles C. Zoltrane, pressed a button on his console to call up his first PowerPoint slide. "Yes, sir. Currently all wings are reporting one hundred percent conventional-combat-ready."

"Conventional only? What's the nuclear side looking like?"

"Due to our conventional mission commitments, the lack of airframes and crews, and lower funding levels, we can meet approximately sixty percent taskings for Single Integrated Operations Plan missions, sir," Zoltrane said. "The crews and the planes are simply not available for certification. The B-2 stealth bombers are in the best shape at seventy percent, but the B-52s are at only fifty percent—and I think that's being generous."

Samson thought about the news for a moment, then shrugged. "Well, if STRATCOM wants more planes ready for SIOP missions, they're going to have to send me more money and more airframes," he said. STRATCOM, or U.S. Strategic Command, was the unified military command in charge of planning and fighting a nuclear conflict. STRATCOM did not "own" any aircraft—like every unified command, STRATCOM "gained" aircraft from other major commands, such as nuclear bombers, intelligence-gathering aircraft, and strategic command-and-control planes, from Eighth Air Force.

"We can bring some planes out of flyable storage to have available for SIOP planning if necessary," Zoltrane said. The fly-stores, or "flyable storage," were the planes held in a sort of maintenance limbo—it was a way to save costs while maintaining a large fleet capable of fighting with minimal preparation. Two-thirds of the long-range bombers allocated to both Eighth and Twelfth Air Forces were in flyable storage at any one time.

"How many planes were we budgeting to come out of fly-store this year?"

"Through the normal rotation? Thirty-six B-52s and—"

"No, I meant planes coming out of fly-store to *augment* the fleet. How many?"

"Well . . . none, sir," Zoltrane responded. "But we're technically non-mission-ready if STRATCOM wants to put any bombers on alert. We'd have to—"

"That's STRATCOM's problem, not mine," Samson said.

"They know hour by hour how many planes we have available. If they notice our shortage, they're not saying anything, which means they don't want to deal with the budget crunch either."

"Sir, we *have* to do something—at least notify the Pentagon that we're low," Zoltrane said. "It'll take weeks, maybe months, for some of those bombers to be mission-ready out of flyable storage. If we start now, maybe we can stop the process before we break the bank, or maybe we'll get interim funding later on. But we can't just—"

"Okay, okay, Charlie, I get the picture," General Samson said irritably. "Have the wings start pulling fly-stores out right away—see if they can put it under an exercise budget, or if they're close enough to their cycle periods anyway, have them pull their allotments early." Planes in flyable storage had to be rotated out every six months, brought back up to full combat readiness, and flown for a specified number of hours before being put back in fly-store. Because of arms-control limitations and other political considerations, there was usually no rush to do this, and in fact many planes in flyable storage went over their six-month time limit or were never brought back up to full combat-ready status. In effect they became "hangar queens," a source of cannibalized parts. It was an unfortunate fact of life for the Air Force's bomber fleet. "I want it done *quietly*. I don't want it to appear like we're mobilizing any long-range strategic forces."

"Yes, sir," Zoltrane said.

"This really sucks," Samson said. "We're forced to spend money on spinning up the fly-stores, while McLanahan and Luger get their pick of the best airframes to do their Q-conversion—and then we can't even use the damned things because no one except the weenies at Battle Mountain knows how they work." The Q-conversion was the outrageous plan recently approved by the Pentagon to modify a number of B-1 and B-52 bombers to unmanned combat-strike missions, reconnaissance, and suppression of enemy air defense. The

111th Bomb Wing at Battle Mountain had developed the capability to control a number of bombers for global-combat sorties without putting one human being in harm's way. "They have code-one airframes and crews out there in Battle Mountain just twiddling their thumbs while the rest of the command has to bust our butts just to get to minimum force levels.

"And even if we had them, we don't even know how to employ robot planes," Samson went on. "It's just like the Turkmenistan UN Security Council surveillance mission all over again—if we want to use them, we have to put one of their Trekkies in charge. I think we could stand David Luger or Rebecca Furness in our headquarters for a short period of time, but if they have to start bringing guys like Daren Mace or their civilian contractors Masters or Duffield in here, they'd drive us crazy in no time. No thanks. I'd rather spend the money and bring some of our fly-stores online before I bring in anyone from Battle Mountain." He turned to the next officer at the conference table. "Gary, I hope you have better news for me."

"Yes, sir, I do," Major General Gary Houser said. "The good news is, one hundred percent of our spacecraft are operational, and we have complete overhead coverage of Central Asia and southwestern Russia; all reconnaissance and surveillance air wings are fully combat-ready, and sortie completion rates are over ninety percent. True, we didn't see the air raid on Bukhara coming, and I will personally find out where the deficiency is and fix it. But now we have almost constant electronic surveillance on the entire region, and if the Russians try to make another move, we'll know about it."

"Good work," Samson said. "I'm going to be relying on you for the best and latest intel, Gary. I expect to be called to the Pentagon soon, maybe even the White House, and I need a constant stream of updates."

"You should let me handle the heat from Washington, sir," Houser said. "You'll have enough on your plate here organizing the force. Leave the intel mumbo jumbo to me."

"Wouldn't be offering just so you can get more face time with the honchos in Washington, would you, Gary?"

Houser smiled conspiratorially. "Never crossed my mind, sir. I'll play it any way you'd like."

"For now I'll take the meetings in Washington or Offutt or wherever they send me, Gary," Samson said. "If we start sending strikers overseas, and they deploy me as part of the air staff, you may have to stand in during the intel briefs. That's your area of expertise."

"Yes, sir."

"Okay, here's my take on the attack, based on what we know, folks," Samson said, addressing everyone in the room. "I believe that this attack on Bukhara was an isolated reaction by General Gryzlov. He got his butt kicked by us at Engels and twice in Turkmenistan, and he lashed out. We've seen this kind of massive aerial assault recently in Chechnya—he does it for show, then backs off.

"But I believe that Gryzlov is under a lot of pressure from his military to retaliate against us, so he won't stand for any more attacks against Russian military forces, but the size and scope of this attack leads me to believe that this is not a prelude to a wider confrontation. Does anyone see any indication that he wants a war with us?" No response from the staff members.

"Then I think we concur. The CIA operation in Turkmenistan was discovered, they had to fight their way out, they killed some Russians, and the Russians retaliated by bombing their field-operations base. I'll recommend to Air Combat Command and the Air Force that we step up monitoring and surveillance, but we feel that the Russians have shot their wad.

"What I need is a profile of Russian forces in Central Asia and the Persian Gulf and a look at other potential targets," Samson ordered. "If you think a fight is possible anywhere in the region, I want analysis on where, when, and how, and I want a plan of action on what we should do about it. Naturally, the plan of action should place Eighth Air Force commanders in charge and assets at the pointy end of the spear, especially intelligence, reconnaissance, and information-warfare activities. Yes, make sure you emphasize joint warfighting—that's the important buzzword these days, and if you use it in your planning, you're likely to get your plan noticed. But the lead agency and the first units in combat should be the Mighty Eighth in every way possible.

"Next I want to make sure that every man and woman in this command—and every piece of hardware from the biggest bomber to the smallest microchip— is one hundred and ten percent ready to deploy and fight on a moment's notice. I want to be able to tell the Pentagon and the White House that we can send any unit, any weapon system, and every airman under my command anywhere on the globe just by picking up a telephone.

"However, it is essential to remember that, until ordered to do so, we must *not* appear as if we are stepping up our posture or readiness for a shooting war," Samson went on. "This means you cannot step up orders for weapons, fuel, and supplies or increase your normal air order of battle. Your units need to prepare as much as possible within the current posture, but no one receives any more planes, weapons, supplies, or fuel than they're currently allotted.

"Finally, I want problems handled in-house, and I want strict, tight control on information and intelligence," Samson said, his voice low and menacing. "Every piece of data that we collect stays in this command unless I authorize its release. If your staffs find a problem or think they find something important, it doesn't leave the command unless this battle staff sees it, deals with the problem, and releases the information with a solution attached. No one, and I mean *no one,* breaks the chain of command. The buck *will* stop right here, and I will destroy the airman and his supervisor if I find out that he or she takes key information and upchannels it outside the command without my signature. If we generate it, it stays with us. Is that perfectly clear?" Heads nodded all around. "Anything else for me?" The battle staff knew better than to speak—they knew that the boss was done with the meeting. Any other questions were expected to go to the deputy commanders. "Good. Dismissed."

As usual, Gary Houser and Charles Zoltrane stayed behind with Terrill Samson after the others had departed. "I apologize for McLanahan's performance today, sir," Houser said. "He's new to the post, and he obviously thinks he can run things like he did at Battle Mountain and Dreamland. It won't happen again."

"You know McLanahan as well as I do, Gary," Samson said. "He's a smart and dedicated young officer who was detoured away from a successful career by some bad influences. He gets the job done by skirting the rules, just as Brad Elliott used to do. It's too bad."

"Don't be sorry for him, sir," Houser said. "I knew him before he joined up with Elliott, and he was an attitude case then, too. But back then the brass was letting guys slide if they made the wing king look good—and McLanahan was good, no doubt about that. He still thinks his shit doesn't stink."

"He's probably better off retiring—in fact, that's what I thought happened with him after I got him bounced out of Dreamland," Samson said. "But he's got balls of steel, loads of brain power, talented friends, and a real lock-and-load attitude that politicians like. He's a survivor. Unfortunately, he's your problem now, Gary."

"We've had a heart-to-heart already, sir," Houser said. "He won't be a hassle for you."

"After today's performance I'd say you still have some work to do," Samson said. "Just keep him in line and out of my face, all right?"

"Yes, sir."

"Who's your deputy, sir?" Zoltrane asked. "Have him give the Nine-sixty-sixth's briefings from now on."

"That's Trevor Griffin."

Zoltrane nodded, but Samson chimed in derisively, "You mean 'Howdy Doody' on steroids? Shit, last time he gave the staff a briefing, all I could think of was Opie Taylor giving a book report in front of the Mayberry schoolmarm. Christ, where do we find these characters anyway?" Houser did not respond. "Just do what you need to do to keep your folks in line and functioning, Gary," Samson went on. "We don't need smart-asses like McLanahan giving us attitude in my battle-staff room. Clear?"

"Yes, sir. I'll take care of it."

"See that you do."

"One more matter for you, sir," Houser said. "I wanted to ask you about the vice commander's vacancy here at headquarters. We talked about moving me here to get some combat command time before we—"

"Everything's on schedule, Gary," Samson said. "The vacancy is still there. I need a firm commitment from the Pentagon about my fourth star and taking over Air Combat Command or STRATCOM. Once I hear for sure, I'll install you here as the vice, so you'll automatically take command when I leave. Don't worry about it. It's in the bag."

"Yes, sir." Houser didn't sound convinced.

"I don't think this recent flap with McLanahan will spoil things," Samson added. "To the command, I jump in McLanahan's shit; to Washington, I tone it down a little. A lot of folks like the son of a bitch. He's still being considered for national security adviser, for Christ's sake. The politicians like getting their pictures taken with a real-life aerial assassin. We're below their radar screen, and we need to stay that way.

"Just keep McLanahan on a short leash. This nonsense about the Russians gearing up their bomber fleet has got to stay in this command, understand me? If word gets out, the politicians will wonder why we're not doing something about it, and then we'll look like jerks. If we play it cool, eventually McLanahan will resign to go work for Thorn, or he'll resign to be with his family on the coast, or he'll be shipped off to Dreamland and put back in his genie's bottle until the next war, like his mentor, Elliott."

"Yes, sir. I agree. You won't have to worry about McLanahan, sir."

Samson pulled out a cigar, lit it, then waved it at the door to dismiss Houser. The Air Intelligence Agency commander practically bowed before he headed out.

"I'll get that order to gin up the fly-stores going right now, sir," Zoltrane said, picking up a phone to his office.

Samson nodded as he puffed away. "It's bad enough dealing with the Russians, Offutt, and Washington," Samson muttered. "Now I have to deal with my own subordinate officers who might be ready to start rolling around on the deck during the storm, knocking guys into the ocean and wrecking my ship."

"Sir, to be perfectly honest with you, I give McLanahan kudos for giving us that analysis so quick," Zoltrane admitted as he waited for the secure connection to go through. "Part of the problem is that our guys are hesitant to upchannel their reports for fear of being labeled a crackpot or a nuisance. We *want* guys to give us educated opinions, and we want them soonest. McLanahan's only been on the job a short time, but he put together a pretty good analysis of Russian bomber capabilities and potential.

"And Trevor Griffin shocked the hell out of me. The guy's . . . what? In his mid to late forties? He climbs aboard an *unmanned* B-52 bomber, flies halfway around the world, then climbs into a high-tech Spam can and lets himself be dropped *out of the damned bomb bay*. Fuckin' incredible. And he made it out of Turkmenistan, too, after the Russians attacked—that's even more incredible. Maybe we should—"

"What? Let him have some satellites and maybe even some field operatives and send them into Russia looking for supersecret Backfire bombers?" Samson asked. "How the hell can you hide a Backfire bomber? And we know damned well the Russians aren't modernizing Backfires—they're scrapping them. McLanahan couldn't possibly have collected enough information from that raid on Bukhara to come up with valid conclusions that warrant additional intel missions. He's *guessing,* Charlie. We don't waste our time or resources on guesses. We need some hard evidence before we can take a field-intel-ops plan to Air Combat Command or the Pentagon. And that goes triple for a proposed operation into Russia. McLanahan is guessing, plain and simple, and he wants to rub our noses in the fact that he's here against his will."

"He doesn't *seem* like the kind of guy to pull shit like that, sir," Zoltrane said, adding the word "sir" to distance himself from his own remark and defer to whatever his boss told him. He really didn't know McLanahan that well, and he certainly knew his reputation—he was not about to defend the guy before he personally saw him in action. "He seems like a straight shooter to me."

"I worked with him long enough at Dreamland to know that he's a sidewinder, Charlie," Samson said. "He's quiet and hardworking, but when he decides he wants to do something, he'll step over anyone to do the job—and if there aren't enough bodies and careers piled up high enough to get him to where he wants to be, he'll create more. The sooner we get his ass out of the Air Force—for good this time—the better."

966TH INFORMATION WING HEADQUARTERS, LACKLAND AIR FORCE BASE, SAN ANTONIO, TEXAS
A short time later

"So how was your first battle-staff meeting?" Trevor Griffin asked when he met Patrick back in his office. The grin on his face told Patrick that he already knew the answer to that one.

"Just peachy," Patrick said dryly.

"If you want me to take those briefings and catch some spears for you, say the word," Griffin said. "I'm used to the abuse."

"Nah, I can handle it," Patrick said, grateful that at least he hadn't been singled out for extra-special abuse. He smiled and asked, "What's the matter—you don't want to go jumping around with the Battle Force anymore?"

"Hey, I'll do that mission again in a heartbeat—just don't tell my wife I said that," Griffin said. "Your guys out there are cosmic. You should be proud of the team you built. If they need me, I'm in."

Patrick liked it when Griffin said "your guys," even though he knew it wasn't true. "You're a Tin Man now and forever, Tagger—they'll be calling on you, I guarantee it. So anything else pop up while I was in the staff meeting?"

"Not a thing."

Patrick loosened his tie. "What about that missile launch that DSP discovered?"

"We're waiting for word from the air attaché's office in Geneva," Griffin responded. "According to the Conventional Forces in Europe treaty, Kazakhstan and Russia are supposed to inform the United Nations if they conduct any tests on missiles with a range longer than five hundred kilometers. There was nothing on the schedule for that missile DSP detected." The DSP, or Defense Support Program, satellites were supersensitive heat-detecting satellites in geosynchronous Earth orbit, designed to warn of ballistic-missile launches. DSP could pinpoint the launch point, report on the missile's track and speed, and predict its impact point with a fair amount of accuracy. The satellites were designed to warn of intercontinental-ballistic-missile attack but had been amazingly effective in warning friendly forces of Iraqi SS-1 SCUD surface-to-surface missile attacks during the 1991 Persian Gulf War and had provided a good amount of warning time in the missile's projected target area. "Naturally, Russia denies that it was one of theirs and told us to contact Kazakhstan; Kazakhstan said they don't have big missiles like that and recommended we talk to the Russians."

Patrick punched instructions into his computer, called up the DSP data on those rocket launches, and studied them for a moment. "Apparently launched north of Bratsk," he muttered. "Any ICBMs based at Bratsk?"

"Not that anyone knows about," Griffin replied. "Mobile SS-25s at Irkutsk and Kansk and silo-based SS-24s at Krasnoyarsk. They could have set up a new SS-25 'shell-game' racetrack out there—it would be worth a look with a SAR or photo-satellite pass."

"I'm going to need an update of all the Russian land-based missile forces, especially the mobile ones," Patrick said. "What do we have to help us on that?"

"We dedicate an entire office to doing just that," Griffin responded. "Six guys and girls in the Seventieth Intelligence Wing at Fort Meade do nothing else but download the latest satellite imagery from the National Reconnaissance Office and track down every Russian SS-24 'Scalpel' and SS-25 'Sickle' road- or rail-mobile missile in the Russian inventory. They study the rail and roadways and monitor every known secure garage where the missiles are sent on exercises. They also keep an eye out for cheating, monitor arms-control compliance, and study the ways the Russians try to decoy or camouflage their missile shelters."

"Oh?"

"We believe that the Russians are doing a deliberate poor-mouth routine to delay deactivating their biggest and best nuclear weapons, claiming they don't have the money to dismantle and destroy some weapons," Griffin explained. "The Scalpel is a perfect example. The SS-24 is a copy of our 'Peacekeeper' ICBM, which was originally designed to be rail-mobile but was converted to silo-launched basing. Like Peacekeeper, the SS-24 has a range of ten thousand miles, has ten multiple independently targetable reentry vehicles, and is extremely accurate—it can threaten targets all across North America and even as far as the Hawaiian Islands.

"According to the Strategic Arms Reduction Treaty number two, the Russian SS-24s and the American Peacekeepers were supposed to be dismantled or converted to single-warhead missiles. Although we no longer have any Peace-keepers on alert, the rockets themselves are still stored in their silos, without any warheads, awaiting removal and disposal. The Russians claim that this is a technical violation, so they said they would keep an equal number of SS-24s on their launchers, without warheads. The Russians recently started moving these SS-24s around, like they move the SS-25s around, so we have to track them as well."

"Is that a problem?"

"The Seventieth has a pretty good record of finding both missiles," Griffin said. "The SS-24s mostly stay in their garrisons. The SS-25s are much harder, because they're road-mobile and they have a fairly good off-road capability and can fire from just about anywhere on the road, thanks to an inertial-navigation system augmented with satellite positioning."

"We have several airborne sensors that can scan wide areas of all sorts of terrain for targets like this," Patrick said. "The Megafortresses have synthetic-aperture radar that can pick out something as large as an SS-25 launcher from three hundred miles away—even concealed in a forest or under netting—and see inside a garage at one hundred miles."

"We can sure use them in treaty-compliance missions—not much chance of them authorizing us to fly a high-tech stealthy bomber over their missile-silo fields, though," Griffin said. "Our imaging satellites do a pretty good job overall, and we correlate signals intelligence with vehicle movements to spot most movements—we keep the count up as high as eighty percent. Weather hampers their movements a bit, especially in the Far East theater, and many units traverse the same areas every time during routine deployments. The good thing is that for the past few years the SS-25s have stayed mostly in their storage areas."

"Reason?"

"It's four times as expensive to maintain the road-mobile missiles than it is the silo-based weapons," Griffin explained. "In addition, the transporter-erector-launchers were built in Belarus, so the Russians have had a hard time getting spare parts and replacements after the breakup of the Soviet Union. The START II treaty limit of just one warhead on every land-launched missile means that the SS-25 has less 'bang for the buck.'

"Of course, its survivability gives it a big edge, and the missiles can be fired from their garages as well, so they all have to be monitored even while parked. We watch the garrison areas carefully for any sign of movement, and we use satellite-based visual, radiological, and thermal identification methods for tracking and identifying each convoy. We think there are only two regiments, a total of eighty missiles, actually deployed in the field at any one time."

"I think I need to get a status briefing from the Seventieth right away," Patrick said. "What else does the Seventieth monitor?"

"Test launches," Griffin said. "There is a missile test-firing range north of Bratsk that has been used in the past to test-launch mobile missiles, so no one was surprised at that DSP detection warning. But Russia hasn't fired a missile into the old Kazakh test ranges since shortly after the breakup of the Soviet Union—they usually fire shorter-range missiles north to the Pol'kino instrumented target complex, and longer-range missiles east to the Petropavlovsk Pacific range complex. Kazakhstan hasn't specifically banned use of their old target ranges, but they haven't allowed it either."

Patrick nodded as he studied the DSP satellite data. After another few moments, he asked, "Can the DSP satellites give us the speed and direction of the missile?"

"Not exactly," Griffin replied. "Lots of folks say that DSP has a 'tracking' function, but in fact it's just a series of detector activations. Certain users, like NORAD, can derive speed and ground track from the detectors, but DSP itself doesn't provide that information. Since DSP is a warning-and-reporting system, not a target-tracking system—ground-based radars like BMEWS and the new National

Missile Defense System are meant for tracking missiles—and since the system is designed to track missiles inbound to North America, not to Central Asia, we don't have that info."

"I'd like to find out how fast that missile was going when it was first detected," Patrick said.

"It may not be a very accurate number," Griffin warned. "In essence, DSP looks directly down at Earth when it spots a missile exhaust plume. Because most missiles go up awhile before heading downrange, the speed turns out to be zero for the first minute or two. That's why we sometimes get excited even when we detect a forest fire or oil-well fire in Russia—they all look the same for the first couple minutes, which is why NORAD is usually quick to blow the Klaxon if it sees a hot dot anywhere in-country."

"Find out for me," Patrick said.

"Sure. What are you thinking about, Patrick?"

"I'm thinking that uncorrelated target has something to do with the attack on Bukhara," Patrick said. He drew an electronic line on the screen between the DSP target-track data points to plot a course—and they saw that the missile's flight path took it directly to Bukhara.

"That could be a coincidence," Griffin said. "The track also goes through the Kazakh missile ranges. We don't know where the missile went after its motor burned out. . . ."

"But you said the Russians haven't been shooting missiles into Kazakhstan—which makes sense," Patrick said. "Kazakhstan cooperates as much with the U.S. as it does with Russia. And we don't exactly know where the missile or its payload impacted—we're *assuming* it was the missile test ranges in Kazakhstan. Maybe it really hit in Bukhara. But if there are no silos and the Russians have never shot a missile from Bratsk before, maybe it wasn't a ground-launched missile."

"What else could it be?"

"An air-launched missile," Patrick responded. "Ever hear of anything like that before?"

"An air-launched Mach-eight missile that can fly almost eighteen hundred miles? I seem to recall something like that, but it's better to ask the expert." Griffin picked up Patrick's secure phone. "This is Colonel Griffin. Get Chief Master Sergeant Saks secure at NAIC, ASAP," he asked Patrick's clerk. To Patrick he said, "Don Saks is one of our 'old heads'—he's been around longer than just about everyone. He's the NCOIC at the National Air Intelligence Center at Wright-Pat, which collects and disseminates information on enemy air-and-space weaponry. If it exists, ever existed, or was once on the drawing board, he'll know all about it." A few moments later, Griffin punched the speakerphone button on the phone and returned the receiver to its hook. "Chief? Tagger here, secure. I'm here at Lackland with General McLanahan."

"Saks, secure. Hello, sirs. What can I do you for?"

"You're the walking Russian threat encyclopedia and the Air Intelligence Agency's *Jeopardy!* champ, so here goes: It's a Russian long-range air-launched hypersonic attack missile."

"Easy. What is the AS-X-19 'Koala'?" Saks answered immediately. "A combination of the obsolete AS-3 'Kangaroo' air-to-surface missile and the naval SS-N-24 long-range hypersonic ship-launched antiship missile. Russian designation Kh-90 or BL-10. First test-launched in 1988. Rocket-boosted to Mach two, then ramjet-powered, speed in excess of Mach eight, range in excess of fifteen hundred miles, cruises at seventy thousand feet altitude. Too big to fit inside a Blackjack bomber, but the Tupolev-95 Bear could carry two externally. The Tupolev-22M Backfire could carry three, although over very short distances—the suckers were supposed to be more than thirty feet long and weigh in excess of eight thousand pounds. The program was canceled in 1992, but rumors persisted that the Russians were going to build a shorter-range conventional-warhead version."

"You mean, this AS-X-19 was supposed to have a *nuclear warhead,* Chief?" Patrick remarked.

"Every Russian air-launched weapon designed before 1991 was supposed to be able to carry a nuke, and the Koala was no exception, sir," Saks replied. "The Koala was inertially guided, but the Russians had terrible inertial nav systems back then—the missile needed a nuke in order to destroy anything. They were experimenting with GLONASS-navigating ultraprecise missiles when the program was canceled. Why, sir?"

"We're looking into a recent Russian missile launch to see if it was an air- or ground-launched bird."

"Got radar data on it, sir?" Saks asked.

"Negative."

"Any data on it? DSP perhaps?"

"That we got."

"Get Space Command to give you the plume-illumination-rate levels from the satellite detectors," Saks recommended. "They'll squawk and say you're not cleared for that info, but tell them you need it anyway. A ground-launched missile will have a huge and sustained first-stage plume, followed by a medium-size second-stage plume, followed by a long unpowered-coast phase. Air-launched missiles like the Kh-90 have a relatively small first stage—the carrier aircraft is actually considered the missile's first stage—followed by a whopping big and sustained second stage, which sometimes continues through reentry and even to impact."

"Would DSP be able to track the Koala during its ramjet-cruise phase?" Patrick asked.

"Probably not, sir," Saks responded. "DSP needs a good hot flame, as from a chemical-reaction motor, versus an air-fuel motor like a ramjet. A ramjet is basically an air-breathing engine, like a turbojet, except it uses the Venturi shape of the combustion chamber, rather than vanes and rotating blades, to compress incoming air. Because there's no moving parts that stall in supersonic air, the ramjet vehicle can fly several times faster than most turbojets or turboramjets. NORAD can tune

DSP to pick up cooler heat sources such as from a ramjet engine, but then it's more prone to false alarms, so they probably wouldn't do it unless they had a really compelling reason. The HAVE GAZE and SLOW WALKER satellites—designed to detect and track stealth aircraft—might be able to pick them up, but they need a pretty solid aimpoint to start with."

"Speed of a ballistic missile, range of a cruise missile—and a nuclear warhead to boot," Griffin summarized. "Did you get the data on the antiradar missiles fired against Kyrgyzstan and Kazakhstan yesterday?"

"Yes, sir. Most certainly AS-17 'Krypton' antiradar missiles, what the Russkies call the Kh-31P. It's a knockoff of the French ANS supersonic antiship and antiradar missile. We've never seen them on Backfires before, but it makes total sense. It's a pretty awesome threat. But if the Russians are flying Koalas now, that's an even greater threat. The Russians practiced launching Koalas from everything from fighters to cargo planes, and even from airliners back in the eighties. Even a Patriot missile can't catch up to it—it's a hypersonic missile almost right up to impact."

"Any more good news for us, Don?" Patrick asked wryly.

"Two things, sir: The Russians know superramjet technology," Saks responded seriously. "If you think you saw a Koala test-fired lately, chances are they've got a bunch of them ready to go."

"What's the other thing, Don?"

"The Koala was originally designed to carry *two* independently targetable reentry vehicles," Saks added. "They'd deploy at seventy to eighty thousand feet, which meant the two targets could be as far as sixty to seventy miles apart. Their accuracy back then was one to two hundred meters—but now, with GPS or GLONASS steering, they could have *ten- to twenty-meter* accuracy. Just thought you should know."

Those words stayed with Patrick long after he hung up. "Tagger, we're going to need to look at those uncorrelated contacts in Siberia," he said finally. "We know that Backfire bombers were involved in that attack on Bukhara, and we know that they can carry both AS-17 and AS-19 missiles. The boss wants to know where that Backfire came from—but I want to know who launched that AS-19, and I want to know what else the Russians are doing with their bomber fleet. If this was some isolated incident, or if this was a prelude to some sort of bigger offensive in Turkmenistan or somewhere else, I want to find out about it."

"I'll get the ball rolling, Patrick," Griffin said. "What's your guess?"

"My guess is that this attack on Bukhara was an operational test mission," Patrick said. "I've flown many of them myself with planes from Dreamland and from Battle Mountain. I think the Russians are getting ready to roll out a whole new attack system, based on long-range bombers. The addition of the Koala missile is the scariest part—with it they can hold thousands of targets in North America at risk."

BATTLE MOUNTAIN AIR RESERVE BASE, NEVADA
Later that morning

David Luger snatched up the secure telephone receiver as soon as he was told who was on the line. "Muck!" he exclaimed after logging in secure. "How are you, sir?"

"I'm fine, and I'm not 'sir' to you anymore," Patrick responded.

"You'll always be 'sir' to me, Muck," Dave said. "How's the Nine-sixty-sixth treating you?"

"Just fine," Patrick responded. "Good bunch of guys. Some of the civilian contractors need a bath and a haircut, though."

"Sounds like our kind of guys. And what's it like to be hobnobbing with the numbered air force brass?"

"Remember the old saying about not wanting to watch how sausage is made?"

"Got it."

"How are things out there?"

"Quiet and busy at the same time," Dave replied. "Our tanker guys are getting plenty of work, but the bomber guys and UCAV operators are going stir-crazy. We had to fly the AL-52s back to the lake." Even on a secure line, both parties hesitated to mention Dreamland or HAWC.

"I expected that to happen," Patrick said. "We were spending their money but not keeping up with the test schedule." The AL-52 Dragon airborne-laser anti-ballistic-missile aircraft was a test program initially begun at the High Technology Aerospace Weapons Center, or HAWC, the super-secret flight-test facility in south-central Nevada known as Dreamland. Patrick McLanahan brought the Dragons, the first operational aircraft to use a laser as their primary attack weapon, to Battle Mountain and created a combat unit based around these amazing planes. They were used over both Libya and Turkmenistan with outstanding results, against both air and ground targets and on targets as small as a heat-seeking missile and as large as a Russian MiG-29 supersonic fighter. But technically the planes still belonged to Dreamland, because Patrick didn't have an official budget.

"Too bad. Are they going to continue the program?"

"Hard to tell. The Cobra program is doing well—they should deploy their first operational aircraft ahead of schedule." The YAL-1A Cobra was an airborne chemical-oxygen-iodine laser set in a Boeing 747 airframe. While the AL-52 Dragon airborne laser had actually been used in combat, the technology used in the YAL-1A was less expensive and far less risky, and so it had much more political and military support than HAWC's version.

"Who's the project officer assigned to the AL-52?"

"There wasn't one when we brought the planes in," David said. "The director of flight ops signed for the birds himself."

"That's not good." If there was no project officer assigned to the flight-test program, there was a very good chance the

AL-52 Dragon airborne-laser program would languish—or, more likely, be canceled. "I'll see what I can do from here."

"Good. Hey, we got the word that the Seventh Bomb Wing is down for their ORI. We put in a request to cover their sorties. Any word on that?"

"It was discussed. They're going to gin up some fly-stores instead."

"That doesn't make sense. We're ready to go now. We can do everything the Seventh can do, plus the SEAD stuff."

"I know. General Hollister stood up for us, but Zoltrane and Samson wanted fly-stores."

"Hmph. Well, it's kind of a moot point anyway—we still need to be certified by Eighth Air Force before we cover sorties. Any word on when we're going to recert?"

"After this Russia thing cools down, I'm sure they'll be out there to get you recertified."

"I hope so—we're definitely ready. The sooner, the better. So what's up, Muck?"

"Dave, I've got a request for you," Patrick said. "Do you have any NIRTSats handy?"

"Sure," Luger replied. NIRTSat stood for "Need It Right This Second" satellite. Up to four of the different types of the small oven-size NIRTSats—reconnaissance, communications, or weapon targeting—were loaded aboard a winged rocket-powered booster, taken up to thirty or forty thousand feet, then dropped from a launch aircraft such as Battle Mountain's EB-52s or EB-1C bombers or from other carrier aircraft, such as Sky Masters Inc.'s DC-10 launch/tanker aircraft. After launch, the booster's first-stage solid rocket motor shot the aircraft to the top of the stratosphere, where the second- and third-stage motors would kick in and propel the booster into low Earth orbit, anywhere from fifty to three hundred miles' altitude. After ejecting its satellites in the proper sequence and spacing, the booster would then fly itself back to Earth for reuse.

Although the NIRTSats carried very little fuel and therefore could not be easily repositioned and could stay in orbit only a short time, they gave a wide range of users—field commanders, aircrews, even small-unit commando forces—their own specialized satellite constellation. But the cost per pound was high; and although Dreamland and the 111th Bomb Wing had launched many NIRTSats over the years, it was still considered an experimental system. "Who's the customer?" Dave asked.

"The Nine-sixty-sixth Wing."

"Air Intelligence Agency? You own every other satellite in the Air Force inventory already, and you control several others I'm sure I don't want to know about. What do you need NIRTSats for?"

"I need a look at some Russian bomber bases to set some baseline database imagery."

"Hold on a sec." David Luger began entering commands into his desktop computer, pulling up a complex grid of lines surrounding the globe at various different levels, then studying the results. "I assume you've looked at your current taskings? You've got them pretty well covered."

"All we have covered now are the reported active bomber bases as of the last CFE and NPT treaty reports; the CFE reports are at least two years old, and the NPT and Open Sky reports are over a year old," Patrick said. "I want all the known bases, active or otherwise—any bases that can still handle a hundred-and-fifty-ton-plus bomber."

"Like the Backfires, eh?" Dave asked. "The planes that apparently came out of nowhere and bombed the hell out of that CIA base in Uzbekistan?"

"Exactly."

"We've actually been doing some looking ourselves, Muck," Dave said. "Obviously, if those bombers reached Bukhara, they can reach the peacekeeping forces in Turkmenistan."

"The Backfire bombers have an unrefueled range of just a

little over a thousand miles with a max combat load," Patrick said. "But none of the Backfires from bases within that radius were used. That means they had to use air refueling. We've believed for years that the Russians wouldn't use Backfires in a strategic role, but if they start putting the air-refueling probes back on and using them for long-range bombing missions, they become a strategic threat once again."

"Agreed."

"So now we have to go back and look at every past heavy-bomber base in Russia to find out where the Backfires came from," Patrick went on, "and also to find out what else is going on. The Tupolev-160 Blackjack bombers aren't supposed to have air-refueling probes either, according to the CFE Treaty, but if they're putting probes back on Backfires, they can just as easily reactivate the retractable probes on Blackjacks, too."

"Sounds like good sound reasoning to me, Muck," Dave said.

"My guess is that the Backfires have been moved east, to somewhere in Siberia," Patrick said. "It's just a hunch, but I would like to get updated pics of the old Siberian bomber bases to see if they've been active lately."

"So what's the problem?"

"I haven't been able to sell my theories to anyone," Patrick replied. "Around here it comes down to cost versus benefit. Retasking a Keyhole or Lacrosse satellite practically needs a papal edict. Landsat is a polar-orbit bird and won't help me; if I move Ikonos, it will decrease its service life too much before a replacement can be launched; and SPOT charges too much for images of Russia." SPOT Image was a private French firm that supplied radar and optical satellite imagery to users all over the world; many governments and military forces, including those of the United States, often purchased up-to-the-minute SPOT images to supplement their own data, or to mask their interest in a particular area. "I can't convince Houser to send my plan up the chain."

David said nothing—mostly because a dull pain was starting to develop in his left temple. He wasn't crazy about the direction this conversation was taking.

"Is the Air Battle Force still heading up the peacekeeping surveillance effort in Turkmenistan?" Patrick asked.

David Luger hesitated a bit before responding. Yep, he told himself, he could clearly see the reason for Patrick's call now—and he didn't like it. "I never received any orders relieving us of command," he said finally, "but with all our planes grounded and the Russians' advances into the interior of the country, no other surveillance assets instead of satellites have been committed. We're in charge of nothing right now."

"The Backfires are obviously a threat to UN peacekeepers—"

"We don't know that for sure, Muck," Dave interjected.

"In any case, we can reasonably argue that there was a violation, so an investigation into where those bombers came from is fully justified. The suspected violation authorizes the Air Battle Force to investigate, according to the terms of the Security Council's cease-fire resolution. That means you're authorized to employ all necessary assets to investigate the violations. You can legally launch NIRTSats anywhere you want. You can—"

"Patrick," David Luger said seriously, "I'm not going to do that."

"Well, you can't launch from the Megafortresses, because they're still grounded—although I think after we make this argument, we can get that restriction lifted—but you can launch from the Sky Masters carrier aircraft," Patrick went on. "I did a preliminary mission plan: two boosters, eight NIRTSats, placed in sixty-five-degree elliptical orbits at two hundred and twenty miles' altitude—we shouldn't need one-meter resolution, so we can afford to go a little higher. We'll get all the baseline shots we need in about twelve days. If we have the fuel, we can reposition whoever's left to an eighty-degree elliptical at whatever altitude they can make it to and get the remaining shots until we lose the birds. We'll then plan to—"

"Get me the okay from the Air Force or from Air Combat Command, Patrick, and I'll do it tomorrow," Dave said.

"But that's what I'm saying, Dave—you don't *need* authorization from anyone," Patrick said. "As the joint task force commander, you have full authority to launch those constellations. Then you can just share the data with the Nine-sixty-sixth here, and I'll—"

"Patrick, I'm sorry, but I won't do that," Luger said tonelessly.

"What?"

"I said I'm not launching anything from Battle Mountain without an okay from Air Combat Command or higher," David said.

"But you have the authority to—"

"No, I don't," Luger said. "I've been ordered to stand down until our activities have been investigated. The fact that the joint task force has not been terminated doesn't mean I can ignore a direct order from my superior officers to stand down."

"But I *need* that imagery, Dave."

"I understand, Patrick, and I'm sure we can get it for you. But until I get an order to launch, I won't do it."

"Dave, Air Intelligence Agency is authorized to request support from any unit or command in the United States military," Patrick insisted. "I can call up Beale or Whiteman or Offutt or Elmendorf and launch any number of reconnaissance and intelligence-gathering aircraft I need."

"Then go ahead and do it, Patrick," Luger said firmly. "I'll watch."

"This isn't funny, Texas. . . ."

"I'm not being funny at all, Patrick," David said. "I would love for you to put in a request for support to Air Force or Air Combat Command, because then we'd get recertified and back into the air again. But the bottom line is, if you thought you could do it through normal channels, you would have done it already. You probably already made the request, and it was turned down."

"Gary Houser is my boss here, Dave," Patrick said by way of explanation. "You remember Gary, don't you? He tormented young lieutenants like you for fun, like a cat toying with a mouse."

"I remember him. He was a great pilot—just not a great person. You protected me from him . . . took a lot of the heat away from me and put it on you."

"Well, he's doing the same shit to me now, here," Patrick went on. "He wants me to find out where the Backfires came from, but he won't give me the tools I need to find them. He's toying with me, hoping I'll fail and retire."

"Maybe you're right, Muck. I wouldn't put it past him."

"Well, I can't let him get away with that shit."

"And maybe he's right, Patrick," Dave said.

"He's . . . *what?*"

"Maybe you *should* retire, Patrick."

Patrick was thunderstruck. He couldn't believe that his longtime friend and partner just said what he said. "Dave . . . you don't really believe that . . . ?"

"Patrick, overflying *four hostile countries* without permission to retrieve that UCAV after it had gone out of control, then crash-landing on Diego Garcia after being ordered by the secretary of defense himself not to. Or when you ordered the bombing of Engels without authority, when you flew back over Russia in direct violation of orders after Dewey and Deverill were shot down—all those incidents happened because *you* made them happen. I'll agree that the situation was desperate, you made a hard decision, and everything turned out for the better for us in the long run. But the fact is, you exceeded your authority each and every time. We don't know what would have happened if you hadn't intervened—maybe lives would have been lost. . . ."

"*Maybe?* Engels bombers were preparing to kill every soul in Chärjew. Dewey and Deverill might still be in a Russian prison if I hadn't gone back for them!"

"You don't know that, Patrick," Luger insisted. "In any case, you had no right to disregard orders."

"I had every right. I was in command."

"I know your arguments, Patrick, and I disregard them all," Luger said. "We all have a superior officer. When he or she gives a lawful order, we're supposed to obey it. The problem is, you don't. Every day I saw more and more of Brad Elliott emerging from within you."

"Oh, Christ, you're not going to give me the 'I'm turning into Brad Elliott' bullshit, too, are you?" Patrick retorted. "I heard that enough from Houser and Samson and half the four-stars in the Pentagon. It has nothing to do with Brad Elliott—it has everything to do with accepting responsibility and taking action." He paused for a few heartbeats, then added, "So you're not going to consider my request for satellite-reconnaissance support?"

"I'll be happy to consider it—but I'll upchannel the request to my superior officers at Air Force, Air Combat Command, and Eighth Air Force," Luger replied. "That's what I feel I have to do."

"You actually think that's the way you should play this, eh, Dave?" Patrick asked. "Make no decision yourself. Don't exercise your authority. Ask permission first—and don't forget to say 'pretty please.'"

"That *is* the way it's supposed to be done, Patrick—you just forgot that somehow. Maybe it *is* Brad Elliott's influence working on you. There's no doubt that Brad was your surrogate father, and he praised and encouraged your success in the military the way you know your actual father never would have done. Your real dad wanted you to join the police force, and you told me many times how disappointed he was when his oldest son wouldn't follow in his footsteps—"

"Don't give me that Freudian psychobabble crap, Dave."

"—or maybe it was just your sense of how the bomber world works . . . no, how *your* world is supposed to work, *your* world of instant justice delivered from above."

"Are you listening to yourself, Dave? Do you really *believe* all this shit you're telling me?"

"But that's not how *my* world works," Luger said, ignoring Patrick's remarks. "In my world, in my command, I need authorization before I commence a risky operation that puts lives and weapon systems in jeopardy."

"Oh, I get it—you have your command now, and you're going to do everything you can not to see it get messed up. You're afraid to take a risk because it might mean you're unsuited to command a combat unit of your own."

"With all due respect, Muck—*eat shit*," Luger snarled. "The *only* reason I got this command is because *you screwed up,* so let's not forget that. I didn't ask to get it; I was your deputy, and I was content to do that job. But now *I* make the decisions here—*not you.* It is my responsibility and my call, and what I say is that I require authorization from higher headquarters before I'll commit my aircraft, satellites, airmen, or ground teams. You must get me that authorization before I commence operations. If you don't, I'll upchannel your request to my superiors before I begin.

"And you know something, Patrick? I have a feeling you already knew the answer to your request, which is why you came to me first," Luger went on hotly. "You thought you'd take advantage of our friendship and ask me a favor, hoping I'd go along just because we've partnered together for so long. Tell me I'm wrong, Muck." No response. "Yeah, I thought so. And you wonder why half of Eighth Air Force wants to see you retire. You've turned into something I never thought I'd ever see you become."

"Dave, listen . . ."

"You take it easy, sir. Air Battle Force, clear." And Luger abruptly terminated the connection.

David Luger sat upright in his chair, hands on the armrests, staring straight ahead, feet flat on the floor. Anyone who might look in on him at that moment might think he was catatonic—and in a sense that's exactly what he was.

Almost twenty years earlier, David Luger had been part of a secret bombing mission into the Soviet Union, along with Brad Elliott, Patrick McLanahan, and three others. After completing the mission by bombing a ground-based laser site, the crew was forced to land their crippled EB-52 Megafortress bomber on an isolated Soviet air base to refuel. Dave Luger sacrificed himself to draw the defenders away, which allowed the Megafortress and its crew to escape.

Luger was captured and held in a secret location in Siberia for many years. Brainwashed into thinking he was a Soviet scientist, Luger helped the Soviets design and build aircraft and weapons that advanced the Soviet state of the art by several years, perhaps several generations. Eventually Patrick McLanahan and the crew of the EB-52 "Old Dog" helped rescue him, but by then he had been held against his will, psychologically and physically tortured, for almost seven years.

During his captivity the rigid position he was in now was a sort of psychological and emotional "happy place"—when he was not being tortured or brainwashed, he was ordered to assume that position, which he equated with rest or relief. To Luger it actually felt good to assume that stiff, tense position. After his rescue and rehabilitation, his doctors and psychologists saw this posture as a manifestation of his emotional damage. But after years of therapy, David was fully aware of what he was doing when he put himself in this rather awkward-looking seated position. In a strange way, it was still a "happy place" for him—in fact, it helped him focus his thoughts more clearly.

Yes, he was angry at Patrick. Yes, Patrick was wrong for not following the proper chain of command, and it was exceedingly unfair of him to use their close personal relationship to break the rules and do something they'd both have to answer for later.

But . . . Patrick McLanahan was the best strategic planner and the best strategic-bombing task-force commander he had ever known. If he had a hunch about where those Russian bombers came from, he was probably correct.

"Luger to Briggs, Luger to Furness," Dave spoke into thin air.

"Briggs here," Colonel Hal Briggs responded via the subcutaneous transceiver system. All of the former Dreamland officers were "wired" with the global satellite datalink and communications system.

"Can you stop by for a chat?"

"I can be there in ten," Hal said.

"I'm in the box and ten minutes to the high fix, Dave," Rebecca Furness responded. "Give me twenty." Furness, the commander of the 111th Wing, in charge of Battle Mountain's fleet of airborne-laser and flying-battleship aircraft, was returning from a pilot-proficiency flight in the "virtual cockpit," the control station for Battle Mountain's fleet of remotely piloted aircraft. With Battle Mountain's combat fleet grounded, the crews maintained proficiency by flying unmanned QF-4 Phantom jet-fighter drones, which were the closest to the unmanned QB-1C Vampire drone's performance. "Get Daren, unless it can wait."

"Roger. Luger to Mace."

"Go ahead, sir."

"You and Hal meet me in the BATMAN. I have a mission I want planned."

"Are we getting a recert?"

"Soon—I hope. Luger to Masters."

"For Pete's sake, Dave, I just sat down to breakfast,"

responded Jon Masters, one of the partners of Sky Masters Inc., a high-tech defense contractor that developed many of the weapon systems and aircraft used at Battle Mountain. "I'm going to program this thing to send callers to voice mail when it detects my mouth full of food."

"Breakfast was over three hours ago for most of the civilized world, Jon," Dave said. "I want one of your DC-10s for a couple weeks. I'm planning on launching some boosters."

"About time you guys started doing something," Masters said. "Send me your equipment list, and I'll load her up for you."

"I'll send over my list, but I'm not ready to upload yet," Luger said. "You'll get the go-ahead from the chief."

"You mean you're actually going to have a budget and I might actually get paid for my gear *before* the mission kicks off?" Masters asked incredulously. "With all due respect to the Old Man, I like the way you do business, Dave." Masters liked to call Patrick McLanahan the "Old Man," an appellation Patrick never seemed to mind.

"Just be ready to go ASAP, Jon," Luger said. "It's important."

At that moment there was a knock on the door, and Colonel Daren Mace, the deputy commander of the 111th Wing, entered Luger's office. He noticed Luger's stiff posture in his chair and tried not to show how sorrowful he felt that Luger had to endure that psychological burden, apparently for the rest of his life. "What's the target, sir?" Daren asked. Dave put his computer-generated map of Russia on the wall monitor and overlaid several satellite tracks on it. "Looks like Russian ICBM bases in the south. Entire country. Are we doing a treaty-verification run? Or does this have to do with that raid on Bukhara?"

"We're looking for Backfire bombers," Luger responded. "We need to find out where the Backfires came from that raided Bukhara. I want a look at all the known bases."

"Are there that many?" Mace asked. "The Russians only have seventy strategic bombers in their entire fleet."

"Which bases are you aware of?"

"Khabarovsk in the east, Novgorod in the west, Arkhangel'sk in the northwest, and Mozdok taking over from Engels in the southwest," Mace replied after a moment's thought.

"So where did those Backfire bombers come from?"

"My guess would be one of those bases."

"Patrick said not. He said AIA has checked, and there's no evidence that any Backfires launched from known bases."

"Well, Backfires are considered tactical bombers, not strategic ones. . . ."

"I'd love to hear the logic the Russkies used to convince us of *that*," Luger remarked.

"The Tupolev-22M bomber is a pig, and everyone knows it—that's why the Russians have been deactivating them in favor of tactical fighter-bombers like the Sukhoi-35," Mace said. Daren Mace had worked around medium bombers most of his Air Force career and, in the past few years, had worked closely with the secretary of defense and the Air Force on developing new bomber technologies. "They'd waste too many resources trying to fly one more than a thousand miles. Sure, they might be able to refuel them, but it would take one Ilyushin-76 tanker for every Backfire to make it across the pole. It's not worth it. The Tupolev-160s and -95s already have much longer legs."

"They have speed, and they have a big payload," Luger pointed out. "Obviously the Russians changed their minds on the Backfires, because they've used them extensively recently over Chechnya, Turkmenistan, and now Uzbekistan. They could easily upgrade the engine and sacrifice a little of payload for added fuel. Screw in the air-refueling probe, reset the circuit breakers, then retrain your crews in how to do a hose-and-drogue refueling—"

"Not easy in a big mother like a Backfire."

"But doable."

"Sure."

"So you agree that it's possible to put a Backfire force together in Siberia, fly them across Central Asia to bomb Bukhara, and fly them back without anyone seeing them?" Luger asked.

"Why not? No one would ever see them coming," Mace surmised. "The Backfires were supposed to dash across Western Europe and destroy NATO airfields with cruise missiles and NATO ships in the Baltic with big-ass antiship cruise missiles. They were forward-deployed in Warsaw Pact countries close to the frontier because they didn't have the range of a Tupolev-95 Bear bomber; hence, they were never considered strategic weapons with the ability to threaten North America."

"Are they a threat?" Luger asked.

"Top one off over Moscow and it can launch a cruise missile against every country in NATO—except the U.S. and Canada, of course," Daren said. "Yes, I'd say it's a threat. If the Russians are turning tactical jets like Backfires out as long-range strategic weapons, that shifts the balance of power significantly in their favor, especially in Europe, the Middle East, and Central Asia. We've assumed that the Russians were mothballing them as they got older and they ran out of money to support them—we'd be in real trouble if it turned out they were not only rehabilitating them but giving them a much greater warfighting capability."

Luger nodded, lost in thought for a moment. He then got up and headed to the battle-staff room to meet the others.

The BATMAN, or Battle Management area, was a large, theaterlike room with a stage flanked by sixteen large full-color computer monitors. The senior staff sat behind computer workstations in the "orchestra" section. Arrayed behind the senior staff were the support-staff members, and in two separate enclosures were the control stations for Battle Mountain's unmanned aircraft. Hal Briggs was already waiting for Luger, and Rebecca Furness was just logging off her QF-4 drone training session. They all met at the commander's workstation in the front row, where Dave Luger quickly ran down the situation.

"Wonder why Air Intelligence Agency won't give Patrick satellite support?" Daren Mace asked.

"I can think of lots of reasons—none of them flattering to the general," Rebecca Furness said. "His reputation has definitely preceded him."

"I told Patrick that an unofficial request for support is not good enough for me—I needed the request to come from either ACC or the Pentagon," Luger said.

"I'll bet he was thrilled to hear you say that, sir," Briggs quipped.

"Nonetheless, that's how I see it," Dave said. "I want to help, but I want the mission to be fully authorized and budgeted. I'm not going to spend money I don't have and use assets I haven't paid for." Rebecca Furness made a show of clearing out her ears, as if she couldn't believe what she'd just heard. "Knock it off, Rebecca. But that doesn't mean I can't plan a mission right now."

He turned to his console and called up the computer images he'd been working with in his office on the "Big Board" in front of the BATMAN. "Assume I'm getting two constellations of NIRTSats aloft in the next few days, and we find something in one of the Siberian or Sakha provinces—I want a plan of action to take a closer look by the Tin Men and, if necessary, destroy the bases."

"A secret Russian base filled with intercontinental bombers?" Furness asked. "The Russians haven't relied on bombers to threaten North America for decades."

"But just in the past year they've used heavy bombers three times, in Chechnya, Turkmenistan, and now against Uzbekistan," Dave pointed out. "Plus, the new president of Russia is the former military chief of staff and a bomber aficionado. Patrick thinks there are too many coincidences, and I agree. Let's build a plan that I can show to Langley right now."

It did not take long—working together and relying on their digital catalogs of preplanned space and aircraft missions along with the computer's real-time inventory of aircraft and weapons, the team had two preliminary plans drafted within an hour: one relying on the 111th's bombers and special-operations transports, which were currently grounded but were ready to go on short notice; and one relying only on Sky Masters Inc.'s research-and-development aircraft and Air Force special-ops transports. Once the plans were signed off on by each element of the Air Battle Force and finally by Dave Luger himself, he spoke, "Duty Officer, get me the deputy commander of Air Combat Command, secure."

"Please stand by, General Luger," the voice of the "Duty Officer," the omnipresent computerized clerk and assistant for everyone at Battle Mountain, responded.

After Luger was routed through several clerks, aides, and chiefs of staff, he finally heard, "General Fortuna, secure."

"General, how are you, ma'am? This is General Luger, Air Battle Force, Battle Mountain, secure."

"Dave! Good to hear from you," General Leah "Skyy" Fortuna, the deputy commander of Air Combat Command, responded happily, her thick New York accent still obvious despite the distortion from the secure telephone line. Leah Fortuna got her call sign "Skyy" both from her love of flying—she'd been a bomber pilot and flight instructor—and her love of blue American-made vodka. "How the heck is the smartest guy ever to graduate from the Air Force Academy?"

"I'm doing okay, thanks."

"Congrats on getting the command out there," Leah said, "although I'm sure you hoped it would be under happier circumstances. No one deserves it more than you, though."

"Thank you, ma'am."

"You're making me feel old with that 'ma'am' crap, Dave—or is this a 'ma'am' phone call?"

"Sort of, yes."

"Okay. So what can I do you for?"

"I received an unofficial request for support from General McLanahan at Air Intelligence Agency," Dave said.

" 'Unofficial request,' huh?"

"That's why I'm calling, ma'am. I have a request for overhead-imagery support that I'd like you to take to General Muskoka." General Thomas "Turbo" Muskoka, a former F-15E Strike Eagle and F-117A stealth fighter pilot and deputy chief of staff of the Air Force, was the new commander of Air Combat Command, the Air Force's largest major command. "Patrick made the request directly to me. I was not comfortable taking that request outside the chain of command, so I denied it. But I believe that Patrick does have a legitimate operational need for the data, and I firmly believe I have the sensors and equipment that can get him the information he needs."

"Why not take it to Eighth Air Force?"

"Air Battle Force's taskings don't normally come from Eighth Air Force," Dave said. He knew it sounded lame, but it was the best excuse he could think of at the moment. Although the EB-52 and EB-1C bombers in the Air Battle Force were not nuclear-weapon-capable, the unit came under the command of Eighth Air Force—although Terrill Samson definitely treated the unit from Battle Mountain, Nevada, as the long-lost ugly stepchild.

"I never really understood exactly *whom* Air Battle Force reports to," Leah admitted. "I assumed it was directly to the Air Force chief of staff's office. But it's okay with me for now—I don't mind being your boss."

"Thank you," Dave said. "Besides, I think Patrick already made the request to his command and was denied. As I said, I think he has a legitimate need that we can fulfill."

"So you decided to go right to Air Combat Command," Fortuna said. "I don't appreciate McLanahan's using you to go over his bosses' heads. You were smart to upchannel his request, Dave. I hate to say this of Patrick McLanahan, but that man is snake-bit these days. No one wants anything to do with him, because they're afraid he'll do something on his own that'll bite *them* in the ass. I know he's a good friend of yours, but I think you should know the buzz about him. He's gone way beyond what even Brad Elliott supposedly did."

"I hear what you're saying, Leah, and I agree," Dave said, "but he's much more than just a good friend of mine."

"I know. A word to the wise, that's all. What kind of satellite support is he requesting?"

"Two constellations of NIRTSats, launched from a Sky Masters carrier aircraft or from one of the One-eleventh Wing's Megafortresses, if I can get them recertified; a mix of visual and synthetic-aperture radar, short duration, low altitude, targeting southern Siberia and Sakha provinces. I also want to forward-position a Battle Force ground team to Shemya for possible ground ops in eastern Siberia."

"Russia, huh? That's going to have to go right up to the Pentagon, probably right past the chief's office to SECDEF himself. And you said that Patrick McLanahan requested it?"

"Is that what I said?" Dave asked. "I believe what I said was *I* was requesting it on behalf of the Air Battle Force, in support of the United Nations peacekeeping operation in Turkmenistan."

"There you go, Dave," Leah said. "I think you'll find that an easier sell, especially after that attack on the CIA base at Bukhara. A little piece of friendly advice, Dave? Don't tie your star too tightly to Patrick McLanahan. He can be your friend—just don't let him be your mentor."

"Can I share the data I get with him?"

General Fortuna chuckled lightly into the secure connection. "Loyal to the end, eh, Dave? Okay, it's your funeral. And it's your data—you do with it whatever you want. Air

Intelligence Agency gets a copy of all overhead imagery for its databases anyway. Send me your ops plan ASAP, and I'll give the boss a heads-up and a recommendation for approval to pass to the Pentagon. Don't send those ground forces farther west than Shemya, or the boss will have your ass for breakfast—after he gets done kicking *mine*."

"Understood."

"Your request will probably need to go to the White House, too—just so you know," Fortuna continued as she made notes on her tablet PC computer. "Your name and McLanahan's will be seen by all the suits as well as the brass. Get ready to take the heat. How soon can you have the plan over here?"

Luger tapped a button on his computer. "Transmitting it now."

"Good. I'll look it over, but if it's coming from you, I don't see a problem."

"Thanks, Leah."

"Hey, I still owe you big-time for all the help you gave me in computer-science and math classes at the Zoo," Fortuna said. "I never would've passed without your help."

"Bull."

"Maybe, but I still owe you," she said. "You were so damned smart—and you are so damned cute. Good thing you're way the hell out there in Nevada."

"Your husband might agree."

"Jeez, Dave, has it been that long since we've spoken? I ditched what's-his-name two years ago," Leah said. "Best thing that ever happened to my career. Men might need loyal, sacrificing wives to get promoted, but women need a good long game on the golf course, and to be able to stay up late, smoke expensive cigars, and bullshit with the politicians and contractors. Once I figured that out, I got my second and third stars with no problem."

"In that case I think I'd like to come out for a visit and play a few rounds," Luger suggested.

"I have a feeling you're going to be busy here real soon," Leah said, "but I'll keep the light on for you, Texas. Stop by anytime, big boy. I'm clear."

When the connection was terminated, David Luger sat quietly, thinking.

Rebecca Furness broke the silence a few moments later. "Sounds like you two were an item, David. So you were the nerdy bookworm at the Zoo who helped all the hard-charging type-A upperclassmen pass the hard-science classes so they wouldn't get kicked out?"

Luger ignored the comment and turned to Hal Briggs. "Hal, I want to position a few of your guys out in eastern Russia as quickly as possible—Shemya, perhaps?"

"Somewhere close to those Russian bomber bases in Siberia?"

"Exactly."

"No problem," Briggs said. "Weather's improving up there. I'll start working on getting plenty of special-ops tanker and combat search-and-rescue support—five minutes after takeoff, we're in no-man's-land. How many troops are we talking about?"

"Everyone you have available," Luger said. "If we find that base, I want to be able to take it down right away."

Furness looked at Luger with an exasperated expression as Briggs stepped over to his console in the BATMAN. "Didn't you hear what your girlfriend said, David?" she asked. "I know you like and respect Patrick, but he's way overstepped his authority, and he's asking you to do the same. Be smart. Don't do it."

"Rebecca, I want a couple Megafortresses available to link up with Hal's ground forces," Luger said. "Get together with him and plan a cover operation with whatever forces he manages to link up with over there."

Furness shook her head. "It's your career, General. You Dreamland guys will just never learn, will you?"

THE KREMLIN, MOSCOW, RUSSIAN FEDERATION
Days Later

General Nikolai Stepashin strode quickly into Anatoliy Gryzlov's office and waited as discreetly as possible just inside the large double doors. Gryzlov was in a meeting with his team of economic advisers; obviously it was not a pleasant meeting at all. When Stepashin finally caught the president's eye, the chief of staff of the Russian Federation's armed forces and chief of military intelligence raised a red-covered folder; Gryzlov adjourned the meeting moments later.

"Practically all of the Central Asian republics of the Commonwealth are threatening to withhold wheat and rice shipments in protest against the attack on Bukhara," Gryzlov shouted, lighting a cigarette and plopping down disgustedly into his chair. "Ukraine and Belarus might follow suit."

"We made it perfectly clear to all of them that we bombed an American CIA base—we were hunting down those responsible for the attack on our forces in Turkmenistan," Stepashin said.

"I made it clear to them, but they insisted that any CIA operations in their countries have been fully sanctioned by Moscow—technically true—and that no operations of any kind have been mounted by Americans from those bases in Commonwealth nations," Gryzlov said. "God, I hate dealing with bureaucrats and politicians! The economic council is panicking, the foreign ministers are panicking—everything is spinning out of control." He paused, then looked at Stepashin carefully through eyes squinting with the sting of the pungent smoke from his Turkish cigarette. "What is it now?"

"We've detected two new visual-reconnaissance satellite constellations, launched within just the past few days," he said. "Probably American. They did not come from one of their government ground-launch sites at Vandenberg, Shemya, or Patrick Air Force Base; they were either launched by a relocatable sea platform or air-launched. Low Earth orbit, small, some radar emissions, deeply encrypted datalinks. One satellite overhead every twenty-five minutes in each orbit."

Gryzlov's face fell. "The target tracks . . . ?"

"Southern and central Siberia—right over the temporary Tupolev-22M bases."

"Damn!" he shouted, slamming his chair's armrest so hard that his cigarette went flying out of his hand in a shower of sparks. "How in hell did they zero in on those bases so quickly?"

"It was a risk using the redesigned -22Ms for the raid on Bukhara," Stepashin said. "It turned out to be a good test of the new birds and the new air-launched weapon, but it raised a lot of questions with the Americans. They're keeping a close eye on our bombers now—and having the refurbished Tupolev-22Ms do such a good job over Bukhara obviously drew their attention." Gryzlov remained silent, fuming, so Stepashin went on. "We detected the new satellites quickly and were able to hide the planes well, so I don't think we have been compromised yet. The Americans will perhaps notice increased activity at bases that have not been in use for a long time, but they will not be able to deduce much more than that. And I don't think they got a good overhead look at Yakutsk—they were concentrating more on the bases in the west and along the Mongolian-Manchurian border."

"We will have to step up our preparations," Gryzlov said. "The modified bombers need to be completed as soon as possible and then dispersed to their secret operating bases."

"The bomber retrofit is proceeding well ahead of schedule," Stepashin assured him. "As soon as the satellite coverage goes away—these new satellites are small, not very maneuverable, and their orbits will decay very soon—we can disperse the Tupolev-22Ms and their weapons to their operating locations. I'm sorry the Americans seem to be zeroing in on the reactivated bases so quickly, but we knew they would be discovered sooner or later."

"I, too, am sorry they apparently have been discovered,"

Gryzlov said, "but at this point I don't care. I'm tired of trying to suck up to the Americans on arms-control issues. The Americans unilaterally abrogate the Anti–Ballistic Missile Treaty in order to build their 'Star Wars' missile-defense system; then they expect us to hurry up and conform to the Strategic Arms Limitation Treaty nuclear-weapon limits so they can impose further arms reductions on us. In the meantime they continue to leap ahead of us in conventional-weapons technology. We cannot compete with the United States. The only way to maintain our position as a world power is to increase, not decrease, our military capabilities."

Gryzlov lit another cigarette, then stubbed it out angrily after taking only one puff. "And that attack on Engels Air Base by those American robot planes—*that was the last straw!*" he fumed. "McLanahan actually dared to mount a preemptive attack against an active Russian air base! That is *completely unacceptable!* And the spineless American president, Thorn, actually had the audacity to *deny* he authorized the attack, and at the same time he rewards McLanahan by allowing him to keep his stars! He should be in *prison*—or dangling at the end of a *noose*—for what he did!

"The Americans want only one thing—complete domination over the entire planet," Gryzlov said. "Well, I will not allow that to happen. I am going to show how weak and defenseless the United States really is. . . ."

3

AIR INTELLIGENCE AGENCY,
LACKLAND AIR FORCE BASE, TEXAS
The next day

"We haven't been successful yet in locating the exact origin of those three Backfire bombers that attacked Bukhara," Patrick McLanahan reported. He was doing the daily morning briefing of the battle staff at Air Intelligence Agency headquarters. Seated beside him was Colonel Trevor Griffin. "The Russians are keeping their entire fleet of long-range bombers out of sight. However, we have recent imagery that might give us some clues."

Griffin hit the slide button. "On this orbit we're examining six bases in particular, all active or former Russian long-range-bomber bases in the south and far east: Omsk, Novosibirsk, Bratsk, Aginskoye, Blagoveshchensk, and Vladivostok," Patrick said. "Vladivostok is the only base known to be operating the Tupolev-95 Bear bomber, primarily in a maritime-reconnaissance role. The last known inventory of Bears at Vladivostok is eighteen, but in the past couple days we've counted as many as thirty-nine. And as you can see, they're not the Tupolev-142M or -MR maritime-reconnaissance planes. You can tell in these photos that the planes highlighted have no magnetic-anomaly

devices on their vertical tail fins, and they have the large
'Clam Pipe' bombing radar under the nose. Only six of the
thirty-nine Bears at Vladivostok have MAD stingers—the
rest are strategic bombers.

"We did not see any planes at the other five bases," Patrick
went on as Griffin changed slides, "nor did we expect to see
any—but, for inactive or closed bases, the five other bases
showed a lot of activity. For instance, in Aginskoye, we see
twelve brand-new and very large bomber-size hangars built.
At one time Aginskoye was one of the former Soviet
Union's main strategic-bomber bases in the south, housing
dozens of Blinder, Backfire, and Bear bombers. But when
the bomber forces were cut, Aginskoye was all but deserted,
virtually overnight. Not anymore.

"Here was the most interesting feature of this particular
shot. Notice the southeast end of Aginskoye's runway. This
base always had a long runway, over ten thousand feet long,
but it was only stressed to handle aircraft as large as the Bear
bomber, which is around four hundred thousand pounds max
takeoff weight. At most bases this means a reinforced-
concrete runway of approximately four feet in depth. Let's
zoom in on the end of the runway." Griffin entered commands into the keyboard, and the digital satellite image
zoomed to a very high magnification, losing only a little of
its original definition.

"You'll see some soldiers or guards climbing down the
riprap supporting the edge of the runway. Note how high
aboveground they are. We estimate about eight feet. That
means this runway has been reinforced even more, perhaps
double its original structure. The only plausible reason for
reinforcing a runway like this is obviously to handle larger
aircraft.

"There are only two aircraft in the Russian military's aircraft inventory larger than the Bear bomber—the Antonov-
124 Condor heavy-lift transport, the largest aircraft in the
world, and the Tupolev-160 Blackjack bomber. These

hangars, gentlemen, don't fit the Condor—they're way too short in height and length. However, each hangar is dimensioned to fit two Tupolev-160 Blackjack bombers perfectly. I believe what we have here are accommodations for as many as twenty-four Blackjack bombers."

"But aren't there only forty Blackjack bombers in the entire Russian arsenal?" General Zoltrane asked.

"Yes, sir," Patrick replied. "Engels and Blagoveshchensk were the two known Blackjack-bomber bases in Russia. The last verified inventory of Blackjacks at Engels had their full complement—twenty-eight planes, most transferred from Belarus. Two were recently verified destroyed, and two more damaged. That's at least twenty-four survivors. Blagoveshchensk had its full complement as well—twelve bombers, transferred from Ukraine and refurbished."

"That doesn't make any sense, McLanahan," Major General Gary Houser said. "Those hangars at Aginskoye could be housing anything—other transports, supplies, even oilpipeline equipment or derricks. You're seeing a big building and assuming there's a couple Blackjack bombers in it."

"The reinforced runway adds to my suspicions, sir," Patrick responded. "Although it's true that Aginskoye's runway could have been reinforced to handle Condor transports, and the hangars could be storage buildings, their dimensions still leave room for doubt. It could be a coincidence, or they could be bomber hangars. The only way to verify it is to check it visually. We're going to need some eyes on the ground to look it over.

"Aginskoye is about a hundred miles from the Mongolian border, about two hundred miles' driving distance by the most direct route, or nine hundred miles from the Sea of Japan."

Gary Houser turned away without further comments; no one else had anything to add.

"Colonel Griffin has some suggestions to make in a moment; I have one more item to present," Patrick said. "We were able to launch a second constellation over Russia, shortly after launching the first over southern Russia," he went on.

This time Houser made an expression of pure disgust, not trying to hide it at all.

"The targets were higher-latitude military bases on the Russian Pacific coast, as well as bases farther in the southwest and in former Soviet republics." Griffin changed Power-Point slides. "Here is the former bomber base at Magadan. This base has always been the Russian equivalent of their far east tanker task force, but the number of Ilyushin-76 and Tupolev-16 tankers there is astounding—well over forty planes are now based there. The imagery also gave us a good look at the submarine base at Petropavlovsk-Kamchatka, which also has seen an increase in the number of Tupolev-95 strategic bombers in recent days. All in all, we've seen a three hundred percent increase in the number of strategic bombers and tankers in the Russian far east theater.

"One more observation was made in these latest images: up here, in the provincial capital of Yakutsk. Yakutsk is the largest northern city east of the Urals and the center of the Siberian oil and natural-gas industry. Air service is the life blood of this city, and we'd be accustomed to a lot of air traffic year-round. The orbit of the second string of satellites didn't cover Yakutsk as well as we'd like, but we were able to get some pretty good oblique pictures—yet even in these shots, it's obvious that air traffic into Yakutsk has more than tripled since official counts were made about a year ago.

"Now, this could be a result of higher oil prices making Siberian crude more valuable, and hence a push to develop the Siberian fields, but this rate of increase has been surprising to all of our analysts," Patrick summarized. "We've seen an overall increase in all types of air traffic, but most notably in military cargo and resupply flights. It's hard to categorize accurately because Aeroflot does as many civil and government flights as it does military, but we regard the increase in air traffic into Yakutsk as significant. And since it coincides with the increases in military activity in other far east locations, we can conclude that the buildups in strategic air assets in the far east theater and the buildups in Yakutsk are related and not just coincidental. We feel that the Russians are engaged in some sort of massive high-tech buildup of strategic air-attack assets, including supersonic and subsonic bombers and air-refueling tankers. The recent attack by Backfire bombers in Turkmenistan could have been a test of some of these assets.

"Most notably we feel that the Russians are building up Tupolev-22M Backfire bombers and Tupolev-160 Blackjack bombers, in violation of Strategic Arms Limitation Treaty rules. The reason for this is obvious—conventional thinking has it that these aircraft are not threats to North America; the Backfires supposedly had insufficient range, and there were only six Blackjacks in the entire Russian arsenal with intercontinental range. The Nine-sixty-sixth feels that these conclusions are no longer valid. We feel that there may be as many as twenty to sixty Backfire bombers with intercontinental range and cruise-missile capability, and between twenty and perhaps thirty Blackjack bombers also with intercontinental range and cruise-missile capability, including nuclear-tipped weapons.

"We don't know precisely what these forces will be used for," Patrick concluded, "but our guess is that these forces pose a significant threat to our Asian allies—and a direct and credible threat to the United States as well. We feel that these bombers, with the massive number of tankers in the theater as well, could easily reach targets all across North America, primarily above forty degrees north longitude and west of ninety-five degrees west longitude—only one-fourth of the United States, but within striking distance of fifty percent of our land-based bombers, fifty percent of our ballistic-missile submarines not presently at sea, and *one hundred percent* of our land-based intercontinental missiles."

The battle-staff conference room rumbled with low murmurs and sounds of utter disbelief—but the loudest voice came from the head of the table. "*Say again?* What did you just say, McLanahan?" Houser asked incredulously. Before Patrick could answer, he went on, "You have got to be shitting me, General McLanahan! You're telling me that you think the Russians are assembling a force of strategic bombers and *intend to attack the United States of America?*"

"It may sound unbelievable, sir, but—"

"It doesn't sound unbelievable, McLanahan—it sounds completely *asinine!*" Houser retorted. "You ought to know better than most of the people in this room that the Russians haven't had a credible long-range-bomber force in over thirty years."

"The Bear bombers are relics, McLanahan," interjected Major General Ralph Nowland, the deputy commander of the Air Intelligence Agency. Nowland had been in AIA longer than almost anyone else and had convinced everyone else that he was the expert on any possible subject concerning the Russian military. "We've never received any credible evidence that the Russians are modernizing the Tupolev-22M Backfire as an intercontinental strike platform—the Russians have been yanking Backfires in favor of continued development of the MiG-29S and Sukhoi-35 fighter-bombers. And for good reason: The Fulcrum and Flankers have more capability, are far less costly to maintain and deploy, and have similar range and combat performance. As for the Blackjacks, there's no evidence whatsoever in any documentation or imagery that proves they've been reactivated and their air-refueling capacity restored enough to give them true intercontinental capability. That's an unsubstantiated rumor only."

"And you haven't given us one shred of evidence or even any plausible conjecture that the bomber that struck Bukhara is some sort of supersecret refurbished Backfire," Houser said. "No one has been able to recover the missile that went off course—the Russians are all over the impact area, so it's unlikely we'll ever get a look at it. We have scoured the intercepts and technical literature coming out of every lab and every aircraft-manufacturing bureau in Russia, and there's not one mention of any programs to upgrade the Backfire fleet. If it exists, it's under a level of secrecy and compartmentalization that hasn't been seen in Russia since the breakup of the Soviet Union." He shook his head. "So let's get down to the bottom line, General: You still don't know where those Backfires came from, is that it?"

"Sir, my guess is that the bombers came from Bratsk," Patrick responded.

"And how did you deduce that?"

"By the number of nonmilitary flights coming in and out of Bratsk," Patrick said. "The Russians have made a big deal out of hiding all their Backfire bombers from satellite view of every base, but the number of Aeroflot flights going into Bratsk has increased almost threefold since the raid on Bukhara. The number of government and civil flights going into Bratsk has increased from an average of twenty per day to an average of sixty-three per day since the raid. Bratsk is a major city on the Trans-Siberian Railway and is a major oil-transshipment point, but its air traffic has remained fairly constant for the past few years—except for the past few days, when all of a sudden its civil air traffic spiked."

"That's *it?*" Nowland asked. "That's all the evidence you have? No sign of Backfire bombers being loaded . . . no bombs, no men and equipment on the field, no signs of increased military activity? Just a few more planes per day taking off and landing there?"

"Sir, these additional flights going into a base that hasn't seen much activity in years could be significant," Patrick said. "It simply raises more questions—and it warrants a look around with HUMINT resources."

"More spy missions inside Russia, is that it?" Houser asked derisively. "McLanahan, you have a lot to learn about the Air Intelligence Agency. We're not the CIA, and we're not a bunch of James Bonds ready to get an assignment to spy on the bad guys. We collect information necessary to build war plans and to defend Air Force assets. We collect information from other intelligence sources, including HUMINT data from other government agencies. The Air Force is not in the business of sending out spies, and sure as hell not inside Russia in peacetime."

"Sir, Colonel Griffin has drawn up a plan that would help us verify our theories on the numbers and capabilities of Russia's Backfires and other long-range aviation forces," Patrick said. "We can send operatives in to three suspected Russian bases—Omsk, Novosibirsk, and Bratsk, launched from Kazakhstan—and verify the existence of modified Backfire bombers. Our other priority is a covert intelligence-gathering mission to Yakutsk, launched from the Sea of Okhotsk."

"Didn't you hear what I said, McLanahan?" Houser said. "It's out of the question."

"Sir, I think we've exhausted all of our signal and overhead-imagery data resources, and all we have to show for it are more unanswered questions," Patrick said. "The only way to discard or verify any of our data is to get guys on the ground to go in and take a look."

"General Houser, I've led Air Force and CIA teams all over the world collecting intel for the Air Force, and I've assisted the Intelligence Support Agency on several missions as well," Trevor Griffin added. "These missions would not be easy, but they're doable, and in a very short time frame. At least it's worth a check to find out if any other agencies have field operatives in those areas. If so, we can combine forces and—"

Gary Houser held up a hand, closing his eyes and shaking his head to emphasize his weariness of this argument. "I understand the reason you feel you need to send operatives in, Colonel, but what I'm telling you is that in the current political climate, the national command authority is not likely to approve an operation like this," Houser said. "Placing eight recon satellites over the heart of Russia rattled nerves and created enough animosity to last an entire generation— exactly the thing we're trying to avoid here. Sending in ground operatives after sending those satellites over the same area would invite disaster as well as heighten tensions even more. You *know* that the Russians will be on guard for such a move. Anyone not passing the most rigorous security screening will be detained on the spot. Or did you think your operatives would just be able to hide in barns and ditches while they make their way to their objectives?"

"Sir, I can have the Nine-sixty-sixth work up a plan of action and brief you and the staff on it in two days," Griffin said. "We have the latest threat assessment, force deployments, topographical and cultural photos of all the target areas. Our staff is already working up ingress and egress options, lining up aircraft and vehicles, mapping out refueling drop points and—"

"I know what goes into planning these types of operations, Colonel," Houser said. "You can have your staff do all the planning they care to do—just be sure you don't make one move off the planning charts without my express permission. Is that understood?"

"Yes, sir."

"Before we leave this subject, General McLanahan, I want to know about these two satellite constellations you got all this information from," Houser went on pointedly. "I don't recall authorizing them, and I don't recall Strategic Command's briefing the staff that they were going to launch such a mission. Perhaps you could enlighten us? Whose are they, and who authorized their insertion?"

All eyes were on him, but Patrick didn't shrink from any of their gazes, especially Gary Houser's. "Yes, sir," he replied. "When my request for overhead-imagery support was denied by Eighth Air Force, in my capacity as Nine-sixty-sixth Information Warfare Wing commander, I requested support from the Air Battle Force commander, Brigadier General Luger, at Battle Mountain Air Reserve Base. I knew that the Air Battle Force had on-demand satellite-reconnaissance assets available. General Luger sent my request to Air Combat Command, who sent it on to the Air Force chief of staff, who sent it on to the joint staff operations office and to the National Security Council liaison office. The mission was approved by the NSC and promptly executed."

"Why wasn't I notified of this request?" Houser asked.

"Sir, you are the deputy commander for intelligence of all these agencies," Patrick said. "I thought you would have been notified every step of the way."

"I mean, why didn't *you* notify *me* that you were going around my office for support on an Air Intelligence Agency tasking?" Houser asked angrily.

"You had already disapproved my request, sir."

"And why did you not inform Eighth Air Force that you were going to go around *them?*" Houser asked. "Did you not receive the directive from General Zoltrane that all requests for operations originating in Eighth Air Force go through his office before going outside the command?"

"Yes, sir, I did," Patrick responded. "But as I understand it, the Air Battle Force reports to Eighth Air Force. My request for support did not go outside the command until General Luger upchanneled it to Air Combat Command."

"Didn't you expect that General Luger would go outside the command to get permission to execute the mission?" Houser asked. Patrick did not reply. Houser nodded knowingly, then added, "Or were you hoping that he *wouldn't* upchannel your request, but just go ahead and launch the mission without permission from his superiors?" Again Patrick did not respond. "Well, it's good to see that someone in Brad Elliott's old organization is obeying orders.

"General McLanahan, I am going to give you a direct

order, so as not to create any confusion or misunderstanding," Houser went on. "You will confine your work and your communications to Air Intelligence Agency units only. If you need information from agencies or sources outside of AIA, you will forward the request to me or General Nowland first. Under no circumstances will you request information or pass information outside AIA without permission from my office. Is that clear?"

"Yes, sir," Patrick replied simply. "May I ask why, sir?"

Heads snapped from Houser to Patrick and back to Houser in surprise at the question. Houser's eyes blazed, but his voice was surprisingly calm. "It's simple, General McLanahan—I don't trust you anymore," he said. "You see, while it is technically correct that you can request intelligence data from any source to create your work product, I'm afraid that you will be using a multitude of unorthodox or nonsecure sources and then not sharing the information with AIA, or not even notifying AIA that you have obtained this information. By doing this you compromise security and break the chain of custody of classified and extremely sensitive information."

"I assure you, sir, that I would never—"

"I don't need your assurances, General," Houser interjected. "Around here assurances are made with actions, not words. You've been here only a short while, but you've already proven you can't be trusted with following our procedures and directives. You give me no choice. My order stands. Is that clear?"

"Yes, sir."

"Good. General, I'd like to see your plans for covert field action against the four targets you mentioned, but don't count on having the operation approved anytime soon. General McLanahan, the information you've given us is interesting, but I don't find enough specific information to support any ground-reconnaissance action. You still have not given the staff any information on where those Backfires came from, only guesses and speculation—and frankly, your ultimate conclusion is pretty far-fetched, bordering on irresponsible. We need to have a talk about your thought processes—maybe you're not cut out to run the Air Intelligence Agency after all. We'll see about that. In any case, I can't present that conclusion to Eighth Air Force and expect anyone to take it seriously."

"Sir, if you're not comfortable presenting my findings to Eighth Air Force or Air Combat Command, I'm prepared to do so," Patrick said firmly.

"That's not the way we run things here, General McLanahan."

"Sir, you can't just sit on the data we've collected. Your job is to collect information and present analysis to—"

"Don't tell me my job, McLanahan!" Houser snapped. "Your job is to shut your damned mouth and do as you're ordered! *Is that clear?"*

Patrick glared at Gary Houser for several seconds, then replied, "Yes, sir."

"Colonel Griffin can take the rest of the staff reports. I may ask him to do so from now on," Houser said angrily. "In the meantime you're dismissed." Patrick pushed his classified reports and photos on the table before him to Griffin, stood at attention, then departed. When he did, Houser said, "Colonel Griffin, plan on taking over the Nine-sixty-sixth shortly. McLanahan's on his way out."

Patrick ignored the surprised stares of his office staff as he hurried into his office and slammed the door shut. He hung up his Class A uniform jacket on the coatrack behind his door, poured himself a cup of coffee, dumped it out, grabbed a bottle of water instead, and nearly squished it as he tried to open the cap. He finally flung himself onto his chair and was on the phone moments later.

David Luger picked up the secure phone and could barely

wait for the encryption circuits to lock in before speaking. "Patrick—"

"Houser ignored my report," Patrick said heatedly. "He's not going to send in any recon personnel."

"Patrick, listen—"

"Dave, I've never been so damned frustrated in my whole life," Patrick moaned angrily. "Houser threw me out of his battle-staff meeting. He's probably going to throw me out of the Nine-sixty-sixth, if not the entire Air Force. . . ."

"Patrick, listen to me," Dave said. "We've been studying the imagery from the NIRTSats today, and—"

"Were you able to move the top constellation?" Patrick asked. "We need better images of Yakutsk. I have a feeling that's going to be the key. We should keep an eye on Bratsk and Aginskoye, too, but all the activity up in—"

"That's what I'm trying to tell you, Patrick, so just listen!" Dave interjected. "We moved the second constellation like you asked, and the orbit dropped down to around eighty-eight miles, and it's only going to be aloft for another few hours, but we finally got some good shots of Yakutsk, and—"

"Good job. What did you—"

"I'm trying to tell you, Muck. It looks like half the Russian air force is parked there all of a sudden," Dave said. "We counted sixteen Tu-16 Blinder tankers and—get this—*twenty-four* Ilyushin-78 tankers. They only have about thirty in the whole fleet!"

"My God," Patrick said. "Ninety percent of the Russian tanker fleet is on one base, in the middle of nowhere in Siberia! Something's going on. What about—"

"I'm getting to that, too, Muck," Luger said breathlessly. "We spotted twenty-four Blackjacks at Blagoveshchensk. We haven't verified if they're all different airframes, but they're sitting there being loaded with some kind of weapons we haven't identified yet—probably cruise missiles."

"We've got to alert Air Force."

"That's not all, Patrick. We counted at least twenty Back-fires out in the open at Bratsk, Novosibirsk, and Agin-skoye—that's at least twenty bombers *at each base.* They're being loaded, too. And they have huge fuel-drop tanks on their external hardpoints—they've got to be five or ten thousand pounds apiece, maybe larger. I mean, all these planes appeared out of nowhere! Twenty-four hours ago there was nothing—today, *boom,* the entire Russian bomber fleet is being readied for takeoff. And we're only counting the ones we can see—there might be twice that number in shelters or hangars or dispersed to other bases we're not watching. Where in heck did they all come from?"

"I'm sure they've been there for a long time, Dave—we just weren't looking for them until now," Patrick said. "Did you report this to anyone else yet?"

"It just crossed my desk, Muck."

"Can you transmit it to me?"

"It's on the way."

At that same moment, Patrick received a message on his computer with the image files. "I got them. Hold on." Patrick punched in a telephone code for the battle-staff area. Colonel Griffin picked up the phone. "Tagger, I need to speak with General Houser right away. I'm e-mailing you photos just taken from the two NIRTSat constellations. The Russians are on the move."

"I'll try," Griffin said, and he put the line on hold. But moments later he came back on: "The general said not now, Patrick. I'm looking at the images. I see lots of planes, Patrick, but these are raw images. We need analysis and verification before we can present it to the staff."

"Tagger, these images were verified by the intel guys at Air Battle Force," Patrick said. "The location and identification data have been verified. It's *real,* Tagger. Houser has to look at them *now.*"

"Hold on." But the wait was even shorter. "I'll be right

down, Patrick," Griffin said. "The general wants me to go talk to you."

"This can't wait, Tagger. I'll come up there."

"Don't, Patrick. Sit tight. I'll be right there." And he hung up.

Shit, Patrick thought, now I've succeeded in getting Trevor Griffin kicked out of the battle-staff meeting also. But this was too important to just sit on. "Houser won't look at the imagery, Dave," Patrick said to David Luger when he got him back on the line. He thought for a moment, then said, "I'm going to send a message to the secretary of defense's office and let them know what's happening. They'll have to contact NORAD to activate the North Warning System, OTH-B, and put every fighter they can find on five-minute alert." But at the same time as he said those words, he knew it was going to be an almost impossible job to convince anyone that the threat was great enough to warrant activating one of the pillars of the Cold War: ADC.

Years earlier the continent of North America was defended by the Air Defense Command, or ADC, which was a joint U.S.-Canadian integrated system of military and civilian ground-based radars and military jet-fighter interceptors that stood poised to stop an attack by enemy bombers or cruise missiles. Its parent organization, the North American Aerospace Defense Command, or NORAD, still existed, but "aerospace defense" had been replaced with "air sovereignty," which generally dealt with detecting and interdicting drug smugglers. Since the late 1980s, the threat that Russian bombers would launch cruise missiles against the United States had all but disappeared, while drug smugglers had virtual free rein over America's skies, so any resources set up to detect and defend against obsolete Russian bombers was shifted to detect, track, and interdict smugglers.

Along with squadrons of jet fighters stationed in Alaska, Canada, and the northern United States, the ADC used a series of long- and short-range unmanned radar sites to detect unidentified aircraft. Called the North Warning System, this system replaced the 1950s-era Defense Early Warning, or DEW Line, consisting of manned radars in Alaska and Canada. The ultimate radar system was deployed in the late 1980s: Called OTH-B, or Over-the-Horizon-Backscatter radar, it could detect aircraft as far away as three thousand miles by bouncing radar energy off the ionosphere. In ideal conditions, OTH-B radar operators in Colorado could see Soviet bombers *taking off* from their Siberian bases. Along with the radar net, there were fighter interceptors on round-the-clock alert, ready to hunt down and destroy any unidentified aircraft. At one time there had been a dozen bases and many dozens of fighters on twenty-four-hour alert.

But as the threat diminished, so did readiness. OTH-B shifted from a full-time system to part-time only, and finally it was placed in "ready" mode, meaning it could be reactivated if needed. The North Warning System radars shifted to part-time mode as well, to reduce annual maintenance and operating costs. Finally, one by one, the fighter-interceptor squadrons were inactivated, disarmed, reassigned to drug-interdiction duties, or placed on "generation recall" status, meaning that the fighters could be placed on the line only after long days of preparation. No one cared: The Russians had only a handful of nearly obsolete bombers that were capable of launching ineffective, inaccurate, and unreliable cruise missiles; the Russian deterrent lay in its arsenal of land- and sea-launched ballistic missiles; the United States had even reactivated and modernized its anti-ballistic-missile defense system.

The problem was soon obvious: Could the air-defense network in North America be reactivated quickly and effectively enough to stop a modern threat? Cranking up the Air Defense Command system was only practiced twice a year, and even so it seemed like a lost and arcane art. Patrick had no idea how to go about ordering an ADC reactivation—and he doubted if it could be effective enough to stop a massive Russian attack against the United States such as the one they were seeing develop right now.

"What do you want me to do, Muck?" David Luger asked.

"You need to get your surveillance and intelligence data over to Air Force as soon as possible," Patrick replied, "because when I hit SECDEF with my concerns, they're going to want proof."

"Patrick . . . Muck, what in hell do you think is going on?" Luger asked. He sounded more scared than Patrick had heard him sound in a long time. Despite his traumatic recent history, David Luger was one of the most unflappable— many called it "emotionless"—persons he knew. Luger possessed a well-trained scientific mind. Everything could be explained, even forecast, by using the proper mixture of research, reasoning, and theory. He never worried about anything, because his finely tuned brain started working on a problem the moment it presented itself. But for any man, especially someone like Dave Luger, the reality of what he knew and the thought of what could happen were finally too much for him to contemplate rationally and analytically.

"Dave . . ."

"I'm looking at the pictures and the analysis, Muck, and I can't fucking believe what I'm seeing!"

"Dave, keep it together, buddy," Patrick said evenly. "I need you one hundred and ten percent on this."

"What in hell can we do?"

"The first thing we need to do is turn on all the air-defense infrastructure in North America, and do it *immediately*," Patrick said. "Next we need to begin twenty-four/seven surveillance of Yakutsk and all the other bases where bombers have been appearing. I need eyes inside those bases, especially Yakutsk. The tankers are the key, and it looks to me like Yakutsk is turning into tanker city. I'm going to talk to the Air Force and get them to crank up the readiness posture, but we need to take a look inside those Russian bases immediately, and the Air Battle Force is the best-positioned unit to get in there. It would take a week just to convince the CIA that what we're looking at is real."

"I've already received permission to forward-deploy Hal and Chris to the region," Dave said. "We're going to send them to Shemya—five hours one way by tilt-jet, but it's the best we can do unless we get some support from U.S. Special Operations Command or the Air Force."

"Do whatever you can to get them out there, as fast as you can," Patrick said. "If you can get in contact with someone at the Pentagon, maybe SECDEF's office directly, we might be able to implement it."

"What is General Houser going to do with the pictures we got from the NIRTSats?"

"Nothing, until he's told to do something with them," Patrick responded. "That's why it has to come from the top down, and higher than Eighth Air Force or Air Combat Command—Houser might even be able to shrug off STRATCOM. Get moving, Dave, and let me know if you make any progress."

"Will do, Muck," Luger said, and disconnected the secure transmission.

Patrick began another secure telephone call to the secretary of defense's office, then hung up the phone before the encrypted connection could go through. Although he had met and briefed the SECDEF, Robert Goff, on more than one occasion, their encounters had been mostly negative—Patrick was usually being reprimanded for some action he undertook with less than full authority. He was losing friends and allies fast, and a phone call to SECDEF's office, in violation of a direct order issued just a few minutes ago in the presence of the rest of the Air Intelligence Agency staff, was not going to win him any more. But this had to be done.

Instead he initiated a secure call to the commander of the Air Warning Center of the North American Aerospace

Defense Command at its command-and-control center at Cheyenne Mountain Operations Center, Colorado, deep inside the underground military base. The Air Warning Center, or AWC, was responsible for monitoring the periphery of the United States, Canada, and parts of Central America and the Caribbean for unidentified aircraft—including cruise missiles—and passing information to the Cheyenne Mountain Command Center. The Air Warning Center controlled the ground-based radars operated by NORAD and also collected data from ground, sea, and airborne military-fighter control radars; other surveillance systems, such as ground- and ship-based radar balloons; Homeland Security radar systems; and civil air-traffic-control radars. Patrick's 966th Information Warfare Wing routinely passed information to AWC on the status of military forces in Russia and on events around the world, which might give AWC a heads-up in adjusting its surveillance to counter enemy incursions.

After several long, excruciating minutes, he was put through to the AWC Charlie-crew commander, Lieutenant Colonel Susan Paige. "It's nice to finally talk with you, General McLanahan," she said after the secure connection was made and verified. "We've received the regular information updates from the Nine-sixty-sixth, and we're very impressed with the quality of work coming from your office. I'd like to—"

"Colonel Paige, I have information provided me by Air Battle Force that shows that Russia may commence a strategic air attack against the United States at any time," Patrick said. "I'm recommending that NORAD implement full air-defense measures immediately, including a full recall and activation of all northern interceptor units and round-the-clock activation of North Warning and OTH-B. It's vital that—"

"Who gave you this information, General? Who is this Air Battle Force?" Patrick knew she was stalling for time—she would be hitting a hot key on her computer that would be tracing and recording this call and perhaps notifying the senior controller at the Command and Operations Center of Patrick's information—or of a crank phone call. After Patrick briefly explained, Paige said, "General McLanahan, you need to take this information to Air Intelligence Agency and have General Houser message—"

"I've already done that. General Houser won't act on it. I need to speak directly with General Lombardi so he can decide if he wants to increase the air-defense posture." General Lombardi was the commander of NORAD and the man who could activate all of the defense systems around North America with one order.

"Maybe you should speak with Air Force or STRATCOM about—"

This was getting him nowhere. "Colonel Paige, this is extremely urgent, or I wouldn't have called the NORAD commander's office directly," Patrick interjected. "I'm having General Luger of the Air Battle Force transmit his overhead imagery to you and to STRATCOM, but I'm calling to advise you that I believe that a Russian combat air operation is in progress, perhaps an all-out attack against the United States using long-range bombers and cruise missiles."

"Is this for real, McLanahan?" Paige asked. "This isn't how AIA issues alerts to NORAD. You should—"

"This alert is from the Nine-sixty-sixth Wing, Colonel Paige, not from AIA," Patrick said. "The information has not been cleared by General Houser. But I decided to contact you directly because I feel there is danger of imminent attack, and when I briefed General Houser a short time ago, he indicated he wasn't going to act on the information. I decided to take a chance and contact you directly. I am now going to try to contact the secretary of defense and give him this same information. McLanahan, Nine-sixty-sixth Wing, clear." Before Paige could say anything more, Patrick hung up.

He had done everything he could with NORAD, Patrick thought. It was up to them if they wanted to act on the information. But even if she didn't believe him, she would certainly sound the alarm—and an alarm from someplace like NORAD traveled up very, very quickly.

Patrick was on hold with the deputy chief of staff of Air and Space Operations—the highest person he could reach at the office of the Air Force chief of staff in the Pentagon—when someone knocked on his door and then entered without being invited in. It was Trevor Griffin. Patrick was about to admonish him when he noticed his stony expression. "I'm on the phone with the Pentagon, Tagger."

"I know, Patrick," Griffin said. "The boss knows, too." Patrick nodded and waved for Griffin to sit, but he didn't put the phone down. Griffin held up his secure cellular phone, which had a long list of SMS messages already on it. "Cheyenne Mountain called a few moments ago, and just now the chief's office called. Everybody wants to know what's going on. All hell is breaking loose. The boss wants you in the battle-staff area, pronto." He paused for a moment, then said with a serious expression, "Sir, what are you doing? You're out of control. You gotta stop this."

"You've seen the pictures and looked over my data, Tagger," Patrick said. "You know as well as I do how serious this is."

"Patrick, it's all speculation," Griffin said. "It's a few buildings erected on bases that haven't been used in a few years, a bunch of tired old Backfire bombers—nothing earth-shattering about that. What are you—?"

"Air Battle Force got new images, Tagger—you saw them yourself," Patrick said. "Yakutsk is wall-to-wall tankers now—dozens of them. Aginskoye, Bratsk, Blagoveshchensk, Ulan-Ude—the Blackjacks and Backfires are massing everywhere. As fast as they've appeared, I think they're going to disappear just as fast—all headed this way."

"Patrick, no one believes that," Griffin said. "No one believes that the Russians would be crazy enough to attack

North America. It's gotta be something else—if there is anything at all."

"The target's not Europe. All the bombers and tankers are in Siberia," Patrick said. "Unless they're going after China or Japan, I think the target is the United States."

"Why? Why would they attack the U.S.?"

"Gryzlov—he wants revenge for my attack on Engels, and he wants to kill ten thousand enemy soldiers for every one Russian soldier we kill," Patrick said. "The guy's crazy, he's in charge, and he wants payback."

"Patrick, this is *nuts*," Griffin breathed. "How in the world are you going to convince anyone of this? They all think that you . . . well, that you . . ."

"That I'm trying to stir up shit, that I'm trying to get back at the guys that took away my command and sent me here," Patrick said. "I know what they think. But there's only one thing that matters: We do everything we can to protect the United States of America." Patrick noticed Griffin's exasperated expression. "Yeah, I know, I sound like some goody-goody comic-book hero, but that's what I believe."

Patrick heard a series of clicks and a rainburst signal on the phone, and then a voice said, "General McLanahan? Stand by for the chief." A moment later: "Kuzner here, secure."

"General Kuzner, this is General McLanahan, Nine-sixty-sixth Information Warfare Wing, secure. I have a possible situation that requires your immediate attention, sir."

"McLanahan, do you have any idea the shit storm you've caused over here?" Charles Kuzner, the Air Force chief of staff, responded angrily. "The NORAD Command Center issued a red alert to the Joint Staff Operations Center, telling us that one of the AIA wing commanders warned them that the United States was under attack by Russian bombers. Did that warning come from you?"

"Yes, sir, it did."

"For Christ's sake, McLanahan . . . where's General Houser? Does he even *know* about any of this?"

"I briefed General Houser and the AIA staff on the findings from two recent satellite-constellation overflights just minutes ago, sir. He indicated to me that I didn't have enough actionable information. I disagreed, and I felt that my information needed immediate attention, so I called Air Battle Force and asked them to draw up a plan for ground reconnaissance. It—"

"Air Battle Force?" Kuzner retorted. "You're with Air Intelligence Agency, McLanahan, not Air Battle Force! We pulled you out of there *specifically* to keep shit like this from happening!"

"Sir, I feel that the information I had needed immediate attention, but I wasn't going to get it from AIA," Patrick went on. "The only recourse I had was Air Battle Force."

"How about Eighth Air—" And then Kuzner stopped—because he knew about Patrick's history with Terrill Samson. He didn't need to mention Air Combat Command either—Thomas Muskoka wasn't a fan of Patrick's either.

"I was informed by General Luger of new data that strongly suggested a massive bomber and tanker mobilization in the Russian far east," Patrick went on. "His new information confirmed my suspicions. At that point I contacted NORAD and gave them the warning, then contacted Air Force. I—"

"Hold on," Kuzner said, and the line went silent. He came back a few moments later. "CJCS wants a briefing later today. *You're* going to give it to him. Let's see if he believes you—because I sure as hell don't. You report to a videoconference center, hook into the Pentagon comm center, and stand by until they send you over to the Gold Room." The Joint Chiefs of Staff Conference Room was nicknamed the "Gold Room" because of its décor and because of all the "brass" inside. "I'm calling the Eighth Air Force staff to meet up with Strategic Command at Offutt to discuss the situation. If you're one second late, mister, I'll personally go out there and kick your ass all the way back to Washington. Kuzner, clear." And the connection went dead.

Patrick got up from his desk and put on his Class A uniform jacket. "This is probably the second command I've given up in less than a month—it's gotta be some sort of record. I'll tell you the same thing I told Dave Luger before I left Air Battle Force, Tagger: Pay attention to what your head and your heart tell you, not what some bureaucrat tells you."

"I will, Patrick," Griffin said, "but you're not going to lose this command."

"I think this time you're wrong, Tagger," Patrick said. He opened his wall safe and extracted a red folder marked TOP SECRET. Griffin knew what it was—and he wished Patrick would put it back in the safe where it belonged. "My last recommendation: Get your ground-recon plan to Kuzner ASAP and press him on it. Get in contact with Dave Luger and Hal Briggs at Air Battle Force for help. They have gadgets and weapons you won't believe."

"We'll plan this thing together, sir," Griffin said. "I'll go with you to the battle-staff area."

"Negative. I want you to get your ground-ops plan forwarded to Air Force right away. I want to see it kicked off in eight hours."

"Okay, I'll take care of it." He stuck out a hand. "You haven't been here long, Patrick, but I already know I'd follow you to hell and back if you asked me to go." Patrick smiled, shook Griffin's hand, nodded, and left to report to the battle-staff area for the videoconference.

Gary Houser showed up moments after Patrick did. Patrick stood at attention as Houser stormed over to him. "I'm getting on a plane in a few hours to report to Strategic Command headquarters to explain what the hell happened here today," Houser said angrily. "My boss and his senior staff, the entire Strategic Command senior staff, half the senior staff from NORAD, the chairman of the Joint Chiefs, and undoubtedly the secretary of defense will be grilling *me* on what *you* did today. What am I supposed to tell them? I think you've flipped out or something. Is that what you think I should tell them?" He stepped toward Patrick until he was almost nose to nose with him. "I just have one question for you, General McLanahan," Houser said. "What in hell do you want?"

"Want, sir?"

"What do you *want*, McLanahan?" Houser barked, standing just inches from Patrick, leaning down to snarl directly into his face. "Do you really want to be in the Air Force, or do you want to go out in a blaze of glory? Do you want to serve your country, or do you just want to soothe your own bruised and battered ego? Do you want to destroy the careers of those around you, or are you crazy enough to believe that what you're doing here is the right thing?"

"Sir . . ." And then Patrick stopped and locked his eyes on his two-star commander. Houser's eyes blazed, and a jaw muscle twitched. "Gary, I'm getting sick and tired of putting up with your bullshit."

"What in hell did you just say?" Houser shouted.

"I said, I'm not going to put up with your bullshit anymore," Patrick repeated. "I gave you information on what could possibly be a major attack against the United States, and all you can do is blow me off. I contacted NORAD and the Pentagon because you're too full of yourself to do it."

"Get the hell out of here, McLanahan, before I—"

"I've been ordered by General Kuzner to brief the Joint Chiefs on the alert I issued NORAD," Patrick said. "I'm staying. You're not going to have a chance to weasel out of this."

"Weasel out . . . ?"

"I'm going to give my information to the JCS, Gary, and then you can tell them why you chose to ignore it."

Houser shook his head. "You've gone off the deep end, McLanahan," he said. "I always knew you were a loner and a little strange, but now I know you've just completely lost it. Your career is over, my friend. Not only have you disobeyed a lawful order, but you have some sort of delusional problem that makes you a danger to the United States in any sort of command position.

"As soon as this briefing is over, pal, you're relieved of duty as Nine-sixty-sixth commander. I will prefer charges against you for disobeying a direct order and for insubordination. You will report to your quarters and await the convening of a court-martial. And if I can, I'll make sure you spend the last remaining years of your career in a military prison camp."

"Gary, all you've done since I've arrived at Lackland is threaten me," Patrick said. "That's not leadership—that's tyranny. I'll be glad to get the hell out of here, even if it's to a prison cell, as long as I don't have to put up with your adolescent nonsense again. *Sir.*"

4

OVER EASTERN SIBERIA, NINE HUNDRED KILOMETERS
NORTHEAST OF YAKUTSK, RUSSIAN FEDERATION
That same time

It was one of the most difficult dances in all of aviation, made even more difficult because all the aircraft and the damned drogues were icing up. Someone once described this exercise as trying to stick your dick into a bull while running across a pasture—except now the pasture was slick with ice and snow.

Aviatskiy Kapitan Leytenant Josef Leborov was very, very good at plugging the bull, but even he was having a tough time of it.

This morning, in and out of clouds heavily laden with ice, a formation of twenty-four Tupolev-95MD Modifikat-sirovanny Daplata aircraft led an even larger formation of thirty-six Tu-95MS-16 Modifikatsirovanny Snaryad strategic bombers on their mission. Spread out over several kilometers, the six formations of four tankers with their six bombers below and behind them made for a very impressive sight. What was not so impressive was watching each bomber trying to plug in to its tanker.

It was Leborov's second try—and he was doing better than the others. The ten-meter-long refueling probe was fixed on the Tu-95's nose, right on the centerline and in plain sight of both pilot and copilot; it had three small lights on the outside edge of the nozzle to illuminate the drogue as it got closer. Once the tanker was forty meters ahead and a few meters higher than the receiver, the tanker's refueling observer in the tail compartment—formerly the tail gunner's station—would slowly unreel the drogue. The drogue would swing around wildly for several meters until it got outside the tremendous prop wash behind the plane, but it would then stabilize and begin to drop slightly as the weight of the hose pulled on it. At maximum extension the observer would flash a green light, and the receiver could move forward and plug the drogue.

The drogue—a large, two-meter-diameter padded lighted steel basket at the end of the fuel hose—did not move around so much. The bomber, on the other hand, seemed never to be in one place long enough to get a good feel for positioning the boom. Unlike Western-style boom aerial refueling, here the tanker's observer could not assist the hookup—it was the bomber pilot's show all the way.

Leborov cruised slowly up to the drogue, trying to make small control and power corrections—but it was no use. The drogue whistled left just enough for the nozzle to hit the rim, which caused the drogue to skitter away. Leborov pulled off a smidgen of power and swore loudly as he backed away for another try. "This fucking pig! I have either not enough control authority or too damned much!"

"Just think of fucking that pretty little waitress you met a few months ago, Joey," said Leborov's copilot and friend, Aviatskiy Starshiy Leytenant Yuri Bodorev. "That's what I do."

"Shut the hell up, asshole," Leborov said, as good-naturedly as he could.

"Refueling behind one of our own planes isn't as easy as it sounded when they first came up with this idea," Bodorev remarked. Without external stores, Tupolev-95 bombers had a maximum range in excess of twelve thousand kilometers—air refueling was usually not a necessity. But several months ago they started practicing air refueling again, using Tupolev-16 tankers. Then, just weeks ago, modified Tu-95 tankers had been brought in. No one understood the reason for all this innovation and experimentation—until now. "Want me to give it a try, Joey?"

"No, no, I'm just out of practice," Leborov said, forcing himself to relax. "How are the gauges looking?"

"RPMs are matched, trims are within limits, power settings are within one or two percent of each other, and fuel tanks are balanced within two hundred kilos," replied the flight engineer, sitting right behind the copilot.

"Just plug this whore and let's go, Joey," Bodorev said. "You're the flight leader—show the other kids how it's done." That seemed to be all the encouragement he needed—along with the image of the long probe protruding from almost right between his legs aimed right for his girlfriend's *manda*—because on the next pass Leborev plugged the drogue smoothly and easily, as if he'd been doing it every day for years. The fuel transfer would be agonizingly slow, just a thousand liters a minute, so they would be plugged in for about fifteen minutes just to get a partial offload and allow the other bombers to cycle through.

It took three hours of formation flying with this huge armada to complete the refueling. Along the way five bombers and two tankers had to drop out, because they either couldn't transfer fuel, couldn't receive fuel, or because of some other major malfunction; one aircraft had a serious weapon problem that forced it to jettison two weapons on two different wing pylons. Fortunately, they were able to divvy up fuel from the remaining tankers to the remaining bombers, so all were able to get their scheduled onloads and continue the mission.

Since one plane had weapons problems, the formation leader decided that all the weapons had to be visually inspected, in addition to the routine safe connectivity-safe continuity checks. "Weapon safety checks complete, all weapons showing safe, no malfunctions," the bombardier in the downstairs nose compartment reported. "Clearing off for visual check."

"Navigator clearing off to assist."

Leborov turned around and said, "Stay put, Arkadiy. I need a stretch. I'll go. Pilot clearing off for visual weapons check." Bodorev donned his oxygen mask—the pilot flying the aircraft was required to wear it while the other pilot was out of his seat—and gave his partner and friend his usual good-luck sign: thumb and forefinger forming a circle, meaning "asshole."

With his parachute, walkaround oxygen bottle, gloves, heavyweight flight jacket, helmet, and oxygen mask on, Leborov stoop-walked past the engineer's and electronic-warfare officer's stations, patted the navigator on the shoulder in the very aft section of the cockpit, undogged the hatch to the lower compartment, climbed down the ladder to the lower deck, sealed the upper-deck pressure hatch, and followed the bombardier aft to the weapons bay's pressurized bulkhead hatch. There were no ejection seats on the Tupolev-95, either upward or downward; the flight-deck crew slid down a pole that extended through the entry hatch that carried them out into the slipstream and away from the aircraft, while the bombardier and gunner simply rolled out through downward escape hatches in their compartments. Now the bombardier unsealed the aft bulkhead hatch, and he and Leborov crawled aft into the weapons bay.

The deck was slick with frozen condensation and leaking coolant from some of the electronics bays, but the men ignored it and continued aft. They could hear the loud *click-click-clack-click* sounds of the navigation system, which used Doppler radar and radar fixes to update an analog computer as big as a refrigerator that still used gears and levers to provide position, heading, and velocity information. The noise from the big dual counterrotating propellers beating on each side of the fuselage was deafening, even through their helmets and ear protectors. Leborov found the switch for the port-side weapon pylon inspection light and flicked it on—and there it was. He had seen it and preflighted it on the ground, of course, but somehow it looked different when the Tu-95 was in the air.

The left weapon pylon held one Kh-90 air-launched attack missile. These were experimental missiles, fielded for the first time when two missiles had been launched at a CIA base in Uzbekistan just recently during an operational test. Then the missiles had carried high-explosive warheads.

But now these missiles carried two one-kiloton thermonuclear devices.

Code-named Sat Loshka, or "Garden Hoe," the warheads were actually copies of American nuclear "bunker-buster" bombs developed after Desert Storm to destroy deep underground bunkers, cave complexes, and biochem-weapon storage facilities without risking large numbers of civilian casualties. The warheads used rocket motors and armored nose caps to drive themselves down as much as thirty meters underground, even through layers of steel or Kevlar armor, before detonating. That meant that the fireballs would be relatively small and that blast and overpressure damage aboveground also would be small. Each cruise missile had its own inertial-navigation system—a system of electronic gyroscopes and pendulums that gave the navigation computers heading and velocity information—but the addition of GLONASS satellite navigation gave the missiles better than twenty-meter accuracy.

The bombardier walked down to another porthole to inspect the aft section of the huge Kh-90 missile. It was as if they were carrying a small jet fighter on their wings, Leborov thought. He saw a tiny bit of ice around the air inlet under the nose, but that would not be of any concern; less than a minute after launch, the exterior of the missile would heat up to several hundred degrees Centigrade as it

approached its top speed of five times the speed of sound.
He nodded to his bombardier, indicating they were done
with their inspection, then shut off the inspection light and
moved to look at the starboard missile. Everything having to
do with nuclear weapons always had to be two-officer, even
if it meant looking at the weapons from inside the plane.

Two thermonuclear bunker-buster missiles, faster than
any antiaircraft missile—and Leborov's sortie was only the
leader of a thirty-one-plane gaggle of similarly armed
Tupolev-95 bombers. Each missile had two independently
targeted nuclear warheads designed to burrow underground
and destroy even the best-protected bunker. The Americans
would never know what hit them. Poor bastards.

The bomb bay itself contained a rotary launcher with six
Kh-31P long-range antiradar missiles. As they closed in on
their launch point, Leborov and three of the other lead
bombers would be responsible for shutting down the local
radar sites along their intended route of flight, including Yel-
lowknife, Pine Point, Uranium City, Lynn Lake, Fort Nelson, Cold Lake, Edmonton, and Whitehorse. The
ramjet-powered Kh-31s had a range of two hundred kilometers and a maximum speed of Mach 3, with a ninety-
kilogram high-explosive fragmentary warhead that would
shred a radar antenna or a building into pieces in the blink of
an eye.

The inspection complete, Leborov and the bombardier
crawled along the narrow catwalk back the length of the
bomb bay and looked in on the gunner, seated in the very aft
tail cabin. They did not ask him to open his pressurized
hatch—that meant he would have had to put on his oxygen
mask and depressurize his compartment—but instead just
knocked on the porthole and got a thumbs-up from him. The
gunner was surrounded by box lunches filled with low-
residue snacks, a small stack of magazines, numerous bot-
tles of water, and metal boxes to store his relief bags.
Normally the gunner stayed up front with the crew in a jump

seat until close to enemy territory, but during formation flying his job was to keep an eye on the wingmen through his large windows and tail radar, so he had to spend the entire mission in his little compartment.

Despite the bone-chilling cold, Leborov was bathed in sweat by the time he'd returned to the cockpit and strapped himself into his seat again. "Pilot's back up," he reported.

"You look like shit," Borodev said cross-cockpit to his aircraft commander. "You didn't *rot yego yebal* with the bombardier again, did you?"

"Screw you."

Borodev looked at his friend carefully. "You okay, buddy?"

Leborov was silent for a few moments. Then, "Ah, shit, Yuri, no one deserves to die in their bed under a fucking nuclear fireball."

"That's not our concern nor our decision, Joey," Borodev said. He liked calling his friend the anglicized version of his name, because he was so obsessed with the dichotomy of Americans—their strange mixture of strength, humor, ruthlessness, and generosity. Some thought his preoccupation with all things American would affect his job performance—and, Borodev admitted, maybe they were right. "Our targets are missile-launch facilities and underground command posts for nuclear-warfighting units, not bedrooms. Besides, what's the difference between dying beneath a fireball and a one-thousand-kilo high-explosive bomb? Dead is dead."

"You know damn well there's a difference. . . ."

"No I don't, partner. I *don't* believe there's a difference. Just like there's no difference between the American attack on Engels and this attack. These are military attacks against military targets. Maybe some civilians will get killed—that can't be helped, and we're doing everything possible to limit civilian casualties, including decreasing the yields on our weapons to limits that very well may not destroy the target.

And you gotta enjoy the irony of attacking the Americans with a mini-nuke that *they* invented and deployed. . . ."

"I'm not in the mood to appreciate irony here, Yuri."

"Joey, we're *more* justified in doing this than the Americans were attacking Engels—we weren't fighting them, we were fighting the damned Taliban that raided our bases in Turkmenistan," Borodev went on, driving the point home as hard as he could without attracting the attention of the others behind them. The last thing they needed to hear was their copilot trying to convince the aircraft commander that what they were about to do was *right.* "The Americans attacked us for no reason. Remember that! *They* attacked *us.*

"Damn it, Joey, *we were there. We* could've been killed in that raid. One-third of our own regiment was wiped out that night, Joey. *One-third.* I lost a lot of good friends in that attack, Joey—so did you—and I know a lot of kids who lost fathers and who can't stop crying at night because they're afraid of American bombs falling on top of their heads again. Russia's finest bomber base is abandoned now—a ghost town. And I'm convinced that the Americans would not hesitate to keep on attacking, using every weapon in their arsenal and threatening us with every *other* weapon they had, including nukes. That's why this attack is necessary. I give President Gryzlov a lot of credit for having the courage to order this mission."

"But why are *we* using nukes, Yuri?"

"You know damned well, Joey," Borodev replied. "It's a tactical decision, not a psychological one—we're doing a job, not trying to send a message. We're using nukes because the Kh-90s wouldn't have the destructive power if we put nonnuclear warheads on them. They wouldn't put a dent in any of the targets we're going after." He looked at the pilot with an exasperated expression. "You *know* all this stuff, my friend. You certified this mission to the commanding general just three days ago, and he chose you to lead this gaggle specifically because you explained it all so well. Don't wuss out on me now, *zalupa.*"

"I'm not wussing out. I believe using nukes and biochem weapons *is* different from using other kinds of weapons, that's all."

"You're a dipshit, Joey. What's going on? You get your girlfriend pregnant and now you dream of a perfect world with no fighting and no war? Wake up, pal." He looked at his friend carefully. "You got her pregnant, didn't you?"

"Worse—I married her."

"You jerk! You never listen to a thing I tell you!" Borodev said, slapping him hard on the shoulder. "Congratulations! When were you planning on telling the general?"

"I submitted the paperwork to him three days ago. He signed us off yesterday."

"The great Josef Leborov, scourge of the gay bars—I mean, the *taverns*—missing in action because he has a wife and a rug rat now. I'm glad I lived to see the day." He patted his friend on the shoulder. "Good man. If we make it, you have someone to go home to . . . and if you don't, your name carries on. Well done, Senior Captain. Now, can we please get back to fucking work?"

"Affirmative," Leborov said. On intercom he reported, "Crew, all weapons have been visually checked and are ready, and we have visually ensured that our gunner is still with us. Station check." Every crew member did an oxygen check, checked his equipment, and reported back in order. "Very well. Naviguesser, position report?"

"Thirty-two minutes to the start-countermeasures point," the navigator responded. The start-countermeasures point was the farthest point from which American radar planes based at Eielson Air Force Base in Fairbanks, Alaska, could detect them. So far their intelligence had not reported any airborne, but Leborov knew that could change at any time, and without warning. "Approximately three hours to the launch point."

"Thank you," Leborov said. Borodev looked at him, and he realized that his voice sounded a little high-pitched and squeaky, a combination of his heavy breathing from crawling around almost the entire length of the plane and from the realization that time was passing quickly and the action was going to start very, very soon. He flashed his friend their mutual "okay" signal, ordered a crew-compartment and oxygen check, then decided to finish off his last box lunch now, before things started getting hairy.

SECRETARY OF DEFENSE'S BRIEFING ROOM, THE PENTAGON
A few hours later

"If you don't mind my saying so—and I don't care if you do or not—you all sound like a bunch of bickering, whining children," Secretary of Defense Robert Goff said, slumping wearily in his seat. He had just received a rundown on the current emergency from the chairman of the Joint Chiefs, the chief of staff of the Air Force, the commander of Air Combat Command, the commander of Air Intelligence Agency, and finally Brigadier General Patrick McLanahan—and his head really hurt now. The emergency meeting was called because of the alert sent by the North American Aerospace Defense Command, sent directly to the chief of operations in the secretary of defense's office.

When the warning from NORAD sounded, the White House was instantly put on alert, and the complex mechanisms put in motion to evacuate the president and other senior members of government. Per the plan, the president, the secretary of defense, the chairman of the Joint Chiefs and any of the service chiefs in close proximity, and any available members of the congressional leadership would get to Andrews Air Force Base as quickly as possible and board an Air Force E-4B aircraft known as the National Airborne Operations Center. The E-4's extensive communications suite allowed anyone on board to communicate instantly with virtually anyone anywhere on planet Earth. If the president was traveling, as he was now, he would take airborne one of the two VC-25 "flying White House" aircraft known as Air Force One and communicate with military commanders from there.

If they couldn't make it to Andrews, key government leaders would be evacuated immediately to an "undisclosed location," which almost everyone in Washington knew to be the Mount Weather Special Facility, code-named "High Point," the 434-acre mountain base near Berryville, West Virginia, operated by the Federal Emergency Management Agency to implement the National Continuity of Government Plan. From the High Point underground-bunker complex, the A-list government and military leaders holed up there had a direct secure videoconference link with the White House Situation Room, Air Force One, the Pentagon, the Navy's E-6B National Command Post, and the Air Force's E-4 National Airborne Operations Center—anywhere the president or the strategic warfighting commanders were likely to be in an emergency. But neither the president nor anyone in his cabinet would evacuate Washington unless absolutely necessary, and it was up to Secretary of Defense Robert Goff and Chairman of the Joint Chiefs of Staff Richard Venti to give the president their recommendation.

After receiving a fast status briefing from Venti—and a slightly more detailed briefing from the commander of NORAD, General Randall Shepard—Goff immediately called the White House operations staff and gave them a "no imminent threat" message. It was not an easy message to send: If he made a wrong decision, it could mean the avoidable loss of hundreds, perhaps thousands of lives, including those in the highest levels of government. Goff was usually ebullient, cheerful, and smiling, but when he was angry, his expression and features turned dark, bordering on wide-eyed maniacal. The Joint Chiefs chairman, Air Force General Richard Venti, had not seen the secretary with such an evil visage in quite some time.

Naturally, the person responsible for giving him this

expression was the same person that caused him to have it the *last* time: Patrick McLanahan.

"I find plenty of fault to go around here," Goff went on, "but let's start with the main instigator of this mess. General McLanahan, to say you overstepped the bounds of your authority is being far too generous. It's as if you have never heard of a chain of command, a direct order, or a commanding officer. Your actions in this entire episode are a disgrace to your uniform, and I think it's about time we investigate whether or not you should be *wearing* an American military uniform.

"However, just because we don't like the person who pulled the fire alarm doesn't mean we can ignore the smell," Goff went on. "General Houser, I understand and concur that you have plenty of reason to be angry at this gross contravention of authority and chain of command. I'm not an analyst, but I tend to agree with your opinion that we don't have enough information to make an accurate assessment. However, your recommendation that we do *nothing* is astounding to me. If it were any other person giving you this information, I think you'd do more, but because the information came from McLanahan, you recommended no action." Goff turned to General Venti. "General? Recommendations?"

"Sir, I know how everyone feels about General McLanahan, but I happen to think the man is a true professional and that his analysis is timely and accurate," Venti said. "If he thinks there is a danger out there, we should do something about it. I recommend that we establish an airborne-radar and fighter patrol over northern Alaska immediately while we fully activate the North Warning System. General Muskoka?"

"The Third Wing from Elmendorf provides AWACS radar coverage for northern Alaska," Thomas Muskoka, commander of Air Combat Command, responded from his headquarters at Langley Air Force Base in Virginia via a secure video teleconference link. "The Three-fifty-fourth Fighter Wing from Eielson provides F-16 alert fighter patrols, backed up with alert F-15s from Elmendorf—fifteen to twenty minutes away, max. This can be set up in a matter of minutes.

"Over the rest of the northern U.S., we deploy AWACS radar aircraft from Tinker Air Force Base in Oklahoma over central Canada, deploy Air National Guard air-defense fighters from Fresno and Klamath Falls to northern bases, and reconfigure other Air National Guard fighters from St. Louis, South Dakota, North Dakota, Montana, Colorado, Michigan, Iowa, and Minnesota for air-defense duties. The AWACS planes can be deployed within a few hours. Reconfiguring the fighters will . . . take some time."

The shock on Goff's face was obvious to everyone, no matter how hard he tried to hide it. "How long, General?" he asked.

"The Fresno and Klamath Falls fighters on ready alert can launch within a few minutes," Muskoka said. "If we can arrange tanker support, which is almost a certainty, we can put them on airborne alert, armed and ready for action." He spread his hands resignedly. "The other aircraft were never meant to be alert aircraft, but respond only to general mobilization and—"

"How *long*, General?"

Muskoka shrugged. "Seventy-two hours at the earliest, sir," he responded. Goff's lips parted in surprise. Muskoka added quickly, "Fresno and Klamath Falls should be able to launch perhaps a half dozen aircraft, F-15s and F-16s, within a few minutes. They'll have to do a unit recall to get more aircraft, but with regular ongoing training sorties, we should have another half dozen aircraft ready to go in an hour or two. If you need more than a dozen fighters right *now*, sir, I'd say we're in deep shit."

"I just never dreamed . . . I mean, I never thought it took

so long for us to get fighters in the air, especially after September eleventh," Goff said.

"Sir, we can get a fighter in the air with guns to cover one hundred percent of the U.S. that'll look real tough and pretty for CNN," Muskoka explained, "but launching a fighter to chase down a Cessna 182 who makes a wrong turn and flies over the White House is a lot different from chasing down a Russian bomber or a cruise missile—doing *real* air-defense work." The frustration on Muskoka's face was obvious. "Besides, I want to know who's going to pay for all this—it sure as hell shouldn't come out of *my* budget!—and mostly I want to know why we're putting so much stock in McLanahan's analysis. He's a bomber guy, not an intel weenie, for Christ's sake!"

"As you *were,* General," Venti warned.

"Excuse me, sir, but you're talking about putting a half dozen air-defense fighters on airborne alert over Canada, plus recalling a bunch more—on *McLanahan's* say-so? With all due respect, sir, I'd prefer a little more reliable confirmation myself."

"You've got all the confirmation you need, General," Venti said. He looked at Goff, who nodded and made an entry into an electronic notebook. "Make it happen."

"Roger, sir," Muskoka said, and he could be seen in the videoconference screen lifting a phone to his ear and giving the orders.

"General Shepard, what's the status of your sensors and radars?"

"Operational and ready to respond, sir." U.S. Air Force General Randall Shepard was the commander of the North American Aerospace Defense Command, in charge of monitoring and defending against a missile or bomber attack on North America; he was also "dual-hatted" as the commander of U.S. Northern Command, in charge of defending against military or terrorist attacks on the United States. "The long-range radars of the North Warning System are currently operational, with a few maintenance exceptions, which should not impact the system's effectiveness. The long-range radars have a range in excess of two hundred miles, depending on terrain and atmospheric conditions. The short-range radars can be activated within a relatively brief period of time, depending on local conditions.

"All NORAD-gained fighter-interceptor units are fully operational: four F-16Cs on alert at Eielson, four F-15Cs at Elmendorf, and four CF-18s on alert at Cold Lake, Alberta, Canada—plus the Klamath Falls and Fresno units," Shepard went on. "I believe each wing can generate one or two more aircraft in a matter of hours, and they can generate their entire force in about two days."

"Only twelve fighters available *for all of western North America?*" Goff asked incredulously.

"Sixteen, including the continental U.S. fighters," Shepard said. "We're at full authorized manning, sir. We have just enough funding to field the units we have out there right now. The southern-U.S. and drug-interdiction duties get all the funding, and have for many years." He looked at Patrick McLanahan's image on the video teleconference screen and added, "I still find it hard to believe we're under a Russian bomber threat, but be that as it may, we can respond to any threat."

"What about OTH-B?" Goff asked.

Shepard at first appeared to be confused, then pained, before replying, 'Sir, I think the staff or General McLanahan is in possession of outdated information. We operate only one OTH-B array, out of Bangor, Maine, which is dedicated only to atmospheric sampling and experiments as directed by the National Oceanic and Atmospheric Administration or on request by the Department of Homeland Security—which, by the way, has never put in a request to use it. The West Coast OTH-B system is in warm storage, and the Alaskan system was canceled about fourteen years ago and was never even completed."

"Can the West Coast system be reactivated, General?" Goff asked.

"Yes, sir—but it would take about two weeks to calibrate it and certify its accuracy and reliability," Shepard replied. "Even then it might not be reliable enough to give you the information you want. The AWACS planes are your best bet, sir. You get them airborne, and we can plug them into the network right away and have wall-to-wall coverage. The AWACS information is merged into North Warning and all the other ground-radar facilities, and it forms a very complete three-dimensional picture."

"The AWACS are on the way, General Shepard," Venti said. He turned to Goff and said, "Sir, I request that NORAD direct Eielson, Elmendorf, and Cold Lake to generate NORAD-dedicated Bravo-force alert sorties as quickly as possible."

"Agreed," Secretary Goff responded. The "Bravo" alert sorties were additional crews and fighters readied for duty behind the frontline planes and crews; unfortunately, it usually took several hours to prepare them for action.

"On the way, sir," Shepard said immediately, picking up a phone. General Muskoka made a note and handed it off-screen to his deputy. NORAD usually requested support from Air Combat Command for additional planes for the fighter-interceptor alert mission, so he wanted his fighter units ready to get the call and start lining up birds.

"General Houser, what other support can you provide for this operation?" Venti asked.

"Sir, the best support Space Command can offer, other than the systems already mentioned, is the Defense Support Program constellation," Houser replied. "The DSP satellites are designed to detect the 'hot dots' from ballistic-missile launches but can be tuned to detect smaller heat sources, such as bomber exhausts, traveling across the cold ocean or polar icecaps. It'll take away from their primary function of ballistic-missile launch warning, and as such I recommend against retuning DSP. Once we get the AWACS planes airborne, sir, I think we'll have all the coverage we need.

"Unfortunately, HAVE GAZE and SLOW WALKER are committed to operations in Central Asia, and it'll take several days to focus them in on any specific area of northern Alaska or Canada." HAVE GAZE and SLOW WALKER were infrared satellites and sensors designed to detect and track small missiles and aircraft. But unlike DSP satellites, in which just three satellites could cover the entire globe, the other two satellites had to be focused on a specific area to be effective. "DSP and AWACS are the best options we have without degrading our strategic surveillance."

"I agree," General Shepard said. "If the Russians really are gearing up for some sort of offensive, NORAD relies on DSP for the first indication of ballistic missile launch, both land- and sea-based. All our other ballistic-missile launch-warning systems are limited because they require the missiles to cross the relative horizon—that reduces launch-warning time anywhere from two to eight minutes. Only DSP gives us instantaneous launch warning."

"Very well—we won't reconfigure DSP," Goff said. He was ready for the meeting to be over with. "All right, we have AWACS planes on the way from Eielson, plus the alert fighters, plus fighters on the way from the CONUS bases, and we're firing up the North Warning radars. Anything else we're overlooking?" No response. "In that case . . ."

"Sir, I'd suggest dispersing the bomber and fighter fleet to alternate-generation bases or to civil airfields," Patrick McLanahan interjected. "If the Russians do attack, I believe they wouldn't go after civilian targets, only military ones. Military aircraft would therefore be safer at civil airfields."

"General McLanahan, I've agreed to the increased surveillance measures because I think that's a prudent step and because we have much of that infrastructure already in place," Secretary Goff said irritably. "But I'm not going to agree to any more moves that would disrupt day-to-day operations or create increased anxiety among our people, our allies, or the Russians until I get more information." He paused, looking around the conference table. "Anything else?"

"Yes, sir," General Muskoka of Air Combat Command chimed in. He looked uncomfortable but pressed on: "General Luger of the Air Battle Force submitted a mission plan to me that could supply you with the information you need. His proposal is to send a small armed recon force into Yakutsk, Russia, to ascertain the exact level of tanker-aircraft activity there. According to the satellite images, Yakutsk is turning into some kind of major Russian tanker base all of a sudden. General Luger feels that we may only be seeing a small portion of the aircraft there."

"That damned Air Battle Force outfit is not an intelligence organization," Houser retorted.

"Pardon the fuck out of me, Houser," Muskoka said, "but I'm not here to listen to your opinions about my operations forces!"

"Knock it off, both of you," Venti warned.

But Muskoka wasn't nearly done shooting back at Houser. "This is what I'm telling you, Houser: Dave Luger's Air Battle Force ground team is in the Aleutians, and they're in position and ready to do a sneak-and-peek operation to Yakutsk," he went on. "Now, unlike McLanahan, I trust Luger." Patrick's face remained stoic despite the direct indictment, but if Muskoka noticed Patrick's lack of reaction, he made no indication of it. "If it was McLanahan, he'd already be in Yakutsk by now raising all kinds of hell. Luger pushed his men to the limit of his authority and *stopped,* and I commend him for it. The question I put forth to the secretary and the Chiefs is simple: Do you want Luger's boys to go forward or not?"

"What's your recommendation, General Muskoka?" Secretary Goff asked.

"Luger's Tin Men are the only assets we have in that

entire region prepared to get us the information we need," Muskoka replied. "His plan is simple, it involves only a few aircraft and men, and it has a fairly good chance of succeeding. In about two hours, we can get the scoop on Yakutsk. I recommend you authorize them to proceed. They might appreciate a Marine Force Recon or Army Special Forces team standing by to back them up."

"I've got a unit ready to go," offered the commandant of the Marines Corps, General Paul Hooks, after quickly studying a report handed to him by an aide. "Bravo Company, First Battalion, Fourth Marines, Eleventh Marine Expeditionary Unit–Special Operations Capable, is right now at Fort Greely, Alaska, finishing up a joint-forces exercise with the U.S. Air Force. We should be able to back up your guys."

"Hold it, hold it," Goff said, raising his hands. "I'm not authorizing an armed incursion into Russia at this time—I don't care how good they are. Tell General Luger to stand by and wait for my word. I don't want to aggravate the situation any more than we already have. Anything else?" Goff asked. Before anyone could reply, he said, "I wish you all could be in the room when I give this to the president—maybe you'd have a better understanding of the consternation you cause when communications break down and personalities and emotions get in the way of clearheaded thinking. General Houser, General McLanahan, stay with me. Everyone else, thank you."

When the others had logged off the secure connection, Goff went on, "General McLanahan, General Houser has requested that you be relieved of command of the Nine-sixty-sixth Information Warfare Wing, pending the results of a court-martial. I think you're familiar with the charges. As is traditional in these cases, I'm offering you the opportunity to resign your commission in lieu of standing for court-martial."

"With respect, sir, I object to the offer," Houser said. "I request that McLanahan be bound over for trial."

"Your objection is overruled," Goff said. "General McLanahan?"

"Sir, before I respond to these charges, I have one last report to make to you and to General Houser concerning this air-defense situation—"

"There is no 'air-defense situation,' McLanahan!" Houser snapped.

Patrick held the classified folder up to the camera. "May I, sir?"

Goff sighed, then nodded. "Make it quick, General."

"Sir, I ran a scenario through the Strike Assessment Catalog computers using the latest intelligence data coupled with the information we now know of deployment of Russian strategic forces in Siberia," Patrick said.

"What scenario?"

"The possibility of success of a Russian bomber attack on the United States of America," Patrick replied.

"Give me a break, McLanahan!" Houser cried.

"It is the absolute latest information available," Patrick went on. "To make it even more conservative, I accelerated defensive time frames in our favor by fifty percent and decreased the size of the Russian forces by fifty percent. The results were the same: The United States can be successfully attacked from the air by Russian strategic air-breathing forces, and about half of all American nuclear-capable forces, especially land-based missiles and bombers, would be destroyed."

"That's *nonsense!*" Houser retorted.

"Sir, my report is done, and I conclude that not only is this attack feasible but it is *imminent*," Patrick said. "The Russians are modifying their bombers for intercontinental missions, repositioning their strike and support forces, and preparing some sort of coordinated attack using long-range aircraft. I believe that their objective is to destroy a good percentage of our land-based nuclear-deterrent forces. This attack could commence at any time. Our only hope of surviving it is to get as many armed interceptors and surveillance aircraft airborne as quickly as possible and to keep them airborne until we determine exactly what the Russians' intentions are."

"McLanahan, you have gone too far this time!"

"Hold it, General Houser," Robert Goff said. "General McLanahan, I've let you have your say, which is more than I should have done, but I think your past record gives you the right to be heard. I know you to sometimes overstep your authority, but I believe you do it for good and true reasons—in your own mind, at least. I don't see any reason to sound the alarm based on a computerized tarot-card reading, but I'm going to do my due diligence here and give you much more of the benefit of the doubt than I think you deserve at this particular time.

"I want you to upchannel that report right away. I want to let everyone take a look at it and offer opinions."

"Sir, I don't think there's time for that—"

"Too bad, General," Goff said heatedly. "That's a direct result of your attitude and the way you conduct yourself and your units. You've stepped out of line so much that no one trusts you. *You* created this mind-set, Patrick—not myself, not General Houser, not General Samson, not the president.

"General Houser, I want McLanahan's report evaluated and passed along as expeditiously as possible from your office. I already know how you feel about McLanahan's analysis—put it in writing, then send the report on up the chain to my office. *No holdups.* Is that clear?"

"Yes, sir."

"That's the best I'm going to do for you now, Patrick," Goff said, "so that report had better be able to stand on its own, because I don't think you'll be around to argue or defend it. Charges and specifications have been brought against you. Because of your rank and outstanding service to your country and to the Air Force, it is within my authority to set aside these charges and avoid a court-martial in exchange for voluntary separation from military duty, to avoid any embarrassment to yourself and your family as well as to the service. How do you respond?"

"I will not resign my commission, sir," Patrick responded. Houser looked shocked, before breaking out into a satisfied grin. "I do request that I be allowed to travel to see my family instead of being confined to quarters, since my family is in Sacramento and did not accompany me to San Antonio."

"General Houser?"

"No objection, sir," Houser replied.

"Very well," Goff said. "General McLanahan, you are hereby relieved of duty. The charges and specifications filed against you by General Houser remain; however, you retain all the privileges of your rank and are free to move about freely within the United States on your own recognizance. You will submit yourself to any hearings or proceedings as directed by the court-martial's presiding officer. That is all."

The video teleconference ended. Houser stood, then snatched the report from Patrick's hand. "I'll read it over, then give it to General Samson while we're on our way to Offutt to meet with STRATCOM, Air Combat Command, and NORAD," he said. "But I don't give it a snowball's chance in hell of seeing the light of day. This is a childish tactic to discredit me and General Samson and focus attention on yourself. Everyone's going to see this report for what it is: a worthless, pointless piece of crap.

"You can fly your little plane back to Sacramento and take a little vacation. Enjoy yourself—because you'll be in prison before you know it. It was nice to know you, Muck. Too bad Brad Elliott twisted your brain into knots. See ya around, nav."

OVER THE BEAUFORT SEA, 450 MILES NORTHWEST OF BARROW, ALASKA
A short time later

"Start countermeasures point, crew," the crew navigator of the lead Tupolev-95 Bear bomber announced.

"Acknowledged," the electronic-warfare officer responded. "My jammers are still in standby mode. All frequencies are clear. I expect to start picking up the North Warning long-range radars in twenty minutes," the EWO added.

Josef Leborov, the aircraft commander, shook his head in surprise and checked his watch and flight plan just to be sure what he heard was correct. It seemed like only minutes ago that the EWO had first given a status report. "Acknowledged," he responded. "Crew, station check. Prepare for ingress procedures." He took a last sip and secured his canteen in his flight bag, hoping like hell he'd have another chance to drink from it. He flipped to the "Start Countermeasures" page in his checklist. "SCM check, Yuri," he ordered.

The checklist was long. It directed them to extinguish all external lights; turn off transponders and any other radios that automatically transmitted a signal, such as the formation distance-measuring equipment and air-refueling rendezvous beacons; make sure radio switches were configured so no one would accidentally transmit on an outside frequency; turn down all interior instrument and cabin lights; and reduce cabin pressurization so any piercing of the fuselage would not produce an explosive decompression. Even the smallest, tiniest lights still left on in the cockpit seemed like searchlights in the ink-black sky, and he found himself checking each light switch two and three times, then finally pulling the circuit breakers to make sure he could not accidentally turn them on. He had done this checklist so many times in training missions and simulators, but it took on a whole new level of importance now.

He had no sooner finished the checklist a few minutes later when he heard a buzzing sound in his headset, and sweat spontaneously popped onto his forehead and the back of his neck, chilling him instantly. "Threat warning, India-Juliett band!" the EWO shouted. "F-16 Falcon interceptor!"

"Low-level-descent checklist!" Leborov shouted, and simultaneously pushed the nose over and pulled the throttles of his four Kuznetsov turboprop engines back to keep the airspeed below red line. "Copilot, notify the formation, evasive action, proceed to opposed ingress routes immediately." In order to ensure that the maximum number of planes made it past the defenses, the four six-ship formations would break apart and go in single-ship, following slightly different routes—some planes were separated by only one or two degrees of track, less than a hundred meters' altitude, or less than a minute's time. Borodev's voice was as excited and high-pitched as a woman's as he got on the radio to notify the rest of their package that enemy fighters were inbound.

That would be the last transmission to his comrades until they all met back at base . . . or in hell.

An F-16! They hadn't expected an F-16 up here for another hour at least. He adjusted the propeller pitch of the rearmost propellers to increase drag so he could increase his descent rate. "Has he seen us yet?" It was a stupid question—they had to assume that the American fighter had them. They also had to assume that there was more than one fighter out there—the American Air Force almost always traveled in two-plane formations. Fortunately, the F-16's radar did not have a true look-down/shoot-down capability, so they had a chance if they could make it to low level. The radar clutter of the Arctic Ocean and then the ruggedness of northern Canada would hide them very effectively.

"I don't think so, sir," the EWO responded. "His radar is still in long-range scan, and his track has not changed. He's heading northeast, across but away from us. He might lose track in a couple of minutes."

But then again, Leborov thought, if he did what he was supposed to do and established a patrol orbit, along the most probable inbound path for bombers from Russia to take—like the one they were on right now—he was bound to find them. They were quickly running out of time. "Any word from our support package, copilot?" Leborov asked.

"Negative," Borodev responded woodenly. "No idea where they are."

"Are we on time?"

"About two minutes early," the navigator responded. "Good tailwinds."

"Good tailwinds, my ass—two minutes is all the time that F-16 needs to sound the alert." Shit, thought Leborov. Soon the entire American and Canadian air forces would be howling after them. Mission and radio security was one thing, but shouldn't they know where the rest of their strike package was? "Okay, we can't stay up here any longer," he said. He put the airspeed needle right on the red line by dumping the nose even lower. "Our best chance is to try to duck under his radar cone before he comes around on his patrol orbit—we may be able to slip past him."

Leborov unconsciously let the airspeed creep up past the red line in an attempt to get down faster, but soon he could feel Borodev pulling back on the control column. "Let's not rip the wings off this old hog, Joey," he said. "We've still got a long way to go." He pulled the nose up to get the airspeed back down below the red line. Damn, Leborov thought, how many of his wingmen had started their descent? How many were still up high? He hoped everyone used proper crew discipline and was ready when that fighter appeared—or they'd be dead meat.

ABOARD AN F-16C FIGHTING FALCON FIGHTER,
OVER THE BEAUFORT SEA
That same time

"Knifepoint, Knifepoint, Hunter Four, blue four."

"Hunter, this is Knifepoint, strangle mode three and Charlie, go active, stand by for mickey check. . . . Hunter, acknowledge. Verify you're single-ship this morning."

"Knifepoint, Hunter checks, I'm single-ship. My wingman will join up later."

"Copy that, Hunter. Negative contacts, cleared into track Gina-two, deploy, advise joker."

"Hunter copies, wilco."

To tell the truth, thought U.S. Air Force First Lieutenant Kelly Forman, she preferred being up here by herself, without having to keep an eye out for a wingman or flight lead. The Alaska sky was an absolute delight to fly in—clear, crisp, and cold, with only the stars above and a very, very few lights below. She sometimes felt as if she were the only person in the sky right now. . . .

Which was obviously not true, or else she would not have been sent up here on such short notice.

The twenty-six-year-old mother of two boys was a newly operational F-16C Fighting Falcon pilot in the Eighteenth Fighter Squadron "Blue Foxes" out of Eielson Air Force Base, Alaska. Although the Blue Foxes were a ground-attack fighter unit, using the LANTIRN night-attack and low-level navigation system, they were often tasked with the air-defense mission as well, operating with the Nineteenth Fighter Squadron's F-15 Eagle fighters and the 962nd Airborne Air Control Squadron's E-3C AWACS radar planes out of Elmendorf Air Force Base in Anchorage. But tonight she was all by herself. Even after an hour, she was *still* by herself—her wingman was still broken, still on the ground. Another F-16 had just taken off a few minutes earlier, with one of the 168th Air Refueling Wing's KC-135 tankers based at Eielson, and wouldn't rejoin for another thirty minutes.

Forman was two hundred miles northwest of Point Barrow, Alaska, over the seemingly endless expanse of the Arctic Ocean. She had just entered her assigned patrol orbit, which was a narrow triangular course aligned northwest-southeast, at an altitude of fifteen thousand feet. She was the "low CAP," or combat air patrol, the altitude that allowed her APG-68 radar to see all the way down to the ocean's surface, at her radar's optimal range of eighty miles, and all the way up to thirty thousand feet, on its normal long-range-scan mode; once her wingman joined her, he would take the high CAP, twenty-four thousand feet, so he could see as high as fifty thousand feet.

As briefed, Forman reduced speed to save fuel and started her turn northwestbound in the triangle. "Hunter Four's established in Gina-two," she reported to Knifepoint. Knifepoint was the call sign of the Alaska NORAD Regional Surveillance Center, based at Elmendorf Air Force Base, which combined radar information from the North Warning System, Federal Aviation Administration, Transport Canada, and other military and civil radars into one regional control center. Knifepoint was different from an air-traffic-control center—unlike air-traffic controllers, who strived to keep aircraft safely *separated,* the Knifepoint controllers' job was to maneuver fighters as *close* as possible to other aircraft.

"Roger, Hunter," the controller responded. "No contacts." Up here, at the top of the United States, Knifepoint relied on the North Warning System radars to see any intruders—the FAA radars in Fairbanks and Anchorage did not have the range to see this far north. The North Warning System, or NWS, in Alaska consisted of four long-range partly attended radars, nicknamed "Seek Igloo," plus eight short-range unattended radars, called "Seek Frost," which closed the gaps in the longer-range systems.

Air patrols were a combination of monitoring the instruments, keeping track of the aircraft in its patrol track, twisting the heading bugs at the corners to head down the next leg, watching the radar and radar-warning receivers for signs of aircraft—and staying awake. Forman enjoyed air-defense exercises because she *knew* there was going to be an intruder, and it was her job to find it. In the real world, she had to *assume* there was an intruder out here in all this darkness. Many times air-defense fighters would be launched after being detected by the FAA or North Warning System, and she would be vectored into position while radar-silent and intercept the intruder from behind to attempt an identification. Those were damned exciting.

Not so this time. She didn't know the exact reason she'd been launched and sent to this patrol, but so far there was no sign of intruders. Often fighters were sent into air patrols because the Russians had spy planes nearby, or because NORAD, the Air Force, or the Canadians wanted to test or observe something. It was impossible to know, so she assumed there was a bad guy out here that needed to be discovered.

But she'd been launched right at the end of her duty day, after studying for a pre-check-ride written exam while doing her normal training duties. An eight-hour duty day followed by several hours' flying in the wee hours of the morning . . . swell. This could turn into a very, very long morning.

She had just turned eastbound after completing her initial fifty-mile northwest patrol leg when she heard, "Knifepoint, this is Hunter Eight, blue four." It was Forman's wingman, finally checking on with the NORAD controller.

"Hunter Four, Knifepoint, your company is on freq."

"Roger that, Knifepoint. Hunter Four checking off to talk with company aircraft. I'll monitor your frequency and report back up."

"Roger, Hunter, cleared as requested."

Forman switched over to her secondary radio: "Eight, this

is Four on tactical. 'Bout time someone showed. Girls don't like being stood up, you know."

"Sorry about the delay—nothing's working right on the ramp this morning. Must be a full moon. We're about two hundred miles out. How's everything going?"

"Nice and quiet. Established in the low CAP. The bird is doing okay." She punched instructions into her navigation computer, checking her fuel reserves. "Joker plus one on board." The "joker" fuel level was the point at which she had to leave the patrol area and head for home; she had one hour left on patrol before she had to head back in order to arrive with normal fuel reserves, which in Alaska were substantial. Because weather and airfield conditions changed rapidly here, and because suitable alternate airfields were very, very few and far between in this big state, every fighter flying in Alaska took as much fuel as possible with it on patrol; Kelly's F-16 had two 370-gallon drop tanks on board, along with four AIM-120 AMRAAM radar-guided missiles, two AIM-9L "Sidewinder" heat-seeking missiles, and ammunition for the twenty-millimeter cannon. Aerial-refueling tankers were precious commodities.

"Roger that. I brought the gas can with me. Any sign of Roadkill?" "Roadkill" was the Blue Foxes' name for their brethren in the Nineteenth Fighter Squadron—their squadron emblem, a stylized gamecock, looked to many folks like a squished critter on the road. The F-15Cs of the Nineteenth, coming with their E-3C AWACS radar plane, were the air-defense specialists; the F-15s had much longer legs, two-engine reliability, and a better look-down, shoot-down radar to find any bad guys that might be up here. They would undoubtedly take over the air-patrol mission once they arrived, although the F-16s liked to play with them as much as possible, too.

"Negative." There was a lot of static on the channel all of a sudden, which was fairly common at the higher latitudes, usually because of sunspot activity. The northern lights were beautiful up here, but the solar flares that caused the sky to light up with waves and waves of shimmering light played havoc with the radios.

"Rog. I'll give you a call if I hear from them. See you in a few." Despite the growing static, Kelly instantly felt much better. Although she enjoyed flying by herself, it sure was comforting to hear a friendly voice on the airwaves, to know that friendly forces were on the way—especially the tanker.

Forman was a couple minutes from her turn to the southeast when the radar target box winked on, at the extreme center-left edge of her heads-up display. Got a nibble, she told herself as she made a hard left turn to center up on the newcomer. It was high enough so it probably wasn't an ice floe or some other—

When she rolled out of her turn, she couldn't believe what she saw: radar targets *everywhere.* She thought she had a radar malfunction, so she turned her radar to STBY, then back to RADIATE—and the targets were still there. Maybe two dozen targets, all at different altitudes.

"Ho-lee *shit,*" she muttered to herself. Frantically, she switched back to the command channel on the primary radio. Through a haze of static, she radioed, "Knifepoint, Knifepoint, this is Hunter Four, 'gorilla,' I say again, 'gorilla,' northwest two-four bull's-eye." "Gorilla" was the brevity code for a large formation of unidentified planes in indeterminate numbers. Forman gave the target's position relative to an imaginary point that changed on every patrol. She couldn't give the targets' altitude, speed, or any more precise information because there were so *many* of them out there.

"Say again, Hunter." There was a loud squeal in the radios that the frequency-hopping communications system couldn't eliminate. "Be advised, Hunter, our status is 'bent,' repeat, 'bent.' Keep us advised."

Jamming—someone was *jamming* them! Forman

switched to her secondary radio and found it hopelessly jammed. The squealing was drowning out all recognizable sound even before she keyed the mike. Maybe whoever was jamming her radios was jamming the North Warning System radar, too—the "bent" code meant that the ground radar was inoperative. So now she was all alone up here with a huge number of planes bearing down on her, with no way to contact anyone.

The only thing she had left were her orders and her tactical doctrine: Any unidentified aircraft entering the Air Defense Identification Zone had to be identified, and if they acted in a hostile manner, they were to be shot down immediately, as quickly as possible before reaching U.S. airspace. She was to continue the interdiction mission until she reached "bingo" fuel, which gave her the minimum fuel state over the intended recovery base only.

Forman thumbed her stick controls and designated the lead aircraft in the lead formation, placed the radar pipper just to the left and below center in her heads-up display, and headed toward it. This guy was screaming for the deck, descending at fifteen thousand feet per minute. Too late, pal, she thought—I got you. . . .

The radar-warning receiver blared again—but this time, instead of a steady electronic tone, they heard a fast, high-pitched, raspy sound. "Fighter has locked on," the electronic-warfare officer said. "Eleven o'clock . . . moving into lethal range."

Leborov couldn't believe the speed of that thing—it seemed only seconds ago that they first got the warning. "What the hell should I do?" he shouted.

"Turn left, head into him!" the EWO shouted. "That'll increase his closure rate, and he'll be forced to maneuver." That wasn't necessarily so with an F-16—they could shoot Sidewinder missiles directly into your face all day long—but he had to give the pilot *something* to do until they got low. "All jammers on and operating . . . chaff and flares ready."

"Passing two thousand for five hundred," the navigator said.

"Screw that, nav—we're going to one hundred meters," Leborov said. "If he wants to come down and play, let's get *way* down into the weeds!" Bravado? Maybe, but he wasn't going to get shot down without a fight, and there was one place the Tupolev-95 liked to fly, and that was down low.

Thirty miles . . . twenty miles . . . the plane was still heading down, passing five thousand feet and descending fast. She was at ten thousand feet, not real anxious to chase this guy down until she started rolling in behind him for an ID. He turned slightly into her, so they were going nose to nose now. She configured her cockpit switches for low-light operations and lowered her PVS-9 night-vision goggles. The view was matte green and with very little contrast, but now she could see a horizon, the shoreline far behind her, details of the outside of her jet—and a spattering of bright dots in the distance: the unidentified aircraft. There were so many that it looked like a cluster of stars.

Forman thought about trying to contact the plane on the international emergency "GUARD" frequency, but the jamming was too heavy and getting stronger as she closed in. Was that considered a "hostile act" right there? Probably so. Fifteen . . . ten . . .

Suddenly one of the other myriad radar targets on her heads-up display scooted across the scope to her right, traveling . . . Shit, the guy was *supersonic*. She immediately pulled up, jammed her throttle to zone-five afterburner, and turned hard right to pursue. The first guy never went above four hundred knots, even in a screaming-ass dive, but this newcomer was going twice as fast! He would reach the coastline way before these others—if she didn't catch him first.

Again she tried to radio Knifepoint and her wingman of

the new contact—but the jamming was still too heavy. Each one of those incoming planes must have *enormous* jammers to take out digital radios and even the North Warning System radars at this range! Even her APG-68 radar was getting spiked, and it had plenty of antijam modes.

The fast newcomer was at forty-three thousand feet, traveling just over the speed of sound, heading east-southeast. Forman locked him up on radar easily after getting behind him and tried to interrogate his Identification Friend or Foe system. Negative IFF—he was a bandit, all right. Supersonic, no modes and codes, flying way off transpolar flight routes through a curtain of electronic jamming—unless it was some Concorde pilot hot-dogging it for his rich passengers, he was a bad guy.

The bandit was passing Mach 1.1, the speed limit for her F-16 Fighting Falcon's external fuel tanks. No Alaska fighter pilot ever wanted to punch off external fuel tanks, especially if there was a tanker anywhere in the area, but she would never catch him otherwise, so, reluctantly, off they went. As soon as this guy was ID'd and the Nineteenth showed up, she was done for the evening—even with a tanker on the way, no fighter pilot played very long up in Alaska without plenty of extra fuel.

It was funny the things you thought about at a time like this, Kelly mused to herself. Here she was chasing down a bandit, in the midst of hostile jamming, and all she could think was that someone was going to have to pay for a couple 370-gallon fuel tanks.

She tried the IFF interrogate switch a couple more times—still negative—then hit her MASTER ARM switch and selected her twenty-millimeter cannon instead of her radar- or infrared-guided missiles. This guy definitely met all the criteria of being a bad guy, she thought, but she had enough gas right now to try to do a visual ID. At Mach 1, he was still fifteen minutes from reaching the Canadian coast. She had forty-five minutes to bingo fuel—a number that was drop-

ping rapidly every minute she spent in zone-five afterburner—so she decided to go in close for a visual.

She kept the power up and was starting to get into visual
range in just under five minutes when suddenly her radar-
warning receiver emitted a high-pitched, fast *deedledeedledeedle* warning tone. An enemy fire-control radar had
locked on to her! The heads-up display categorized it as an
"unknown," position directly ahead of her. But there were no
other aircraft except the guy in front of her. . . .

A tail gun! That's the only thing it could be! The damned
bandit had locked on to her with a tail-mounted fire-control
radar.

And sure as hell, moments later she saw winks of light
coming from the still-dark silhouette of the bandit in front of
her. *The bastard was firing a tail gun at her!* She immediately punched out radar-decoying chaff and flares and broke
hard right to get away. She heard a couple hammer taps
somewhere on the fuselage, but there were no warning messages.

Kelly was not scared—she was *incensed!* She'd been shot
at by Iraqi surface-to-air missiles while doing patrols for
Operation Southern Watch, and she'd taken on plenty of
simulated surface-to-air missiles, antiaircraft artillery, and
every kind of air-to-air missile possible in training—but
she'd never been shot at by a tail gunner. She didn't even
know that any planes *had* tail gunners anymore! Furious, she
flipped her arming switch from the cannon to her
Sidewinder missiles and tightened her turn, getting ready to
line up on the bandit.

No question any longer—the guy was a hostile. She
wished she could tell her wingman or the Nineteenth about
the other bogeys heading in, fearing they all might have tail
gunners, but the jamming was still too heavy. No matter—
this guy was going *down.*

But as she lined up for her first shot, her night-vision goggles blanked out a tremendous burst of light coming from

the bandit. It was a missile launch—but the missile was *huge,* hundreds of times larger than an air-to-air missile. The tail of fire had to be two hundred feet long! The missile shot straight ahead for a mile or two, then pulled up abruptly. A few moments later, she heard a sonic boom, followed by a large flash of light, and the missile accelerated and disappeared in the blink of an eye. Oh, Christ, Forman thought, he's firing attack missiles toward Canada. They were too fast to be cruise missiles. They looked like . . . like . . .

Like air-launched ballistic missiles.

As soon as Kelly got a lock indication, she fired a Sidewinder. Seconds later another big missile launched from the bomber. "Oh, my God," she muttered, and she fired her last Sidewinder. The first Sidewinder veered from the attack plane and went after the second missile, but it accelerated off too quickly. The Sidewinder couldn't reacquire the plane and fell harmlessly away until it exploded. Just milliseconds before the second Sidewinder hit, the bandit launched a third big missile.

Her second Sidewinder hit the enemy aircraft directly in its right engine. The bandit veered right, stabilized, veered right again, started to turn left, then made a slower, steadier right turn, crossing directly in front of her. Forman closed in for the kill. At four miles, as the bandit made its turn, she recognized it as a Russian Tupolev-22M bomber, nicknamed "Backfire," its variable-geometry wings slowly swiveling forward. It had two large external fuel tanks beside the fuselage on each side. Smoke and fire were trailing from the right engine, getting heavier each second. She switched to her cannon, zoomed down on him, and opened fire. Shells peppered the fuselage and left wing, and now through her night-vision goggles she could see puffs of fire coming from the left engine. The Backfire aimed right for the Canadian coast, still over a hundred miles away. She doubted if it would stay aloft for—

Her attention was drawn to a bright streak of fire above and to her left. She realized with horror it was *another* one of those huge air-to-surface missiles. In her desperation to shoot this guy down, she forgot she was single-ship, that there might be *more* bombers out there—and that she was responsible for them all until help arrived! That was probably why this Backfire turned right instead of left—to distract her enough so the wingmen could launch their missiles.

Forman turned sharply left and started a climb, selected her AMRAAM missiles, and quickly locked on to the second bandit just as it launched a second big air-to-ground missile—but then her radar-warning receiver screeched again, and this time the hammer blows and shudders she'd felt before came back twice as hard. In her drive to hose the first Backfire and then diverting her attention to the second bandit, she'd flown too close to the tail end of the first Backfire and gotten into its kill zone.

The engine instruments were still okay, but she could feel a vibration in her control stick and rudder pedals—and then she noticed it, the right-wing fuel gauge dipping well below the level of the left. She immediately started transferring fuel from the right wing to the fuselage and left-wing tanks, but there was probably no room in the other tanks for the right-wing fuel—she was going to end up losing it. Fuel was life up here in the Arctic.

And as she fretted about her fuel state, the second bandit launched a third missile, then started to do a one-eighty. Now she assumed that each Backfire carried three of those big honking missiles, and she assumed that there were more up here, so instead of pursuing the second bandit, she searched farther west and south for more high-flying fast-movers. Sure enough, two more supersonic bogeys appeared.

She quickly verified that they were not transmitting any friendly IFF codes—they were not. She had to fly west a few minutes to get within range, which was not the direction she needed to be flying. Kelly didn't have to check the nav computer to know that if she didn't turn around now, she might not make it back to base. Even though Alaska had the best search-and-rescue units in the world, there was no way you wanted to eject over northern Alaska—and sure as heck not over the Beaufort Sea. She had to turn back. . . .

But the Backfire she didn't attack might be the one that launched a missile and destroyed Eielson, Fairbanks, Anchorage, Elmendorf, or Washington, D.C.—and there was *no friggin' way* she was going to let that happen! She started a gradual climb and turned westward to get within position to attack with whatever ammunition she had left.

As quickly as she could, she maneuvered and locked up both Backfires, interrogated for friendly IFF codes once again, received a negative reply, then fired one AMRAAM missile at each. Both Backfires immediately started ejecting chaff and flare decoys, but she was close enough for the decoys to have no effect and the missiles to stay on target. The first Backfire was hit on the left side of the fuselage and started to spin almost straight down into the Beaufort Sea. The second was hit in the belly, and the hit must've detonated the missile in its belly, because the Backfire blew apart in a spectacular cloud of fire. The explosion then ignited the two external missiles, adding their destruction to the tremendous fury of that blast. Forman had to peel off to the north to stay away from that massive blast—she swore she could feel the heat right through her bubble canopy and winter-weight flight gear. Kelly repeated the attack with two more supersonic targets. One AMRAAM missed; she scored another hit on a Backfire but couldn't see what happened to it because she had removed her night-vision goggles due to the longer ranges involved. Next . . .

"Warning, fuel low," the computerized "copilot," nicknamed "Bitching Betty," intoned. One more glance at her fuel gauges: The right wing was almost empty, and the left wing and fuselage tanks were less than half full. Crap. She was right at emergency fuel level—sixty minutes of fuel,

sixty minutes' flying time to Eielson. But the tanker was on its way, and there was one emergency airfield at Fort Yukon that she might be able to use. She still had plenty of ammo in the cannon. Time to get busy.

Forman lowered her night-vision goggles and did strafing runs on two more Backfires, scoring hits on both but unsure if she'd done any damage. She then turned farther to the west to look for more targets—and there they were. As she saw it, there were several waves of attackers—multiple levels of slower-moving planes, most of them descending to low altitude, and another wave of high-speed attackers at higher altitude that appeared to be blowing past the slow-movers and launching huge hypersonic missiles, perhaps to pave the way for the slow-movers.

"Warning, fuel emergency," Bitching Betty chimed in. In her drive to get as many enemy planes as possible, Kelly had ignored her fuel state. She knew that her wingman was coming, but he was still at least twenty minutes away. She was almost out of ammunition—admittedly having been a little excitable and trigger-happy on her first gun pass, but being more frugal as her supply got lower and lower. She tried the radios again—still jammed. The datalink hadn't activated yet, meaning that the AWACS plane from Elmendorf hadn't arrived yet. There was no indication that her wingman was anywhere in the area, so she couldn't even lead him to the bandits.

With the sky full of enemy planes all around her, she came to the horrifying realization that she was done for the day—she had no fuel and no weapons. The enemy aircraft were heading farther to the southeast, within visual range of the Canadian coastline by now. They were heading away from Eielson, so she couldn't pursue. It was the hardest thing she'd ever done in her life, but she had no choice except to break off and head for home.

And then she saw them: more missiles flying overhead. The Backfires that she couldn't down were launching their missiles! And she was powerless to stop them.

Forman pointed her F-16's nose toward Eielson, entered the emergency beacon code into her transponder, and throttled back to max-range power. On radar she could see even the slow-movers down low passing her easily. Her radar tracked twelve bandits cruising on their way toward North America, and it detected even more missile launches. She kept trying her radios, but it would be no use until every one of the bandits had disappeared from radar.

As she slowed to her best-range power setting, the vibration in her stick and rudder pedals got worse. She couldn't go below three hundred knots without the fighter's shaking so violently that she thought she could lose control at any second. That was not good. It meant that air refueling was probably out of the question.

"Hunter Four, this is Hunter Eight on company, how do you read?"

Thank God the jamming had subsided enough to hear human voices, she told herself. "Two by, Eight," she responded. "How me?"

"Weak and barely readable," her wingman said. "We tried to raise you earlier, but no response. I have you tied on, three-zero at one-two bull's-eye, base plus eleven. What's your state?"

"Eight, I engaged seven, repeat, seven bandits," Forman said breathlessly. "Do you copy?"

"*You engaged seven bandits?* Did you make visual contact?"

"Affirmative. Russian Backfire bombers. Two of them launched what appeared to be very large air-to-surface missiles. I got six of the bandits. There were several groups of bandits, the Backfires up high and slower-movers that descended to low altitude. They were headed southeast. I have been unable to contact Knifepoint. Can you try? Over."

Hunter Eight was farther south, away from the Russian planes that were jamming them—she hoped he'd have better luck. Now Forman's wingman sounded as breathless as she did.

"Stand by," he said. On the primary radio, she heard, "Knifepoint, Knifepoint, this is Hunter Eight." It took several tries to reach the NORAD controller. "Hunter Four has engaged large hostile attacking bomber force." He gave the approximate position and direction of flight.

"We copy all, Hunter flight," the controller responded. "We encountered heavy MIJIing on all frequencies. We have lost contact with all SEEK IGLOO and SEEK FROST sites. Unable to provide service at this time." The controller paused, then said, "We saw the gaggle go by, but we couldn't talk to anyone—and then we lost our radars. There wasn't a damn thing we could do."

NORTH AMERICAN AEROSPACE DEFENSE HEADQUARTERS, CHEYENNE MOUNTAIN AIR FORCE STATION, COLORADO
That same time

"Triple-C, this is ADOC, we have a situation," the intercom announcement began. "Alaska NORAD Region has just submitted a radar outage report. They report losing contact with four long-range radars and seven short-range radars of the North Warning System. They've also submitted a Fighter Status Report and indicate they have lost contact with one of their fighters scrambled out of Eielson. This is not a drill. Both Alaska NORAD and Eielson report communications outages as well."

"ADOC, Command copies," responded U.S. Army Colonel Joanna Kearsage, the command director of the Combined Control Center. "All OCs, stand by. Systems, warm up the hot lines. This is not a drill." Kearsage was a former Patriot air-defense-brigade commander from Fort Hood, Texas, and a twenty-two-year Army veteran. She once thought that nothing compared to deploying her brigade out to the field on short notice and putting her beloved Patriot missile system through its paces—and then she got the assignment to the Mountain. She'd been wrong. For eight hours every day and a half, information from all over the world flowed right to her fingertips, and she made decisions that affected the lives of two great democracies and the peace and freedom of the entire world. There was nothing else like it.

At first the idea of living in a huge underground bunker was not very appealing. The Cheyenne Mountain Operations Center was a series of massive excavations covering four and a half acres deep inside the Mountain. Inside the granite excavations was a rabbit's warren of fifteen steel buildings, most of which were three stories tall, all mounted on springs to absorb the shock of a nuclear blast or earthquake. There was no contact between the buildings and the rock; flexible corridors connected the buildings. The complex had its own emergency power generators and water reservoirs, along with its own dining halls, medical centers, and barracks, and even such creature comforts as two exercise centers, a barbershop, a chapel, and a sauna. The whole complex was enclosed behind massive steel doors, each weighing over twenty-five tons but so precisely balanced on their hinges that only two men could push them open or closed if necessary.

The command director of the Cheyenne Mountain Operations Center was the person in charge of the round-the-clock global monitoring network of three major military commands: the North American Aerospace Defense Command, the U.S. Strategic Command, and the U.S. Northern Command, all responsible for the defense of the United States and Canada. Kearsage's forty-person Charlie crew manned the extensive communications and computer-network terminals that collected information from everywhere in the world and from space and merged it into the displays and readouts presented to the command director and her operations staff.

Her battle staff was broken up into operations centers within Cheyenne Mountain: Missile Warning, Air Warning, Space Control, Intelligence, Systems Control, and Weather. Each center's combined data was displayed in the command center on several computer monitors of various types and sizes.

Kearsage was seated in the command center along with her deputy commander, Canadian Forces Colonel Ward Howell, and the noncommissioned officer in charge of command communications. Dominating the command center were four wall-size monitors with graphical compilations of the global threat and continental defense picture. The left-center screen showed the current threats for North America, and the right-center screen showed threats around the world. Flanking the two large center screens were two other screens showing the status of air-defense and strategic-attack forces. Two rows of computer monitors in front of Kearsage and her deputies showed up-to-date information and reports from the individual operations centers themselves.

Her attention was riveted on the North America display, which showed the circles representing the optimal range of the long-range radars, or LRRs, and short-range radars, or SRRs, of the North Warning System in northern Alaska and northern Canada. The circles were blinking red, indicating a malfunction or degradation. The North Warning System was the first line of defense against air-breathing threats to the North American continent—and for some reason a good chunk of it was suddenly shut down.

In addition, there was a blinking red inverted V, indicating the last known position of the F-16 scrambled out of Eielson Air Force Base on cryptic orders from the Pentagon. She could still see the two other groups of symbols, representing other airborne assets: one F-16C and a KC-135R tanker from Eielson, which were supposed to rendezvous with the lone F-16; and two F-15Cs and an E-3C AWACS radar plane flying northeast from Elmendorf Air Force Base in southern Alaska to temporarily set up a long-range radar and fighter picket northwest of Alaska over the Arctic Ocean. But the other two groups of symbols were steady green—on course, on time, and in contact. What happened to the first F-16?

"ADOC, talk to me," Kearsage said, using the acronym for the Air Defense Operations Center inside the Mountain, her group responsible for tracking and identifying all air targets over North America. "What do we have? And where is that fighter?"

"Village is trying to ascertain the status of those radars and to make contact with the fighter," the Air Warning Center's senior controller responded. "Remote transmissions appear to be experiencing heavy interference." "Village" was the call sign for the Alaska NORAD regional headquarters at Elmendorf Air Force Base.

"SOLAR, would sunspot activity be responsible for the comm interference?" "SOLAR" was the nickname for the Weather Support Center at nearby Peterson Air Force Base, which provided weather support to Cheyenne Mountain.

"Unknown at this time, ma'am, but we're not experiencing any abnormal solar activity."

"Triple-C, this is MWC," the controller at the Missile Warning Center at NORAD reported. The Missile Warning Center was responsible for detecting, identifying, and monitoring any possible missile launches anywhere on the planet, using heat-seeking satellites, and predicting if the missiles posed a threat to North America. "We're looking at some events near the long-range and short-range radar sites in northeastern Alaska and northwestern Canada. Not very high threshold readings—definitely not ballistic-missile launches. Stand by." "Events" were how they referred to whatever hot spots the heat-sensing Defense Support Program satellites could pick up—anything from oil-well fires and forest fires to ballistic-missile launches.

"Village, this is Anchor, what do you think?" "Anchor" was Kearsage's code word for NORAD headquarters.

"Ma'am, we're in contact with the fighter's wingman,

who took off from Eielson, and we're in contact with the F-15s and AWACS that launched out of Elmendorf," the senior controller at the Alaska NORAD Region headquarters responded. "Some sort of localized interference over the Beaufort Sea."

"Are you going to submit an ECTAR?"

"Negative. Not at this time," the senior controller responded.

Kearsage allowed herself to relax a bit. An Electronic Countermeasures Tactical Action Report, or ECTAR, was an important notification, because it was often the first indication of an enemy attack. If there was some kind of jamming, the NORAD Regional Operations Centers were supposed to launch airborne-radar planes and prepare to transfer control to them. So far they had not lost tactical command—that was a good sign. "MWC, what you got for us?"

"Triple-C, we recorded a few brief hot events," the Missile Warning Center's controller responded. "Not sunlight glints, but very brief flares. Perhaps a fire or explosion."

Kearsage and Howell turned and looked at each other. "Electronic interference, loss of contact with both the radars and our fighter, and now possible explosions near the LRRs—looks pretty suspicious to me," Howell said.

"But we don't have any indication of a threat," Kearsage said. "And we have contact with all other airborne assets. . . ."

"Colonel, that message from Air Intelligence Agency was pretty specific—a possible bomber attack against the United States, similar to the attack on that CIA base in Uzbekistan."

She looked at him, looked at his eyes to read the seriousness of his words—and what she saw scared her. Howell was the former fighter pilot on this command crew. He'd been involved in strategic air defense for almost his entire career. He was always the stoic, unflappable Canuck—and if he thought this was a real emergency, he meant it. He also rarely called her by her rank, except if VIPs or commanding officers were in the Mountain—if he used her rank now, he was probably scared, too.

That warning from the U.S. Air Force was certainly weird. Normally intelligence data flowed directly from whatever source, usually Air Intelligence Center or sometimes directly from the U.S. Space Command, to NORAD. This time a warning had been issued by the chief of staff of the U.S. Air Force. This indicated some kind of turmoil in the Pentagon. That was usually very, very bad news. Someone had broken the chain of command, which usually resulted in confusion and chaos.

She heard through the grapevine that it was a flap in Air Intelligence Agency, involving its powerful commander and the new commander of one of its information-warfare wings, none other than Patrick McLanahan. That, Kearsage thought, explained a lot. McLanahan had the worst reputation of any general officer since Lieutenant General Brad Elliott. He was, simply, a flakeoid. He couldn't be trusted. He'd obviously said or done something that got everyone at the Pentagon riled up—his specialty. Now they had to expend lots of time, energy, manpower, and resources proving how stupid the guy was.

Kearsage studied the map of North America. The lone F-16 and the tanker from Eielson would soon be in the last known area of the first F-16, and the E-3C AWACS and the two F-15s from Elmendorf would join up a few minutes later. Assuming there was a big outage of several North Warning System radars, their first priority would be to fill in those gaps.

She looked over at the list of available assets in Canada and was pleased to see that two NATO AWACS planes were based at Four Wing, Canadian Forces Cold Lake, Alberta, probably deployed there to support a MAPLE FLAG air-warfare exercise. "Let's get an AWACS and a couple CF-18s airborne from Cold Lake moving north to cover that gap in the North Warning System," she ordered.

"Roger that." Howell picked up his telephone and hit the button that would connect him immediately to Canadian Air Defense Forces headquarters in North Bay, Ontario. The NORAD-tasked fighter units in Alaska and Canada were very accustomed to these sudden air-sovereignty missions—they would have those three planes launched in less than half an hour.

"MWC, I'm about to wake up the world," Kearsage said seriously. "I need to know if we have an attack, an incident, or an anomaly. Give me your best guess."

There was a slight hesitation before he responded, "Triple-C, MWC believes we do not have an attack. We may have sustained some sort of large-scale power outage or malfunction of a communications network, but without further investigation, I'm not prepared to say it was an enemy or terrorist attack on our radar sites."

"Very well," Kearsage said. The first rule of NORAD surveillance: When in doubt, report it. Even though it could be nothing more than a short circuit or a polar bear eating through a power cable—that happened all the time—the loss of those radars needed to be reported.

She flipped open her checklist, filled in some blanks with a grease pencil, used her authenticator documents to insert a date-time group, had Howell check it over, then picked up the telephone and dialed the Air Force Operations Support Center in Washington. When she was connected, she read from the script: "Monument, this is Anchor with a Priority Secret OPREP Three BEELINE report, serial number two-zero-zero-four-four-three. We have lost contact with three LRRs and five SRRs of the North Warning System, and we have lost contact with a single Foxtrot-sixteen assigned combat air patrol, reasons unknown. DSP reports brief unexplained infrared events with no tracks taking place near the radar sites. We are investigating further but do not believe that these are attacks against NORAD assets that would require a PINNACLE FRONT BURNER report.

"We have deployed additional air-defense and airborne-surveillance assets in the affected area, and we are investigating the radar and radio outages." She ended the message with the date-time group and the proper authentication code. A BEELINE message was an alert notification to the U.S. Air Force only, letting them know that there was a problem and what NORAD was doing to fix it. It was one step below a PINNACLE FRONT BURNER report, which was a notification of an actual attack or deliberate action against NORAD.

Kearsage received an acknowledgment from the Air Force Operations Center—they were now responsible for channeling the report to the proper agencies. She would surely get a phone call in the next few minutes from the National Military Command Center at the Pentagon, asking for updates and clarification. "MWC, anything?" Kearsage asked after she received an acknowledgment that the report had been copied and understood.

"Negative," came the response. "No further events. Village still reports negative contact with their LRRs and their F-16s, reason still unknown."

"Roger, Triple-C copies." Joanna sat back in her chair, wishing she could light up a cigarette. There was nothing else to do but wait and see what the troops in the field could find out next.

5

OVER THE CHUKCHI SEA, 150 MILES NORTH OF NOME, ALASKA
That same time

NORAD's long-range early-warning radars at Point Hope and Scammon Bay couldn't see them, and even RAP-CON's—Nome Radar Approach Control—precision approach-control radar didn't spot them until they were well over Kotzebue Sound, heading away from the Seward Peninsula and into the forbidding Arctic wastelands of Alaska. The groundspeed readout for the target did indeed say "540"—540 knots, over 570 miles per hour—but the electrically charged atmosphere, magnetic anomalies, and terrain often confused and scrambled radar plots in Alaska.

Still, with a few sketchy reports of some kind of air-defense activity up in the northeast part of Alaska, reporting even likely radar anomalies was far better than making no report at all. The Nome Approach controller issued a "pending" contact report to Fairbanks Approach Control, with an estimated time of radar contact. At the same time, the RAP-CON supervisor issued a similar report to the Alaska NORAD Region headquarters at Elmendorf Air Force Base near Anchorage. NORAD would in turn alert the short-range radar station at Clear Air Station in central Alaska to watch for the contact as well.

Except those manning the station would never get the chance to see it.

The activity wasn't a radar anomaly or magnetic disturbance—it was a formation of two Russian Tupolev-160 supersonic bombers, which had been flying nap-of-the-earth for the past hour, since well over the Chukchi Peninsula of eastern Siberia.

It originally started as a formation of four bombers, but one could not refuel and another suffered engine failure and had to abort the mission. Their route of flight took them not over Siberia but along the Bering Sea close to the commercial polar transoceanic flight routes, where their presence would not cause alarm until the flight approached the American Air Defense Identification Zone. By then the two remaining bombers—fully refueled and with weapon, flight, engine, navigation, and defensive systems all working perfectly—descended below radar coverage and drove eastward toward their objective. Flying at very low altitudes—sometimes just a few meters above the sea—the bombers successfully slipped through the gaps in the long-range NORAD radars along the western Alaskan coastline.

By the time the bombers were detected, it was too late . . . but even if they had been detected earlier, there were no fighters to intercept them and no surface-to-air missile systems to shoot them down. The two alert fighters at Eielson Air Force Base near Fairbanks had already been committed to the air patrol over northern Alaska with the E-3C AWACS radar plane; the four F-15C Eagle fighters being prepared for alert duties were still being armed and manned and wouldn't be ready to respond to an alert call for several minutes. The bombers were completely unopposed as they headed east, into the heart of the Alaskan wilderness.

EARECKSON AIR FORCE BASE, SHEMYA, ALASKA
That same time

U.S. Marine Corps Sergeant Major Chris Wohl stuck his head in the door, letting light from the hallway spill across the bed inside the small room within. "Sir, you're needed in the ready room," he said loudly and without preamble.

Air Force Colonel Hal Briggs was instantly awake—a trait that, although it served him well as a forward combat air controller and chief of security at HAWC, was irritating because he knew that now that he was awake, it would be nearly impossible for him to go back to sleep. He glanced at the glowing red numerals on his bedside alarm clock and groaned theatrically. "Top, I just got to bed five friggin' hours ago. What the hell is—?"

"Sir, you're *needed* in the ready room. *Now.*" And the door slammed shut.

Hal knew that Chris Wohl wouldn't awaken his boss if it weren't pretty damned important—usually. He quickly dressed in pixelated Arctic battle dress uniform, cold-weather boots and gloves, wool balaclava, and a parka, and headed to his unit's ready room.

Shemya Island was only six square miles in area, the largest of the Semichi Group of volcanic islands in the western Aleutian Island chain. Much closer to Russia than to Anchorage, the Aleutians were barely noticed before 1940; Russian blue foxes far outnumbered humans along almost the entire chain. But the islands' strategic location did not go unnoticed at the start of World War II. The Japanese invaded them in 1942, occupying Adak Island and attacking Dutch Harbor on Unalaska Island. If the Aleutians could be captured and held, the Japanese could control the entire North Pacific and threaten all of North America.

Admiral Chester Nimitz ordered the construction of an airfield on Shemya in 1943 to enable the staging of air raids on Japanese positions on Adak and Kiska Islands; Shemya was chosen because it was relatively flat and was not bothered as much by fog as were most of the other Aleutians. By 1945 Shemya housed over eleven hundred soldiers, seamen, and airmen, plus a fleet of B-24 bombers and P-51 fighters. Its tremendous strategic importance as the guardian of America's northern flank was in direct inverse proportion to the level of morale of its troops, who endured years of stark isolation, lack of resources, the worst living conditions of any base in the American military, no promotions, and severe psychological depression. It was without a doubt America's version of a Soviet-style gulag.

After the end of the Korean War, Shemya's importance steadily declined, as radar and eventually satellites took over the important job of watching the Arctic skies for any signs of attackers or intruders. At the end of the Cold War, with the Russian threat all but eliminated, the Air Force station was closed and put into caretaker status, with just a handful of civilian technicians on hand to service the massive COBRA DANE ballistic-missile tracking radar, nicknamed "Big Alice," and other intelligence-gathering systems. The island became a massive dumping ground for all of the Aleutians, since it was far easier to dump even expensive equipment than it was to haul it back to the States. Shemya became "The Rock" once more.

But since the advent of President Thomas Thorn's "Fortress America" initiative—eliminating overseas military commitments and building up the defense of the North American continent—Shemya, fifteen hundred miles west of Anchorage on the western tip of the Aleutian Island chain, was busier and more important than ever. Already vital as an emergency-abort base for transpolar and Far East airline and military flights and as a location of ballistic-missile tracking radars and other intelligence-gathering facilities, Eareckson Air Force Base, formerly just an air station but now advanced to full air-base status, was the location of the Aerospace Defense Command's long-range XBR, or X-band radar, and the In-Flight Interceptor Communications System, which provided ultraprecise steering information to ground-based interceptor missiles fired from silos in Alaska and North Dakota.

Eareckson Air Force Base was now in an almost constant state of upgrade and new construction. Nearly two thousand men and women were based there in modern concrete dormitories, connected by underground tunnels and interspersed with comfortable, albeit subterranean, offices, computer rooms, laboratories, and other amenities. The runway facilities could now handle any aircraft in the world up to a million pounds gross weight and could land a suitably equipped aircraft in almost any weather, including the frequent and usually unexpected near-hurricane-force windstorms that were as much a part of life on Shemya as were Russian blue foxes, the cold, and the loneliness. Every aircraft that arrived in Shemya was housed in its own hydronically heated hangar—sometimes in better facilities than at its home base.

Along with the construction workers and engineers assembling the new missile-defense network, Shemya was host to many other government and military organizations—and that included the Air Battle Force. It was not the first time they had been there: Rebecca Furness's 111th Bombardment Wing, from where all of the Air Battle Force's B-1 bombers originated, had been deployed there during the War of Reunification, to prevent an outbreak of nuclear war on the Korean Peninsula. Shemya's strategic location against Russia, China, and all of Far East Asia—especially now that all bases in Korea and Japan were closed to permanent American military forces—made the little island the stepping-off point for most military operations in the North Pacific theater.

Hal decided not to take the tunnel to the ready room out on the flight line—and almost instantly regretted it. Although nights were fairly short in early spring, the changing seasons meant changing weather. In the short walk to the ready room, Hal experienced almost every possible climatic change: It went from cold and frosty to horizontal snow and stinging ice to horizontal freezing rain to windy but clear in a matter of a couple minutes. Once he had to brace himself against a light pole to keep from being knocked off his feet by an errant blast of wind.

There was one consolation: Hal was able to see a rare Aleutian sunrise, the first one he'd ever seen. The golden light illuminated the nearby islands and turned the sea from dark and forbidding to an unbelievable crystal blue. He was almost breathless with amazement—until another gush of icy wind brought his attention back to the here and now.

Hal was hesitant to remove his balaclava to speak, but when he did, he found that it was warming up quickly outside now that the sun was up. All part of living and working in Alaska. As the old saying went, "If you don't like the weather on Shemya, wait five minutes." "Duty Officer," Hal spoke into thin air, "get the door for me, will you?"

"Yes, Colonel Briggs," the female computerized voice of the Duty Officer responded, and Hal felt the click of electronic locks disengaging as soon as he touched the door handle. The "Duty Officer" was a computerized all-around assistant, handling everything from routine radio messages to complex top-secret mission planning from Air Battle Force headquarters at Battle Mountain Air Reserve Base in Battle Mountain, Nevada. Relayed via satellite, the Duty Officer tracked the location and identity of every person assigned to Battle Mountain and instantly responded to requests, even if the person was far from the main base. As it did at Battle Mountain, the Duty Officer constantly monitored and operated all security systems wherever the Air Battle Force was deployed—personnel never carried pass cards or had to worry about passwords or codes. The Duty Officer knew who and where you were and made sure that if

you weren't cleared to enter a particular area—from an aircraft hangar to an individual file drawer—you didn't get in.

Of course, Hal realized, it would've been far easier, faster, and more efficient for the Duty Officer to awaken him if there was something urgent happening—but getting the boss's ass out of bed was a pleasure Sergeant Major Wohl obviously reserved for himself, no matter what the weather.

The ready room for the Air Battle Force was actually their aircraft hangar, where barracks, planning, storage, and communications rooms had been set up. Two MV-32 Pave Dasher tilt-jet aircraft waited inside. The MV-32 resembled the MV-22 Osprey tilt-rotor special-operations transport—with a big, boxy fuselage; stubby, high-mounted wings; large tail structure; and a drive-up cargo ramp—except the MV-32 was larger and used four turbojet engines, two on each wingtip and two on the tips of the horizontal stabilizer, in place of rotors. Like the MV-22, the Pave Dasher could take off and land vertically yet fly like a conventional fixed-wing aircraft, but the MV-32 could fly 50 percent faster than the -22 on just a little more fuel. The MV-32 was air-refuelable and had an infrared camera and radar for terrain-following flight and precision navigation and targeting. It could carry as many as eighteen combat troops and also carried two retractable and reloadable weapon pods on the landing-gear sponsons, along with a twenty-millimeter Minigun in a steerable nose turret with five hundred rounds of ammunition.

Hal Briggs threw his parka and hood onto a chair. "Someone get me coffee, and someone else talk to me," he said, "or I'm about to get very cranky."

"Some increased NORAD activity, sir," Chris Wohl responded.

"We know that already, Top," Hal said irritably. "That's why we're here. The general convinced NORAD to put fighters on patrol until they can push out the radar surveillance."

"It's something else, sir," Wohl went on, handing Briggs a

large mug of steaming coffee. "NORAD just issued a BEE-LINE report for sudden, unexplained radar outages along the North Warning System."

That didn't sound good. "Where are the fighters?"

"NORAD put one fighter from Eielson on patrol over the Arctic Ocean—his wingman should be airborne shortly," Wohl responded. "An AWACS radar plane and a couple F-15 interceptors from Elmendorf are on their way now to fill in for the long-range radars that are out."

"So at the present time, all the surveillance we have north of Alaska is *one fighter?*"

Wohl nodded. "Thought you'd need to know that right away, sir," he said.

He did. Hal thought hard for a moment, then spoke into the air, "Briggs to Luger."

"I was just going to give you a call, Hal," Brigadier General David Luger, commanding the Air Battle Force, responded via the secure subcutaneous-transceiver system. "I got the message just now."

"What do you think is going on?"

"Whatever it is, it's not good," Dave said. "What's your status?"

"I just need to get the children out of bed and the planes rolled out, and we're off," Hal responded. "Fifteen minutes max."

"Good. Stand by." There was a slight pause. Then Luger said, "Civilian approach controllers just issued a 'pending' notification to NORAD—an unidentified target heading east, altitude unknown, groundspeed five hundred and forty knots."

"A plane at low altitude going point-seven-two Mach over Alaska?" Briggs remarked. "Either it's Santa Claus on a training flight—or it's trouble."

"It's trouble," Luger said. "I'll see if the Navy can get any look-down eyes out there. Get your guys airborne. Disperse them someplace nearby. Adak?"

"The bad guys are the other way, Dave," Hal said. "The

Coast Guard said we can use their hangar on Attu Island, so that's where we'll go." Attu Island, about fifty miles west of Shemya, was the largest and rockiest of the Near Islands, and the westernmost of the American Aleutians. It also had the worst weather in the Aleutians—if it wasn't having driving rain or snow with hurricane-force winds, it was blanketed in thick, cold fog. The U.S. Coast Guard maintained a small search-and-rescue, maritime patrol, communications, and ground navigation facility there, with just twenty people manning the small site—they welcomed visitors and encouraged all services to use their facilities. "They usually have plenty of fuel and provisions, too. We've made a few resupply flights for them just since we arrived."

"Good. Disperse there and keep in touch."

"You think Shemya could be a target?"

"No, but it doesn't hurt to be safe—and that big old radar out there plus all the ballistic-missile defense stuff sure are pretty inviting targets," Dave said.

"Rog," Hal said. He turned to Wohl and twirled his index finger in the air, telling the master sergeant to get his men ready to fly. "What are you going to do?"

"I'm not sure," Dave said. "I'm not authorized to fly my bombers. . . ." He thought for a moment, then added, "But no one said I couldn't fuel them and hoist them to the surface, just for a systems-test run. Maybe I'll see how fast my guys can get them upstairs." Unlike any other air base in the world, Battle Mountain Air Reserve Base was built twelve stories underground in an abandoned national alternate military command center first built in the 1950s. The facility was originally constructed to house an entire fighter-bomber air wing and over five thousand men and women and protect them from all but a direct hit by a one-megaton nuclear device. Aircraft were raised up to the surface on eight large elevators located at the end of the airfield's twelve-thousand-foot-long runway and at the mass parking ramp.

"Sounds like a good idea to me," Hal said. "We'll report in when we're safe on Attu."

"Roger that."

"Any word from the general?" Even though Patrick McLanahan had been gone for several weeks now, everyone still referred to him as "the general."

"He's not at AIA headquarters anymore," Dave said. "He may be heading back to Sacramento. I think he may have gotten spanked for going around Houser and Samson about what the Russians are doing."

"I have to admit, it's quite a stretch to see a bunch of tankers at one base in Siberia and conclude that the Russians are going to bomb the United States," Hal said. "But that's the general. He's a smart guy and one hell of a leader, but he does tend to lead with his chin sometimes."

"Hal, it scared the hell out of me when I saw all those bombers and tankers at those bases—and now with that BEELINE report about the North Warning System radars down, I'm more scared than ever," Dave Luger said. "We'll know what happens this morning. In the meantime I want to make sure our unit is safe."

"We're on our way, boss," Hal said. "We'll report when we're on alert on Attu. Briggs out."

Back at Battle Mountain, Luger thought about the situation for a moment, then spoke, "Duty Officer, set condition Alpha-Foxtrot-one for the Air Battle Force Alpha alert team, and set condition Echo-Foxtrot-two for all other aircraft. Then get me Colonel Shrike at Elliott Air Force Base."

"Roger, General Luger, set condition Alpha-Foxtrot-one for the Alpha team and Echo-Foxtrot-two for all other aircraft," the Duty Officer responded. *"Please stand by for counterorder."*

"Furness to Luger," Rebecca Furness radioed excitedly a

few moments later. "I didn't hear an 'exercise' classification. What's going on?"

"This is not an exercise, Rebecca," Dave said. "I want all the Alpha-alert aircraft into Foxtrot-one."

"Luger, I damned well shouldn't have to remind you that we're not authorized to fly our aircraft *anywhere*," Rebecca said angrily. "You remember that little order from the secretary of defense, don't you?"

"By the time the crews arrive and the planes are hoisted to the surface, I'll have authorization," Luger said.

"Then why not order an Echo generation for all aircraft?" Rebecca asked. "You ordered an Alpha launch for the Alpha force—that's a survival launch for our aircraft with weapons aboard." Even though the planes were decertified and declared non-mission ready, David Luger and Rebecca Furness had directed that the Air Battle Force's Alpha force—composed of two EB-1C Vampire bombers, four EB-52 Megafortress bombers, and four KC-135R tankers—remain loaded with weapons, fueled, and ready to respond at short notice for combat operations. These planes could be airborne in less than an hour. The other planes were all in various stages of readiness, but in general the Bravo force could be ready in three to six hours, and the Charlie force could be ready in nine to twelve hours.

"Rebecca, something's happening up in Alaska," Dave said, "and after what we've seen in Siberia, that's enough warning for me. I need you to countersign the order to launch the Alpha team right away."

"You're going to end up out on your ass even faster than McLanahan," Rebecca said.

"Rebecca . . ."

"I want your word that you won't launch any aircraft, even the tankers, without my counterorder," Rebecca said. "Otherwise I'll defer my countersignature to higher headquarters."

"Agreed." A moment later he heard the Duty Officer

report, *"General Luger, generation order verified by General Furness, A-hour established."* A moment: *"Colonel Shrike is on the line, secure."*

"Put him on."

"Shrike here, secure," Colonel Andrew "Amos" Shrike was commander of Elliott Air Force Base at Groom Lake, Nevada, the supersecret weapon- and aircraft-testing facility north of Las Vegas.

"This is General Luger at Battle Mountain."

"What do you need, General?" Shrike said testily. Shrike was a twenty-three-year veteran of the U.S. Air Force. He'd received an Air Force commission through the Officer Training Corps program after graduating from Texas A&M in electrical engineering. Through hard work and sheer determination, he rose through the ranks all the way to full colonel, wrangling a pilot-training slot for himself at a time when the Air Force was RIFing (Reduction in Forces) pilots left and right. He was hand-selected by Terrill Samson to take over the High Technology Aerospace Weapons Center, with strict instructions *not* to turn it into a secret combat base—specifically, not to let McLanahan, Luger, Furness, Mace, or Cheshire turn it into their private combat-operations center.

But on a personal level, Shrike resented the young, brash men and women like Luger who got promoted by doing outlandish, audacious things that Shrike himself would've been busted for in his early years. He had been taught that the way to get promoted was to follow orders and run a tight ship, not contravene orders and disregard the chain of command. Luger was ten years younger but was already a one-star general—in Shrike's book that was pure crapola.

"I'd like my AL-52s fueled and ready to load the laser as soon as possible," Luger said now. "I'm flying flight and technical crews down on a KC-135 in one hour."

"I'd be happy to give them to you and get them the hell

out of my hangars, General—as soon as I see some paper-work," Shrike said. To call Andrew Shrike "anal" would be an understatement: He took a personal, direct interest in every aspect of all operations at the High Technology Aero-space Weapons Center. Nothing happened there without his express knowledge and approval. "But since I haven't seen or heard anything from you guys in weeks, it won't happen. It'll take you an entire day just to get authorization for your tanker to land here—and another week at least to get per-mission to launch those things out of here."

David Luger could feel that familiar tension creeping into his brain and spinal cord—the feeling of dread, of abject fear, of impending pain—and he felt his body start to move into self-defense mode. He found he couldn't speak, couldn't react. He just looked straight ahead, feet planted firmly on the floor, arms becoming rigid. . . .

"Anything else, General? It's early, and I've got a lot of work to do."

"I . . . I . . ." Dave stammered, but no words were com-ing out.

"Nice to talk to you, sir," Shrike said flatly, obviously not meaning one word of it. "Good—"

"Colonel," Dave finally spit. He blinked, gritted his teeth, and willed his back and neck muscles to move.

"Yes, General? What is it?"

"I want . . . those planes ready for my crews in one hour."

"I told you, General, it won't happen," Shrike said. "You need the proper—"

"Damn it, Colonel, *you do as I goddamned tell you to do!*" Luger suddenly blurted out. "You don't need authoriza-tion to fuel those planes and open the fucking hangar doors, and you don't need authorization for an R&D team that already has clearance to both the aircraft and the facility to arrive there. I'll get all the other authorizations. Now, *move those planes* like I told you to do, or I will nail your ass to my front gate, warning all you other insubordinate assholes *not to mess with me!*" And he disconnected the line.

When he looked up, he saw most of his senior officers—Rebecca Furness; Colonel Daren Mace, her ops officer; Colonel Nancy Cheshire, commander of the EB-52 Megafortresses and the AL-52 Dragons of the Fifty-second Bomb Squadron; and Lieutenant Colonel Samantha Hellion, commander of the EB-1C Vampire bombers of the Fifty-first Bomb Squadron—staring at him as if he had grown an extra head.

"What are you standing around for?" Luger snapped. "I want the Alpha force ready to launch into the Foxtrot One airborne-alert area in one hour, and I want the rest of the force on the roof and ready to fly in two hours. Nancy, get your Dragon crews loaded up on a KC-135 and ready to fly to Dreamland to get the birds ready for combat operations."

"Are you serious, sir?" Nancy Cheshire asked incredulously. Cheshire was a veteran Dreamland test pilot and one of the original program directors of both the EB-52 Megafortress airborne battleship and the AL-52 Dragon airborne laser, both modified B-52 bombers. "We're going into combat even though we haven't been recertified?"

"Not quite—I said I want all our planes 'ready' to go into combat," Luger said. "But I'm authorized to do everything necessary to have my force survive an attack against the United States, and that's what I plan to do."

"What attack against the United States?" Cheshire asked.

"The one that very well could be happening right now—if what Patrick thought might happen really *does* happen," Dave said. "I've got a feeling he's correct. And if he is, I don't want my planes sitting around here on the ground like wounded ducks. Let's roll, folks." He paused, then said, "Duty Officer, get me General Muskoka's office at Langley right away—urgent priority."

CLEAR, ALASKA
A short time later

The Tupolev-160 supersonic bombers accelerated to twelve hundred kilometers per hour and climbed slightly to five hundred meters above the ground shortly before crossing just north of Wolf Mountain in central Alaska. They received a READY indication moments later, but the navigator/bombardier knew well enough to wait until the designated launch point, because his Kh-15 missiles would lose valuable range if they had to climb over or circumnavigate the mountain.

At the preplanned launch point, the bombardier flipped a switch from SAFE to COMMIT, which started the Kh-15 missile countdown. The Tu-160's attack computers immediately downloaded navigation, heading, and velocity information to the missiles, which allowed the missiles' gyros to perform their final transfer alignment to prepare them for flight. As soon as the missiles reported ready, the aft bomb-bay doors flew open, and four Kh-15 missiles were ejected down into the slipstream, one every fifteen seconds. Each one fell about a hundred meters in a slightly nose-low attitude while the air data sensors sampled the air, computed roll and bank velocities, set the rear fins for stabilization, and then fired its first-stage solid rocket motor. The Kh-15 shot ahead of the bomber in the blink of an eye, sped ahead for a few kilometers, then started a fast climb. The second Tu-160 fired four missiles from its rear bomb bay as well.

In fifteen seconds the missiles were at twenty thousand meters' altitude, where they began to level off as the second-stage motor ignited. They cruised at twice the speed of sound for another forty-five seconds, then started a descent. Their precision inertial accelerometers kept them on course for their target, now less than eighty kilometers away.

Like Shemya, Clear Air Station in central Alaska was a rather isolated location that was growing in importance and development with the advent of the Aerospace Defense Command's ballistic-missile defense system. Along with the existing Ballistic Missile Early Warning System radar, Clear Air Station hosted civilian air-traffic-control radars and NORAD surveillance radars. As part of the national missile-defense system's expansion, the Air Force was also constructing a Battle Management Command and Control Center and an In-Flight Interceptor Communications System, plus eight silos, each housing four ground-based interceptor (GBI) rockets, spread out over eight hundred acres. The rockets were modified Minuteman II ballistic missiles fitted with a kill-vehicle warhead, designed to track and destroy ballistic-missile warhead "buses" outside Earth's atmosphere. Three hundred military and over five hundred civilian contractors and construction workers lived and worked at the base.

Clear Air Station was definitely a "soft" target—perfect prey for the Kh-15 missiles.

In less than two minutes from launch, the first Russian attack missile reached its target. When the Kh-15 missile was still a thousand meters aboveground, its warhead detonated. The fireball of a one-kiloton thermonuclear device was very small and barely reached the ground, but the shock and overpressure of the explosion were enough to destroy every surface structure within four kilometers of ground zero. Every fifteen seconds another explosion ripped across the Alaskan wilderness, burning, crushing, or sweeping away buildings, radar antennae, and trees—and killing every living thing standing within a sixteen-square-kilometer area.

Each bomber's third and fourth missiles were fitted with a deep-penetrating warhead and a delayed-action fuze and programmed against the ground-based interceptor silos. Although these were not as effective as the air-burst warheads programmed against aboveground targets, over half of the thirty-two GBIs were destroyed by the burrowing Kh-15 nuclear warheads.

* * *

"For the alert force, for the alert force, scramble, scramble, scramble!"

The radio announcement came as a complete surprise. The four F-16C Fighting Falcon alert crews were inside the ramp-maintenance supervisor's truck, sipping coffee while they reviewed their jets' Form 781 maintenance logs prior to accepting the aircraft for alert status. Coffee cups dropped to the floor, and confused, scared eyes turned to each other inside the truck.

"Holy shit!" one of the younger pilots shouted as they all collected their flight gear. "What do we do?"

"Get your ass airborne, that's what!" answered one of the other pilots, the flight commander. "Get rolling as fast as you can!" He dashed for the door, hoping like hell the others were right behind him.

The alert ramp at Eielson Air Force Base was in a state of slight disarray. With the two alert aircraft airborne in support of the newly established air patrols over northern Alaska, the wing was still in the process of preparing more aircraft for alert. The Third Wing at Eielson kept two F-16 interceptors in preload status, ready to be armed and fueled, but with no crews assigned, in support of the air-sovereignty mission for Alaska. Normally it took anywhere from one to three hours to get the preload birds ready to fly, but in this heightened state of alert, with the alert aircraft suddenly committed to fly airborne patrols, the two preload aircraft were almost ready, and two more F-16s were less than an hour away from ready-five status as well.

The four aircraft being preflighted were in alert shelters, with both forward and rear doors open and with many different teams of maintenance technicians inside checking systems and running checklists. The crew chiefs were furiously racing around their aircraft, yelling at the maintenance teams to finish up and get out of the hangars, removing streamers and plugs, and closing inspection and access panels. Their precocking checklists were not yet complete, so they had to be sure that all steps in several other checklists were done, as well as the "scramble" checklist itself. The pilots did the same, following right behind their crew chiefs, running several checklists simultaneously in a mad dash to get their jets ready to fly. But in less than ten minutes, pilots were climbing inside the two ready-five interceptors, and soon engines were started, the taxiways cleared, and the two Falcons started taxiing to the active runway.

But they would not make it airborne.

Two minutes after the last warhead detonated over Clear Air Station, the Tu-160 Blackjack bombers screamed overhead, continuing their missile run. With the NORAD and FAA radars down, they would be virtually invisible as they pressed their attack. Five minutes after passing over Clear, the Tupolev-160 bombers were in position to begin their second missile run.

Each bomber launched four missiles against three separate target areas around the city of Fairbanks, Alaska: Fort Wainwright, Eielson Air Force Base, and Fort Greely. Like Shemya and Clear, all these three locations had components of the new ballistic-missile defense system under construction; in addition, Eielson was the location of the Alaskan battle-management headquarters, which was a mirror to the main command headquarters located in North Dakota. All eight missiles were bunker-buster weapons, designed to explode deep underground—but the blast effects were more than powerful enough to heavily damage all three military bases.

As soon as the two Russian bombers launched the remaining weapons in their aft bomb bays, they headed southwest across Alaska, staying clear of the radar sites around Anchorage, Bethel, and Dillingham. In twenty minutes they were feet-wet over the Bering Sea. Two F-15C Eagle fighters launched from Elmendorf Air Force Base near Anchorage to pursue, but they never got within range to spot them at low altitude.

And the Russian bombers still were not finished with their attacks.

ABOARD THE RUSSIAN TUPOLEV-95MS BEAR BOMBER
A short time later

"Feet dry, crew," the navigator radioed. "Ninety minutes to launch point."

Leborov was in the middle of his attack briefing when the navigator gave his report. The cabin got instantly quiet. They still had a long way to go before this part of their mission was over, but actually making it into North America was simply an incredible feat in itself. Even the most optimistic planner gave them a one-in-ten chance of getting this far—and, as far as Leborov could tell, every Tupolev-95MS in his formation that had completed an air refueling had made it. The old rattletraps had done their jobs nicely so far.

The Tupolev-22M bombers had done their job admirably, too. They had created a curtain of electronic jamming that screened the attack force from detection until their long-range Kh-31 antiradar missiles were in range to destroy the North American Aerospace Defense Command's North Warning System radar sites. As far as he could tell, they had lost just six -22Ms, and no -95Ms.

"R . . . roger, nav," Leborov responded after a few moments. "Station check, crew." Each one of his crew members responded with his crew position and then performed the routine check, which included switches, oxygen, safety equipment, lights, radios, and required logbook entries. They had done a station check just a few minutes earlier, but doing that simple yet important task, Leborov hoped, would get their minds back on the mission and away from the danger they were continuing to fly into.

When everyone had finished, Leborov went on, "Okay,

crew, let me get through this damned briefing, and then you can have some quiet time to yourselves before we do our thing.

"After weapon release we'll head directly west toward the Rocky Mountains, then northward along the military crest to evade any surviving radars. We still have all of our antiradar missiles on board, so we'll attack and destroy any military radars we encounter, such as AWACS, fighter-intercept, or fire-control radars, and secondarily any ground-surveillance radars. If possible, we'll retain any unused weapons for force reconstitution.

"Our primary forward landing base is Norman Wells, which is located on the Mackenzie River west of Great Bear Lake—in fact, we'll be flying close to it on our inbound leg. We have SPETZNAZ commandos and mechanics on the ground waiting for our signal to help us refuel—"

"Has that been confirmed, sir?" the flight engineer cut in. "Are they really there?"

"They were in place when we departed, but we haven't heard a thing since," Leborov responded. "We won't know for sure until we're getting ready to land. If we get no word from them, we'll decide what to do as a crew—either land and attempt a refueling ourselves, land and abandon the plane, bail out and crash the plane, or risk flying across Alaska attempting to make it back into eastern Siberia." Again the crew got very quiet. "Anyway, as soon as possible, we'll take on as much fuel at Norman Wells as we can and, as the Americans say, 'Get out of Dodge'—whatever the hell that means. We then will try to make it past any American fighter patrols and across to any friendly base. Anadyr is the primary recovery base. If we top off our tanks at Norman Wells, we will have enough fuel to make it all the way to Novosibirsk or Petropavlovsk with no problems.

"Weapon-disposal procedures: If we have any of the Kh-90 weapons still on board, and we can't launch them against secondary targets, we'll take them with us," Leborov went on. "If there is any danger whatsoever of their falling into enemy hands, we'll jettison them safe over isolated enemy territory, open ocean, or ice pack. If we're on the ground, we'll jettison them prearmed on the ramp—they won't detonate, and they'll be useless after their chemical batteries run out. Lastly, if the weapons cannot be jettisoned at all, our only option is to bail out of the aircraft and let the weapons crash with the plane. If we do make it on the ground, *under no circumstances* shut down power to the weapon-arming panel. I will stay in the pilot's seat, and I will have full authority on whether to retain or jettison the weapons. Bottom line: We don't let viable nuclear weapons fall into enemy hands. Of course, none of this applies to the Kh-31s, since they are nonnuclear.

"Survival and evasion: If we are forced to bail out, crash-land, or ditch, it is each individual crew member's responsibility to survive and to make your way to a designated recovery or exfiltration point. Our poststrike exfiltration zones are near Norman Wells, Pine Point, Inuvik, Prince Rupert, Whitehorse, and Fort Nelson. If you don't know how to get to them by now, you had better learn fast, because we're destroying all maps after we launch our missiles. You are all well trained in cold-weather survival, and I should think our chances of surviving off the land and making it to one of the planned exfiltration points is very good. Try to link up with one of the others if possible, but don't travel together unless you need assistance. The exfiltration points will be visited from time to time by friendly forces, hired escorts, or SPETZNAZ combat-rescue teams, as conditions warrant, so sit tight once you make it to an exfil point, and look out for your contact. Most of all, remember your training and keep a cool head.

"Resistance and escape: If you're captured, remember

that your first and foremost responsibility to your crew and your country is to survive; second, to resist to the best of your ability giving up vital state secrets; and third, to escape, so you can return to friendly forces and fight again. You must protect your fellow crew members and support your country, but if you feel you will be killed if you do not talk, then talk—but say as little as possible. The Canadians and Americans are generally not considered brutal captors, but the outposts and field-intelligence officers will be the most unpredictable, and of course we'll have just launched nuclear weapons against them, so they're likely to be very, very angry.

"If necessary, give them the most minimal information possible—name, rank, serial number, and date of birth— then beg for mercy. Try anything and everything to avoid being abused, tortured, or interrogated: Remind them of their legal responsibilities, speak about the Geneva Conventions, ask to talk to the Red Cross, plead with them to be fair and humane, tell them you are a family man, pretend you're injured, blah blah blah, and they will likely not hurt you. This is no time to be a hero and get yourselves maimed. Remember, we are not talking about the Chechens or the Afghans—the Americans and Canadians respond to pleas for help. Again, rely on your training and keep a cool head, and you'll come out of it okay. Hell, you might even star on one of their television reality shows, sign a Hollywood movie deal, marry Pamela Anderson, and get famous defense lawyer Johnny Cochran to represent you in court within a day or two." That got a laugh that Leborov could hear even in the noisy cabin.

"If you escape, your chance of finding support from the civilian population is unknown," the aircraft commander went on. "You may encounter some Russian-speaking individuals, but don't assume they are pro-Russian. Generally, people who live in the Arctic, as in Russia, support strangers they find in the wilderness—it is an unwritten code for those who live in inhospitable regions. Still, it is best to stay away from strangers and make contact only if your situation becomes desperate. We assume you'll be treated as an evading combatant as defined in the Geneva Conventions; as such, remember that if you kill a civilian while evading or in custody, even if you are being pursued by armed individuals or are being mistreated or tortured, you may be subject to the death penalty, even though Canada does not have it. Is that understood?"

Leborov asked for questions. They discussed this and that, mostly the weather and ground conditions in northern Canada and a little about their poststrike refueling base. Norman Wells was in the heart of Canada's vast western oil fields, so there was a lot of jet traffic and a lot of aviation fuel stored there. It was doubtful they'd be able to steal enough gas for all twenty-one Tupolev-95 bombers to refuel—in that case they'd pick the best planes, fill them up with crew members, and take whomever they could. The SPETZNAZ commandos would be exfiltrated by submarine from Mackenzie Bay, so some of the crew members could go with them if they chose.

"Fuck all that," Borodev said cross-cockpit after their discussions were concluded. "I'm staying in Canada."

Leborov couldn't believe his ears. "What did you say?"

"I said, if I can't fly out, I'm staying," the copilot said. "I speak pretty good English—I can even speak some Canadian, hey? I'll be a bush pilot. I'll fly tourists in the summer and supplies in the winter. Or maybe I'll put on a Russian fur-trapper music show with a dancing bear in Sitka, Alaska, for the tourists coming off the cruise ships. I'll hide out right under their noses."

"You're crazy," Leborov said. "Do you think they'll still have dancing bears and music shows after what we'll do to them today?"

"More than ever," Borodev said.

"You have a life back in Russia, my friend, remember? You're an airman and an officer in the Russian air force."

"You made a life for yourself back home—if they let you have one," Borodev said, turning serious. "Wherever they send us after this is over, at least you'll have your family with you. I won't have shit."

"You'll be a hero," Leborov said. "You'll spend the rest of your military career explaining how in hell you survived penetrating Canadian and American air defenses and bombing the shit out of them."

The copilot laughed. "I think I prefer the dancing bear, Joey," he said. "But I'll make sure you're on your way home first, don't worry." Leborov didn't respond—he didn't want to continue this line of discussion at all.

"Coming up on the turnpoint," the navigator said.

"There's another good reason to stay in Canada, my friend," Borodev said. "Great Bear Lake. One of the largest freshwater lakes in the world, and by far the best trout fishing on Earth. I read they catch trout out of that lake that take two men to carry. A busboy at one of their fishing lodges makes more money in one month than flying officers in the Russian air force make all year."

"You're fucked in the head, pal."

The navigator gave a heading correction that would take them east of the lake. Although there was nothing in the area this time of year except caribou, grizzly bears, and oil rigs, overflying the lake would highlight them from any air patrols they might encounter.

"Forty minutes to launch point, crew," the navigator said.

"Stop with the damned countdown, nav," Leborov said irritably. He took a few whiffs of oxygen to try to calm his nerves. "Just let us know when you're starting your check-lists—everyone else is configured for weapon release. Let's do a station check and then—"

Suddenly they all heard the slow warning tone over their

headphones. "UHF search radar, two o'clock," the electronic-warfare officer reported.

"*Search radar?* From where?"

"Airborne radar, probably an AWACS," the EWO said.

"Want to step it down to one hundred meters?" Borodev asked.

"If it's an AWACS, it won't matter how low we go—it'll find us," Leborov said grimly. "Our only hope is to try to shoot it down before they—"

Just then they heard another warning tone. "Fighter radar sweep, two o'clock," the EWO reported. "X-band, probably a Canadian CF-18 Hornet. It's down—AWACs will take over the hunt."

"—send in fighters," Leborov said, finishing his sentence. "Let's get up to launch altitude." They had no choice. They had to climb to one thousand meters aboveground to launch a Kh-31 from the bomb bay.

"Airborne search radar changing from long-range scan to fast PRF height-finder scan. I think they spotted us. Jammers on. All countermeasures active."

"I need a fire-control solution *right now,* EWO," Leborov said.

"No azimuth or range data yet."

"Damn it, EWO, you gave me the azimuth a moment ago!"

"That was a rough estimate off the warning receiver," the electronic-warfare officer retorted. "The fire-control receiver hasn't computed a launch bearing."

"I don't want excuses, I need to attack!" Leborov shouted. "That Hornet will be on us any moment now!"

"No azimuth yet . . ."

"Don't wait for the fire-control computer!" Leborov screamed. "Fire a missile at the last known azimuth. Make them take the first move!"

There was a short pause, then, "Stand by for missile

launch, crew! Consent switches."

"Consent!" Leborov shouted, flipping three red guarded switches up. "Shoot, damn it!"

"Bomb doors coming open!" the EWO shouted. Seconds later there was a deep rumbling sound as the Tupolev-95's massive bomb doors swung open. *"Missile away!"* Both pilots shielded their eyes as a tremendous streak of fire illuminated the cabin and an impossibly loud roaring sound drowned out even the thunder of the Tu-95's turboprops. The first Kh-31P missile fired ahead of the bomber on its solid rocket booster, then started its climb.

Seconds later: "AWACS radar down!" the EWO crowed. The missile launch had its desired effect—the AWACS crew shut down its radar to escape the missile. Moments later: "X-band radar, CF-18 Hornet, three o'clock!"

Leborov immediately performed a "notch," turning the Tu-95 hard right, directly over Great Bear Lake. He was hoping to maneuver until he was flying perpendicular to the Hornet's flight path, which would blank out the Russian bomber from the Hornet's pulse-Doppler radar. It seemed a little ridiculous trying to hide a huge, lumbering rhinoceros like the Tu-95 from an advanced interceptor like the CF-18 Hornet, but for the sake of his crew, he had to try everything.

"Hornet's at nine o'clock . . . wait . . . fast PRF, Hornet has reacquired . . . Hornet is locked on . . . *chaff, chaff,* pilot hard turn left." Leborov threw the Tupolev-95 into a hard left turn, hoping now to cut down on their radar cross-section and make the enemy fighter's radar track the decoy chaff and not the plane. "Hornet's . . . wait . . . Hornet's turning northeast . . . Hornet's locked on . . . *missile launch, missile launch, break* . . . Wait . . . he's not tracking us . . . I'm picking up the uplink for an AMRAAM launch, but it's not aimed at us . . . another missile launch!"

Leborov twisted the microphone-select switch on his

intercom panel to the formation frequency. "Heads up, guys, the bastard's firing!"

"Second Hornet, eight o'clock. Hard turn left, heading one-two-zero . . . possibly a third Hornet in formation . . ."

Suddenly they heard on the command channel, *"We're hit, we're hit, One-seven.* Initiating bailout. We are—" And the radio went dead.

"We lost One-seven," Borodev said.

"Bandits, seven o'clock high, six K!" their tail gunner shouted over the intercom.

"No RWR contact," the electronic warfare officer said. "He must be using a night-attack system, or night-vision goggles." They heard the chatter and felt the heavy vibration as the Tu-95's big twin twenty-three-millimeter tail cannons opened fire. Moments later they heard the roar of powerful jet engines overhead as the Hornets sped past. Like a shark that brushes up against its prey to taste it before attacking, the crew knew that the Hornets' first pass was an identification run—they'd close in for the kill on the next pass.

"AWACS radar back up," the EWO reported. "Our first missile must've missed."

"Nail that bastard, EWO!" Leborov shouted.

"No fire-control solution yet."

"Bandit, five o'clock, seven K," the gunner reported. "Coming in fast . . . six K, five K . . ."

"Fire-control solution resolved and entered!" the EWO shouted. "I got it! Stay wings-level! Bomb doors coming open!" Seconds later they launched their second Kh-31 missile. The two pilots watched as the missile seemed to shoot straight up in front of them, and they heard the sonic boom as it broke the sound barrier. "AWACS radar down . . . -31 is going active . . . -31 is homing, it's locked on!" The pilots were surprised when, in another instant, they saw a tremendous flash of light off in the distance, and a large streak of fire slowly tumbled across the night sky, with burning pieces of debris breaking off and fluttering to Earth.

"You got it!" Borodev shouted. "You got the AWACS! Good shoo—"

At that moment they heard the tail guns firing again. *"Bandit five o'clock four K!"* the tail gunner screamed. They couldn't maneuver while the Kh-31 was being launched, and so they were sitting ducks for the Canadian Hornet. Seconds later the Tupolev-95 rumbled and vibrated as several huge sledgehammer-like blows rippled across its fuselage and wings. One engine on the left wing surged and bucked, yawing the bomber violently from side to side as Leborov fought for control. "Second bandit is at seven o'clock high, six K. . . . He's coming down . . . five . . . four. . . ." The tail guns opened fire again—and then abruptly stopped. It seemed there was a moment of eerie silence.

And then more hammer blows pelted the bomber. A flash of light illuminated the cabin. *"Fire, fire, fire, engine number four!"* Borodev screamed. As Leborov pulled the appropriate prop lever to FEATHER, brought the throttle to idle, and pulled the condition lever to SHUT DOWN, Borodev pulled the emergency fire T-handle, shut off fuel to the number-four engine, and isolated its electrical, pneumatic, and hydraulic systems.

"The number-two -90 is still reporting okay," the bombardier said. "I can see the fire on number four—it's still on fire! I'm preparing to jettison the number-two missile."

"No!" Leborov shouted. "We didn't come all this way just to jettison the missiles!"

"Joey, if that missile cooks off, it'll blow us into a billion pieces," Borodev said.

"Then launch the bastard instead!"

"We're still forty minutes from our launch point."

"Forget the planned launch point!" Leborov shouted. "Replan the missiles for closer targets."

"But . . . how can we . . . I mean, which ones?"

"Get on the damned radio and coordinate retargeting with the rest of the formation," Leborov said. "We've been discovered—I think we can break radio silence now. Then radio to the other formations and have them retarget as well. You're the formation leader—you *tell* them what targets to hit. Hurry! Navigator, help him."

"Ack-acknowledged." The bombardier switched radio channels and immediately began issuing orders to the other planes. Each bomber's attack computers had been programmed with the same set of target coordinates, so it was a simple matter to look up the targets farther north within range and reprogram the computer. Finally the bombardier radioed the second flight of Tu-95 bombers that they were changing their targets and taking their target sets, so the second formation could reprogram their computers for targets farther south.

It was very quiet in the cockpit for several long moments, but suddenly the pilots saw a large red RYADAM light illuminate on their forward eyebrow panel. "I have a SAFE IN RANGE light, bombardier."

"Acknowledged. Consent switches."

"Bandit, eight o'clock high, seven K . . ."

"*Consent!* Launch the damn missiles!"

The RYADAM light began to blink. "Missiles counting down . . . Start a slow climb, pilot, wings-level. . . ."

"Six K . . . five K . . ."

The RYADAM light went to steady as the tail started violently swaying from side to side. "Hold the nose steady, pilot!"

"I think we're losing the number-three engine," Borodev said. "Oil pressure is surging . . . losing control of prop pitch on the number-six propeller. . . . Should I shut it down?"

"No. I'll hold it." Leborov took a crushing grip on the control wheel, and he was practically lifting himself off the seat as his feet danced on the rudder pedals to keep the tail following the nose.

The RYADAM light began to blink once more—the first

missile was counting down again. Suddenly the light flashed brightly. "Missile one away!" the bombardier shouted. There was nothing for what seemed like a very long time—and then there was an earsplitting roar that seemed a thousand times louder than the Kh-31's rocket-motor ignition, and the first Kh-90 missile fired ahead, then started a steep climb and fast acceleration, disappearing quickly into the night sky. "Missile two counting down . . ."

Just then they heard the gunner yell something—and then an instant later the number-one engine blew apart in a dramatic shower of fire. An AIM-9L Sidewinder missile launched from one of the Canadian CF-18 Hornets had found its mark.

"Fire, fire, fire on engine number one!" Leborov shouted as he pulled prop, throttle, and condition levers. "Shut down number one!" He glanced at the RYADAM light—it was steady, the missile holding its launch countdown until the proper aircraft flight parameters were met. Leborov struggled to keep the plane steady, but it seemed to be swaying, yawing, and turning in every direction at once.

"Number one isn't shutting down!" Borodev shouted.

"What?"

"Fuel control must've been cut—I can't shut off fuel to the engine. It's still burning. I can't isolate hydraulics or bleed air either."

The cabin started to fill with smoke, getting heavier and heavier by the second. "Crew, bail out, bail out, bail out!" Leborov ordered.

"I'll take it, Joey," Borodev said, grasping the control wheel.

"Negative. Blow the hatch and get the hell out."

"I told you before, Joey—I'm staying here, in Canada," Borodev said, a smile on his face. "You have someone to go home to, remember? You're a family man now. I'm staying."

"Yuri . . ."

"I have the airplane," Borodev said. He jabbed a thumb aft. "Get going, Commander."

Leborov could see that he wasn't going to change his copilot's mind, so he quickly unstrapped, pressed the ESCAPE button, then patted Borodev on the shoulder. "Thank you, Yuri," he said.

"Maybe I'll see you on the ground, Joey. Get going. I've got work to do." Borodev started concentrating on keeping the plane steady so that the last remaining missile could continue its countdown.

Caution lights illuminated on the forward instrument panel as both the bombardier and gunner blew their escape hatches. The flight engineer, navigator, and electronic-warfare officer were already on the lower deck. The lower entry hatch was open and the escape slide rail extended. They attached their parachute slide rings to the rail, faced aft, put one hand on the emergency parachute D-ring, one hand on the rail, and dropped through the hatch. The escape slide rail kept the crew members from getting caught in the bomber's slipstream and sucked back into the fuselage. At the end of the rail, a mechanism pulled the automatic parachute-activation knob, which used a barometric device to control parachute opening—since they were at very low altitude, the pilot chute came out immediately, followed by the main chute less than a second later.

Leborov was the last man under a parachute. At first he couldn't believe how quiet it was. He could hear a faint humming sound, probably his Tupolev-95 flying away, but he thought it must be very far away, because he could barely hear the sound. He wondered how far. . . .

And then the silence was shattered by an incredibly deafening roar, and a tongue of flame seemed to erupt right in front of his face. It was the last Kh-90 missile: Yuri Borodev had managed to keep the stricken bomber straight enough for the missile to finish its countdown.

Leborov pulled a parachute riser so he could turn around—and then he saw the missile streaking away into the night sky, followed by a stream of fire arcing off to the right. It was the Tupolev-95, its leftmost engine burning fiercely. As he drifted down in his parachute, he saw the fire completely consume, then burn apart, the left wing. Leborov scanned the underside of the fuselage in the glow of the fire, hoping he could catch a glimpse of his copilot sliding out of the hatch. But soon the bomber spiraled into the darkness and crashed into the tundra below, and Leborov never saw if Borodev exited.

He hit the hard, half-frozen ground a few moments later, in the typical aircrew member's parachute-landing fall—feet, butt, and head. Dazed, Leborov just lay on his back, not daring to move. The still-billowing parachute tugged at his harness, asking to be released, but he ignored it. If the parachute dragged him, he didn't much care right now.

As he lay there trying to recover his senses, he saw them—streaks of fire across the clear night sky. His teammates had done it—one by one they were launching their missiles, too. He lost count after fifteen, but they kept on coming. He blinked every time a sonic boom rolled across him, but it was a happy sound.

The sound of success.

CHEYENNE MOUNTAIN OPERATIONS CENTER
That same time

"Tell Village to launch every plane they've got to their patrol orbits *now*," Joanna Kearsage said. "Armed or unarmed, get them up in the air before they get their asses blown away. Order Ferry and Argus to get their alert planes up into their patrols as well, and tell Vigil and Feast to disperse all available aircraft." Those were the other air-defense units in central Canada and the western United States—she needed to get as many planes into the sky as she could to deal with the bombers attacking Alaska.

"Warning, MWC detects multiple strategic events via DSP three in central Canada," the Missile Warning Center's senior controller reported. "MWC determines the events are hostile. This is not a drill. We confirm, repeat confirm, multiple missile launches. Track and impact estimations in progress."

Joanna Kearsage nearly catapulted out of her seat as she saw the numerous lines beginning to appear over the map of Canada. Swearing softly to herself, she lifted a clear plastic cover on a button on her console and pressed it, waiting for it to turn from red to green. When it did—signifying that everyone on the NORAD Aerospace Reporting System network was online—she said, "Warning, warning, warning, this is Anchor with a Flash Top Secret PINNACLE FRONT BURNER report. Missile Warning Center has detected numerous events over central Canada and is resolving track and impact predictions. This is not a drill. All stations stand by."

It was her second warning in just the past few minutes—the first being the attacks in Alaska by bombers carrying cruise missiles. This was no rogue or terrorist action—this was an *all-out attack on the United States of America!*

"Triple-C, ADOC, Village reports fighters have engaged multiple Russian bomber aircraft, Tupolev-95 Bear-H bombers," the senior controller of the Air Defense Operations Center cut in. "The bombers are launching small missiles from their bomb bays and have apparently shot down the AWACS—"

"They *what?*"

"—and the Bear bombers have also launched larger missiles from wing pylons. Each Bear seems to have two very large wing missiles and an unknown number of the smaller missiles in its bomb bays."

"How many Bear bombers, ADOC?"

"They've counted over a dozen so far, Triple-C, and there may be many more," the ADOC controller replied. "They've shot down three so far. There's only two CF-18 Hornets up there, and without the AWACS they don't have a complete picture."

Kearsage keyed the Aerospace Reporting System button again: "Warning, warning, warning, all stations, NORAD air forces have engaged multiple Russian bomber aircraft, position near Great Bear Lake in Alberta, Canada. Enemy aircraft have been observed launching multiple hypersonic attack missiles. All NORAD regions are being ordered to launch alert aircraft to their assigned patrol orbits and to launch all other flyable aircraft to dispersal or survival anchors immediately."

The phone lights started blinking, but all Kearsage could see were the growing track lines of missiles speeding south toward the United States. She flipped open her codebook to the next section and started to compose a new missile-track report, working as quickly as she could: "Warning, warning, warning, all stations, Missile Warning Center issues the following special hostile track report Sierra-Bravo-seven. AWACS issues Flash special hostile track report Tango-Alpha-one-three, stand by for—"

And then she stopped. Because now the computers were issuing their predictions for missile impacts. Her mouth dropped open in surprise. The codebook forgotten, she pressed the ARS button and spoke, "All units, this is Anchor, inbound track reports . . . missile targets—Oh, my God, we're under attack! America is under attack. For God's sake, *America is under attack!*"

6

KANSAS CITY, MISSOURI
That same time

The chief of the Presidential Protection Detail of the Secret Service didn't call first before rushing into the president's hotel suite, but he wasn't surprised to see President Thomas Thorn hurriedly putting on his trousers in the sitting area. The president had always exhibited a weird second-sight ability to anticipate events before they happened. "What's happened, Mark?" the president asked.

"NMCC called a 'campfire,' sir," the PPD chief said, his voice wavering in terror. The president's mouth dropped open in surprise, and he was going to ask the PPD chief to repeat, but one look at the man's face told him that he'd indeed heard the right code word—the one for an "enemy nuclear attack on the United States under way"—and that this was no exercise. In moments the president was dressed for quick travel, wearing his dark brown leather flying jacket over a white shirt, a dark blue Air Force One ball cap, dark gray business slacks, and thick-soled casual shoes.

"Let's get moving, gents," the president said, and he rushed past the astonished agents and out into the hallway, toward the staircase. Members of the Secret Service were trained to physically take control of their charges in the process of evacuation—usually the evacuees were too confused, sleepy, or scared to know which way to go, and they *never* moved fast enough to suit the PPD—but Thorn, an ex–U.S. Army Green Beret, was moving so quickly that the agents couldn't get a grasp on his arms.

Inside the armored limousine, Thorn met up with the U.S. Navy officer who carried the "football," the briefcase containing coded documents and communications equipment that would allow him to issue orders to America's nuclear forces anywhere in the world. "Marine One is ready to fly, sir," the chief PPD officer said as they peeled out of the hotel entryway, surrounded by police cars and flanked by Secret Service armored Suburbans. "We'll be at Union Station pickup point in three minutes." He listened to the reports through his earpiece. "Your staffers are asking us to return to pick them up."

"Negative. Let's roll," the president said. He obviously did not want to wait for anyone—which suited the PPD just fine. The chief made a report on his secure cell phone, then handed it to the president. "This is Séance," he responded, using his personal call sign. "Go ahead."

"Thank God you're all right, Mr. President," came Vice President Lester Busick's voice. When he was excited, Busick's thick South Florida drawl became obvious, almost indecipherable. "Are you okay?"

"Fine, Les. What's going on?"

"I don't know yet. The Secret Service blew the whistle, and I've been on the move ever since," Busick replied. "I thought those bastards were going to rip my arms off carrying me out of the residence. I do know we're on our way to Andrews, not High Point. I think I'm going airborne."

"Who's with you?"

"Nobody," Busick responded. "Hell, I couldn't even get the old lady out of bed."

"I'll talk to you after I'm airborne, Les."

"Okay, Thomas. I'll see you back at the ranch after they're

done screwing with us." The heaviness in his voice said much more than his words—they both knew that something serious was happening, and they most likely wouldn't be going back to Washington for quite some time.

"Everything will be okay, Les," the president said. "I'll call as soon as I hear anything."

"You take care, Thomas," Busick said. Thorn was about to hang up when he heard, "Thomas?"

"Go ahead, Les."

"You need to be tough now, Thomas," Busick said. "I got a feelin' the shit's hittin' the fan. I want you to be strong, Thom—I mean, Mr. President."

"Since when do you call me 'Mr. President' when we're—?"

"Damn it, Mr. President, please listen," Busick said earnestly. "We may not be able to talk for a while, so just listen. I've seen this before, sir—"

"Seen what?"

"Seen this shit that's happenin' right now," Busick said. "The last time was in '91, when we thought the Iraqis were launching biochem weapons at Israel and we were getting ready to drop a nuke on Baghdad. I was the Senate majority whip. We were hustled out of Washington faster than shit from a goose. And it wasn't just to the Mountain—we were dispersed to preserve the government, sir."

"What are you talking about, 'preserve the government'?" Thorn asked. "This is a precaution, a contingency. With all that's happening in Turkmenistan and the Middle East, the heightened tensions, the saber rattling, it's understandable—"

"Mr. President, with all due respect, sir, you have no friggin' idea what's about to happen," Busick said seriously. "As soon as you step aboard Air Force One, you will become the executive branch of the United States government—not just the White House but every department and every executive agency that exists. You may be alone and isolated for days, maybe weeks. You may not be in contact with your cabinet or advisers.

"What I'm tryin' to tell you is that I think this is it, Mr. President," Busick went on. "The warning came right from NORAD. They were talkin' about missile tracks and flight times. They—"

"What are you saying, Les?"

"I'm tellin' you, Mr. President, I think we just caught the bolt from the blue," Busick said. "And I'm telling you that you need to be strong and you need to be tough. Because there will be a lot of hurt people in this country very, very soon, and they'll be looking to you for leadership. You've got to give it to them. And sometimes being the leader means doin' the most horrific thing you can damned well think of."

"Les . . ." Thorn tried to tell him again that everything was going to be okay, that this was just some sort of mistake or false alarm, but he didn't know what it was, and he would sound silly trying to reassure the veteran politician of something he himself knew absolutely nothing about. Finally he said, "Les, my family . . . ?"

"Helicopters picked them up from Rutland minutes ago. They should be launching from Burlington International about the time you go airborne." The first lady was a former state supreme court justice from Vermont, and she visited her family near the Vermont state capital whenever the president went out on his infrequent political travels.

The phone buzzed, interrupting their conversation—a higher-priority call than the vice president had to be pretty damned important. "I'll talk to you soon, Les."

"Yes, sir," Busick replied. Then he added, "Be tough, Thomas. You're the fucking president, sir. Shove it down their throats." Thorn was going to ask him to elaborate, but by then Busick had hung up.

Thorn hit the TALK button. "This is Séance."

"Mr. President, this is General Venti. I'm en route to the

NMCC, but I've received the latest from NORAD. I request permission to change your escape routing."

"Whiteman . . . ?"

"Sir, Whiteman is not secure." Whiteman Air Force Base, an hour's drive east of Kansas City in Knob Noster, and the home of the B-2A Spirit stealth bomber, was where Air Force One was based while the president was in Kansas City.

"Tell it to me straight, General."

There was a slight pause before Venti said, "Yes, sir. NORAD has issued an air-defense emergency. The Missile Warning Center is tracking a number of high-speed, high-altitude cruise missiles, launched by Russian Bear bombers. We count twenty-seven tracks so far. We believe that each missile carries two nuclear warheads, yields unknown. One track is definitely headed for Whiteman Air Force Base. Time to impact, approximately thirty-five minutes."

"Oh, my God . . ."

"Other confirmed tracks are headed for Offutt Air Force Base in Nebraska; Ellsworth Air Force Base, South Dakota; Minot Air Force Base, North Dakota; Twentieth Air Force headquarters at F. E. Warren Air Force Base in Wyoming; and several missile-launch control facilities in Wyoming, Montana, and Colorado. It appears that the Russians are attempting to take out all of our land-based strategic nuclear-strike weapon systems—our ICBMs and bombers—in one massive preemptive strike."

"I . . . I can't believe it," Thorn muttered. "This can't be happening. . . ."

"It's confirmed, sir," Venti said, his voice a bit shaky and strained. "The first missile will hit Minot Air Force Base in less than thirty-four minutes. Minot has thirty-two B-52 bombers, twenty-eight KC-135 aerial-refueling tankers, and other support aircraft; plus, they serve as Ninety-first Space Wing headquarters, controlling one hundred and fifty Minuteman III missiles."

"Can . . . can any of those bombers escape?"

There was another slight pause. "We're trying to get as many aircraft as we can off the ground, sir, any way we possibly can—maintenance troops, students, transient alert crews, anybody who can start the engines and take the controls and have any chance at all of landing it afterward. We have no strategic strike aircraft on ready alert. I'm afraid that the only survivors might be aircraft that are ready to launch on training or operational-support missions, are deployed, or already airborne."

"My God . . ."

"Mr. President, our first consideration is to be sure you can escape," Venti said. "Whiteman is definitely out. The other Air Force base within range of Marine One is McConnell, near Wichita, but it was once an Air National Guard B-1 bomber base and might be a target as well." He was silent for a moment. "The staff recommends you be evacuated to Fort Leavenworth, Kansas. It's the most secure location nearby. Once Angel escapes, we can arrange a rendezvous."

"Sounds fine to me," the president said. "Angel" was the unclassified code word for the Air Force VC-25 transport planes, known as "Air Force One" when the president was aboard. Both planes in the fleet were always deployed with the president on his travels, and at least one was always kept ready to fly at a moment's notice.

"Is Foghorn with you, sir?"

Thorn looked at the Navy officer with the "football." "Yes."

"Sir, I recommend you change the national defense configuration to DEFCON One," Venti said. "All surviving military forces will begin preparations for war, should you order it in the future. You don't need to give me an authorization code—your verbal order is enough until we can formalize it in writing."

"Very well. Issue the order," Thorn responded immediately.

Venti barked out an order over his shoulder, then returned to the phone: "I also recommend you increase the strategic force posture to red, sir," he said.

Thorn hesitated. The Defense Configuration, or DEF-CON, ordered all military units to various readiness states, with DEFCON One being maximum readiness for war. The "posture" told the units with weapons exactly what state or operational status their weapons and delivery systems should be in. The exact state varied by unit and weapon system but was broken down into three stages: red, yellow, and green, with green meaning that weapons in secure storage and coded documents and launch or enabling devices locked away; to red, which meant that weapons were loaded and the crews had all the documents and devices they needed to prearm and launch live nuclear weapons. The crews still needed the execution order from the president to release live nuclear weapons, but under a Posture Red, the crews were just a few switches away from unleashing hell on the enemy.

"Sir?"

"Go to Red Posture, General Venti," Thorn said finally.

"Yes, sir. Understand. Posture Red." Again he gave a verbal order to his deputy to issue the posture change to military forces around the world. Then he said, "Sir, I know we've game-planned this out in advance, but I still want to ask you: Do you wish to order any retaliatory or preemptive strikes at this time?" Any particular combination of DEF-CON and posture initiated a series of actions by various military units around the world, depending on the nature of the emergency. Several actions were automatic—dispersing ships and aircraft, retargeting missiles, activating shelters, and sending commanders to alternate and airborne command centers—and other actions were optional. Among the optional actions were nuclear and nonnuclear strikes on selected important targets.

Thorn had made it clear early on in his administration that he would not initiate nuclear retaliation based on just an attack notification—the so-called launch-on-warning option—but the plans were still in the bag sitting on the shelf anyway, and Venti thought it his duty to ask. There were several targets he'd like to see vaporized right now, he thought.

"No. Proceed as planned, General," Thorn replied. The president's standing order to any attack on the United States, from another September 11–style terrorist attack to a massive nuclear attack, was the same in all cases: Ride it out, then plan a response based on all available intelligence and advice. It assumed that every other aspect of emergency planning remained the same: survival of key government officials, ensuring constitutional succession, and maintaining positive and unambiguous control of the nation's nuclear weapons; but in any case, Thomas Thorn insisted on complete and absolute control over his nuclear forces. "Any word from Gryzlov?" Thorn asked.

"Stand by, sir. . . ." A moment later: "Yes, sir, there are numerous hot-line messages, both voice and e-mail."

"Have Signal connect me to President Gryzlov, General," Thorn ordered.

"Sir, we don't have time—"

"Link us up, General."

"Mr. President, I . . . sir, whatever they say, I hardly think they have the slightest bearing on what our response should be!" Venti said. "The Russian Federation has initiated a sneak attack against the United States of America, and the first weapon impacts in about thirty minutes. They certainly didn't consult us before launching this attack!"

"General . . ."

"With all due respect, sir, it doesn't goddamn matter what Gryzlov has to say!" Venti stormed. "You know he's going to come up with some cockamamie reason, invent some crisis or trigger event, blame the whole event on us, and warn us not to retaliate. What the hell difference does it make if he apologizes, if he says it was a mistake, if he's sorry, if he's angry? He still launched an attack on us, squarely aimed to take out most if not all of our land-based long-range attack forces!"

"It's all right, Richard," the president said, trying to soothe his obviously agitated Joint Chiefs chairman. "I'm not going to make a decision without consulting the Joint Chiefs and the Cabinet. Now, get him on the line. I'll be on Marine One in a few minutes."

"Yes, sir," Venti finally responded, the outrage obvious in his voice. "Stand by." It took several minutes, during which time Thorn had transferred to Marine One and was on his way across Kansas City to Fort Leavenworth, about thirty miles to the northwest. It was risky making such a call—although the circuit was encrypted to protect eavesdroppers from listening in, the bearing to Marine One could easily be measured and the helicopter tracked across the sky.

"Marine One, this is Signals, your party is on the line, secure," the Army communications officer announced.

"President Gryzlov, I assume you have an explanation for this attack," Thorn said without preamble or pleasantries.

"President Thorn, listen to me very carefully," the voice of the Russian interpreter said. Anatoliy Gryzlov's voice could be heard in the background. He did not seem to be agitated in the least, as if launching missiles at the United States were an everyday occurrence. But he was the former chief of the general staff of the world's second-largest military, and he was accustomed to giving orders that sent thousands to their deaths. "This action is nothing more than retaliation for the attack against Engels Air Base, Zhukovsky Flight Test Center, and our paramilitary forces near Belgorod, perpetrated by Major General Patrick McLanahan and his band of high-tech aerial terrorists, acting under your full authority and direction—"

"That's sheer nonsense, Mr. President," Thorn said. "I've taken full responsibility for each and every one of those attacks, all of which were provoked by Russian military hostilities; and may I remind you that the United States has paid millions of dollars in reparations and legal claims as a result of those attacks. I want you to abort those missiles immediately and—"

"President Thorn, I asked you to listen to me," Gryzlov's interpreter said. "This is not a negotiation, only a notification. The missiles cannot and will not be aborted. The targets are offensive bomber and missile bases and combat command-and-control facilities only. The warheads are one-kiloton nuclear devices with bunker-penetrating technology, designed to destroy armored underground facilities—"

"My God!"

"They are no more powerful than the plasma-yield devices you used over Korea and only a few magnitudes more powerful than the thermium-nitrate weapons you used on Engels Air Base, and I predict that the death toll will be much lower in this attack than from the one on Engels," Gryzlov went on. "At least I gave you the courtesy of notifying you ahead of time, Mr. President."

"What?"

"If you'll check your hot-line messages, I notified the White House of the targets of the attack shortly after the missiles were launched," the interpreter said. "You have the entire target list, exactly as programmed into the attack computers of every aircraft in our strike force. I *had* intended to give you a full hour to evacuate those targets, but our strike force was discovered, and the flight leader ordered his force to retarget and launch early.

"You are more than welcome to try to shoot down the warheads, since I am certain that you can accurately predict the missiles' flight path, but I am assured that it is almost impossible to do so even with your impressive Patriot PAC-3 surface-to-air missile. Of course, you might have a chance to do so with the AL-52 Dragon anti-ballistic-missile laser aircraft under General McLanahan's command, but our intelligence tells me that you have grounded his entire fleet of air-craft. Unfortunate."

"McLanahan is no longer in command of the Air Battle Force, Gryzlov," Thorn said angrily. Marine One banked sharply, lining up for its final approach to landing. "You're doing all this to avenge yourself on a man that's not even in the picture anymore!"

"That does not matter, Mr. President," the interpreter said. "For too long you and your predecessors have sanctioned McLanahan's actions, and when he performs some heinous attack without your authority, you choose not to punish him—even when his actions kill thousands of innocent men, women, and children and terrorize the entire civilized world. McLanahan is nothing but a wild dog—but *you* are the dog's handler. It is your responsibility, and you have failed. Now it is time to accept your punishment.

"I know you have absolutely no reason to trust me, President Thorn," the interpreter went on, "but what I am about to tell you is the truth, and if your officers will check the data I have provided, you will see that I have told you the truth all along. I will continue to do so until I perceive that you will not be truthful with me. I do not want to start a nuclear war with you, Mr. Thorn—"

"But that is exactly what you're doing!" Thorn retorted. The noise level inside the cabin rose as Marine One began its hover approach to its landing zone on the parade grounds outside the Fort Leavenworth headquarters building. "What do you expect me to do, Gryzlov—sit still while Russia drops dozens of nuclear warheads on the United States?"

"That is *precisely* what I expect you to do—for the sake of the world," Gryzlov said. "I promise you, on my mother's eyes, soldier to soldier, that I will not launch any further attacks on the United States of America, its allies—what few allies you have left—and its territories, unless you decide to retaliate. This attack is a response to your attacks against Russia. It is merely payback. Remember that.

"And if you study the effect of this attack, Mr. President, you will see in very short order that it leaves the United States and Russia with *exactly* the same number of strategic weapon systems—in other words, nuclear parity, with an equal number of delivery vehicles on both sides."

"Are you actually going to present to the world that this attack is an *arms-control exercise?*" Thorn asked incredulously. "Do you honestly expect anyone on Earth to believe that?"

"Nonetheless, it will be true, and you may verify it yourself," Gryzlov's interpreter said. Thorn could hear papers shuffling—the interpreter was likely reading from a prepared script. "Now, I know that you have eight to ten *Ohio*-class nuclear ballistic-missile submarines on patrol at the present time, plus an equal number at port or undergoing maintenance. That is five times more than Russia has and, as much as I hate to admit it, I fear that our submarines will probably blow themselves up the moment they try to launch a missile. That gives the United States a substantial deterrent capability."

"What's your point, Gryzlov?"

"The point is, sir, that even if our attack is one hundred and ten percent effective, the United States would still have a substantial advantage over Russia. We could then—"

"Gryzlov, you don't understand a thing," Thorn snapped. "I don't give a damn about the weapons. I'm all for reducing our nuclear arsenal to below two thousand warheads, maybe even lower. I would have been happy to work with you to draft a new Strategic Arms Limitation Treaty. But what you're doing is killing potentially thousands of people in a sneak attack against the United States. No American president would allow that to happen unavenged."

"So a sneak attack against Russia is acceptable to you, but a sneak attack against the United States is not?"

Thorn found he had no answer for Gryzlov. He felt that the Russian president was right: McLanahan *had* staged a sneak attack against Russian border guards in Belgorod, trying to rescue two of his crew members who'd been shot down over Russia—after he was specifically ordered to return to base. McLanahan *had* launched a sneak attack against Engels Air Base, moments before Russian bombers were to launch and execute a massive attack against Turkmeni military forces that had defeated a Russian battalion in Turkmenistan. McLanahan *had* destroyed a Russian air-defense site in Turkmenistan without proper authorization.

He hadn't used nuclear weapons, of course—but did that really matter? The attack on Engels had killed thousands, including some civilians, and nearly destroyed one of Russia's main military air bases. McLanahan's attack on the air-defense site had killed almost two dozen, and that was against a completely defensive weapon system. Was Gryzlov a worse leader just because he was using nuclear weapons? Was Patrick McLanahan the real provocateur in this entire matter after all?

The door to Marine One opened, and two Secret Service agents, a general officer, and several armed soldiers stood outside in the driving rain, waiting excitedly for the president to alight. He did not need to glance at his watch to know that time was running out—no, time had run out a long time ago. Time had run out when he'd failed to deal with McLanahan, when he'd let his secretary of defense, Robert Goff, talk him out of punishing the general.

"Listen to me, President Thorn," Gryzlov went on. "I need to know what you decide. Will you retaliate?"

"What if I do?"

"Then, depending on the threat to my government and my people, I will have to respond in kind," the interpreter responded.

"Following your sneak attack with more threats, Gryzlov?"

"Allow me to remind you again, Mr. President: This attack, although preemptive and heinous, makes us *even*. For the first time in history, Russia and the United States are at a strategic parity, with the United States definitely holding a technological and, at least for the time being, a moral advantage. If you retaliate, you'll be condemning the world to nuclear disaster. *You* will be the aggressor."

There was a rustling of sound on the phone, and then General Anatoliy Gryzlov's voice, speaking in halting and heavily accented English, took over from that of the interpreter. "Mr. President, you have made remarks in the past saying that a limited nuclear war is not just possible but probable. You have seen nuclear weapons used by the People's Republic of China, the former North Koreans, and even Ukraine against Russia itself. Surely you have given this topic much thought. You know your answer. You know that the risk I have taken is great, but the risk you take by retaliating heightens the danger to the world a thousandfold."

"Mr. President, I want you into a shelter in five minutes," the chief of the Presidential Protection Detail said sternly. Thorn's internal "commando clock" told him there was less than twenty minutes before the first warhead would hit. "We have to go *now*."

"President Thorn?" Gryzlov asked. "What will you do?"

Thorn looked at his PPD chief, then at the floor of the VIP cabin of the helicopter. Taking a deep breath, he raised his head and said, "What I'm going to do . . . is not talk to you any longer, Gryzlov," the president said. "You launch nuclear weapons at my country and then tell me that you won't launch any *more* unless we do—and you say it as casually as apologizing for accidentally splashing mud on someone? I'll do what I have to do, without conferring with you beforehand." Gryzlov was saying something in Russian in the background, but Thorn hung up before the interpreter could translate.

He leaped out of the helicopter. The general officer saluted, and Thorn returned his salute. "Mr. President, I'm Major General Robert Lee Brown, commanding general," he said. "This way, sir, *quickly*." Brown motioned to a waiting staff car, and they drove off, surrounded by Army military-police escorts. They drove to a traditional-looking three-story brick building; inside, it looked any-thing but traditional. There was a welcome area featuring several large computer screens where visitors could watch images of computerized tank and helicopter battles, with captions underneath showing which units were participat-ing in the mock battle. All of the screens were dark now, shut down to prevent damage in case of an electromag-netic pulse, and the area was deserted except for a few worried-looking soldiers in battle-dress uniforms stepping hurriedly past.

The group took a concrete-and-steel stairway down two floors, followed a long minimally decorated corridor, and entered an office complex with a secretarial staff area flanked by several large office suites. "This is the computer operations hub for the National Simulation Center, which conducts several different types of battlefield combat simu-lations," Brown said. "This office complex is the most secure location on base, and it is also equipped with secure high-speed communications facilities. You should be safe down here for as long as you need to stay. We're not hard-ened against EMP, nor are we equipped with biochem filters, but this is the safest place on post. We should be safe if Whiteman or McConnell is attacked."

"That's okay, General," Thorn said. "We'll be on our way as soon as we're able. Thank you. Please see to your com-mand now—make sure everyone is safe." The general saluted the president, shook his proffered hand, then departed. "Mark, get me the NMCC."

The Secret Service agent got a quick briefing on the phone system, then dialed the National Military Command Center, checked in, and activated the speakerphone. "This is the president, secure," Thorn said. "Situation report."

"Sir, this is General Venti. Secretary Goff and I are en

route to Andrews to take the NAOC airborne." The NAOC, or National Airborne Operations Center, was the flying version of the National Military Command Center at the Pentagon, a converted Boeing 747 able to communicate with government, civil, and military forces around the world. "We are still in an Air Defense EMERCON. Four bases in Alaska have been struck by small-yield nuclear missiles—all radar sites and ballistic-missile defense installations. NORAD is now tracking several dozen inbound very-high-speed cruise missiles over south-central Canada. Estimated time to first impact: nine minutes, twelve seconds; target: Minot Air Force Base, North Dakota."

"I spoke with Gryzlov—he confirmed he launched the attack and warns us not to retaliate," Thorn said grimly. "Status of the government and military command-and-control network?"

"Good and bad, sir," Venti said. "Most of the cabinet and congressional leadership have checked in with the comm center. Most are staying in Washington, unless there's evidence that they might try to strike the capital. Since there are no tracks detected heading toward Washington or anywhere east of the Mississippi, the vice president relocated to High Point instead of going airborne. We'll take several members of Congress and other agencies airborne with us. Secretary of State Hershel is airborne in a C-32 from Phoenix. Attorney General Horton hasn't checked in, but his deputy said he was en route to Andrews, along with the director of the FBI."

"I want you and Secretary Goff airborne ASAP, General, as soon as you arrive at Andrews," the president said. "As soon as both of you are on board, lift off. Don't wait for stragglers."

"Understood, sir."

"What's the bad news, General?"

"The bad news, sir," Venti said grimly, "is that we're going to get clobbered, and there's nothing we can do about it except watch—and wait for the casualty counts to come in."

SITE 91-12, NORTH DAKOTA
That same time

Their day had started at seven-thirty the previous morning. Captain Bruce Ellerby and Second Lieutenant Christine Johnson, his assistant crew commander, met at the 742nd Missile Squadron to review tech-order changes and alert notes. They wore royal blue Air Force fatigues with white name tapes and insignia, along with squadron scarves.

After a series of briefings to the entire oncoming crews, including launch-facility status, intelligence, weather, and standardization/evaluation reports, the crews piled their tech orders, manuals, and other bags into assigned vans and headed out to their assigned launch-control facilities. Both Ellerby and Johnson were taking correspondence classes while on alert, so they brought backpacks filled with books: Ellerby was working on his master's degree in aviation-maintenance management from Embry-Riddle Aeronautical University, while Johnson was working on both Squadron Officer School and her master's degree in computer science from the University of North Dakota.

After dropping off another crew, Ellerby and Johnson made their way to their facility and checked in with the security-forces commander around noon. A security-alert team was sent out to check ID cards and access badges, and the van was allowed to approach the launch-control facility. The crew checked in with the "House Mouse," the noncommissioned officer who controlled access to the facility, to get the security and operational status of the site, and then placed a lunch order with the cook. By then the House Mouse had checked in with the offgoing crew, received verification of crew change and code words, then opened the elevator-shaft access door for the ongoing crew.

Despite its being only an eight-story ride, it took four minutes for the elevator to reach the bottom. Their first task after reaching the subterranean level was to manually pump open the locking pins securing the ten-ton outer blast door leading to the launch-control electrical bay. Despite being heavy, the door was so well balanced on its hinges that it was easy for Ellerby and Johnson to pull it open. Once inside, the crew completed their preflight checks of the high-voltage electrical systems, switching panels, generators, and batteries, which would supply electrical power to the launch-control facility in case city power was disrupted. Once the checklist was complete, the crew closed the big door and pumped the locks back in.

Meanwhile, the offgoing crew in the launch-control capsule was pumping open the blast door to the capsule. By the time Ellerby and Johnson were finished, the door was open, and they walked across a narrow tunnel leading to the launch-control capsule, an egg-shaped room suspended from the ceiling by enormous spring shock absorbers designed to protect the crew from the blast effects of all but a direct hit by a nuclear weapon.

The offgoing crew commander briefed the ongoing crew on the status of the facility and on any scheduled maintenance or security-team inspections that were to be performed on the facility itself or any of the ten primary and ten secondary missiles under their supervision. The final task was for the offgoing crew to remove their combination locks from the red safe above the deputy commander's launch console and cut off the tamper-evident truck seals securing the safe. The oncoming crew checked the authentication documents and launch keys, logged the new seal numbers, then closed, locked, and safety-sealed the safe. With the changeover complete, the offgoing crew turned over their sidearms to the new crew and departed. A final one hundred pumps on the handle, and the capsule was closed. After a check-in with the squadron's other four launch-control facilities and assessment of equipment status, the twenty-four-hour alert tour began.

Normally, pulling alert in a missile launch-control facility meant hours and hours of boredom, punctuated by a few hours of busywork and a few minutes of excitement. This tour was anything but normal. After a fairly quiet day and early evening, the communications system became more and more active as the evening wore on, with several communications and status-report queries from wing and Twentieth Air Force headquarters. Tensions were obviously high. The crews were fully aware of the events that had taken place in Central Asia in recent weeks and months, and of the overall heightened degree of distrust and suspicion of the Russians.

The tension exploded early the next morning with a loud, rapid *deedledeedledeedle!* warning tone, signaling receipt of an emergency action message. Christine Johnson, taking a nap in the crew bunk, immediately bolted upright and hurried over to her deputy crew commander's seat. Ellerby was already in his seat, and he had his codebook out and open. Seconds later a coded message from the wing command post was broadcast, and both crew members copied the message in their codebooks with grease pencils and began decoding it.

The first indication that this was not going to be a normal day: The message decoded as an "Actual" message, not an "Exercise," and although they had received several "Actual" messages already that shift, getting another so early in the morning was not normal. "I decode the message as a Message Eleven," Ellerby announced.

"I concur," Johnson said, her mouth turning instantly dry. She stood up and removed her lock and the truck seal from the red safe while Ellerby joined her. He removed the proper authentication card from the outer compartment. "Card Bravo-Echo."

"Checks," she said. He snapped open the foil card and tore off the top, exposing a combination of six letters and numbers underneath the foil, then laid it down on the message book. The characters were exactly as Johnson had copied.

"Authenticators match and are in exact sequence," Ellerby said.

"I concur," Johnson said, her heart pounding now.

This time both crew members did everything together, slowly and carefully. They decoded the rest of the message, entering the proper date-time group and instructions on another page in the message book. When they were finished, they looked at each other—and realized they were about to do something neither one of them had ever done except in a simulator.

Ellerby removed his lock from the red safe, cut off the second truck seal, and opened the main compartment. He handed Johnson a key and three more authenticator cards, then took a key and his cards back to his console. The two consoles were fifteen feet apart, separated to avoid any one person from touching the other's console—especially the switch into which the launch keys were inserted. Meanwhile, Johnson looped the launch key over her neck, strapped herself into her steel seat with a four-point harness, and tightened the straps.

Both crew members began running their checklists as directed in the emergency action message: They notified the other launch-control facilities in the squadron that they had copied and authenticated a valid message; they began the power-up and data-transfer and alignment sequence; and they alerted the aboveground security and maintenance crews that they had received a launch-alert message. The crew was in a hair-trigger readiness state, waiting for the next message.

The next message arrived a few moments later, with retargeting information. On day-to-day alert, the Minuteman III missiles at Minot and elsewhere had "open-ocean" coordinates programmed into the missiles, so in case of an accidental or terrorist launch, the warheads would not hit any real targets. Now real targets had to be entered back into each missile's warhead. It did not take long to do, but it was scary for the crew members to realize that they had taken the next step toward actually firing their missiles in anger. If the missiles left their silos now, they would strike their assigned targets minutes later—there was no abort, no recall, and no retargeting while in flight.

After the retargeting was completed, there was nothing to do but sit back and wait to copy and authenticate an execution message, which would direct them to complete their launch checklist. The final step was to insert their launch keys into the launch switch and perform simultaneous key turns, which would enter a launch vote into the time-shared master computer. Successful key turns by at least two launch-control capsules with no INHIBIT commands from any other squadron LCCs was necessary to launch the missiles; three successful key turns in the squadron would send a launch command, no matter how many other INHIBIT commands were entered. The master computer would then decide when each missile would launch, automatically holding some missiles while others launched so the warheads would not destroy each other after—

Suddenly the entire launch-control capsule heaved. The lights blinked, then went out, then came back one by one. The air became heavy, then hot, then seemed to boil with moisture and red-hot dust. The capsule banged against something solid—probably the bottom of the facility—and then bounced and shook like a bucking bronco. Both crew members screamed as their bodies were hurled against their restraints. Equipment, books, and papers started flying in every direction around the capsule, but Ellerby and Johnson didn't notice as they fought to stay conscious against the tremendous pounding. The heat began to build and build. . . .

And then it all exploded into a wall of fire, which mercifully lasted only one or two heartbeats, until everything went forever dark and silent.

OVER CENTRAL UTAH
That same time

"Attention all aircraft on this frequency, this is Salt Lake Center, I have received an emergency notification from the U.S. Defense Department and the Department of Homeland Security," the message on the radio said suddenly. "You are instructed to divert to the nearest suitable airport and land immediately. Any aircraft not in compliance within the next twenty minutes is in violation of federal air regulations and will be prosecuted, and you may be shot down by ground or airborne air-defense weapon systems without further warning."

Patrick McLanahan, sipping on a bottle of cold water while at the controls of his own Aerostar 602P twin-engine airplane, nearly gagged when he heard that announcement. He immediately punched the NRST button on his GPS computer, which gave him a list of the nearest airports. Luckily, there were a lot to choose from in this area—a few minutes farther west, out over the vast high deserts of western Utah and eastern Nevada, and he'd be in big trouble.

His Aerostar was a rather small, bullet-shaped twin-engine plane, built for speed, with short wings that needed a lot of runway for takeoff, so he had to choose carefully or he might have trouble departing; Patrick also remembered that thousands of air travelers had been stranded for several days after they were grounded following the terrorist attacks on September 11, 2001, and several hundred general-aviation aircraft were grounded for weeks if they were based near Boston, New York City, or Washington, D.C. The nearest airport to him now, Nephi Municipal, was only six miles away, which would take him about two minutes, but Provo

Municipal was only twenty-eight miles farther north and would only take him an extra nine minutes to reach; it had a longer runway and better airport services. He figured he'd be much more likely to get a bus or train ride home from Provo than he would from Nephi.

The channel was clogged with voices, dozens of pilots all trying to talk at once. "All aircraft on this frequency, *shut up!*" the controller shouted. It took several such calls for the frequency to clear. "Everyone, listen carefully and cooperate. Don't acknowledge my calls unless I ask you to, and keep all channels clear unless it's an emergency—and by God, it had *better* be a *big* emergency.

"All VFR aircraft using radar flight following: Radar services are terminated, squawk VFR, and land immediately at the nearest suitable airfield," the controller went on, struggling to remain calm and measured. "Aircraft below flight level one-eight-zero on IFR flight plans in VMC, remain VMC, squawk VFR, and land at the nearest suitable airfield immediately." Patrick was on an IFR, or Instrument Flight Rules, flight plan, which meant his flight was being monitored by federal air traffic controllers. Because the controllers were responsible for safe aircraft and terrain separation, IFR pilots had to follow precise flight rules. All aircraft at or above eighteen thousand feet were required to be on such a flight plan.

Below eighteen thousand, pilots flying in good weather (called VMC, or "visual meteorological conditions") had the option of filing an IFR flight plan or flying under VFR, or Visual Flight Rules, which allowed much more freedom. Pilots flying VFR were responsible for their own traffic and terrain separation, but could request radar service, called "flight following," which controllers would provide if they weren't too busy with their IFR responsibilities.

"IFR aircraft in positive control airspace, if you are so equipped and can ensure your own terrain and traffic separation, squawk VFR and proceed immediately to the nearest suitable airport for landing—I should be able to figure out which airport you're headed for and change your flight plan.

"All other aircraft, I am going to be giving you initial vectors, so listen up. Approach controllers will be giving you further vectors for landing. Do not acknowledge radio calls, just do what I tell you to do. As soon as you descend below one-eight thousand feet in VMC, squawk VFR and proceed to the nearest suitable airport for immediate landing. Keep your eyes and ears open for traffic advisories and monitor GUARD for emergency messages."

Patrick adjusted the autopilot for a quick descent, set his transponder to "1200," which meant he was accepting responsibility for his own navigation and collision avoidance, pulled out his approach charts, and began running his checklists for landing. The Center frequency was hopelessly clogged with radio calls, despite the controller's pleas, so Patrick tuned the radio to Salt Lake City radar approach control, checked in, and received approach instructions. Weather was good. He popped the speed brakes to increase his rate of descent, careful not to pull too much power off, because his engines were warm and a rapid descent plus low power settings might damage the Aerostar's big-bore turbocharged engines.

He knew he should be concentrating on his plane, approach, and landing, but he couldn't help it—he had to find out what had caused the air-defense emergency.

"McLanahan to Luger," Patrick spoke into midair. His original subcutaneous transceiver had been removed—"hacked out" would be more accurate—by the Libyans two years earlier, but the new one, implanted into his abdomen to make locating and removing it more difficult, worked perfectly. All personnel assigned to the High Technology Aerospace Weapons Center wore them for the rest of their lives, mostly so the government could keep track of them in case the need arose.

"Patrick!" Dave Luger responded. "Where the hell have you been?"

"On my way to Sacramento to meet up with my family," Patrick said. "I'm in the Aerostar, about to land in—"

"Muck, all hell is breaking loose," Luger said. "I've just launched four Vampires, five Megafortresses, and six tankers to escape orbits off the coast."

"What?"

"Muck, the damned Russians actually did what you predicted—they launched a gaggle of Blackjack, Bear, and Backfire bombers and attacked with AS-17s and -19s, exactly like over Uzbekistan," Luger said. "First they sent two Blackjack bombers in low-level and wiped out Clear Air Station in Alaska, then shot nuclear missiles at Fort Wainwright, Fort Greely, and Eielson—"

"What? Oh, *Jesus . . . !"*

"Looks like the targets were all ballistic-missile defense sites, Muck," Dave went on. "Then they blasted a hole in the North Warning System radars with missiles from Backfires and drove about thirty Bear bombers through. They were caught by the Canadians about three hundred miles after feet-dry and started firing missiles. The Canucks got a couple, but DSP estimates at least fifty hypersonic cruise missiles are on their way."

"Oh, *shit!*" Patrick swore. His throat and lips turned instantly dry, there was a buzzing sound in his ears, and his heart felt as if it were to jump right out of his chest. He could not believe what he'd just heard—but then, he'd been so certain it would happen that he really wasn't that surprised. "Wh-when will they hit?"

"First CONUS missile hits Minot any minute now," Luger responded. "Looks like they're going after ballistic-missile defense bases, bomber bases, missile launch-control facilities . . . and STRATCOM headquarters at Offutt."

"My God . . . what about Washington . . . ?"

"Not yet," Luger responded. "Just Alaska and the Midwest bomber and missile bases. Where are you, Muck?"

"Getting ready to land in Provo, Utah."

"It'd be safer for you here, and it won't take you long in your Aerostar—maybe an hour and a half. Got enough gas to make it?"

"I just refueled in Pagosa Springs, so I have plenty of gas," Patrick said, "but air-traffic control ordered all aircraft to land. I've got ten minutes to be on the ground."

"I'll give them a call and see if they'll let you come on in. Stand by." But less than a minute later, he came back. "No good, Muck. Every phone line is jammed."

Patrick hesitated—but only for a moment. He retracted the speed brakes, pushed in the mixture and prop levers, then slowly moved up the throttles, while at the same time continuing his descent. Soon the radar altimeter, which measured the distance between the airplane and the ground, clicked in at two thousand feet above ground level.

"Aerostar Five-six Bravo Mike," the approach controller radioed a few moments later, "you are below my radar coverage, radar services terminated, frequency change approved. Land immediately and remain on the ground until specifically cleared for flight again by the FAA. Do not acknowledge."

Don't worry, I won't, Patrick said to himself. When the radar altimeter read one thousand feet aboveground, Patrick leveled off—and then he punched the DIRECT-TO button on his GPS navigator and entered "KBAM," the identifier for Battle Mountain, Nevada. He had to adjust the routing to stay away from restricted airspace around the Dugway Proving Grounds, but soon he was heading westbound as fast as the Aerostar could carry him, as low as he could safely go in the mountainous terrain. "Dave, I'm coming in, ETE one hour twenty-five minutes," Patrick reported.

"How'd you manage that, Muck?"

"The old-fashioned way—terrain masking," Patrick replied. "I just hope no interceptors think I'm a bad guy. Send a message to NORAD and tell them what I'm doing so their fighter jocks won't shoot me down." Undoubtedly the

North American Aerospace Defense Command would set up air patrols around the entire region in very short time. "After you do that, you can brief me on the status of your forces."

"They're *your* forces, Muck," Luger said.

"I've been bounced out of my last command, Dave," Patrick said. "Houser has preferred charges against me. I'm not in command of anything."

"These are *your* forces, Muck—always were, always will be," Luger repeated. "I'm just keeping them warm for you. You realize, of course, that I never received orders confirming me as commander of Air Battle Force?"

"Yes you did. The message from the Pentagon—"

"Only directed that I take control of the force while you were called to take command of the Nine-sixty-sixth," Luger said. "You're still the boss—and I think the powers that be wanted it that way. Come on in, and we'll figure out what we're going to do next—if we survive this, that is."

"We'll survive it," Patrick said. "Were you able to deploy any of the Tin Men?"

"I've got two teams deployed to Eareckson right now," Luger said. "I'm just awaiting an execution order."

"Get them out of there—if the Russians are going after ballistic-missile defense bases, it's likely to be next."

"Already done, Muck," Luger said. "We dispersed them to Attu as soon as the air-defense alerts were broadcast."

Patrick made several rapid mental calculations and quickly determined that the mission was nearly impossible. It was around fifteen hundred miles from Eareckson Air Force Base on the island of Shemya in the Aleutian Islands of western Alaska to Yakutsk, Russia. For the MV-32 Pave Dasher tilt-jet aircraft, it meant five hours and at least two aerial refuelings one way, flown over open ocean as well as over some of the most inhospitable terrain on the planet. The team's tanker aircraft, a U.S. Air Force HC-130P special-operations tanker, would have to fly over the Kamchatka Peninsula, the Sea of Okhotsk, and probably a good portion of Siberia to rendezvous with the MV-32 on its return leg.

If the Pave Dashers missed any of their refueling rendezvous, they would not make it back home.

From the moment the MV-32 and the HC-130P left Shemya, it would be virtually over enemy territory—there was nothing between Shemya and Yakutsk except icy-cold oceans and Russian territory. It was suicidal. No one would ever imagine that such a mission could succeed.

Which made it perfect for the Tin Men. "Have the team stand by, Dave," Patrick said. "I want to get them airborne as soon as possible—but they're not going in alone."

SIXTY MILES EAST OF OFFUTT AIR FORCE BASE, BELLEVUE, NEBRASKA
That same time

The intercom phone next to Lieutenant General Terrill Samson's seat buzzed. He, along with Major General Gary Houser of the Air Intelligence Agency and several of their senior staff members, were flying to Offutt Air Force Base south of Omaha, Nebraska, to meet with General Thomas Muskoka of Air Combat Command and the staff of the United States Strategic Command to discuss activities in Russia and what sort of plans they should recommend to the Pentagon to respond. Samson glanced at Houser, who was seated across from him in the club seating of the small jet, silently ordering him to answer it. Houser reached forward and picked up the receiver. "This is General Houser."

"Major Hale up on the flight deck, sir," the copilot of the Air Force C-21 transport jet responded. "We've received a notification of an air-defense emergency over the United States."

"*What?*" Houser exclaimed. "What's the emergency?"

"Unknown, sir," the copilot responded. "Air-traffic control is ordering us to land immediately. Offutt Air Force Base has closed its runway because of operational requirements. The nearest suitable base for us is Lincoln Municipal."

"We're not landing at a civilian airfield, Major—we're a military SAM flight, for Christ's sake," Houser retorted. A SAM, or Special Air Mission, was a designation that gave government or military flights priority handling by air-traffic controllers, almost on a par with Air Force One itself. "And what the hell does 'operational requirements' mean?"

"They wouldn't say, sir."

"Tell ATC that we're going to land at Offutt unless further notified," Houser said. "Remind them, *again*, that we're a military SAM flight. Then get the Fifty-fifth Wing commander on the line immediately."

"Sir, we've already tried to communicate with him directly—no response."

"I've got General Samson with me. He'll authorize us to divert to Offutt."

"Sorry, sir, but this directive comes down from NORAD through the FAA."

"Then request General Samson speak with General Shepard at NORAD ASAP—he's probably already at Offutt for the meeting we're supposed to attend, for Christ's sake. If he's not available, get General Venti at the Pentagon. We're *not* going to divert to a civilian airfield, especially not if an emergency exists that we need to respond to. Hurry it up."

"Yes, sir."

Samson looked up from his laptop computer. "What's going on, Gary?"

"ATC says someone's declared an air-defense emergency," Houser said. "They're trying to get us to land at the nearest civilian airfield."

"They know we're a SAM flight?"

"Yes, sir."

"Base ops at Offutt will have to contact FAA directly."

"The crew has tried to contact the Fifty-fifth Wing commander directly. They're going to try to get General Shepard to get us permission to land. He should be right there at the STRATCOM command center."

The phone buzzed again, and this time Samson picked it up. "General Samson."

"Major Hale up on the flight deck, sir. ATC says to divert immediately to Lincoln Municipal. Offutt is out. They say base ops at Offutt advised ATC not to allow anyone to land there, including inbound SAMs. No response from General Shepard."

"What in hell is going on, Major?"

"I don't know, sir," the copilot responded, "but I'm monitoring the radios, and it sounds like Offutt launched one of their AOCs." AOCs were the Airborne Operations Center E-4Bs based at Offutt, modified Boeing 747 airliners with the ability to communicate with and direct military forces worldwide.

"So the runway itself is okay?"

"Sounds like it, sir."

"Then advise ATC that we're landing at Offutt," Samson ordered. "If they still want you to divert, declare an emergency for national security reasons and proceed to Offutt."

"Yes, sir."

Samson hung up the intercom, picked up the in-flight phone, and dialed his command post's number. No response. He tried his office number—still no response. "Well, what the *hell* is going on?" he muttered. "I can't get through to anyone."

"Maybe we ought to land at Lincoln as they ordered," Houser suggested nervously, "and then sort it out on the ground."

"We're less than forty miles from landing—we're not going to divert an extra fifty just because ATC has got a bug up their ass about something," General Samson said. "Besides, if something's going on, the best place for us to be is at Offutt in the command center. We'll go there, even if we have to land on the taxiway." Samson had a bit of trouble relaying that desire to the pilot, but once the C-21 pilot was reminded exactly who in the back of the plane was calling the shots, the decision was quickly made.

They watched out the small jet's windows as they broke through a thin overcast layer and caught a glimpse of the air base off in the distance. Nothing looked out of the ordinary—no smoke or fire from a plane crash, no signs of any sort of terrorist attack or of an approaching tornado or severe thunderstorm. They appeared to be lining up for a straight-in approach. Gary Houser felt relieved when the landing gear came down, indicating they were cleared to land.

On the five-mile final, Houser was busy packing up his briefcase and getting ready for landing when he noticed a bright flash of light, like a nearby bolt of lightning. At that exact moment, the lights inside the airplane cabin popped out.

"Holy crap!" Terrill Samson said, "I think we just got hit by lightning."

"It sounds like the engines are spooling down, too," Houser said. It was hard to tell with the noise from the landing gear and flaps—or *was* that noise from the gear . . . or something else? This was bad. They might be able to drag it in from this altitude, but these jets didn't glide too well. He tightened his seat belt and waited for the impact. He could hear the jet engine's starters roaring and the igniters clicking as the pilots frantically tried to restart the engines. They *had* flown through that thin overcast, but there didn't seem to be any thunderheads nearby—where did the lightning come from? He glanced out the window.

And saw what he thought was a huge tornado, like something in a disaster movie, that had instantly materialized out of nowhere right in the middle of the base. It was an immense column of dirt rising vertically, at least a mile in diameter—with what looked like orange, red, and yellow volcano-like rivers of fire mixed in. He opened his mouth to yell out a warning to the cockpit when he heard an earsplitting blast, like a thousand crashes of thunder.

Then he felt, saw, and heard nothing.

7

ABOARD AIR FORCE ONE
A short time later

President Thomas Thorn sat at his desk in the executive office suite in the nose section of Air Force One, staring at a computerized map of the United States. Several dots on the map, representing military installations, were blinking; others had red triangles around them. Another flat-panel digital monitor had images of the vice president at the Mount Weather Continuation of Government Special Facility, known as "High Point," in Berryville, Virginia; another showed images of Secretary of Defense Robert Goff and Chairman of the Joint Chiefs of Staff General Venti, both airborne aboard the E-4B National Airborne Operations Center, orbiting out over the Atlantic Ocean with two F-15C Eagle fighters in formation with it. Several members of the Joint Chiefs of Staff—the ones that managed to make it to Andrews in time for takeoff—were also present in the NAOC's conference room and listening in on the teleconference, but were not visible on the screen.

"NORAD is showing no more tracks, Mr. President," Goff said somberly over the secure videoconference link. "Looks like the attack is over."

It was over, all right—over for thousands of military men

and women, their families, and many thousands more innocent civilians living near the military targets.

As hard as he tried, Thomas Thorn found himself growing angrier by the second. He knew before receiving any estimates that the death toll was going to be huge—ten, twenty, maybe thirty times greater than the number of lives lost in New York, Washington, and Pennsylvania on September 11. How could the Russians do something like this? It was such an unbelievable act of pure homicidal madness. Calling this an "act of war" just didn't seem to cut it. This was an act of insanity.

"You okay, Thomas?" Vice President Busick asked over the secure video teleconference. "You look like you're flying through some rough air."

"I'm okay," Thorn replied.

"I know what you're feelin', Thomas," Busick said. "You wanna go wring someone's neck." Thorn glanced at Busick's face in the monitor. "Get over that, Thomas. You have a lot of dead Americans out there, and a lot more that want to know what's gonna happen next. You're the man that's going to need to have some answers. Let's get organized."

Thorn stared blankly at a window—thick silver curtains had been installed over all the windows in Air Force One to prevent injury by flash blindness, should any more nuclear warheads explode nearby. He felt helpless, overwhelmed. He and a handful of military and government advisers were locked up in an airplane, flying over the ocean, far away from the capital. Bits of information were dripping in, but for the most part they were disconnected from the rest of the country. They were cut off.

No, even that wasn't exactly true. They were *running*. They had abandoned the capital and were doing nothing more than fleeing to save their own lives, while the rest of America had to sit and take whatever the Russians were going to fire at them next.

He had faced many such unexpected disasters in his years as a special-operations officer in the U.S. Army. When an operation went wrong or when they were discovered, the team went into a sort of mental shock. They had planned and sometimes rehearsed many alternate and emergency-contingency missions, but when the shit hits the fan for real, the only plan they usually thought of was escape. It was confusing, chaotic, and, frankly, it didn't look very heroic. Weeks and sometimes months of planning gave way to a headlong, almost irrational fleeing instinct. Some of the more experienced troops remembered to tell the others important things—like which way to go, what to watch out for, and to remember to collect up things like maps, comm gear, weapons, and fallen comrades. But for everyone the bottom line is simple: Get out. Save yourself. Run.

Once they had escaped, rendezvoused, and inventoried themselves and their equipment, the very next thing they did was look to the team leaders, the officer and NCO in charge, for guidance and a plan of action. They didn't want anger, or vows of revenge, or signs of grief and sorrow—they wanted and needed leadership. That's what President Thomas Thorn had to provide—*now*. Even if he didn't know exactly what he wanted to do, he had to have the strength and courage to gather up his forces and get them moving.

Thorn drew in a deep breath, retrieved a bottle of water, took a deep swig, then turned back to the video teleconference camera, "facing" his team of advisers. "Analysis?" the president asked simply.

"I've got a very preliminary tally, Mr. President," General Richard Venti, chairman of the Joint Chiefs of Staff, responded. He took a deep breath, steeling himself to deliver a report he thought he would never, ever have to present:

"First to be hit was Clear Air Station in Alaska," he began. "Clear is . . . was . . . is a major radar and command-and-control base for the entire state of Alaska and the approaches into North America. The attack destroyed several radar systems, communications facilities, and a ground-based interceptor silo complex being built for the ballistic-missile defense force. Clear was the main ballistic-missile and aircraft-tracking station in the north, manned by approximately one thousand men and women. It was hit by a total of eight low-yield nuclear weapons, some with air-burst fuzes to destroy aboveground facilities, others with penetrating bunker-buster fuzes to destroy the ground-launched interceptor silos.

"Next was an attack against three major military bases in eastern Alaska, near Fairbanks," Venti went on. "Eielson Air Force Base is the home of the Three-fifty-fourth Fighter Wing, an F-16 and A-10 attack wing, but it also houses several components of the national missile-defense infrastructure, including the Alaskan headquarters for the system. Fort Wainwright and Fort Greely are Army installations housing several infantry units, but they also contain several key NMD facilities. The bases were hit by eight nuclear-tipped missiles."

"How many men and women at those bases, General?" the president asked woodenly, dreading the answer.

"About . . . approximately fifteen thousand in all four bases, sir," Venti responded.

"My . . . God . . ." Thomas Thorn felt his face redden, and tears flowed into his eyes. He could barely fathom such a number killed all at once. His voice cracked as he said, "Those *bastards* . . . !" He rested his head on his fingers, blankly staring straight ahead. After a few moments, with his head still bowed, he asked, "Do we know what kind of bombers they used?"

"The attacks against Alaska were accomplished by an unknown number of high-speed bombers, probably Tupolev-160s, code-named 'Blackjack,' " Air Force Chief of Staff General Charles Kuzner responded. "The Blackjack's standard strategic attack armament is sixteen AS-16 'Kickback' missiles, inertially guided, short range, high speed, similar to our obsolete AGM-69 short-range attack missiles that used to arm our strategic bombers. The bombers probably came in at treetop level all the way from Siberia. FAA and NORAD spotted them as they came ashore, but we couldn't get any more interceptors in the air fast enough." The president raised his head and stared accusingly into the camera, which prompted Air Force General Kuzner to blurt out, "Sir, we had already launched fighters from Eielson and Elmendorf because of the air-defense threat farther north and—"

"I'm not blaming anyone, General," Thorn said.

"We had four fighters rolling at Eielson when the base came under attack," Kuzner went on. "We had two more coming up from Elmendorf searching for them, but the electromagnetic pulses from the aboveground nuclear explosions were scrambling radar and communications for hundreds of miles. The F-15s couldn't see a thing, couldn't talk to anyone, couldn't do a damned thing to stop them. . . ."

"I said I'm not blaming you, General Kuzner," the president repeated. He could see Kuzner's Adam's apple bobbing up and down and his facial muscles slacken as he silently tried to deal with the horror—the horror that his forces might have prevented, had they been more prepared.

Venti waited until he could see the president look at him, silently asking him to continue, then cleared his throat and went on. "The first CONUS base to be hit was Minot Air Force Base, thirteen miles outside the city of Minot, North Dakota. That base is the home of the Fifth Bomb Wing, with twenty-four B-52H Stratofortress bombers and twelve KC-135R Stratotanker aerial-refueling tankers. Minot is also the home of the Ninety-first Space Wing, a Minuteman III missile wing, which comprises fifteen underground launch-control centers spread out over eighty-five hundred square miles of North Dakota. Each LCC controls ten LGM-30G Minuteman intercontinental ballistic missiles; in compliance with the START II treaty, each Minuteman has been downgraded from three independently targeted warheads to just one W78 nuclear warhead. We have detected direct hits on the base itself and several hits near the LCCs, but we don't yet know how many were knocked out."

"What about the base?"

"Unknown yet, sir," Venti responded somberly. "It took two direct hits."

"How many personnel on that base?"

"About . . . about five thousand military." Left unsaid was the obvious fact that perhaps two to four times that many military dependents and civilians living near the base could have perished.

"My God," the president breathed. He could scarcely believe that this was happening—and yet he reminded himself that the death toll had not even *begun* to be calculated. "What about the city?"

"A few reports of damage, a few casualties, but it appears the city itself was not affected."

"Thank God."

"The attacks on the continental U.S. appear to have been done by Tupolev-95 Bear bombers, launching very long-range AS-19 hypersonic missiles, code-named 'Koala,'" Venti said. "The Bear bombers are not supersonic, but their range is almost twice that of the Blackjack bomber. Several Bear bombers were intercepted and shot down over Canada by Canadian air-defense forces."

"AS-19—isn't that the same missile supposedly used over Uzbekistan?" Vice President Busick asked.

"Yes, sir," Secretary of Defense Goff said. "Apparently the attack against our CIA station in Uzbekistan was an operational test launch."

"Oh, shit . . ."

"Next to be hit was Grand Forks Air Force Base, sixteen miles west of the city of Grand Forks, North Dakota," Venti went on. "Grand Forks is the headquarters of the new

U.S. National Missile Defense Command, the agency that will control our ballistic-missile defense forces. The base also has a reserve nuclear-weapon storage facility that houses approximately four hundred and forty Minuteman-missile warheads, air-launched cruise-missile warheads, and B61 and B83 nuclear bombs, all in secure storage. It was hit by a single Russian cruise missile with great accuracy. It's possible the direct casualty count here is very small, although that doesn't take into account the fallout and contamination from the warheads that were not incinerated in the blast. The base was also home to the Three-nineteenth Air Refueling Wing, with twenty-two KC-135R tankers."

The president could do nothing but shake his head, almost overwhelmed by the enormity of this disaster. The effect of the fallout—dirt and debris bombarded by gamma radiation, making it radioactive, then carried aloft by the force of the blast, spreading over hundreds of thousand of square miles by high-altitude winds, then falling back to Earth—was something to which very little attention had been paid since the collapse of the Soviet Union and the end of the Cold War. Thorn remembered the civil-defense exercises he'd participated in as a child, and fallout was one of those fearsome things that caused nightmares in impressionable young children. Now they had to face it for real—and he found he was still scared of the harm it might cause.

"Next was Malmstrom Air Force Base, just six miles east of Great Falls, Montana," Venti went on. "The Three-forty-first Space Wing there deploys two hundred Minuteman III missiles in twenty LCCs spread out over twenty-three thousand square miles of Montana. The base itself, which does not have an operating runway, did not appear to be hit. Unfortunately, the missile-silo fields surround the city of Great Falls on three sides, and we have detected explosions all around the city. It's possible casualties could be relatively small here, too, but it's too early to tell.

"Next was Ellsworth Air Force Base, twelve miles east of Rapid City, South Dakota. Ellsworth is the home of the Twenty-eighth Bomb Wing, a B-1B Lancer-bomber base. It was hit by a single missile. This target is somewhat unusual, in that all the other places targeted by the Russians were related to nuclear warfighting—Ellsworth's B-1 bombers were made nonnuclear eight years ago to conform to Strategic Arms Reduction Treaty limits. Although it's possible to make them capable of carrying nuclear weapons, it would take many months to do it, and it would greatly downgrade our conventional bombing capability. This signals a flaw in the Russians' intelligence matrix— either they forgot that we made the B-1s nonnuclear or they thought we were about to turn them back into nuclear bombers."

"Which is precisely what we should be doing, sir," Kuzner interjected, "along with the aircraft in flyable storage. As soon as we convert them and train crews to man them, we should put them on alpha alert."

"I have no intention of putting nuclear-loaded bombers back on alert, General," President Thorn said. "Those days are over."

"With all due respect, Mr. President, it looks to me like those days are back again," Kuzner said bitterly. "Without the ICBMs we have no choice but to put every aircraft we can back on nuclear alert—not just the bombers but every tactical jet capable of carrying a thermonuclear weapon."

"General Kuzner . . ."

"Mr. President, we can't waste any time on this. It'll take four to eight weeks to recertify a new B-1 aircraft with positive-control switches and devices for nuclear weapons, plus twenty to thirty weeks to train a new aircrew and forty to sixty weeks to train a new maintenance technician. We need to—"

"That's enough, General," Thorn said sternly. "We'll discuss this when the time comes."

"Will we? Or are you just going to let another six thousand airmen on one of my bases die?"

"I said *that's enough,* General," Thorn snapped. He noticed that neither Vice President Busick, Secretary of State Goff, or Joint Chiefs chairman General Venti attempted to shut Kuzner down—they wanted him to go off, and they wanted to see how Thorn would handle it. "I assure you, when the time comes, we'll plan an appropriate response and use every weapon in our arsenal to implement the plan. In the meantime I want to hear what we've lost and what we might have left before I start loading nuclear weapons on bombers again. Is that clear, General?" Kuzner said nothing and responded with the faintest of nods. Thorn noticed this and gave Kuzner a stern glare but decided not to argue further. "General Venti, continue your report."

"Yes, sir. Next was Francis E. Warren Air Force Base, adjacent to the city of Cheyenne, Wyoming. F. E. Warren is Twentieth Air Force headquarters, responsible for all of America's land-launched intercontinental ballistic missiles, and is also the home of the Ninetieth Space Wing, which controls one hundred and fifty Minuteman ICBMs. One cruise missile hit on the base itself—we don't know exactly where yet. Most of the other missiles were targeted on the fifteen launch-control centers spread out over almost thirteen thousand square miles of Wyoming, Colorado, and Nebraska.

"The next target was Whiteman Air Force Base, located in a relatively rural area of western Missouri, about forty-five miles east of Kansas City. Whiteman is the home of the Five-oh-ninth Bomb Wing, with nineteen B-2A Spirit stealth bombers and fourteen KC-135R tankers, plus an OA-10 Thunderbolt II close-air-support fighter wing. Two Russian warheads hit the base itself. Again, approximately four to five thousand personnel were stationed at Whiteman.

"The last target was Offutt Air Force Base, eight miles south of Omaha, Nebraska. Offutt has the Fifty-fifth Wing, which controls all of the nation's strategic electronic reconnaissance and electronic command-and-control aircraft, and of course it is the headquarters of U.S. Strategic Command, the Joint Intelligence Center, the Air Force Weather Agency, and the Pentagon's National Airborne Operations Center—all important military agencies necessary in planning and executing strategic combat missions, such as what we would employ if we fought a nuclear conflict with Russia. The base was hit by at least four warheads."

"Military contingent at Offutt?" the president asked woodenly.

Venti hesitated, swallowed, then responded, "Over eight thousand, sir."

"*Jee*-zus," Vice President Busick exclaimed.

"There was one clean miss, sir—unfortunately, it could be the greatest disaster of the attack," Venti said. "Two warheads from one missile were apparently targeted for the weapon-storage facility at Fairchild Air Force Base near Spokane, Washington, which stores approximately five hundred nuclear gravity bombs, and warheads for cruise missiles, naval missiles, and torpedoes. The missile fell short and hit outside the city. No specific casualty reports yet, but damage is extensive.

"DSP reports a total of sixty-three explosions in the United States," Venti summarized. "Thirty-one warheads targeted against Minuteman III launch-control centers, obviously intended to prevent the missiles from being launched; sixteen against ballistic-missile defense installations; ten warheads targeted against nuclear-capable bomber bases and weapon-storage facilities; and six against strategic command-and-control bases, mostly involving nuclear warfighting. The Air Warning Center tracked over fifty missiles inbound on the attack against the CONUS, so perhaps as many as ten Russian cruise missiles malfunctioned and failed to detonate; one missile malfunctioned but its warheads did detonate, with disastrous results."

"Still no contact with anyone at STRATCOM?" the president asked.

"No, sir—it looks like Offutt took a direct hit with three warheads," General Venti said. "The airfield took one, and two hit the underground command center. No word yet if anyone survived. One warhead exploded north of the city of Bellevue—damage and casualty estimates are not in yet. All of the warheads used in these attacks were very small, perhaps one or two kilotons—less than a tenth the size of the bomb that was dropped on Hiroshima."

"What are the chances anyone survived at STRATCOM?"

"The command center was designed to take the shock and overpressure from a one-megaton warhead," Venti responded. "Many of the warheads used on this attack were designed to explode deep underground. It's very possible anyone inside the underground facility could have survived, if the complex was sealed up and fully disconnected from all external power and air in time. Same with the Minuteman-missile launch facilities. They are built on shock absorbers that are designed to survive tremendous overpressure. But they can't survive inside the fireball. If the earth and the facility shielding couldn't stop the fireball from forming underground, they couldn't make it."

"Just one aircraft made it away from Offutt?"

"One E-4B Airborne Operations Center, which was on alert at the time. They have checked in and are fully functional, although they do not have a complete battle staff. Rear Admiral Jerrod Richland is the battle-staff director. Although it does not have a complete crew, it can do all the command-and-control functions of the STRATCOM command center. No other aircraft made it off in time."

"So I can still talk to our subs and military headquarters?" the president asked. "I still have control of the nuclear warheads?"

"The E-4 is a global communications platform, able to communicate directly with any civilian or military person on planet Earth with a radio receiver or computer—it took over for the old Strategic Air Command EC-135 'Looking Glass' aircraft, which were designed to 'mirror' operations in SAC's underground command center," Venti responded. "The E-6B is a communications aircraft, designed to communicate with military units and ballistic-missile submarines deep under the ocean, but the difference is that the B-model can format and send execution messages to nuclear forces and can also monitor and launch land-based ballistic missiles."

"Can't I do all that from Air Force One?" the president asked.

"You can communicate easily with the E-4 and E-6 aircraft and issue orders to them and to any military command centers and government operations centers; you can also break in on civil television and radio frequencies to speak with the American people," Venti explained, "but Air Force One was not designed as an airborne military command post, only as an airborne White House. You cannot actually launch a nuclear strike yourself."

"So do I have control of our nuclear forces or not?" the president asked, struggling to keep his head clear through the enormous jumble of information he was absorbing. "Exactly what am I left with here?"

"You can issue orders to the ballistic nuclear submarine force at any time through coded messages to the E-6A TACAMO aircraft that are airborne over the Atlantic and Pacific Oceans," chimed in Admiral Charles Andover, Chief of Naval Operations, who was back in the National Military Command Center at the Pentagon. "The E-6A's job is to talk with the boomers while submerged with extremely low-frequency transmitters, and that network is still in place and operational."

"We issued a change in posture and DEFCON—"

"So the boomers know that tensions are high," Andover said. "Under DEFCON One and a Posture Red, the boomers will proceed to their launch positions and wait. After several days, if they don't receive a 'withhold' or 'termination' message, they'll launch." Andover saw the concern in President Thorn's face and added quickly, "That is the procedure under these circumstances, sir. In case an attack completely wipes out the leadership, under DEFCON One the subs are authorized to launch if they don't hear from us again. It ensures maximum stealth and maximum deterrent effect—the subs don't have to expose themselves to enemy forces just to receive another execution message, and the Russians know they can't completely destroy our most survivable nuclear forces just by killing the president."

"What else do we have left?"

"We don't know how many land-based ICBMs we have left yet," General Venti responded. "With STRATCOM and Twentieth Air Force headquarters destroyed, the U.S. Space Command will need to hook into alternate communications lines to assess the status of the individual Minuteman launch-control centers and the weapons themselves. That should be done shortly."

"If any survived, can we control those missiles?"

"The B-model Mercury aircraft should be able to take control of the ICBMs, sir," Venti said. "Stand by one, sir." He studied his status-of-forces report for a moment, then said, "The E-6Bs are based at Tinker Air Force Base in Oklahoma City. Normally, they embark a battle staff at Offutt and then disperse to various locations around the United States. The relief aircraft was destroyed at Offutt, but the alert E-6B was dispersed to ground alert at Naval Air Station Dallas, and it launched as soon as the air-defense alert was sounded. They'll fly to their monitoring-and-control orbit over Wyoming and try to make contact with the launch-control centers to find out how many of our land-based missiles made it."

Venti nodded to an off-camera screen. "As far as the bomber fleet goes: If you'll look at the DSP satellite readouts, sir, you'll see that three very critical bases were destroyed: Minot Air Force Base in North Dakota, Ellsworth Air Force Base in South Dakota, and Whiteman Air Force Base in Missouri," he went on. "We don't know how many bombers based at those locations survived. This leaves just one B-52 wing at Barksdale, near Shreveport, Louisiana, capable of executing a nuclear strike."

"How many bombers are based there?"

"Eighteen, sir."

"*That's it?* That's all the heavy bombers we have left?"

"Those are all the nuclear-capable bombers we have left, sir," Venti said. "There may be other surviving bombers that were airborne at the time of the attack. General Kuzner, what other forces do we have available?"

"We have just one base with B-1B Lancer long-range bombers left—Dyess Air Force Base just outside Abilene, Texas," Kuzner responded. "It has about twenty aircraft, plus their air-refueling tankers. However, we deployed four of Ellsworth's B-1 bombers to Andersen Air Force Base on Guam and six to Diego Garcia in the Indian Ocean as part of a contingency fast-strike and naval surface action group air support force for the Middle East and Asia. So it appears we have a total of about thirty B-1 bombers left. We also have another twenty to thirty B-1 bombers in flyable storage, which is the most ridiculous oxymoron ever invented—most of those planes would take months to make flyable, and some will *never* fly again.

"Keep in mind, sir, that B-1s cannot carry nuclear weapons without significant and lengthy work. However, they can now carry cruise missiles—they have always had the capability of carrying cruise missiles but were prevented from doing so by the START treaty. I think it's safe to say that all treaties with the Russians are null and void at this point."

"*I* will inform *you* about which treaties are in force and which are null and void, General Kuzner," President Thorn snapped.

"Of course," Kuzner went on angrily, ignoring the president's remark, "we've converted so many nuclear cruise missiles to conventional-warheads-only that there aren't enough for the B-1s to carry. Barksdale lost all of their ALCMs and has only enough advanced cruise missiles to equip its own fleet of B-52s—"

"General Kuzner, go get yourself a cup of coffee," General Venti said, and he reached over and punched a button that deactivated Kuzner's video-teleconference camera. He turned back to his own camera. "I apologize, Mr. President. He's a little upset. General Kuzner's family is from Cheyenne."

"We're all a little upset, General," Thorn said. "Have him resume his duties as soon as he can think and speak clearly. Understood?"

"Perfectly, sir."

"So what do we have left to retaliate against the Russians with, General?" Vice President Busick asked.

Venti added up the numbers. "At the present time, sir, we have six *Ohio*-class ballistic-missile submarines on patrol, three each in the Pacific and Atlantic, each loaded with twenty-four D-5 Trident II sea-launched ballistic missiles—SLBMs—each of which has five independently targeted nuclear warheads," he said. "We have another four subs that can be deployed in a short amount of time."

"Where are the other subs?"

"Undergoing extensive overhauls, sir. Each overhaul takes about a year."

"What sort of targets?"

"On day-to-day patrol, each SLBM has target coordinates only for ice packs," Andover responded. "That's a safety measure set in case of accidental or terrorist launch. But when we changed the DEFCON level, the crews would have changed to normal SIOP targets—military bases, command-and-control facilities, and major lines of communications."

"You mean cities?"

"Yes, sir—telephone and data-switching stations, power plants, gas and oil pipelines and distribution systems, highways, railroads, ports—any civilian infrastructure that could support sustained military operations," Andover said. "The goal is to eliminate Russia's ability to fight an intercontinental war."

"Even though it obviously means greater civilian casualties?"

"We don't specifically target civilians. We don't attack cities or towns indiscriminately," Venti said.

"What other nuclear forces do we have left that we know about?" the president asked.

"We have fifteen heavy bombers that can be generated for nuclear strike missions, plus two more undergoing depot-level maintenance and one in extended local-level maintenance status—meaning it's the 'hangar queen,' being used for spare parts until more come in.

"*Fifteen bombers?* That's it?" the president exclaimed. "My God!"

"And the thirty surviving B-1s are not nuclear capable," Venti reminded him. "The only long-range nuclear air-attack forces left are the eighteen B-52s left at Barksdale, plus any other bombers that were airborne or deployed during the attack. We think only two B-2 stealth bombers survived. That could leave us with about twenty nuclear-capable long-range bombers.

"We do have other forces capable of delivering nuclear weapons, but it will take time to generate those forces, and they're not as survivable as the heavies," Venti went on. "As I mentioned, there are about thirty B-1B bombers that can be converted back to carrying nuclear weapons. The Air Force also has about one hundred and seventy-five F-15E Strike Eagle tactical fighter-bombers that are capable of delivering nuclear weapons, based at six locations in the continental U.S. and Alaska—unfortunately, we closed the F-15E base at RAF Lakenheath in England and brought all of the nuclear weapons stored in Europe back to the U.S. Although no warships except the ballistic-missile subs carry nuclear weapons, ships can be quickly supplied with nuclear cruise missiles and gravity bombs—the F/A-18 Hornet carrier-based fighter can deliver nuclear weapons."

"I think it would be wise to disperse those bombers and any other bombers that survived around the country," Secretary of Defense Goff said, "to make it harder for the Russians to attack them. If they want to go after bomber bases, they'll be next."

"I sent a message to Air Combat Command to suggest exactly that," Venti said. "We can phone or instant-message all the commanders from the NAOC, just as you can from your phones and computers aboard Air Force One. General Muskoka of ACC is on his way back to Langley. He *was* en route to Offutt Air Force Base for a meeting with STRAT-COM, NORAD, Space Command, First Air Force, and Eighth Air Force commanders to discuss reestablishing a tighter air-defense network in the continental U.S. and perhaps putting the bomber force back on twenty-four/seven alert." He paused, swallowed, then added, "I've received no response from General Samson of Eighth Air Force, who is the commander of the bomber forces. His staff thinks he had just arrived at Offutt when the attack took place. Air Force has also not heard from General Shepard of NORAD, General Wollensky of Space Command, General Craig of First Air Force, and General Houser of Air Intelligence Agency. They may have been at Offutt as well."

"Oh, Christ," Goff breathed. "That's most of the Air Force's senior commanders."

"We need replacements for the dead and missing generals, and we need them *fast*," the president said. "Then I need to talk to them right away. I can't even begin to try to plan a response to this attack before I know what we have and what *they* have."

"My staff is working on all that as we speak, Mr. President," General Venti said. "I've already been in contact with the deputy commander of the Nine-sixty-sixth Information Warfare Wing, Colonel Trevor Griffin. He's taking a military jet from San Antonio and will be at the Pentagon in a few hours. The STRATCOM ops detachment here at the Pentagon can brief us on the status of strategic forces anytime you're ready."

"Have Griffin contact me as soon as he's briefed, General," Thorn said. "What about civil defense and securing the blast sites?"

"The governors of each affected state and several of the neighboring states have activated their national guards," Secretary Goff responded, "and we're working with the Federal Emergency Management Agency and U.S. Northern Command to secure the impact sites and provide relief services. It's too early to tell the extent of contamination—the weapons were detonated underground but were extremely small, so the hazard of radioactive fallout might be minimal."

"Thank God," the president murmured. He rubbed his eyes wearily. "All right, everyone, my first order of business is to find out what we lost and what we have left. I can't say much of anything to the American people or to the world right now, except that I'm alive and our capital and government are still functioning. But very soon everyone's going to wonder what our first move will be. That's what I need to figure out. We'll talk again in one hour, or sooner if conditions warrant." And the connection was broken.

BATTLE MOUNTAIN AIR RESERVE BASE
A short time later

"Nice to see you again, Tagger," Patrick McLanahan said. He was in the Battle Management area of the command center, speaking to Colonel Trevor Griffin at Air Intelligence

Agency headquarters via a secure video teleconference. Patrick McLanahan was busily checking the streams of data being fed to Battle Mountain from the Seventieth Intelligence Wing, Fort Meade, Maryland, which had several technicians and experts poring over intelligence-satellite imagery recently received from space. "Glad to have you running the show there now."

"I just wish it hadn't happened because of a damned Russian sneak attack," Griffin said.

"We'll take care of that problem shortly, Tagger," Patrick said. "I damned well guarantee it." There was then a brief moment of silence as they thought about the devastation that had come down on Offutt, Minot, Ellsworth, Whiteman, and all the other targets of Russian cruise missiles. America had suffered its worst-ever attack on its own soil—and now it was their job to find a way to give the president of the United States some options other than initiating a nuclear response.

"The data feed is looking good," Patrick said to break the reverie.

"This stuff is hot off the presses," Trevor Griffin said. "The last NIRTSat overflight was just five minutes ago. Man, you guys have the best toys."

They did indeed, Patrick thought. The four-satellite NIRTSat—"Need It Right This Second" satellite—constellation launched just a few hours ago by Jon Masters was speeding over southern Siberia, photographing hundreds of thousands of square miles of territory with ultrabroadband radar and high-resolution imaging infrared cameras every twenty minutes, then instantly beaming any returns back to Battle Mountain. The images were analyzed by comparing their size, density, and heat signatures to a catalog of known military objects.

"Okay, guys, here's what we got," Tagger began. "Let's start with the bombers. The Russians took some serious hits with their bomber fleet on their attack, but they were very effective and bit a big chunk out of our asses. They easily have over a hundred and fifty or so planes left, spread out across ten bases. They lost about a quarter of their fleet in the initial attack, but it's not slowing them down one bit. It definitely looks like they're reloading and rearming and getting ready for another swipe—and this time they'll have an easier time of it. Their next attack could well reach every base and every government office in North America.

"Their tanker tactics are very impressive—they're using a level of organization and sophistication that equals ours," Tagger observed. "They launch the bombers with maximum ordnance and minimal fuel, refuel them with unit tankers as they cruise-climb to altitude, then top them off with task-force tankers from Yakutsk before they begin their launch run. They're tanking all the way to feet-dry, and they have a huge reserve. By the time the bombers return to Siberia, the tankers have loaded up at Yakutsk, and they go out and meet the bombers and just repeat the whole process back to landing. Questions?"

Patrick said nothing, but he nodded slowly as he studied the satellite imagery of the bases Griffin had just briefed.

"Let's take a look at the Russian land-based missiles now," Tagger went on. "The SS-18s at Aleysk and Uzhur are definitely warmed up and ready to go. Uzhur has the largest deployment, with four launch-control centers each controlling twelve silos. Aleysk has just two launch-control centers.

"Patrick, you asked about the composition of the launch-control centers. The Russians did away with modernizing their SS-18 LCCs in favor of improving their mobile-missile survivability. They assumed we were going to smack their LCCs hard, so they emphasized fast-reaction silo launches versus the idea of riding out an attack and then launching. So the answer is, yes, a weapon like a Longhorn with bunker-busting technology—a hardened penetrating nose cap, delayed fuze, and booster motor—along with an enhanced-yield but nonnuclear payload such as a thermium-nitrate warhead can, we believe, take out an SS-18 launch-control center. We just have to be sure that we get to them before they launch.

"The real trick has been the SS-25s," Trevor Griffin went on. "Those bastards are road-mobile, and they've had plenty of time to deploy. We took a chance and started checking out every known garrison location for the SS-25s, and I think we've hit pay dirt.

"The largest missile wing, Kansk, has forty-six units, but all of them relocated to their garrisons. Although they can still launch from a garrisoned position, we're hoping that's a sign of either equipment malfunctions or crew disillusionment. The smallest wing, Drovyanaya, hasn't even moved their missiles off the base yet—they're all in their security garages. Both of these wings are the most geographically isolated, so I think without a lot of adult supervision, the local commanders decide on their own whether to deploy their rovers or not. Looks like in these two cases they decided on very limited deployments.

"The other three missile wings are more difficult to surveille," Tagger admitted. "They dispersed their units quickly, and they're not using their garrisons as much— perhaps only a quarter of the units are in garrison locations. Barnaul, Novosibirsk, and Irkutsk's missiles are likely to escape. We can get the ones in the garrisons, but that still leaves over seventy units unaccounted for."

"We'll target the ones in the garrisons and hope we catch a break on the rest," Patrick said.

"We've got the garrisons covered," David said. "The SS-25s may be mobile, but in their garrisons they're detectable and stoppable, and out in the open they're still detectable and as vulnerable as a tree. StealthHawks fitted with ultrawide-band sensors can look inside the garrison shelters easily, and millimeter-wave radar and imaging infrared sensors can spot transporter-erector-launchers under foliage and hidden by camouflage."

"We definitely got a surprise here," Tagger went on. "We

weren't looking for them, but they popped up on our over-flights anyway: activity at the old SS-24 garrisons at Kras-noyarsk."

"What?" Patrick remarked. "SS-24s on the move?" The SS-24 "Scalpel" rail-mobile intercontinental ballistic missile was the weapon that changed the course of arms-limitation-treaty talks in the 1990s. The SS-24 was a copy of the American Peacekeeper ICBM, a long-range missile designed to carry ten independently targeted nuclear warheads to ranges out to ten thousand miles. Like the original Peacekeeper missile, the SS-24 was designed from the outset to travel on the national railway system, mixing in with Russia's substantial train population and making targeting virtually impossible. At the beginning of the 1990s, Russia had 150 three-missile units deployed throughout the country. They could be launched anywhere with just a few minutes' warning time, and the warheads they carried were the most accurate carried by any Russian ballistic missile.

The second Strategic Arms Reduction Treaty signed between the United States and Russia was supposed to eliminate the long-range rail-mobile SS-24 and Peacekeeper missiles, and to make all land-based ICBMs carry only single rather than multiple warheads. The United States deactivated its last Peacekeeper missile in 2002 and destroyed its silos; the Russians were supposed to transfer the rail-mobile SS-24s to older SS-18 silos and make them carry single warheads only.

"Obviously the Russians have been cheating on START II," Tagger summarized. "I think we might have as many as twelve SS-24s on the move."

"Dave?"

"The SS-24s are the biggest threats," Luger said. "They have the longest range, carry more warheads, and are more accurate than anything else the Russians have." He sat back in his seat and finally shook his head. "It's not going to work, Muck," he said. "Even before we found the SS-24s, we were pushing it—now I don't think we have a chance. Even if we gain all of the Air Force's surviving bombers, we just can't surge enough airframes to drive ten thousand miles and take all these locations at once. Some will leak through."

Patrick remained silent for a few more moments, then turned to Luger. "I know how to surge our planes," he said. "I need Rebecca, Daren, Hal, and the entire staff ready to do some planning—but I think I know how we can do it. I'll need to speak with General Venti in about an hour." He nodded his thanks to Trevor Griffin, then asked, "Anything else, Tagger?"

"Sure," Griffin said matter-of-factly. His face broke out with a sly, boyish smile. "Want to know where Anatoliy Gryzlov is now?"

"*What?* You *know* where Gryzlov is?"

"Air Intelligence Agency routinely tracks his command posts and monitors radio and data traffic from Russia's forty-seven various alternate military command centers scattered around the country," Tagger said. "Gryzlov is crafty. He launched two sets of airborne military command posts before the attacks began, and there's a lot of confusing and conflicting radio traffic, meant as diversions. But I think we've pinpointed his actual location: Ryazan', at an underground military facility next to a deactivated military base, about a hundred forty miles southeast of Moscow. We noticed shortly after the base closed that a substantial amount of work was being done on Oksky Reserve, a game and forest preserve adjacent to the old military base; when we saw a lot of dirt being moved but didn't see any structures being built aboveground, we suspected the Russians of building either an underground weapon-storage facility or a command center. Gryzlov also happens to be from Ryazan' Oblast."

"How certain are you that he's there?"

"As certain as we can be, boss."

"Which is . . . ?"

Tagger shrugged. "Sixty percent sure," he admitted.

Patrick nodded, thankful for Griffin's honesty. "Thanks for the info, Tagger," he said. "Let's concentrate on nailing those ICBMs, and then maybe we'll get a shot at the general himself. But I *want* those missiles—especially the SS-24s."

ABOARD THE E-4B NATIONAL AIRBORNE OPERATIONS CENTER AIRCRAFT
Hours later

"McLanahan is on a secure link, sir," General Richard Venti said to the secretary of defense, Robert Goff. Along with them were members of the Joint Chiefs of Staff or their designees—all of the chiefs did not make it on board the NAOC before it departed Washington.

"Oh, brother!" Goff exclaimed. "Wonder what in hell he wants? Where is he?"

"Battle Mountain, sir."

"I should have known," Goff said. He wearily massaged his temples, but nodded. Venti pointed to the communications technician, and moments later Patrick McLanahan appeared on the video-teleconference monitor, wearing a flight suit. Goff recognized most of the officers seated with him: David Luger, the new commander of McLanahan's old unit; Rebecca Furness, the commander of the high-tech bomber wing at Battle Mountain Air Reserve Base; her ops officer, Daren Mace; and one of Furness's squadron commanders, the one in charge of the modified B-52 bombers, Nancy Cheshire. "I see you are alive and well, General," Goff said.

"That's correct, sir," Patrick replied.

"I also see you're in flight gear. I hope it's just for convenience's sake, General. I believe you're no longer on flight status, pending the outcome of your court-martial."

Rebecca Furness looked at McLanahan in some surprise—obviously she hadn't heard *this* development. "I'll fly only if I'm ordered to do so, sir," McLanahan responded.

"That would be a first," Goff said dryly. "I don't have much time, General. What's on your mind?"

"Upon General Luger's authority, our attack and support forces are holding in secure survival orbits off the West Coast until we can determine what the Russians intend to do," Patrick replied. "We have a total of eight strike and six support aircraft airborne, plus five more strike aircraft and two support aircraft safe on the ground, operational and ready to go."

"That's good news, General," Goff said, "because right now you represent about one-third of America's surviving bomber force."

Luger's and Furness's faces turned blank in surprise, but Patrick's was as unflinching and stoic as ever. "We count two B-2As, two B-52Hs, and four B-1B bombers that survived the attacks on Whiteman, Minot, and Ellsworth," he said.

"How do you know that so quickly, General? We don't even have that information yet."

"The Air Battle Force routinely monitors all military aircraft movement, sir, especially the heavy bombers and tankers," Dave Luger said. "We keep up with where every aircraft is, even those that aren't active—in fact, we keep track of where every aircraft component and part is, right down to the tires. We build a lot of equipment from off-the-shelf parts and non-mission-ready airframes."

"Impressive," Goff muttered. "So what's the purpose of the call, General McLanahan?"

"Sir, I'm ready to take command of Eighth Air Force and begin a counteroffensive against the Russian Federation," Patrick said.

"I'm not in the mood for jokes, McLanahan," Goff said. "I've already picked officers to replace the men we lost in the attack. Besides, you're not in line to take command of anything."

"That's . . . not exactly true, sir," General Venti said.

"What are you talking about, General?"

"Sir, Patrick McLanahan was the senior wing commander of Air Intelligence Agency," Venti explained. "Upon the death of General Houser, Patrick assumes command of Air Intelligence Agency—"

"What?"

"—and he also becomes the deputy commander in charge of intelligence of several units and agencies, including Air Combat Command, Space Command, the Air Force, and U.S. Strategic Command, and even reports to the National Security Council, the Joint Chiefs, and the White House."

"Not unless *I* say so!" Goff snapped. "I'll put someone else in that position—someone who's not about to be court-martialed!"

"As commander of Air Intelligence Agency, General McLanahan is an ex officio deputy commander of Eighth Air Force, in charge of intelligence operations," Venti went on. "And since there was no vice commander, the senior ranking deputy commander takes charge."

"McLanahan."

"Yes, sir. And as commander of Eighth Air Force, McLanahan also becomes a deputy commander in charge of bomber forces for U.S. Strategic Command."

"Wait a minute—are you saying that McLanahan is going to advise the STRATCOM commander on the bomber force—or what's left of it?" Admiral Andover asked. "With all due respect, sir, you can't allow that to happen. No one in the Navy trusts McLanahan. Sir, McLanahan is the *last* guy you should choose to represent the Air Force or the bomber force in STRATCOM."

Goff was thunderstruck—but not for long. He thought for a moment, then waved a hand at Andover. "I don't trust him either, Admiral. But he saw the signs and called this conflict a long time ago, and he was frighteningly accurate." He paused, then turned to General Venti. "Dick, you know I can make all this hocus-pocus chain-of-command shit go away like *that*. What are your thoughts on this?"

"Technically, McLanahan should take command because of his rank, but General Zoltrane does have more command and headquarters experience than McLanahan, and I think he knows the force better," Venti admitted. "Charlie Zoltrane would definitely be the better choice. We're at war here, sir—we need someone with true command experience to take charge of the strategic nuclear air fleet."

Goff thought for a moment, then nodded. "I agree. Dick, direct General Kuzner to order Zoltrane to take command of Eighth Air Force, and have him report to us via secure video teleconference as soon as possible," Goff ordered. "He'll have to reorganize his staff and line units on the fly. Then have Kuzner direct Colonel Griffin to take command of Air Intelligence Agency, and have him prepare to brief the leadership by video teleconference."

"Sir, I have a way to downgrade or perhaps even effectively neutralize Russia's strategic nuclear forces that might threaten North America," McLanahan interjected. Robert Goff paused and swallowed, but he was going to repeat his order to upchannel his plan through the proper chain of command, when McLanahan added, "I can set it in motion in less than thirty-six hours—and I can do it without using nuclear weapons."

"I'm going to be perfectly honest with you, General McLanahan: No one, including myself, trusts you," Robert Goff said seriously, ignoring McLanahan's words. "You have certainly set a record for how many times a line officer can be busted, driven out of office, demoted, and charged with insubordination, refusing to follow orders, and conduct unbecoming. I think you have even managed at your young age to eclipse Bradley James Elliott as the biggest uniformed pain in the ass in U.S. history."

"Sir, I'm not asking for a leadership position—let Zoltrane and Griffin keep on doing what they know best," Patrick said. "But put me back in the field where I belong—here, in charge of the Air Battle Force."

"Why should I do that, General?" Goff asked.

"Sir, neither General Zoltrane nor the two surviving bomb-wing commanders have any experience with the Megafortresses based out here at Battle Mountain. Generals Furness, Luger, and myself, along with Colonels Mace and Cheshire, are the only ones capable of employing the weapon systems here. On the other hand, all of us have experience leading B-52, B-1, and B-2 bombers into combat."

"McLanahan, I don't have time for this. Put it in writing and submit it to—"

"Sir," General Venti said with a firmness that surprised the secretary of defense. He turned away from the camera, speaking directly to Goff as privately as he could in front of a camera. "Whatever you think of Patrick McLanahan, sir, may I remind you that he *predicted* exactly what has happened," Venti said. "He saw the signs and wasn't afraid to make the call. We all saw the same data, but we never allowed ourselves to believe it would happen."

"So what, General?"

"At the very least, sir, McLanahan deserves a listen," Venti said. "We're threatening to put the guy in prison—I wouldn't have blamed him if he went home, packed up his family, and hightailed it up to Lake Tahoe. But he didn't. He made it to Battle Mountain, got into a flight suit, and put a plan together to deal with this emergency."

Venti was right, Goff thought, but he wasn't ready to admit it. He turned to the chief of naval operations. "Admiral Andover?"

"I've made my opinions known already, sir—McLanahan is a menace and should not even be in a military uniform, let alone being considered to lead a military unit into combat,"

Andover responded. "Sir, give me a few days and I'll brief a combined-forces operation—"

"How many Russian targets can the fleet hold at risk without using nuclear weapons, Admiral?" Goff asked. "A couple dozen? A couple hundred—as long as the shooters can safely move within a few hundred miles of the shore? And how much time do you think we have?"

"We've got as much time as we need, sir—and we sure as hell have enough time to consider options other than sending Patrick McLanahan. And I damned well know that the U.S. Navy can put many more targets at risk than one Reserve unit can. And if a nuclear strike is necessary, the Navy can exercise that option, too—McLanahan can't."

"Sir, Battle Mountain's planes, the Megafortresses, are some of the most high-tech aircraft left in our arsenal," Venti went on. "They are designed for SEAD—suppression of enemy air defenses—and antiballistic-missile defense, but they also pack a considerable precision standoff attack capability. Although the unit itself is not operational and all of its aircraft are considered experimental, McLanahan's Air Battle Force and Furness's One-eleventh Attack Wing of the Nevada Air National Guard have proven themselves in combat many times, from United Korea to Libya to Central Asia to western Russia." He shrugged and added, "And no one else in the Air Force except General Terrill Samson knows much, if anything, about them—and Samson is apparently one of the casualties at Offutt."

Goff shook his head. He expected Venti, an Air Force general, to support his fellow blue-suiters. Most Joint Chiefs chairmen had biases toward their own services. "And I'm supposed to forget the fact that he disregards directives and busts the chain of command to suit himself?" Goff asked. He rubbed his eyes in exasperation. "Richard, McLanahan is a good guy, but I just can't trust him. He's the definition of 'loose cannon.' The president doesn't trust him. Even Gryzlov wants his head on a plate. Why on earth should I allow him back in uniform? Damn it, General, I sure as hell shouldn't allow him back at Battle Mountain, with access to all those fancy high-tech aircraft and weapons—God knows what he might do, or what he might be doing *right now!*"

Venti took a deep breath, ready to argue—but he couldn't. He found himself nodding agreement. "Sir, at least consider this: It'll take Zoltrane and Griffin a few hours to get up to speed and report in—and they won't have a plan ready until they can assemble their own battle staffs and pull packages off the shelf. Until we assess the status of the ICBM and bomber fleets, the only other option is the sea-launched nukes. Long before we have a plan, the subs will be in position—and the Russians know this."

"So?"

"Whatever the Russians will do next, sir, they'll do it before the boomers get into launch position," Venti said. "The sub bases in Washington State and Georgia, the remaining bomber bases, Europe, NATO, Washington, they'll all be at risk—unless you believe that the Russians really *will* stop?"

Goff's eyes unconsciously widened. "Do you think this could be the prelude to a wider attack?"

"I don't know, sir—but right now we're totally on the defensive until the subs get into launch position," Venti said. "The Russians have the complete advantage of surprise and position. We can't do much no matter where they move next. It could take us days or weeks to plan and organize a response by sea or a special-operations mission, and weeks to months to plan a ground offensive." He took another deep breath. "I see two options right now, sir: Listen to McLanahan's plan, or plan a strike using the subs in about forty-eight hours."

"A nuclear strike?" Goff asked.

Venti nodded. "But I don't think the president will authorize it," he said. "Do you, sir?" Goff responded with silence. "Then I recommend we hear what McLanahan has to say."

ONE HUNDRED FIFTY KILOMETERS NORTHEAST OF SHEMYA ISLAND, ALASKA
That same time

"Stand by for final launch run, crew," radioed the bombardier aboard the lead Tupolev-160 Blackjack bomber. "Final radar fix in progress, stand by for transfer-alignment maneuver. Radar to radiate . . . now."

The bombardier activated his radarscope, already preset to the proper range and tilt for the fastest and sharpest return—and there it was, right where he predicted it would be: the American island of Shemya, almost at the very end of the Aleutian Island chain. This little flat rock in the ocean was one of America's most important surveillance outposts: Its COBRA DANE radar could monitor each and every Russian land- and sea-launched ballistic-missile test fired into the Pacific instrumented target range, and electronic listening posts collected broadcasts from Russian and Chinese military bases half a world away. It was also a linchpin in America's new and highly illegal ballistic-missile defense system.

In short, it was going away—right now.

Although they had initiated their attacks on America's bases in Alaska hours ago, it had taken this long to fly back across the Bering Sea to get into position to strike this last but no less important target. After this, it was an easy cruise back to the air-refueling track to rendezvous with the tankers operating out of Yakutsk, and then an easy ride home.

The radar crosshairs were less than a hundred meters off the aimpoint—the COBRA DANE antenna itself—so the bombardier laid them back on, magnified the image to ensure they were on the right spot—the northernmost corner of the massive array—checked the aimpoint coordinates, and then pressed the RADAR FIX button. The precise radar fix, combined with GLONASS satellite-navigation signals, would help keep the Tu-160's inertial navigator properly aligned. Thirty seconds later the navigation computer dumped velocity, heading, and position information to the four remaining Kh-15 nuclear missiles in the forward bomb bay.

"Fix complete," he reported. "Stand by for TAL maneuver. Left turn, thirty degrees of bank, ten seconds . . . now." The pilot commanded the autopilot to accomplish the turn. The TAL, or transfer alignment maneuver, "exercised" the inertial-navigation system and allowed a known quantity of velocity readings to fine-tune it. "Hold heading for twelve seconds. . . . Good, now right turn, center up the heading bug. Remaining on this heading. Three minutes to launch point. TAL complete, all remaining missiles reporting ready for launch. Confidence is high."

The Tu-160 was traveling at one thousand kilometers per hour at an altitude of one hundred meters above the Bering Sea. His course would take him about a hundred kilometers north of Shemya, out of range of any Patriot surface-to-air missiles the Americans may have placed there. The American naval base at Adak Island had been closed for a few years now, but there was no use taking chances; besides, they had plenty of fuel to make it back to the refueling anchor and to the first alternate landing site if they couldn't make their refueling. They'd had training missions twice as long and many times more complex than this. But it was strange that the Americans didn't place defensive weapon systems around their own bases. Obviously, they thought themselves invincible to attack—even way out here along the Aleutian Islands, where Shemya was half as close to Russia as it was to Juneau, the Alaskan capital.

Russia had proved this day how very wrong the Americans were. America was *not* invincible. In fact, this attack was unbelievably easy. They had detected just two American fighters during their entire two-hour attack run into Alaska, and the fighters had zoomed right over them without locking on even for a second. True, the electromagnetic pulses created by the multiple nuclear detonations around Fairbanks had helped degrade their radar. But launching only two fighters for the *entire state of Alaska?* Didn't the United States have any love or respect for their forty-ninth state? Did they think so little of this big, beautiful, mineral-rich place that they chose not to defend it with every weapon system in their arsenal? Heading outbound toward Shemya was even easier, as if the Americans never even tried to look for them. Could they really be this completely disorganized?

The bombardier took a few radar sweeps of the ocean, scanning for American warships. Nothing straight ahead, just a few small vessels, probably fishing or patrol vessels—nothing with the size to suggest they had the surface-to-air missile capacity to threaten a Tupolev-160. "This is lead. You see that surface target at eleven o'clock, fifty kilometers?" the bombardier radioed.

"I see it," the bombardier aboard the number-two Tu-160 responded. "Less than twenty-five meters long, I'd say. Shaped like a trawler. No threat."

"We'll keep our distance anyway," the lead bombardier responded. But he did not alter his flight-plan routing. They would be at least five kilometers north of the sea target at their closest point—well out of range of Stinger or other shoulder-fired antiaircraft weapons, which were not very much of a threat to a Tupolev-160 anyway. "Two minutes to launch."

"Acknowledged. Search-radar contact only—no targeting radars."

"EWO?" the pilot radioed to the electronic-warfare officer. "Check those radar contacts."

"Search radars only," the electronic-warfare officer aboard the lead Tu-160 reported after double-checking his readouts. "Echo-band air-traffic control radar from Shemya,

X-ray band phased array search radar also from Shemya—the COBRA DANE long-range radar—and F-band search radar from just offshore, probably a surface-search radar from that trawler. No height finders."

"One minute to missile launch."

The pilot's voice sounded much more apprehensive. "Where's that trawler?" he asked.

"Eleven o'clock, thirty-two kilometers."

"And you say it's painting us with radar?"

"Search radar only, pilot," the EWO responded.

"Can he see us?"

"Probably."

"Then let's deviate around him," the pilot said. "Bombardier, give me a vector."

"Negative. Less than forty seconds to launch. Deviating might put us outside the footprint. Hold heading."

"If that trawler lights us up with a height finder, I want him blown out of the water," the pilot ordered.

"With a one-kiloton nuclear warhead? You want to nuke a little fishing boat with a ten-million-ruble nuclear missile?"

"Have number two target that trawler—he's got four missiles to spare. That's an order."

"Roger." On the interplane radio, the bombardier relayed the order from the flight commander. The number-two Blackjack's bombardier laid his radar crosshairs on the radar return, hit a button to engage the moving-target designation mode, waited thirty seconds for the crosshairs to drift off, then placed them back on the target. The attack computers automatically calculated the trawler's speed—less than ten knots—and computed a set of target coordinates for where the trawler would be at the end of the missile's very short flight time.

Not that it mattered much: A one-kiloton nuclear warhead would create an eight-cubic-kilometer hole in the ocean that would suck millions of kilos of seawater into it within seconds, crushing anything inside that was not already vaporized in the blast. The missile could miss by several kilometers and still destroy the little trawler.

"Stand by for missile launch," the lead bombardier reported. "Missile counting down . . . Doors coming open . . . Missile one away . . . Launcher rotating . . . Missile two away . . . Doors coming closed . . . All missiles away."

At this range it would take just over one minute for the first missile to hit. "Double-check curtain seals," the pilot ordered. The pilots made sure that the silver-and-lead-lined anti–flash blindness curtains covering the cockpit windows were closed and securely fastened in place. "Crew, sunglasses secure, dark helmet visors down, interior lights full bright." They turned the inside lights full bright so they could see their instruments through all the eye protection and to constrict their irises as much as possible. "Autopilot is off, climbing to one thousand meters. Prepare for—"

Just then the bombardier radioed, "Lost contact with missile one . . . Missile two still on track . . . Thirty seconds to second missile impact . . . twenty . . . Stand by for shock wave from first missile detonation . . . ten . . . Shit, I lost contact with the second missile. . . . Shock wave impact, *now*." There was nothing. "Stand by for shock wave from missile two. . . ."

"What happened, bombardier?" the pilot asked.

"Unknown. I just lost contact. . . . Shock wave coming up, *now*." Still nothing. "No detonation. I don't understand it, pilot. I had two good missiles until just before detonation, and then nothing."

The pilot started pulling off the anti–flash blindness curtains from his cockpit windscreen. "I'm going to look for a mushroom cloud or signs of detonation. Copilot, shield your eyes." The pilot gingerly opened his curtains a few centimeters. There was no sign of a nuclear explosion. "Nothing! What could have happened?"

"Want me to launch the last two missiles at Shemya?"

"We were supposed to save the last two for surface targets we'd encounter on our way back," the pilot reminded him, "and then save any unexpended weapons for contingencies." But Shemya was a very important target, he thought. "Have our wingman cancel his attack on that surface target and launch two missiles at Shemya—then we'll both have two missiles remaining. That's better than one plane having four left but being unable to launch."

"Acknowledged. Break. Two, this is lead, put a couple on Shemya. Our two missiles malfunctioned."

"Acknowledged. Changing to left-echelon formation." Since his missiles would be flying south, the number-two Blackjack bomber crossed over to the lead bomber's left side and prepared to launch two Kh-15 missiles at Shemya.

"Zagavn'at!" the pilot swore aloud. "How could we fuck up that bad?"

"We didn't do anything wrong, pilot," the bombardier said. "Who knows? Maybe the missile's electronics got beat up too badly during the long low-level cruising. Maybe the fuze malfunctioned."

"Any air defenses on Shemya?"

"None whatsoever," the electronic-warfare officer responded, puzzled.

"And even if there were, even a Patriot missile would have a hard time shooting down a Kh-15," the bombardier says. "The Kh-15 flies faster and lower than the Patriot can—"

"Uyobyvay!" the copilot suddenly swore. "What in hell was that?"

The pilot saw it too—a streak of blue-yellow flashed by the windscreen, so fast that it seemed like a beam of light— except the streak left a thin, white, steamy contrail. *"Was that a surface-to-air missile?"*

"I'm not picking up any uplink or height-finder radars," the electronic-warfare officer said immediately. "Scope's clear except for a surface-search radar at eleven o'clock, ten kilometers."

"That trawler is still painting us?"

"It's not a SAM radar, just a—"

At that instant the crew felt a tremendous *bang!* reverberate through the aircraft—very quick and sharp, almost like clear-air turbulence. "Station check, crew!" the pilot ordered as he snapped his oxygen mask in place. "Everyone on oxygen."

"Offense in the green."

"Defense in the green."

"Copilot is in the— Wait, I've got a tank low-pressure warning in the fuselage number-two fuel tank," the copilot reported as he continued scanning his instruments. "Pressure is down to ten kilopascals. . . . Fuel quantity is dropping, too. I'm initiating transfer to the main body and transferring wing main fuel to the outboards."

"Any other malfunctions?"

"Negative, just the fuel pressure and—"

At that moment there was another sharp *bang!* The air inside the cabin turned instantly cloudy, as if a thick fog had appeared out of nowhere. The pilot felt air gush out of his nostrils and mouth so loudly that he barked like a dog. "What was that? Station check again! Report!"

"My God!" the electronic-warfare officer screamed. *"Oh, my God . . . !"*

"What is it? Report!"

"Igor . . . the bombardier . . . God, he's been hit . . . Jesus, *his entire body exploded!"* the EWO screamed over the intercom. "I felt that second thud, and I looked over, and . . . oh, God, it looks like his body was blown in half from head to toe. Something came up from the bottom of the aircraft and blew Igor into pieces!"

"Copilot . . . ?"

"Explosive decompression, two alternators and generators offline, and I feel a tremor in the fuselage," the copilot reported.

"I have the airplane," the pilot said. "I'm turning north."

He keyed the mike button. "Two, this is lead, I think we've been hit by ground fire. We're taking evasive action north."

"We're thirty seconds to missile launch, lead," the second Blackjack bomber pilot responded. "We're not picking up any threats. We'll stay on the missile run and rendezvous when—"

And the radio went dead.

The pilot strained forward in his seat to look as far to his left as he could—and he saw the second Blackjack bomber start a tail-over-head forward spin, flames tearing through the bomb bay, its burning wings breaking off and cartwheeling across the sky. *"Oh, shit, two just got hit!"* he cried out. "He's on fire!" He shoved his control stick farther right. "We're getting out of here!"

"He's turning, Top—don't let him get away," Hal Briggs radioed.

"I can see that, sir," Sergeant Major Chris Wohl said. He was standing atop the MV-32 Pave Dasher tilt-rotor aircraft as it bobbed in the choppy and gently rolling Bering Sea, sixty miles north of Shemya Island. Wohl, along with one more commando in Tin Man battle armor and eight more commandos in advanced ballistic infantry armor seated in the cargo compartment, had raced across the Bering Sea to a spot where they predicted they could intercept any Russian attack aircraft returning from Alaska that might launch a similar attack against Shemya. The MV-32 crew then deployed its emergency-survival flotation bags, which resembled a gigantic raft surrounding the entire lower half of the tilt-jet aircraft, and set the aircraft down on the Bering Sea.

Wohl smoothly tracked the target through his Tin Man electronic visor display, which showed the Russian Blackjack bomber in a steep right turn. The display also showed the predicted impact point for one of his hypersonic electromagnetic projectiles, fired from his rail gun. Wohl's microhydraulically powered exoskeleton covering his Tin Man electronic body armor allowed him to easily track the bomber while holding the large, fifty-eight-pound weapon. He lined up the impact reticle onto the radar depiction of the bomber as precisely as a conventional soldier would sight the main gun on an Abrams battle tank.

"Fire five," he said, and he squeezed the trigger. A pulse of electricity sent a seven-pound aerodynamic depleted-uranium projectile out of the large rail-gun weapon at a muzzle velocity of over eighteen thousand feet per second. The heat generated by the projectile's movement through the atmosphere turned it into blue-and-yellow molten metal, but the supersonic slipstream kept the bolus together, leaving a long, hot vapor trail in its wake. When the molten uranium hit the Blackjack bomber, the bolus cooled and decelerated. The collapsing supersonic cone caused the bolus to break apart, scattering thousands of pellets of red-hot uranium in a wide circular pattern through the Blackjack's fuselage, like an immense shotgun blast.

The Blackjack was obviously hit, but it unsteadily continued its northbound turn. In a few seconds, it would be out of range. "Crap, not a fatal shot."

"Don't let it get away, Top," Hal Briggs warned. He and another of his Tin Man commandos had returned to Shemya from Attu Island to help defend the island against the expected Russian attack. They had successfully shot both Kh-15 missiles out of the sky with their rail guns. The other Battle Force commandos, along with as many of the island's personnel as they could carry in several trips with the MV-32, had evacuated Shemya for Attu.

"Don't worry, sir," Wohl responded. "Got it, Sergeant?"

"Roger that, sir," responded the second commando in Tin Man armor, alongside Wohl. "Fire six." Even at such a great distance, it only took three seconds for the projectile to hit. This time the shot had a more spectacular effect—the entire aft end of the fuselage sheared off the aircraft, sending the big bomber tumbling out of control.

"Good shooting, boys," Hal Briggs said. "Control, splash two Blackjacks and a couple cruise missiles. Sensors are clear."

"Copy that," Patrick McLanahan responded. "Nice work. Glad you made it out there in time."

"We couldn't just sit out there on Attu and watch Shemya get blown to bits by those Russian muthas," Hal said. "So what's the plan now, boss?"

"You guys are on," Patrick said. "I need you refueled, equipped, and on your way as soon as possible. We're in the process of recovering all our planes and loading them up. The Dragons will be headed out from Dreamland in a couple hours."

"All *right!*" Briggs exclaimed. "Those are my *honeys!*"

"We're going to launch everything we got and get some help from a few planes from off-station," Patrick went on. "You'll have as much backup as we can provide, but you guys are going to have to be the pointy end of the spear. Take those bastards down, and get the place ready for visitors."

"You got it, boss," Hal Briggs said. "Good to have you back on the team."

"Good to be back, guys," Patrick said proudly. "It's damn good to be back."

8

RYAZAN' ALTERNATE MILITARY COMMAND CENTER, RUSSIAN FEDERATION
A short time later

"First indications are confirmed, sir," said Chief of the General Staff and Minister of State Security Nikolai Stepashin. "Two Tupolev-160s missing after they successfully attacked their targets on the Alaskan mainland. Presumably lost while making their final run on Eareckson Air Base in the Aleutians. Probably surviving fighter jets from Eielson or Elmendorf, deployed or dispersed to Eareckson because it's the only surviving military base in Alaska."

Gryzlov thought for a moment, then shook his head. "It has begun, Stepashin. American fighters who survived the attacks on the mainland would not deploy fifteen hundred kilometers out to a windswept island at the end of the Aleutians. I believe the counteroffensive has begun, Nikolai—McLanahan's war."

"Who, sir?"

"McLanahan. Thorn will send Patrick McLanahan and his modified long-range bombers into battle. They will deploy to Eareckson Air Base and launch attacks on us in the far east."

"Perhaps the bombers were shot down by a Patriot or I-Hawk surface-to-air missile? . . ."

"We have been watching Eareckson Air Base for months—there was never any indication they were going to install Patriots on that rock. We would have seen it," Gryzlov said. "No. I believe that McLanahan has been activated—his planes are already on Shemya, or soon will be. He will commence attacks on our Siberian bomber bases very soon—they may already be under way."

"That's crazy, sir," Stepashin said. "Why attack bases in the far east? Why not Moscow, St. Petersburg, or any of dozens of active bases in the west?"

"Because McLanahan has discovered our secret—that we are using long-range bombers launched from Siberian bases," Gryzlov said. "It was he that sent those small satellites over our bomber bases." He thought hard for a moment, then said, "You must assume that all of our eastern sub bases will be attacked soon, probably first by long-range bombers launching cruise missiles, followed by commandos—if McLanahan is involved, they'll probably use their Tin Man commandos in small groups." He paused again, then corrected himself. "No—McLanahan will attack air bases, not naval bases. He'll go after Anadyr, Blagoveshchensk, Ulan-Ude, Bratsk, or maybe even Kavaznya again."

"How do you know that, sir?" Stepashin asked skeptically. "If I were he, I'd go after the ballistic-missile sub bases—Rybachiy and Vladivostok. He should know that all of our Pacific ballistic-missile subs are based there, and that we keep most of them in port. Our bombers have scattered—there's nothing to hit at any of those bases except for a few empty planes."

"I know him, and I challenged him, so that's what he'll do," Gryzlov said confidently. "Even if the bases are empty, he'll bomb them just to show us and Thorn that he *can* bomb them. Thorn will keep him on a tight leash. He won't want to provoke a nuclear counterattack by striking our nuclear-sub bases—that would be an overt act of aggression, and Thorn isn't built for that."

Gryzlov picked up the telephone to the communications center. "Get me President Thorn immediately on the hot line." To Stepashin he said, "Listen to me carefully, Nikolai. You may get only one chance to stop him. I have studied McLanahan, his weapons, and his tactics. I believe that this is the best way to stop him:

"First, his stealth technology is second to none," Gryzlov began. "He will come at you from every direction, even from behind. It is absolutely critical that your defensive forces not use radar, except for long-range surveillance. The first targets he will attack are surface-to-air missile-defense systems. Activating surface-to-air missile radars will only result in their being destroyed. It is important not to waste your defensive-missile systems, because the initial attacks are designed only to clear a path for follow-on forces—*those* are your main targets. They will attempt to degrade or destroy your defensive systems enough to allow less stealthy special-operations transports to fly in, and you cannot allow that to happen.

"The fighters are your first line of defense. You must mass your fighters around your important bases, use long-range-surveillance radars only, and have the fighters use just optronic sensors to the maximum extent possible. The minute they turn on radar, they will be shot down. Any targets you see on surveillance radar are your *real* targets, but you must assume that they are being escorted by stealth aircraft with substantial air-to-air capabilities. Therefore you must have your fighters go in fast, strike at long range, and then get out of the area. There is no use in doing visual identifications or trying to close in to dogfight-missile range—McLanahan's stealth aircraft will eat your forces alive. Knocking down as many of the special-operations transports as possible is more important than knocking down the bombers.

"However, you must assume that some special-operations forces will sneak in—most likely McLanahan's Tin Man armored commandos," Gryzlov went on. "Unless you receive intelligence information that indicates otherwise, I suggest you augment forces at every bomber base with additional heavy infantry. Don't bother with heavy armored vehicles: The Tin Man commandos are far too fast, and they carry penetrator weapons that can disable even main battle tanks with ease. Light, fast armored reconnaissance units, helicopters with precision-standoff antiarmor weapons, and dismounted infantry with antitank weapons can deal with them effectively.

"More important is the Tin Men's ability to vector unmanned bombers and attack aircraft, so you must supplement your ground forces with as much antiair weaponry as possible," Gryzlov said. "Use passive infrared and optronic sensors, not radar. Don't try to detect their aircraft from long range—you won't see them until the attack has begun. The Americans will go after command and control, communications, power generation and distribution, air defenses, radar, and airfields first, so have each base decentralize and disperse its resources, and have alternate, backup, and emergency networks in place.

"McLanahan's forces hit fast, hit hard, then disengage," Gryzlov summarized. "The better your forces can ride out the initial standoff attack and then give chase as they try to withdraw, the more success they'll have in whittling down his Tin Man forces. Killing one Tin Man is equivalent to destroying an entire mechanized infantry platoon or tank squadron. Do you understand, General?"

"Yes, sir." Stepashin picked up a telephone and began issuing orders.

"Mr. President, Thomas Thorn is on the line for you," the

command center's operator announced. "An interpreter is standing by."

Gryzlov picked up the phone and nodded for the connection to be opened. "Is this Thomas Thorn?" he asked.

"This is President Thorn. To whom am I speaking?"

Gryzlov paused a moment to collect his thoughts, took a deep breath, then said through his interpreter, "This is President Gryzlov, Mr. Thorn." He purposely tried to keep Thorn off balance by not using his title of "president," addressing him as just another bureaucrat or functionary. "I just wanted to call to inform you that we have detected movement of General McLanahan's forces from Battle Mountain."

"Do you expect me to confirm that information for you, Gryzlov?" Thorn asked. "Or did you call just to make more threats?"

"I am glad to see you did not attempt to deny it," Gryzlov said. "You are not very good at lying, and your truthfulness is your most endearing virtue. It will also be your downfall."

"Let me guess, Gryzlov," Thorn said. "You will say that I should recall all my special-operations forces immediately; that any forces in your country will be caught; that if caught, they will be summarily executed; and that if there are any attacks on any base in Russia, then you will have no choice but to retaliate with all weapons under your command. Is that what you called to tell me, Mr. President?"

"I am calling to tell you, Thorn, that you will be responsible for triggering more death and destruction, and it is totally and completely unnecessary," Gryzlov said. "Our attacks on your bases were done out of frustration and desperation. It is not a sign of an all-out war between our countries, I swear it. I hereby promise to you that I will order a complete stand-down of all Russian strategic and tactical forces around the world immediately."

Thorn paused for several moments. Finally he said, "I am very glad to hear it, Mr. President."

"I know that McLanahan's bomber forces and most

assuredly his Tin Man commandos are even now moving toward staging locations at Eareckson Air Base on Shemya Island, and that a number of his Tin Men are already located there," Gryzlov went on. He thought he detected an uneasy rustling and a slight intake of breath on the line and was pleased that he'd apparently guessed correctly. "Our intelligence also indicates that McLanahan intends to strike our bomber bases at Ulan-Ude, Vladivostok, and Blagoveshchensk. These attacks are not necessary, Thorn. I wish to do everything in my power to convince you to stop these attacks from commencing."

"I'm sure you do, Gryzlov."

"I will order all Russian strategic and tactical forces to stand down—but not our defensive forces. All air, coastal, and base-defense and -security forces will remain at one hundred and fifty percent manning and at full alert."

"I think that is a very wise and reassuring move, Mr. President."

"But it would not look wise or reassuring for my base defenders to have to fight off your attack planes and armored commandos after I announce a cease-fire," Gryzlov said. "I think it would be most wise to recall McLanahan's forces and any other military, paramilitary, or intelligence operations you have ongoing against my country. We certainly cannot commence negotiations for a complete end to hostilities with foreign military troops on our shores."

"Now that your military objectives have been met, you want to negotiate an end to hostilities, is that it, Gryzlov?"

"I told you before, Thorn: Our actions were not premeditated," Gryzlov said. "They were born of desperation and frustration on our part—not of American hegemony but of our inability to make any progress in reversing our own economic misfortunes. As the only remaining true world superpower, you must certainly understand the enormous pressure on myself and my government to come up with results. The military response was unfortunate and miscalculated, and I take full responsibility for it. Russia will do everything possible to compensate the United States for its loss and ensure that such a horrendous, unspeakable catastrophe never happens again."

"What do you propose we do to decrease the likelihood of another attack on one another, Mr. President?" Thorn asked.

"Russia's actions will be unilateral," Gryzlov said. "I will immediately order all ballistic-missile submarines to unload American targeting data from their missiles' computers, leave their alert launch positions, and return to their bases; I will order all land-based ballistic-missile forces to unload target data and return to normal alert; all mobile land-based missiles will unload data and return to their shelters; and all strategic and tactical aircraft will unload their nuclear weapons and return them to storage. I will hope that the United States will follow suit, but there is no condition for our own actions."

"The United States will certainly cooperate, once we observe your forces returning to normal alert and once their status can be verified," Thorn said.

"I thank you, Mr. President," Gryzlov said. "I think this is an important first step in ensuring peace." He paused for a moment, then added, "But as I said, Mr. President, there remains the problem of McLanahan's attack forces. They are undoubtedly already on their way and ready to close in on our bomber bases. You of course understand that it would look very, very bad for myself and my government if I announce a unilateral stand-down and then several of our most important eastern bases come under attack. Ordering McLanahan's forces to withdraw to Eareckson Air Force Base or to the continental United States would help me convince the parliament and my people that my actions truly are in the best interests of peace."

"Negotiating a cease-fire with Russia when in eight American states radioactive fires caused by Russian nuclear warheads are still burning will not look good for me either,"

Thorn said. "Besides, I'm not confirming or denying any national-security activities in Russia or anywhere else in the world."

"I understand, Mr. President," Gryzlov said. "I'm sure you understand my position as well, and you will do the appropriate and right thing. All I can offer is this: If you give me their location and egress-route information in a timely manner, I will guarantee their safe passage out of Russian territory and airspace. They will not be harmed. I will publicly guarantee this. If they are downed or captured, I will return them to American control immediately, with no recourse whatsoever to the Geneva Conventions. They will be treated as noncombatants and turned over to you or to a third party you designate who can guarantee their safe return."

"This will be discussed, Mr. President," Thorn said simply.

"Very well," Gryzlov said. "In any case, the order to stand down Russian strategic and tactical strike forces will be issued within the hour; a copy will be sent to your Department of State via our embassy in Washington, which will be addressed to all affected Russian military forces. In that way you can verify that all of our forces that can hold American targets at risk have been notified. We will also send copies of acknowledgments and unit positions on a daily basis, so that your space reconnaissance forces can pinpoint our withdrawing forces as well. We will be happy to negotiate implementation of any other verification programs you care to propose. All the information we send is releasable to the world media."

"I think this is an important and forthright first step, President Gryzlov," Thorn said, "and I look forward to receiving the notifications and data from you."

"We shall be in touch, Mr. President," Gryzlov said, and disconnected the call.

Thorn replaced the phone in its cradle, then leaned back in his chair and stared at a far wall. Behind him was a plain light blue drape, which had served as the camera backdrop when he made his last address to the American people from his office in the converted Boeing 747. Since the attack he had made four addresses, which were broadcast around the world in many different languages. All of them had been messages seeking to reassure the American people that he was alive, that he was in control, and that their government and military were still functioning despite the horrific loss of life and destruction of American military forces.

"Mr. President," Les Busick said, breaking the president's reverie, "talk to us." The vice president was on a secure videoconference line at "High Point," the Mount Weather Special Facility in West Virginia, along with Director of Central Intelligence Douglas Morgan and other cabinet officials and members of Congress. "You're not going to cooperate with that rat bastard, are you?"

Thorn was silent for a very long moment. "General Venti, where are McLanahan and his team members now?"

"Mr. President, with all due respect—are you *serious?*" Secretary of Defense Robert Goff interjected. He, along with Venti and other members of the Joint Chiefs of Staff, was also airborne in the National Airborne Operations Center aircraft, now orbiting over central New Mexico. "You can't recall them now!"

"I know, Robert."

"Besides, Gryzlov can't and won't guarantee their safety," Goff went on. "The minute they exposed themselves, he'd blow them all away."

"I would never order them to reveal their location," Thorn said. "I would expect them to execute their egress plan and get out as stealthily as they got in."

"Mr. President, *there is no egress plan,*" Goff said. "The team had a due-regard point—a point of no return. Once they crossed that line, there was no plan to get them out again unless their operation was successful."

"I was never told that!"

"McLanahan never briefed it, and there wasn't enough time to staff the plan before it was time to issue the execution order," Goff said. "Once McLanahan's team goes in, it's a one-way mission unless they succeed."

"Every mission has a contingency plan and an emergency egress plan," Thorn said adamantly. "Even McLanahan has enough experience to know this."

"There's an outside chance that special-ops forces could pull them out, but flying that far inside Siberia, retrieving several dozen men, and getting out again is difficult and dangerous for even our best guys," Richard Venti said. "There was barely enough time to organize what forces we had. Communications are still screwed up, and every American military unit is in complete COMSEC and OPSEC lockdown—no one is talking or sharing data with anyone unless they know exactly who they're talking to." A base in total COMSEC (Communications Security) or OPSEC (Operational Security) status would be virtually cut off from the rest of the world—no one allowed on or off the base, no outside unencrypted telephone or data lines, and no movement on the base itself without prior permission and only under strict supervision. "No contingency plan was ever built into McLanahan's operation—there just wasn't time to get all the players organized." He paused, then said, "Aside from a complete nuclear-attack plan, sir, I think McLanahan's operation is the best chance we've got."

"How in hell could Gryzlov discover McLanahan's plan?"

"He's guessing, Mr. President," Busick said. "He's bluffing. McLanahan's whole damned operation is a hundred feet underground—no Russian satellite can see what he's doing. He's bullshitting you."

"Gryzlov is smart, I'll give him that," Robert Goff said. "He's a bomber guy, too, like McLanahan. He's certainly smart enough to guess McLanahan's next move."

Thorn nodded, then turned to another camera and asked, "Maureen? Your thoughts?"

"Mr. President, I don't know the details of McLanahan's plan," Secretary of State Hershel began. She had at first returned to Washington, but then, in the interest of safety and security, she'd been flown to Atlanta, Georgia, where a Joint Strategic Information Operations Center had been set up during the 1996 Summer Olympic Games. The Atlanta JSIOC was a combined federal, state, and local command-and-communications center that securely combined information from the CIA, FBI, State Department, Pentagon, and other agencies to allow law enforcement to more effectively track down and stop suspected terrorists.

Since the Olympics the JSIOC had been redesignated as a Federal Continuity of Government facility and used during exercises to relocate several governmental agencies in times of crisis. This was the first time the facility had been used for the real thing: the virtual evacuation of the Department of State from Washington, the first time that had happened since the War of 1812.

"But I trust the general to plan and execute missions that are very limited in scope, swift, effective, and deadly. I'd trust my life with his decisions." The president masked the thought that flashed in his mind: She said that, he was sure, because she was developing a very close personal relationship with McLanahan.

"On the other hand, I do *not* trust Anatoliy Gryzlov," Hershel went on. "He rules the government by fear and the military by blind, almost mythic fealty—an arrangement more akin to a military dictatorship, like Saddam Hussein's Iraq or Kim Jong Il's North Korea. Gryzlov's Russia will probably end up like those two regimes—destroyed and disgraced. Unfortunately, also as in both those regimes, the dictator will probably attempt to scorch most of his adversaries on the way out, without any thought to the fate of any innocent persons, including his own people." She paused, then ended by saying, "I recommend you let the general proceed with his plan, Mr. President. Bargaining with Gryzlov is an absolute no-win situation."

"Lester?"

"I hate to say it, Mr. President, but that big Russian asshole has got you by the balls," Vice President Busick said. "If you let McLanahan go ahead, he can claim you escalated the conflict instead of negotiating. If you agree to his demand, you could be tossin' away McLanahan's life—and that motherfucker could *still* hit us from the blind side again. It's the wacko in the catbird seat, sir." He sighed, then said, "I recommend you let McLanahan proceed. We've always got the sea-launched nukes. If Gryzlov commences another attack, he'll be signing his own death warrant. This time, though, I suggest you launch on alert—the second we see any more missiles comin' at us, we pound Moscow and every military base in our sights into carbon atoms."

Thomas Thorn turned away from the camera and stared off toward the door to the office suite aboard Air Force One. He hated making decisions like this alone; he'd always had Goff, Venti, or his wife nearby to query or from whom to get opinions on something. Even though he was electronically connected to everyone, he felt completely isolated.

He turned back toward his teleconference monitors. Goff looked angry, Venti as calm and as unruffled as ever, and Maureen Hershel appeared determined and aggressive. "Robert, what's the chance of McLanahan's successfully accomplishing this mission?" he asked.

"Mr. President, it's impossible to guess," Goff replied. "It's a good plan—simple, modest, and audacious enough to surprise the heck out of everyone. I don't believe for a moment Gryzlov knows where our boys are or what they're doing, or else he would've paraded shot-up aircraft and bodies out for the world press in a heartbeat. McLanahan's teams are small and rely too much on high-tech gizmos for my taste, but if anyone knows that arena, it's him. However, the sheer scope of what they have to do . . . hell, sir, I don't give them more than a one-in-ten chance."

"That's *it?*"

"But considering our only other options, I think it's the best chance we've got," Goff said. "Gryzlov's a mad dog, sir—totally unpredictable. If he were worried about the destruction of his regime and the Russian government, he never would have attacked us. The bottom line is, he could strike again at any moment. We've got to move before he does. McLanahan's our only option, other than an all-out nuclear attack."

"And if I chose to recall McLanahan and wait to see if Gryzlov really will stand down his strategic and tactical nuclear forces?"

"Sir, you just can't trust Gryzlov," Vice President Busick said. "More than likely he's hoping that we'll try to recall or freeze McLanahan, which will give the Russians an opportunity to pinpoint his location. The guy is obsessed with tacking McLanahan's scalp up on his wall, sir—you heard him yourself. My God, the bastard probably murdered Sen'kov and then attacked the United States of America with *nuclear weapons* just to lash out at McLanahan—he wouldn't hesitate to lie to your face if it meant getting a shot at McLanahan, dead or alive."

Thorn nodded his thanks to his onetime political adversary, thought in silence for a few moments, then said, "I don't want to play Gryzlov's game, but I don't want to provoke another nuclear attack either. And if there's any way to ensure peace, even if it means entering into negotiations with the Russians before we attempt a counterstrike, even if it means sacrificing a good man, I'll do it.

"McLanahan can continue to his objective—but he holds short before he attacks. He must contact Secretary Goff, General Venti, or myself for an update and instructions. If we have positive evidence that Gryzlov has stood down his forces and is ready to negotiate a verifiable arms deal, we'll recall McLanahan—preferably by getting permission from Gryzlov to fly a transport plane in and get him, rather than make McLanahan evade the Russian army halfway across Siberia. Under no circumstances can McLanahan or his forces commence their attack without a go signal from one of us."

Reluctantly, Secretary Goff turned to Richard Venti and nodded. Venti picked up a telephone. "Get me General Luger at Battle Mountain." Moments later: "Dick Venti here, secure, Dave."

"David Luger, secure, ready to copy, sir."

"We're going to issue written orders in a moment, but I'm relaying orders to you now directly from the president: Patrick's teams go in, but they hold in place and contact the National Command Authority or myself before initiating action."

"That would be extremely hazardous for the team, sir," Luger responded. "With their fuel states and reaction times, they're counting on a very precise sequence of actions to occur. Stopping someplace outside the fence to hide and wait wasn't in the game plan."

"Unfortunately, that's the order, General," Venti said. "Transmit yours and Patrick's concerns to me once you get the written orders, but get a message out to Patrick right away and give him the update. Ask him to acknowledge the orders immediately."

"Yes, sir. Can I ask what prompted this change of plan, sir? Communications from President Gryzlov?"

"Affirmative."

"Sir, I assure you, the team is still on schedule and still one hundred percent mission-ready," Luger said. "If Gryzlov told you that agreeing to call off this mission is the only way to save the team's lives or to ensure peace, he's lying."

"Issue the orders, General," Venti said simply. He knew for damned sure Luger was right, but the president had already made his decision. It was a dangerous but prudent compromise—putting a small group of commandos at great risk in the hope of averting a nuclear exchange at the same time. "If you have any questions or concerns, put them in writing and send them along. Out."

"You can't be serious, sir!" General Nikolai Stepashin exclaimed. "You are going to unilaterally *stand down our strategic and tactical forces?*"

"Of course not, General," President Anatoliy Gryzlov said as he replaced the phone back on its cradle. He lit up a cigarette, which only served to make the cramped, stifling meeting room even gloomier. "Do you think I'm stupid? Give the Americans the locations of the missile bases, silos, and garrisons they already know about and monitor; move a few planes around; scatter around some inert weapons, fuel tanks, or ammo boxes on the ramps besides a few bombers—anything to make it appear as if we are disarming."

"Such trickery will not fool the Americans for long."

"It doesn't have to, Nikolai," Gryzlov said. "All I want is for Thorn to issue the order to McLanahan to halt."

"Halt? Why do you think he will tell him to just stop?"

"Because Thorn is a weak, spineless, contemplative rag doll," Gryzlov responded derisively. "He sent McLanahan on some mission—more likely McLanahan *himself* launched a mission—so he does not want to order him to just turn around and come home, because it represents the only offensive action he's taken during this entire conflict. But at the same time, he wants to avoid confrontation and distress and will therefore clutch onto any possible hope that a concession from him will end this conflict.

"My guess is that he will not order McLanahan to turn back, but he will not order the mission to be terminated either—it is part of his pattern of indecisive thinking that will result in defeat for the Americans and disgrace for Thorn and all who follow him," Gryzlov said confidently.

"He will order McLanahan to stop at Eareckson Air Base and stand by until Thorn sees if we are serious or not. This will give us several hours, perhaps even a day or two, to find McLanahan and crush him. All of our strike forces will still be in place and still ready to deliver another blow against the Americans if they decide to counterattack."

Gryzlov looked at Stepashin and aimed a finger at him menacingly. "You have your orders, Stepashin—it's up to you and your men now," he said. "Find McLanahan, his aircraft, and his Tin Man commandos. Don't worry about taking them alive—just blast them to hell as soon as you find them." He thought for a moment. "You have a force of bombers standing by for follow-on attacks, do you not, Stepashin?"

"Yes, sir," the chief of staff replied. He quickly scanned a report in a folder in front of him. "I think we have adequate forces ready, sir. What is the target, sir?"

"Eareckson Air Base on Shemya Island."

Stepashin nodded. That order was not unexpected: The two Tupolev-160 bombers originally assigned to destroy Shemya obviously were shot down or crashed sometime between their successful strikes over Alaska and their planned attacks against Eareckson; satellite reconnaissance reported much air activity over Shemya, so the base was obviously still operational. As America's closest base to Russia's eastern military bases, Shemya had to be dealt with. "We will plan another air strike using MiG-23s from Anadyr."

"Fighter-bombers? What about the rest of our heavy-bomber fleet, Stepashin?"

Nikolai Stepashin swallowed apprehensively. "The initial attack on North America was most successful, sir, but the casualty count was high," he said. "The heavy-bomber units will need time to reorganize and reconstitute their forces."

"How high?"

Stepashin hesitated again, then responded, "Forty percent, sir."

"Forty percent!"

"Approximately forty percent of the force that launched on that mission was shot down, failed to return to base, or returned with damage or malfunctions significant enough to make them non-mission-ready," Stepashin said. "Against the United States, I count that as a major victory."

"You do, do you?" Gryzlov asked derisively. "It sounds like a tremendous loss to me!"

"It is a tremendous loss to our bomber force, sir," Stepashin said. "But we scored an amazing victory and accomplished eighty to ninety percent of our stated objective—crippling America's strategic strike force. Initial reports estimate that we have eliminated seventy-five percent of its long-range bomber force and perhaps half of its strategic nuclear-missile force, plus all but eliminated America's capability to launch its surviving land-based missiles and its ability to control its nuclear forces in the event of an all-out nuclear war. I consider it a great victory for you, sir."

"I don't share your optimistic assessment, Stepashin," Gryzlov said angrily. "Forty percent casualties *in one day* is far too much, and initial assessments of successes are always too optimistic. What nuclear forces remain?"

"Virtually all of our land- and sea-based nuclear ballistic force is operational," Stepashin said. "You can be assured that—"

"I am assured of nothing when it comes to our missile fleet, General, and you know it," Gryzlov said. "Why do you think I put so much trust in our bomber fleet? I was in your position two years ago, damn it. I visited the bases, interviewed the crews—not the suck-ass commanders, mind you, but the launch and maintenance crews themselves!—and saw for myself the deplorable condition of our nuclear forces. I wouldn't give our missile forces more than a sixty percent success rate—and that's a sixty percent chance of *even leaving their launch tubes* successfully, let alone hitting their assigned targets with any degree of accuracy!"

"That is simply not the case, sir. . . ."

"*Nye kruti mnye yaytsa!* Don't twist my balls!" Gryzlov snapped. "I relied on the modernization of our bomber forces to save this country, Stepashin. The Americans disassembled virtually all of their bomber defenses—the attacks should have been cakewalks." Stepashin had no response for Gryzlov's accusations, just silent denial. "How many planes are in reserve?"

"We committed no more than one-third of the fleet to the initial attack," Stepashin replied, then quickly added, "at your order. That leaves us with a long- and extended-range bomber force of approximately one hundred and eighty aircraft. Two-thirds of these are based in the Far East Military District, safe from tactical air attack and positioned so they can mount successful raids on North America again if necessary."

"It's necessary," Gryzlov said. "You failed to destroy Eareckson Air Base in the initial assault, and now it is being used against us by McLanahan and his Phoenix bombers. Plan a strike mission on Eareckson. Completely destroy the airfield, intelligence-gathering, and surveillance facilities. Plan another mission to attack any military air-defense or airfield facilities on Attu Island as well."

"Yes, sir."

Gryzlov thought for a moment, then said, "Launch the attack on Shemya using the MiG-23 tactical bombers from Anadyr only. Mass those forces if you must, but I want Eareckson turned into *glass* as soon as possible. I want the long-range bombers readied for follow-on attacks over North America."

"Targets, sir?"

"The targets that failed to be struck by our initial attack force: the Cheyenne Mountain Complex, Barksdale Air

Force Base, Fairchild Air Force Base, Nellis Air Force Base, Battle Mountain Air Reserve Base. . . ." Gryzlov paused, gazed off into the distance distractedly, then added, "And Sacramento, California, as well."

"Sacramento? You mean, Beale Air Force Base, sir?"

"That can be our *intended* target, of course," Gryzlov said. "But I want the warhead to land in the city of Sacramento, not on the military base."

"For God's sake, sir, *why?* The city itself is no longer a military target—all of the bases located near it were turned into civilian airports. There is a small rocket-motor research company there, and some computer-chip research firms, but they don't . . ." Then he remembered the general's previous remarks about his twisted motivations for this entire campaign—and he remembered that same look Gryzlov had now, and he knew why Gryzlov wanted to target a major American population center, before the president started to speak. "Not *McLanahan* again, sir . . . ?"

"Another of our missiles will go off course, Stepashin, just like the one that 'went off course' and hit Spokane, Washington," Gryzlov said. "But that strike, the loss of his son and what remains of his already fractured family, will be the final event that will drive Patrick Shane McLanahan mad."

"Sir, you cannot tell me that you would kill hundreds of thousands of civilians just to lash out at—?"

"It will be a missile malfunction, damn it!" Gryzlov retorted. "I will apologize, offer my condolences, perhaps even offer to resign from office in an attempt to atone for the miscalculation. The Duma will reject that offer, of course. But McLanahan will suffer far more than any other man or woman on the planet." He glanced at Stepashin's incredulous expression and shook his head. "You think I'm crazy, don't you, General? McLanahan is perhaps even now preparing to strike our forces, and you still believe that I'm crazy for taking such a personal interest in this man?

"It is *you* who are mistaken, Stepashin," Gryzlov went on.

"McLanahan is like a crocodile, like a rattlesnake. He lies quietly, moves slowly, barely creates a ripple in the water or disturbs a leaf on the ground when he moves. But when he moves, it is with speed, power, and tenacity. His jaws clamp on, and he will not let go until he has killed his prey. And then he returns to his lair or his river, lies quietly, and watches and waits for the next opportunity to strike."

"Mr. President, with all due respect, I suggest you take some time to get a little more perspective on this conflict," Nikolai Stepashin said. He knew that it was dangerous to try to admonish or correct a man like Gryzlov, but in order to sustain any semblance of control or leadership in this conflict, he had to be sure of exactly where the president's head was right now. "I understand your campaign against McLanahan—I agree that the man has been at the root of so many major conflicts in past years that it is a wonder he's still alive, let alone not in prison or dangling at the end of a rope. But this war is far beyond one man now. *We are at war, Mr. President!* Let us focus on the American war machine, not on this one disgraced Air Force officer. You must meet with the general staff and hear what they have to—"

"I'm well aware of what's at stake and what must be done, Stepashin," Gryzlov said. "Your job is to get the information and opinions from the general staff and present them to me, and for me to pass along my orders to the general staff. I have followed the staff's recommendations to the letter. I have invested the money, built up and modernized our forces, and garnered the support of the Duma—everything my military and political advisers told me I would have to do before this campaign could be successful. Do not question my motivations, Stepashin!"

"I . . . I do not question your goals, nor your commitment to them, sir," Stepashin said. "But talking about going to war and destroying one city just to lash out against *one man* is not rational. Disrupting the American strategic nuclear triad and regaining parity with American nuclear forces—that is a goal I and the members of the general staff agree with completely. But it is . . . disheartening to hear you rattle on about this McLanahan as if he were some demigod that needs to be destroyed."

Gryzlov looked as if he were about to explode in a fit of rage . . . but instead he lit another cigarette, took a deep drag, stubbed it out, and nodded through the haze of blue smoke. "Do not worry, Stepashin," he said. "The battle in which Russia is engaged is real. The battle I fight on Russia's behalf with McLanahan will not interfere with that. Now give the order to strike Eareckson Air Base on Shemya Island, and have the plan ready for my approval as soon as possible."

"That's the order, Muck," Dave Luger said. "I just got the hard copy." There was no response. Luger waited a few more moments, heard nothing, then asked, "You copy, Patrick?"

"Loud and clear," Patrick McLanahan responded via his subcutaneous satellite transceiver.

"It sucks, but all the players will still be in position, and we can move fast from Eareckson when we get the go-ahead," Luger said. "Should I give the word?"

There was another long period of silence. Luger was about to ask the question again, but Patrick finally responded, "No. Everyone continues as planned."

"Patrick . . ."

"No arguments this time," Patrick interjected. "The brass signed off on the operation—and damn it, we're going to complete it. Unless Gryzlov is confirmed dead or in custody by American officials, I'm not trusting him to make peace with the United States."

"Muck, they may have signed off on the plan originally, but they're changing it now," David argued. "We have a decent alternative: The ground units move forward, and the air units get a chance to refuel and rearm at Eareckson."

"It's *not* a good alternative, Texas. The president is grasping at any options that would mean an end to hostilities. He still believes that Gryzlov was desperate when he attacked the United States, and that if everyone stops right now, we can have peace. Gryzlov doesn't *want* peace—he wants to destroy the U.S. military, plain and simple. He obviously suspects we're coming after him, and he's telling the president anything he can think of to get us to stop."

"I hear you, Patrick, but we have no choice," Luger said. "You can't send in a force this size and with this large an objective without an okay from the White House, and we don't have it now."

"I sure as hell can. . . ."

"This is different, Patrick," Luger argued. "Attacking Engels, Zhukovsky, Belgorod—those were all preemptive strikes designed to defend our own forces or to prevent an imminent attack from taking place."

"So is this operation, Dave."

"Ultimately yes, but the first step is definitely an invasion, not a preemptive strike," Luger said. "There's no defensive aspect to the operation—we take the offensive all the way. I want full authority to do this. We had it; now we don't. We have no choice but to hold until we get the word to go."

Again Patrick hesitated. Luger fully expected Patrick to give him an order to continue the current mission, and he was ready to obey the order. But to his surprise, Patrick said, "Very well. Make room for the Air Battle Force and the Marines to refuel and rearm at Eareckson. Let's plan on getting a second and third ground contingent on their way as well."

"Roger that, Muck. I don't like it any more than you do, my friend, but I know we're making the right decision."

"We'll see," Patrick said simply. "McLanahan out."

NEAR SHEMYA ISLAND, ALASKA
Several hours later

"Eareckson Approach, Bobcat One-one flight of two, passing twelve thousand for eight thousand," radioed Lieutenant Colonel Summer "Shade" O'Dea, the aircraft commander aboard Patrick McLanahan's EB-52 Megafortress bomber. "Check."

"Two," responded Colonel Nancy Cheshire, the aircraft commander aboard the second aircraft in the flight, an AL-52 Dragon airborne-laser. The AL-52 Dragon was a modified B-52H bomber with a three-megawatt plasma-pumped electronic laser installed inside its fuselage, which could project a focused beam of laser energy powerful enough to destroy a ballistic missile or satellite at a range of three hundred miles, an aircraft at one hundred miles, or ground targets as large as an armored vehicle at fifty miles. Although the fleet of Dragons had grown to three in less than two years, the weapon system was still considered experimental—a fact that never stopped Patrick McLanahan.

Nancy Cheshire was the squadron commander of the Fifty-second Bomb Squadron from Battle Mountain Air Reserve Base, the home of all of the Air Force's modified B-52 bombers—and, as Nancy reminded herself often, one of only two B-52 squadrons left in the world right now, after the nuclear decimation of Minot Air Force Base by the Russians. She was determined to do everything she could—use every bit of her flying skills and leadership ability, *whatever it took*—to make the Russians pay for what they'd done to America.

"Bobcat One-one flight, roger, radar contact," the air-traffic controller at Eareckson Air Force Base responded. "Cleared for Shemya Two arrival, report initial approach fix inbound. Winds two-four-zero at twenty-one gusting to thirty-six, altimeter two-niner-eight-eight. Your wingman is cleared into publishing holding and is cleared to start his approach when you report safely on the ground."

"One-one flight cleared for the arrival, will report IAF inbound. Two, copy your clearance?"

"Two copies, cleared for the approach when lead is down," Cheshire responded.

"It's an unusually nice day on Shemya," O'Dea said on intercom. "The winds are only gusting to thirty-six knots. We've been cleared for the approach. Check in when ready for landing, crew."

Patrick turned in his ejection seat and looked back along the upper deck of the EB-52 Megafortress. Six aft-facing crew seats had been installed for carrying passengers—aircraft-maintenance and weapon technicians from Battle Mountain and the Tonopah Test Range in Nevada. Six more technicians were seated on the lower deck. These twelve men and women were key in accomplishing their mission. Unfortunately, their mission was on hold, on order of the president of the United States himself.

"Lower deck ready," one of the techs radioed.

"Upper deck ready," another responded.

"MC ready for approach," Patrick chimed in. "Aircraft is in approach and landing mode. Sixteen miles to the IAF. I'm going to do a few more LADAR sweeps of the area before the ILS clicks in."

"Clear," O'Dea said.

Patrick activated the Megafortress's LADAR, or laser radar. Emitters facing in every direction transmitted electronically controlled beams of laser energy out to a range of three hundred miles, instantly "drawing" a picture of every object, from clouds to vehicles on the ground to satellites in near-Earth orbit. The composite LADAR images were presented to him on his main supercockpit display, a large two-foot-by-three-foot color computer monitor on the right-side instrument panel. Patrick could manipulate the image by issuing a joystick, by touching the screen, or by using voice commands. The attack computer would also analyze the returns and, by instantaneously and precisely measuring objects with the laser beams, compare the dimensions with its internal databank of objects and try to identify each return.

Immediately Patrick noticed a blinking hexagonal icon at the northernmost edge of the display, at the very extreme of the LADAR's range. He zoomed his display so the contents of the hexagon filled the supercockpit display. The attack computer reported the contact as "unidentified aircraft." "Shade, I've got an unidentified air target, two-thirty position, two hundred and seventy-three miles, low, airspeed four-eight-zero, three-five-zero-degree bearing from Shemya."

O'Dea hit a button on her control stick. "Go around," she ordered. The flight-control computer instantly advanced the throttles to full military power, leveled off, configured the Megafortress's mission-adaptive skin to maximum climb performance, and started a climb. "Approach, Bobcat One-one is on the go," she radioed. "Alert Eareckson. We may have unidentified aircraft inbound from the north at two-seven-zero miles. Break. Bobcat Two-two."

"We're looking for your target, lead," Cheshire replied.

"Roger. We're on the go." On intercom, O'Dea said, "Crew, strap in tight and get on oxygen. Give me a vector, General."

"Heading two-eight-zero, climb to fifteen thousand feet," Patrick said. "LADAR coming on." He activated the laser-radar system, this time focusing energy on the returns to the north after making a complete sweep of the skies and seas around them. "I've got numerous bogey out there, counting six so far. They're right on the deck, accelerating past five hundred knots. I'd say they're bad guys." He switched over to the command channel. "Two-two, you have them yet?"

"Not yet, but we're receiving your data and maneuvering to set up an orbit," Cheshire responded. "Did you notify Eareckson?"

"Just approach control, not the units. Tell them to get everyone into shelters." Patrick knew that it was a futile move—one or two bombs the size of the warheads that were dropped on Eielson or Fort Wainwright would obliterate Shemya Island, shelters and all. "Fire up the lasers, Zipper."

"They're already warming up, boss," responded the AL-52 Dragon's mission commander, Major Frankie "Zipper" Tarantino. The Dragon's electronic laser really didn't need to "warm up," like less sophisticated chemical or diode lasers, but the system stored electrical power in massive banks of capacitors to use during the firing sequence, and the more power that could be stored prior to the first shot, the more shots the laser could fire. "Two-two has LADAR contact, two-five-zero miles bull's-eye. I count six targets as well, but at first the computer counted seven. We may have a big gaggle of multiple contacts coming at us."

"Checks," McLanahan said. "I still count six. Let me know when you're in attack position."

"Roger," Tarantino said. The AL-52 departed its holding pattern, flew northwest toward the oncoming targets, and then began a long north-south racetrack pattern at twenty thousand feet altitude. By the time the Dragon was in its racetrack, the unidentified aircraft had accelerated to six hundred knots' airspeed and were less than one hundred miles away. "Two-two is ready to engage. I now count six groups, but I believe there are multiple contacts in each group."

"You are cleared to engage," Patrick ordered. "Take out the lead aircraft in each group if you can break it out."

"Roger," Tarantino said. He selected all six groups of unidentified returns as targets, then zoomed in on the nearest group. The airborne laser used an adaptive-mirror telescope to focus laser energy on its target, but it also allowed the user to get a magnified and extremely detailed visual look at the target. "I've got a visual, lead," he reported. "Looks like Russian MiG-23 fighters. Each formation looks like it has four fighters in very close formation. Three big fuel tanks and two gravity weapons each. I can't identify the weapons, but they look like B-61 gravity nukes."

Patrick called up the datalinked image from the AL-52

Dragon's telescope on his supercockpit display. "That checks," Patrick said. "RN-40 tactical nuclear gravity bomb, the only one cleared for external carriage on supersonic fighters. Start weeding them out, Zipper."

"Roger that, sir. Fire in the sky." He hit his command button and spoke, "Attack targets."

"Attack targets, stop attack," the computer responded. Seconds later: *"Attack commencing."*

In the tail section of the AL-52 Dragon, pellets of tritium fluoride dropped into an aluminum combustion chamber under computer control and were bombarded by beams from several diode lasers. The resulting cloud of gas was compressed and further heated by magnetic fields until the gas changed to plasma, a highly charged superheated form of energy. The plasma energy was channeled into a laser generator, which produced a tremendous pulse of laser light that was amplified and focused through a long collimation tube through the AL-52's fuselage and directed forward. A four-foot diameter mirror, controlled by laser-radar arrays on the AL-52's fuselage, predistorted and steered the laser beam toward its target, correcting and focusing the beam to compensate for atmospheric distortion.

Even after traveling almost a hundred miles through space, the invisible laser beam was focused down to the size of a softball by the time it rested on the fuselage of the lead Russian MiG-23 fighter-bomber. Precisely tracked by the laser-radar arrays, the beam quickly burned through the fighter's steel surface on the left side just forward of the wing root. Before the laser burned through fuel and hydraulic lines under the skin, the sudden structural failure caused the MiG's entire left wing to peel away from the fuselage like a banana skin. Before the pilot or any of his wingmen knew what was happening, their leader disappeared in a tremendous ball of fire and hit the icy Bering Sea a fraction of a second later.

The sudden loss of their leader caused the first attack formation to scatter. Executing their preplanned lost-wingman maneuvers, the three wingmen turned away from their original track and started a rapid climb to be sure they got away from the ocean, from their doomed leader, and from the other members of their attack group. They had no choice but to completely clear out of the way, then rejoin using radar or visual cues or execute their strike as single-ship attackers.

The other three four-ship formations saw the first plane explode and go in. Thankful it wasn't them, they activated their electronic countermeasures equipment, tightened their oxygen masks and seat belts, and prepared to take on whatever enemy antiair weapons were in the vicinity—until the second lead MiG-23 exploded right before their eyes, moments after the first, and again with absolutely no warning whatsoever.

"Bobcat, I've got six single-ships and four more attack formations still inbound," Tarantino reported. "I've also got a caution message on my laser. I might have just two or three shots remaining before the magnetron field strength is below safety limits."

"Copy that, Two-two," Patrick responded. "I'm engaging now. You can reposition to engage any bandits that leak through." Patrick activated his laser-radar arrays, designated the third attack formation, and, at a range of about sixty miles, commanded, "Attack aircraft."

"Attack aircraft command received, stop attack," the computer responded. Moments later, when Patrick did not countermand his order, the computer announced, *"Attack aircraft Anaconda."* The forward bomb-bay doors swung inward, and the first AIM-154 Anaconda long-range hypersonic air-to-air missile dropped free from the bomb bay. The weapon fell for less than a hundred feet, then ignited its first-stage solid rocket motor and shot ahead and skyward. By the time the motor burned out, the missile was traveling at over twice the speed of sound, and a ramjet sustainer engine kicked in, accelerating the missile to more than Mach 5. A second and third missile followed seconds later.

Now flying faster than sixty miles per minute, it did not take long for the first Anaconda missile to reach its quarry. Seven seconds before impact, the missile activated its own terminal-guidance radar—that was the first indication to the MiG-23 crews that they were under attack.

The third attack formation scattered, leaving trails of radar-decoying chaff in their wakes. The first Anaconda missile's radar was now being hopelessly jammed, and it switched guidance back to the signals from the EB-52 Megafortress's laser-radar system. The missile abandoned the third formation of MiGs and steered itself toward one of the single-ship aircraft. The missile ran out of fuel and detonated several hundred feet away from its target, but that was enough to create fear and confusion in all of the remaining attackers.

The second and third Anaconda missiles did not miss. They picked off single-ship attackers one by one as they maneuvered to get on their bomb-run tracks. "Splash two," Patrick announced. "I count three large formations and . . . hell, at least fifteen or twenty single-ship attackers lining up for bomb runs. I've got nine Anacondas remaining."

Just then he heard, "Time to bug out, sir," on the command channel.

Patrick studied his supercockpit display—and his eyes widened in surprise as his sensors finally identified the weapon approaching them from behind. "Left turn heading one-five-zero, and do it *now*, Shade!" he ordered.

O'Dea didn't hesitate but threw her EB-52 into a hard left turn, cobbing the throttles to full military power and keeping back pressure and bottom rudder in to tighten the turn. She could hear one of their six passengers on the upper deck retching and hoped to hell it was into a barf bag. Shade completed her turn first and only then asked, "What's going on, General?"

"Lancelot in the air," Patrick said simply.

"Roger that," O'Dea said. That was enough for her.

One hundred miles behind Patrick's formation of modified B-52s was a second formation of three modified B-1B bombers called "Vampires." Commanded by Brigadier General Rebecca Furness from Battle Mountain Air Reserve Base, the EB-1C Vampires were the next generation in flying battleships, specifically designed to carry a large variety of standoff weapons into combat.

The Vampires' primary weapon was the ABM-3 Lancelot air-launched anti-ballistic-missile weapon. Designed to be an interim weapon for use against ballistic missiles until the airborne-laser aircraft weapon system was perfected, the ABM-3 was in effect a four-stage air-launched Patriot missile, using the Vampire bomber as its first-stage engine. Steered by the Vampire's laser-radar array and by its own onboard terminal-guidance radar, the Lancelot missile had a range of nearly two hundred miles and could attack targets even in near-Earth orbit.

But the Lancelot missile itself was only part of the effectiveness of the weapon; its primary deadliness came from its plasma-yield warhead. Unlike a high-explosive or thermonuclear warhead, Lancelot's warhead created a large cloud of plasma gas that instantly converted any matter within its sphere into plasma, effectively vaporizing it. Even though the size of the superhot plasma sphere was limited when created in Earth's atmosphere—the warhead was designed to explode in space, where the plasma bubble was thousands of feet in diameter and could even be electronically shaped and steered by computer control—the kill zone in the lower atmosphere was still hundreds of yards wide.

And when it exploded now, in the midst of the fourth formation of MiG-23 attackers, all four fighter-bombers simply, instantly ceased to exist.

"My God," Patrick breathed. He had seen the effects of the plasma-yield warhead many times—he was the first to use one in test launches over the Pacific—but it still never failed to astound him. It was a totally fearsome weapon. The plasma-yield detonation had taken out not just the fourth formation of MiGs but several of the single-ship bombers as well. "I see two formations and eight stragglers," he said.

"Keep coming south, sir," Rebecca Furness said, and at that moment Patrick saw another Lancelot missile heading north toward the Russian planes. Her second Lancelot missile malfunctioned and failed to detonate, but a Lancelot fired from one of her wingmen destroyed another complete formation. By then the sixth formation of MiG-23s and all of the surviving single-ship aircraft were heading west, toward Petropavlovsk Naval Air Base on the Kamchatka Peninsula, their intended recovery base.

"Good shooting, Rebecca," Patrick radioed. "Looks like they're on the run."

"Thanks, boss," Rebecca said. "We'll stay on patrol while you guys land and reload."

"I'll send the Dragon down to have the laser looked at," Patrick said, "but we're not going to land. I'm going to air-refuel the rest of the package and press on."

"But you were ordered to land, boss."

"And I fully intended to comply—until Gryzlov tried a sneak attack on Eareckson," Patrick said. "Our mission is back on. I'm going to take the fight to Gryzlov and make him negotiate—with the barrel of a gun pointed right in his face."

RYAZAN' ALTERNATE MILITARY COMMAND CENTER, RUSSIAN FEDERATION
That same time

President Anatoliy Gryzlov, seated in the center of a raised row of seats behind Chief of the General Staff Nikolai Stepashin and his senior aides, could immediately see that something had happened. The staff officers with the headsets listening to reports had suddenly stiffened, then looked furtively at Stepashin, then quickly turned away before they were noticed; the technicians working on the grease boards froze, looked at their symbols with angst, then stepped away from the boards as if unsure what to do. "What has happened, General?" he asked.

"I . . . er, reports are still coming in, sir," Stepashin stammered.

"Damn it, Stepashin, *what happened?*" Gryzlov thundered. Heads snapped up at the command, then lowered quickly back to consoles and papers.

"One of our flight leaders of the Shemya attack force reports that he has lost contact with . . . with all of the other flight leaders," Stepashin said. "Flight Six is leading his group plus five stragglers back to their poststrike base at Petropavlovsk."

"One flight plus five . . . *nine aircraft?*" Gryzlov exclaimed. "We sent *twenty-four* planes on that strike mission!" Stepashin could do nothing but nod. "Was Eareckson destroyed?" Stepashin didn't need to respond to answer the question. "Was Eareckson even *hit?*" Stepashin shook his head. "Damn it, General, I thought we had intelligence that said there were no aircraft except a few tankers and transport planes at Eareckson—probably an advance force preparing for the arrival of a large number of aircraft, but certainly not a base-defense force. What in hell happened?"

"Our flight leader said they were intercepted by air-defense aircraft firing air-to-air missiles, some with nuclear warheads," Stepashin said.

Gryzlov was about to continue his tirade but stopped short. "Nuclear weapons? I don't think so," he said. He shook his head, thought for a moment, then nodded knowingly. "No, I think what the squadron encountered was McLanahan's attack force of Megafortresses and Vampires and his other high-tech aircraft. It was just plain bad luck, Nikolai. Either McLanahan's forces were deploying to Eareckson or President Thorn really did order those planes to return to Eareckson, and McLanahan was obeying his order—rather uncharacteristic of him. They may have even used one of their plasma-yield weapons when they found they were in danger of being overrun—one detonation could have easily destroyed a close formation of MiGs."

The Russian president shook his head, and Stepashin was surprised to see a smile creep across his face. He lit up a cigarette, the same crocodile smile still on his face, although his voice was now seething with anger. "You know what else, Stepashin? We will never get a phone call from Thomas Thorn. He will never accuse us of breaking the agreement or even acknowledge that anything untoward happened. If he didn't realize it before—and I'm positive he was sincere when he said he would recall McLanahan's forces in the interest of peace—he knows it now: The fight is on."

"What do you want to do, sir?" Stepashin asked.

"McLanahan will come now—no doubt about it," Gryzlov said. "It could happen at any time. Start a watch from the last report from our MiG bombers, set aside enough time for McLanahan to refuel those forces at Eareckson and rearm the ones that expended weapons, and then compute flight time to Vladivostok, Petropavlovsk, Kavaznya, or Anadyr— that is how long you have to get your air-defense forces in place. Whatever he has in mind, he'll come, and he will come hard and fast."

9

PETROPAVLOVSK, KAMCHATKA PENINSULA, EASTERN RUSSIA
The next evening

The direct-line phone was one of those hot-line connections that would ring continuously until answered, which meant that the call was from headquarters. The sector commander fairly lunged for the phone, snatching it up as fast as he could; he didn't even bother to say anything as he did, because he knew that the caller would start the conversation right away.

"Report, Major," the voice of the regional air defense commander said over the secure line from his office at the Far East Military District Air Defense Headquarters at Petropavlovsk Naval Base on the Kamchatka Peninsula.

"Target S-3 is still heading three-zero-zero true, altitude twelve thousand meters, speed five-seven-nine kilometers per hour, no evasive maneuvers, sir," the sector commander responded. He had reported the contact moments after it appeared, so he knew that headquarters had been alerted—and no doubt the air-defense commander of Pacific Fleet, based at Vladivostok, would be listening in, too. "No reply to our warning broadcasts."

"Any jamming signals?"

"None, sir."

There was a long pause. The regional commander knew exactly what air-defense assets he had and their capabilities—undoubtedly he was going over this engagement in his head right now:

Primary among Petropavlovsk's defenses was the Antey S-300V1 surface-to-air missile system, the world's best long-range antiaircraft missile system. An entire S-300 brigade was situated at Petropavlovsk, one of Russia's largest and most important Pacific naval and air bases, with almost two hundred antiaircraft and anti-ballistic-missile rounds deployed between six launcher sites around the sprawling base complex on the southeast corner of the Kamchatka Peninsula. Normally, the S-300 missiles had a nominal range of only one hundred kilometers, but against slow, high-altitude, nonmaneuvering targets such as this one, they had a maximum effective range of almost double that—the unidentified aircraft was already within the S-300's lethal range.

It was not the only missile site on the Bering Sea. Another S-300 brigade was stationed at Ust'-Kamcatsk, three hundred kilometers to the north; another at Ossora; and yet another at Kavaznya, the site of Russia's newest long-range anti-ballistic-missile laser system, still several years from completion but proceeding despite the country's financial woes. Kavaznya was being rebuilt on the site of an old Soviet research facility that was suddenly and mysteriously destroyed in the late 1980s, before the fall of the USSR. The official explanation was that the original site was destroyed when an earthquake ruptured the containment building of the nuclear plant there, causing a catastrophic explosion.

But local Eskimo and Aleut folklore claimed that the laser facility was destroyed by an American air raid using, of all things, a lone 1960s-era B-52 bomber. No one believed that outlandish story, even though the rumors still persisted after almost two decades.

But it didn't matter right now, because Moscow had ordered that the fighters, rather than the long-range surface-to-air missiles, handle any intruders. A squadron each of MiG-27 and MiG-29 fighters had been deployed to Petropavlovsk since the initiation of hostilities less than two days ago. Four flights of four fighters were assigned a wedge of airspace about four hundred kilometers long. One fighter was airborne continuously; the others would launch as necessary, usually one more fighter upon radar contact by the first fighter and the last two if multiple targets were detected. Two full flights were held in reserve, but in this deployment no one was considered off duty—all air and ground crews were either on crew rest, ready to be called up, or ready to respond. Other air-defense units were based at Magadan and Anadyr and could be called into service if any intruders made it past the outer defenses.

Petropavlovsk also had a squadron of twelve Tu-142 long-range maritime-reconnaissance planes—upgraded Tu-95 Bear bombers designated for antiship, antisubmarine, long-range sea patrol, and electronic-warfare duties. Six bombers were flying at all times on thousand-kilometer-long patrol legs. The bombers had already attacked two vessels, assumed to be intelligence-gathering ships, that refused to turn away from Petropavlovsk.

Yes, the ships had been in international waters—but this was war. They obeyed orders or suffered the consequences. It was the same with this newcomer, the sector commander thought. He was either a hostile or an idiot if he kept on cruising closer to one of Russia's most important bases. Whichever was the case, he had to die: If he was hostile, he had to be stopped before he attacked; if he was an idiot, he had to be killed before he was allowed to breed.

The Pacific Fleet was one of the most powerful of the Russian navy's arms, with almost two hundred surface ships, strategic ballistic-missile submarines, and nuclear and nonnuclear attack submarines. Whatever targets the fighters could not get, the SAMs and sea-based antiaircraft units would. But the fighters would not miss.

"Am I clear to engage unidentified aircraft, sir?" the sector commander asked. Even though Russia was excluding aircraft and vessels out to three kilometers, this newcomer had already made it in to two-fifty. The range of the American conventional air-launched cruise missile was over eight hundred kilometers, and the nuclear-armed version was well over four thousand kilometers, so if it was a warplane armed with either weapon, it would have already attacked. The Americans' next most powerful air-launched weapons—the air force's AGM-142 TV-guided rocket-powered bomb and their navy's turbojet-powered Short-range Land Attack Missile-Extended Range—both had a maximum range of about two hundred kilometers, so this unidentified aircraft had to be stopped before it got within range of those two weapons.

"Authorized," the regional commander said. "Get your fighters airborne, and destroy any target immediately, from long range."

The surveillance radar at Petropavlovsk had a range of well over five hundred kilometers, and the unidentified aircraft had been spotted cruising in at high altitude at just over four hundred kilometers. The MiGs accelerated to Mach 2. They didn't need their radars yet—they were receiving datalinked signals from Petropavlovsk showing them exactly where the enemy aircraft were, and once they were within missile range, they could attack without ever revealing themselves. Textbook engagement so far.

But Moscow said they would not be alone: The Americans had stealth aircraft up here, and the word from air force headquarters was that some of them could launch air-to-air missiles. The best tactic, Moscow said, was to rush any aircraft that was detected at high speed with as many fighters as possible, engage at maximum range, get away from the area right after missile launch using full countermeasures, then reengage from a completely different axis of attack.

They had also switched missiles along with changing procedures: Instead of four short-range heat seekers and two semiactive radar missiles, they now carried four long-range R-77 radar-guided missiles, plus two extra fuel tanks. These advanced weapons had their own radars that could lock on to targets as far as thirty kilometers away. This meant that the MiG-29s could simply designate targets, let the missiles fly, then maneuver and escape—they no longer needed to keep the fighter's radar locked on to the target all the way to impact.

They had only a limited number of the expensive R-77s at Petropavlovsk—more had been sent to air-defense bases in the west and to fighters deployed to active bomber bases at Ulan-Ude, Blagoveshchensk, and Bratsk—but air-defense command had ordered every one of them loaded and sent aloft right away. This was obviously no time to hold back. Every enemy aircraft downed meant that the chances of America's mounting any sort of counteroffensive against Russia in the far east were slimmer and slimmer.

"Tashnit Two-one, this is Detskaya," the radar controller said, "initial vector thirty right, your target is one-two-zero K, low, cleared to engage. Acknowledge."

"Two-one acknowledges cleared to engage," the lead fighter pilot responded. Flying at well over the speed of sound, the two advanced Russian interceptors from Petropavlovsk closed in on their target rapidly. They already had their orders: no visual identification, no standard ICAO intercept procedure, no warning shots, no radio calls. All Russian air traffic had already been ordered to clear out of more than one hundred thousand cubic kilometers of airspace over the Sea of Okhotsk, the Bering Sea, and the Kamchatka Peninsula—anyone else up here was an enemy, and he was going to down them without any warning whatsoever.

"Da, Detskaya. Ya ponimayu."

"What is your state, Two-one?"

"Base plus two, control," the pilot responded. That meant he had forty minutes of fuel remaining, plus one hour of reserve fuel that was inviolate—because the closest emergency-abort base, Magadan, was about an hour's flight time away.

"Acknowledged. I will launch Two-two. Continue your approach to the target, Two-one."

"Acknowledged."

They had just passed within one hundred kilometers of the target. No sign of any other players up here yet, but they *had* to be up here—the Americans would not send an aircraft into the teeth of the Russian air defenses like this without having another plane ready to sneak past. Maybe it was a decoy? Whatever it was, it was making a large and very inviting target for the MiGs. Just over forty seconds and they could engage from maximum range.

At that moment the radar controller reported, "Sir, target turning south . . . Continuing his turn, looks like he's turning around."

"Too late, *aslayop*," the sector commander said under his breath. "I still want him to go down. Have Two-one continue his attack."

"Acknowledged, sir." But a few moments later: "Sir, the target is off our scope! Radar contact lost!"

"*Lost?*" The sector commander could feel the first prickles of panic under his collar. "How could you lose such a big contact less than one hundred and fifty kilometers out? Did he descend? Is he jamming you?"

"Negative, sir," the controller replied. "Just a weak radar return."

Shit, shit, *shit* . . . The commander fumbled for the mike button on his headphones: "Two-one, control, are you tied on yet?"

"Negative, control," the MiG pilot responded. "I was expecting to pick him up any second now."

"We have lost contact," the commander said. "Advise when you have him either on radar or IRSTS." The Infrared Search and Track System on the MiG-29 was a very accurate and reliable heat-seeking sensor that could detect and track the hot dots of large engine exhausts at ranges out to two hundred kilometers away—it was so accurate that it was used to guide active air-to-air missiles close enough to their targets so they could lock on with their terminal-guidance radars. This unknown target was flying *away* from the MiG—its hot engines should show up clearly on IRSTS.

"Status, Captain?" the regional commander radioed once again.

Better to confess right away, he thought: "Sir, the target has disappeared from our scopes," he replied. "The target turned away from shore and was flying away from the interceptors. The target was beyond the radar's optimal range, and we did have some weather recently—a slight heading change and a little frozen moisture in the air could easily cause him to drop off our screens."

"I don't need excuses, Captain—I need a visual ID on that aircraft, or I need him crashing into the Bering Sea," his commander told him. "The interceptor should be using his infrared sensor to track him."

"No contact on IRSTS yet, sir, but if he did make a heading change, the sensor might not pick up his engine exhausts until closer in. The interceptor should be picking up his heat trail soon, and he'll be in radar contact soon afterward. He can't simply have disappeared, sir—we'll get him."

"How long until Two-one gets into firing position?"

"About five minutes, sir."

"Call me when the fighter has radar contact," the regional commander ordered, and he abruptly disconnected the line.

Crap, the sector commander thought, the old man is *really* pissed now. He switched to the brigadewide radio network, which connected him to all of the different regiments under his command. "Attention all units, this is Brigade. We have lost radar contact with an unidentified aircraft, last seen two hundred and thirty-five kilometers west of Petropavlovsk. All units, stay alert. Immediately report any outages or jamming to Brigade. That is all."

He knew it was a lame message. His men were already on a hair-trigger alert and had been ever since the attack on the United States—they didn't need to be told to stay alert. But this was serious . . . he knew it, he *felt* it. Something was happening out there.

"Not even the old guys ever blew lunch in their helmets, Breaker," Hal Briggs said. He didn't need to turn around in his seat to know what had happened—even through the filtration system in the Tin Man electronic battle armor's helmet, he could smell that unmistakable smell.

"Damn it, I'm sorry, sir," First Lieutenant Mark "Breaker" Bastian said. Bastian, a former Air Force combat air controller, was a nephew of Colonel Tecumseh "Dog" Bastian, the former commander of the High Technology Aerospace Weapons Center and originator of the special-ops team code-named "Whiplash" that was the progenitor of the Battle Force ground-operations team. He was a big, muscular guy, with incredible speed and stamina for someone his size. He had excellent eyesight, was an expert marksman, and had made over two dozen combat jumps in his short military career.

He also had an extraordinarily queasy stomach. The poor guy got airsick even before boarding an aircraft. Fortunately, his vasovagal episodes occurred only *after* or just *before* he was about to do something dangerous, not *during*, so his jumpy stomach didn't usually interfere with his performance.

"It's okay, Lieutenant," Sergeant Major Chris Wohl said. He had loosened his restraints and turned to help Bastian remove his battle-armor helmet. "Just make sure you clean out the inside of the helmet carefully—the thing is filled with electronics, and you don't want crap interfering with any of it. If you can't clean it well enough, use the spare helmet."

"Take your time," Hal said. "We have a *long* way to go."

"Someone open a window," Marines Corps Staff Sergeant Emily Angel said after Bastian began cleaning his gear. Emily had no call sign because everyone called her by her very apropos last name: Angel. With short dark hair, glittering dark eyes, and a body honed by five years in some of the toughest infantry units in the U.S. Marines Corps, Angel had been handpicked by Chris Wohl to join the Battle Force ground team after he'd watched her compete in an urban-warfare search-and-destroy course competition at Quantico. The reason for recruiting new members there was simple: The Battle Force stressed small-unit tactics, speed, and maneuverability over strength and endurance. It was no surprise to Chris Wohl that the winner was a woman.

"Bite me, Angel," Bastian said, but he gratefully accepted her help as he began cleaning. They all helped because they knew that, but for the grace of God, they could've been the ones who'd thrown up in their helmets.

The four members of the Battle Force team were aboard an MQ-35 Condor special-ops infiltration/exfiltration aircraft. They had just been dropped about eighty miles east of the Kamchatka Peninsula over the Bering Sea from an altitude of thirty-six thousand feet from inside an unmanned EB-52 Megafortress bomber. Briggs, who flew on the first Condor flight over Uzbekistan and Turkmenistan, was ready for the gut-wrenching descent after dropping from the bomb bay, but no one else on board had ever had that experience before—and no amount of briefing could prepare someone for it.

"Condor, Control, you are at best glide speed," Major Matthew "Wildman" Whitley, the remote piloting technician controlling the Condor from Battle Mountain, reported.

Matt Whitley of the Fifty-second Bomb Squadron was one of the first technicians, or "game boys" as they were called, trained at Battle Mountain to fly the Megafortresses, Condors, and the other experimental aircraft without first being a pilot—his background was in computer-simulation programming. He was proud of his accomplishment, and he was looked up to by all of the other nonrated fliers in the unit as a junior god.

"How's everybody doing?" asked Brigadier General David Luger, commanding the Air Battle Force from the Battle Management Center at Battle Mountain.

"Except for one smelly helmet, fine," Briggs reported.

"They let us get an extra sixty miles closer to the coast than we figured," Wilde said. "We can use every mile we can get."

"How are we looking, Matt?" Briggs asked.

"Stand by." He checked the computer's flight plan, which updated their flight profile constantly, based on glide performance, winds, air temperature, and routing. "Right now we're looking at a six-one glide ratio—six miles for every thousand feet. That means if we descend you down to ten thousand feet, you can glide for about one hundred and fifty miles, or one hour flight time, before we have to fire up the engine. That will put you roughly over the Central Kamchatka Highway just west of Mil'kovo. Then it's a thousand-mile cruise into Yakutsk on the turbojet, or about three hours.

"You'll have less than ten minutes of fuel remaining—if everything goes to plan. Any shift in the winds, ice buildup, or malfunctions can put you on the wrong side of the fuel curve fast. We'll keep you up as high as we can, but as soon as you leave Magadan's radar coverage you'll be in Yakutsk's, so we'll have to contend with that. At ten thousand feet, you can glide for another sixty miles once the engine quits, so that's probably all the reserve you'll have."

"Sounds lovely," Briggs said wryly. "What are the bad guys up to?"

"The threat situation looks about the same as before," Luger responded. "Numerous fighter patrols all around you. The Russians have set up a picket of patrol and warships every fifty to seventy miles across the Sea of Okhotsk. We'll reroute you around the ones we detect, but be prepared to do some more gliding down to lower altitudes if necessary. They're being very careful and not radiating with anything but normal surface- and air-search radars. Long-range surveillance radars at Petropavlovsk, Yakutsk, Komsomol'sk, and Magadan are active, but all of the previously known SA-10 and SA-12 sites along the coast are silent. They're not exposing any of their air-defense stuff, which will make it harder for us to target them."

"Was this supposed to cheer us up, Dave?"

They proceeded in silence for the next hour, but the tension built up quickly and precipitously as they cleared the coastline of the central Kamchatka Peninsula and approached the engine-start point. "Okay, crew, listen up," Briggs said. "The emergency-egress procedures are as briefed: If the engine fails to start, we'll turn south and continue our glide to the planned emergency landing zone along the Central Kamchatka Highway. We then make our way to Petropavlovsk and wreak as much havoc there as we can from the ground. There are no plans at this time for anyone to rescue us, so we're on our own. Our mission will be to disrupt air-defense and surveillance operations on the Kamchatka Peninsula in order to offer follow-on forces an easier ingress path. Questions?"

"Has the engine ever not started, sir?" Angel asked.

Briggs turned to glance behind him, then replied by saying, "Are there any *other* questions?" Not surprisingly, there were none.

"Coming up on engine start," Whitley reported. "Stand by. . . . Engine inlet coming open . . . inlet deicers on . . . starter engaged . . . fifteen percent RPMs, igniters on, here comes the fuel. . . . Stand by. . . . Ignition, engine RPMs to thirty . . . thirty-five . . ." Suddenly the engine's whirring sound stopped. "Igniters off, fuel off. We got a hot start, guys. The engine inlet might be blocked with ice."

The crew felt the Condor turn, and shoulders slumped. "Okay, guys, here's the plan," Dave Luger said. "We've turned you southbound on the planned emergency routing. We've got to wait three minutes before we can attempt another start. You'll lose about two thousand feet altitude and go about twenty miles. We'll keep the inlet deicers on longer in case we got some ice restricting airflow for the three minutes, then try one more restart. We might have time for another restart if the second one doesn't work, if the battery doesn't run out with all the starter activations. We—"

"Caution, airborne search radar, seven o'clock, sixty-five miles," came a computerized voice—the threat-warning receiver.

"Petropavlovsk—the fighter patrols," Luger said. "They've got fighters everywhere. Hopefully they're looking out over the ocean and not up the peninsula. We should be—"

"Warning, airborne search radar and height finder, seven o'clock, sixty-four miles."

"How about we give that engine restart a try now, Dave?" Hal Briggs suggested nervously.

"I think that's close enough to three minutes," Dave said warily. "Starter on, igniters—"

"Warning, radar lock-on, MiG-29, eight o'clock, sixty miles."

"C'mon, baby, *start,*" Matt Whitley breathed. "Time just ran out."

SIX HUNDRED MILES NORTH OF THE CONDOR, OVER FAR EASTERN SIBERIA
That same time

"Control, Yupka-Three-three flight has radar contact on unidentified air target, five-zero kilometers, low," the lead Mikoyan-23B pilot reported.

"That's your target, Three-three," the ground-intercept controller said. "No other targets detected. Begin your intercept."

"Acknowledged. Wing, take the high CAP, I am turning to intercept."

"Two," the pilot of the second MiG-23B responded simply. His job was to stay with his leader and provide support, not chat on the radios.

Based out of Anadyr, the easternmost military air base in Russia, the MiG-23B Bombardirovshchiks were single-seat, swing-wing, dual-purpose fighter-bombers, capable of both medium-range attack and air-interceptor missions. All interceptor-tasked MiG-23s based at Anadyr were armed with twin twenty-three-millimeter cannons in the nose with two hundred rounds of ammunition, two R-23R radar-guided missiles on fuselage hardpoints, two R-60 heat-seeking missiles on wing pylons, and one eight-hundred-liter external fuel tank.

The thirty-eight bomber-tasked planes at Anadyr had different weapon loads: three external fuel tanks on the fuselage hardpoints for extra-long range—plus two RN-40 tactical nuclear gravity bombs on the wing stations, each with a one-hundred-kiloton yield. If the United States tried to attack Russia, their orders were to launch and destroy military targets throughout Alaska and Canada. The fighter-equipped MiGs were there to hold off an attack by either American planes or cruise missiles long enough for the bombers to launch and get safely away from the base.

This unidentified radar contact may have been a prelude to such an attack, which was why nerves were on edge all over the district. The first counterattack by the United States had to be blunted at all costs, and the MiG-23s at Anadyr and the MiG-29s at Petropavlovsk were the first lines of defense against the expected American attack.

The lead MiG pilot kept his PrNK-23N Sokol attack radar on long enough to get a firm idea of the unknown aircraft's position in his mind, flicked it to STANDBY so his radar wouldn't give away his position, then rolled right and started a descent into firing position. The target was moving slowly, far more slowly than a jet-powered aircraft. It was also flying at extremely low altitude, barely two hundred meters above the coastal mountain range. It was too dark to be able to see it, so a visual identification was not going to happen.

It was far too late for that anyway—this guy was already well inside Russia's borders and was not squawking any identification codes. An intruder, no doubt about it. He was going down in flames.

The MiG-23 pilot rolled out and continued his descent. He wished for night-vision goggles so he could see the rugged terrain below, but those were luxuries left for the MiG-29 pilots and the bombers, not the old fighter guys. The pilot had already checked his minimum terrain-clearance altitude, which would keep him safe within a fifty-by-fifty-kilometer box—plus, he added a few dozen meters' altitude as an extra safety measure "for the wife and kids," as he and his fellow fighter pilots liked to say. He would be low enough to lock on to and engage this target and still clear the terrain.

As he continued in on his intercept run, the MiG pilot activated his ship's TM-23 electro-optical sensor, and a blip appeared right away, exactly where he thought it would. The sensor did not display an image of the target, just a simple dot on a screen when a bright or hot object was detected; once locked on, the system fed target bearing and altitude to his fire-control computer, allowing him to give his air-to-air missiles almost all the data they needed to attack.

Using his skill and situational awareness, he kept the dot on the lower edge of the screen and mentally calculated when he would be in firing range. A few seconds later, he flipped on his Sokol attack radar, which was also slaved to the enemy aircraft's azimuth by the TM-23 sensor. The radar locked on instantly. As soon as he selected an R-23 missile, he received an IN RANGE indication. He flipped open the red cover to the arming switch and then—

At that instant his Sirena-3 radar-warning receiver blared and a red LAUNCH light snapped on—his threat-warning receiver had picked up the uplink signals transmitted to steer surface-to-air missiles, meaning that a missile was in flight and aimed at his plane! His reaction had to be instantaneous: He immediately punched out several bundles of radar-decoying chaff, chopped the throttle, and threw the fighter in a hard right break. In ninety degrees of bank, he pulled on the control stick until he heard the stall-warning horn, leveled out, punched out more chaff, and then hit his afterburner to speed up again. When the radar-warning receiver blared again, he did another break, again to the right, hoping to turn around far enough to lay his radar on his attacker. The stall-warning horn screamed quicker this time, so when he leveled out, he dipped the nose to help speed up.

The second time, he saw it—an explosion, just a few meters away. A missile had missed him by a fraction of a second! Another moment's hesitation and he could be dead right now.

He had no choice but to bug out; he had received no warnings from his ground controller, and his radar had not locked on to anything—he was completely blind. He pulled the throttle back to full military power to help conserve fuel, then started a turn to the north and a fast climb away from the terrain. His only choice was to disengage, hope the newcomer would follow him up to altitude so the ground radar could see him, then try to reengage.

Kurva! Where in hell did he come from? "Control, Yupka

Three-three, I'm under attack!" the pilot radioed frantically. "I was painted by fire-control radar, and I just evaded a missile!"

"Three-three, Control, we do not show a second aircraft, only your target at your seven o'clock position, twenty-eight K."

"I tell you, Control, I was under attack!" He tried but failed to get his head back into the fight. His brain was hopelessly jumbled—he had a wingman up there to worry about, one known enemy target, and another completely unseen foe that had just attacked him. "Three-three wing, I've lost the attack picture, so you engage the target. I'll take the high CAP."

"Acknowledged, Lead," his wingman radioed. "Control, give me a vector."

"Three-three wing, steer forty right, your target will be at your one o'clock, forty-three K, low, lead will be at your two o'clock, eighteen K. Clear to descend to your minimum vector altitude. Three-three lead, come twenty right, continue climb to your patrol altitude, your wingman will be at your three o'clock, eighteen K, in a descending turn."

"Wing acknowledges. Turning right."

"Lead acknowledges." The lead MiG-23 pilot was quickly regaining his mental picture of the battle space—minus the newcomer, of course. Or did he just imagine that "attack"? Maybe it was some spurious signal from the radar site on the ground or from his wingman, perhaps checking his weapon stores or briefly firing up his radar? Just forget about it, he told himself. Concentrate on getting the one *known* target and then—

Suddenly he saw a flash of light and a short trail of fire off in the darkness—and he knew he hadn't been imagining anything. "Oleg!" he shouted on the command radio. "Attacker at your six o'clock position! *Break! Do it now!*"

"I'm not picking up any—" And at that instant the threat-warning receiver blared. Unlike the MiG-23, this attacker could launch a missile without having a radar lock-on.

"Chaff! Flares! Break!" the lead pilot shouted. But he

knew it was pointless. His wingman's reaction had to be immediate and aggressive, with no hesitation or second-guessing whatsoever. By the time he thought whether or not he should react and then how to do it, it was too late. The lead pilot spotted a bright flash far off to his right, followed by a large explosion, and then a trail of fire that wobbled briefly through the night sky before being swallowed up by the darkness.

"Splash one, Crowbar."

"Thank God—and thank the propellerheads," the mission commander aboard the U.S. Air Force MC-130H Combat Talon transport plane, Marine Corps First Lieutenant Ted Merritt, said half aloud with a rush of relief. He felt as if he hadn't taken a breath of air in several minutes, and his throat was dry and scratchy. A veteran special-operations officer of the Twenty-fourth Marine Expeditionary Unit, Special Operations Capable, Merritt was accustomed to handling any kind of contingency on the ground—what he couldn't handle was being engaged by the enemy while still aboard the transport plane.

Merritt was leading a force of forty-eight Marines on a covert insertion mission deep inside Russia. Their MC-130H had lifted off from Kirtland Air Force Base near Albuquerque, New Mexico, shortly after being given the warning order from U.S. Special Operations Command headquarters at MacDill Air Force Base near Tampa, Florida. Its seven-member crew flew to Camp Pendleton, California, and embarked Merritt's Marine Special Purpose Force platoon of fifty-one men, including three thirteen-man infantry squads and three four-man fire teams, that were part of the Fifteenth Marine Expeditionary Unit. The Fifteenth MEU had just completed its twenty-four-week qualification course and had just earned its Special Operations Capable designation before preparing to deploy on a six-month Pacific Ocean cruise.

The Marine Special Purpose Forces, once known as Direct Action Platoons, were composed of highly trained and experienced special-operations soldiers who specialized in light, mobile, and highly destructive missions deep inside enemy territory. Their job was to go in ahead of a Force Reconnaissance battalion or other heavy Marine unit to map out the forward edge of the battle area, hunt down and kill enemy scouts, pinpoint and relay locations of air defenses and fortifications, and create diversions to confuse, exhaust, and harass enemy forces.

The MC-130, using in-flight refueling, had flown nonstop since leaving Camp Pendleton, receiving hourly intelligence briefings and mission updates and plans via satellite while en route on the torturous fifteen-hour flight across the northern Pacific. The plane made several in-flight refuelings, with the last one just north of the Aleutian island of Attu, right before entering Russian radar coverage. Once within range of Russia's long-range airborne early-warning radars at Kavaznya and Petropavlovsk, the MC-130 descended to just a few hundred feet above the ocean using its satellite-navigation system, then used its terrain-following radar once over land to stay at treetop level.

Merritt was hopeful: They hadn't had one indication of any threats during the entire long overwater cruise through Russian offshore airspace. But just minutes after going feet-dry and hugging some of the roughest terrain on the entire route of flight, where they should be the best protected from radar, they were jumped. Combat Talon II birds had an extensive electronic defensive suite, including jammers and decoys that were effective against ground and airborne threats, but the highly modified C-130 turboprop transports were very large, slow, inviting targets.

Thank God for their guardian angel. He was out there somewhere, blazing a trail for them.

The threat-warning receiver blared once again. The second MiG had already found them.

* * *

"Control, Three-three, my wingman is hit, repeat, my wingman is hit!" the lead MiG-23 pilot shouted. "Give me a vector! The second target is somewhere at my twelve o'clock! Do you see him?"

"*Vy shutitye,* Three-three, *nyet!* Proceed with the attack. We will launch—" And then the radio was drowned out by an earsplitting whistle. The automatic frequency-hopping mode on the radio cleared the jamming for a few seconds, but then it returned again with full force.

He was alone—no wingman, and now no ground controller. It sounded as if the controller was going to vector in some help, but at maximum speed it would take them over fifteen minutes to arrive.

The MiG pilot activated his radar. There, right in front of him, was a radar target. Again he didn't hesitate. He immediately got a lock-on, centered the aiming pipper on the lock box, and squeezed the trigger just as he got an IN RANGE indication on his heads-up display. He reached down to select his second radar-guided missile.

When he looked up, his radar was a jumble of targets that filled the entire scope. The radar lock box on his heads-up display was flitting from one false target to another, whichever one it thought was the strongest return or the most serious threat. The MiG pilot hit a button on the radar panel to activate the electronic counter-countermeasures mode. That cleared up the radar screen—but only for a few sweeps, and then the enemy jamming signals locked on again to his radar's new frequency and started false-target jamming it all over again. He had no idea where his missile was heading. For all he knew, it could be heading back toward *him*.

"Control, Three-three . . ." he tried, but the radio was still unusable, a hopeless jumble of screeches, pops, and whistles. The MiG pilot immediately started a climb and made a slight right turn—he'd been on that one heading too long, exposing himself to attack. What in hell was it? An enemy fighter over eastern Siberia with both air-to-air weapons *and* jammers strong enough to take out a Sokol PrNK-23S radar?

He had just a few minutes of fuel left before he needed to head back to base. Without a ground controller, he had only one option left: try to find his original target on his own. Kill something before he had to get out of there—or before *he* was killed, like his wingman. The MiG pilot's strength was forming the mental map of the battle space in his head—visualizing where all the players were and correctly guessing what they might be doing, even many minutes since getting their last exact position. That's what made him such an important and trusted flight lead. He had to put that skill into use right now.

His original target was slow-moving, flying very low but not terrain-masking, and pretty much flying in a straight line. Maybe he would still be doing the same thing now.

The MiG-23 pilot turned slightly left and aimed the nose of his jet slightly nose-low, aiming for the spot he imagined the original target had moved toward. His guess was that the first target was a large American turboprop special-ops aircraft, like an MC-130 Hercules, probably loaded with troops and fuel but having to stretch that fuel a long way—which meant he was going to continue to fly slow and low and not make a bunch of course reversals, climbs or descents, or even very many turns if he could avoid it. Maybe if he was concerned about—

Suddenly a dot appeared on the TM-23 electro-optical sensor screen. *There it was!* He couldn't believe his luck. The radio was still being jammed, so he assumed his radar would be jammed, too, so there was no use turning it on and giving away his position. No messing around this time—he slammed the throttle forward, lowered the nose, and started a rapid descent at the slow-moving target.

He had no definite idea how far away he was from the target—he was relying strictly on his own internal "radar screen" as he selected his R-60 heat-seeking missiles and closed in. All he had to do was keep the dot centered and continue moving in—the R-60 would report to him when it had locked on to a hot enough heat source. It had to happen any second now. His situational-awareness "chart" told him he couldn't be any farther than five or six kilome—

A red light flashed on, and he flipped open the safety cover and squeezed the launch button—before realizing that it wasn't the IN RANGE indicator, but the MISSILE LAUNCH warning. The Sirena-2 radar threat detector had picked up the specific frequency of a radar-guided missile in flight. He had to get out of there! He had only a fraction of a second to react.

But at that same moment, he heard the raspy growl of the R-60 locking on to its target, and moments later he saw the IN RA—

The AIM-120 AMRAAM missile plowed into the center of the MiG-23's fuselage, tearing open its fuel tank and blowing the fighter into pieces in the blink of an eye. The pilot stayed conscious long enough to grasp his ejection handles before the fireball created by his own exploding jet engulfed him, instantly vaporizing him.

"Splash Atwo, Crowbar," Matthew Whitley radioed a few moments later. He was also the "game boy" for the unmanned EB-1C Vampire "flying battleship" bomber, flying in protection mode to cover the MC-130 Combat Talon II transport as it flew through long-range radar coverage from Anadyr and Kavaznya along the Russian coastal area. "Your tail is clear."

"Thanks, Bobcat," Merritt radioed back on the secure radio frequency. "We owe you big-time."

Merritt's "guardian angel" was an unmanned EB-1C Vampire long-range bomber. Launched from Battle Mountain Air Reserve Base twelve hours earlier, it was one of the most advanced SEAD weapon systems ever developed. A modified B-1B strategic bomber, its three bomb bays were loaded with a mix of defensive weapons: twelve long-range

radar-guided AIM-120 Scorpion air-to-air missiles on a
rotary launcher in the forward bomb bay; six AGM-88
HARMs—high-speed antiradiation missiles—on another
launcher in the center bomb bay; and eight AGM-65M
Longhorn Maverick TV- and imaging-infrared precision-
guided missiles in the aft bomb bay. The Vampires also had
advanced ultraprecise laser radar systems that could locate
and identify enemy targets at long range, even spacecraft in
low Earth orbit.

"We can hang with you for another thirty minutes," Whitley said, "and then we'll have to reverse course and hit our
tanker. But after we refuel, we'll head back in to cover your
approach into Yakutsk and your egress."

"Copy that, Bobcat," Merritt said. "We'll be waiting for
you. What's the word from Condor?"

There was a slight, strained pause. Then: "They may be
having some problems. Stand by. . . ."

*"Warning, airborne radar in target-tracking mode, eight
o'clock, fifty-five miles,"* the threat-warning computer
announced.

The commandos inside the little Condor heard a loud
baarkk! sound coming from the rear, followed by a very substantial shudder, another animal-like cough, and then a faint
whirring sound. "Engine up to thirty percent . . . thirty-five
percent . . . forty . . . forty-five   percent . . . Starters   off,
temps in the green, looks like we got a good light," Matt
Wilde reported. "Power's coming up . . . generators coming
online." At that moment the rumbling and shuddering completely disappeared—it was as if they had suddenly been
firmly planted on solid bedrock. "Mission-adaptive system
active, guys. Power up to eighty-five percent. Looks like the
engine swallowed a chunk of ice, but everything looks
okay."

" 'Looks okay,' huh? *You're* not being chased by a damned
Russian MiG!" Hal Briggs retorted. "Where is that sucker?"

"Eight o'clock, less than forty miles," Dave Luger said. "Stand by. . . ."

" 'Stand by'? Dave, what's happening out there?"

"I think the fighter has you guys," Luger radioed from Battle Mountain. "We're working right now to buy you some time."

"He's got one MiG lining up on Condor and another that'll get within firing range soon," Whitley reported.

Luger had no choice. "Deploy the towed array on the EB-52, open target fins, and send out a beacon signal," he ordered. Whitley reluctantly complied. A small, bullet-shaped device unreeled itself from a fairing on the EB-52 Megafortress's tail. When the device was about two hundred yards behind the bomber, it opened up several fins and began sending out a tracking beacon. The device was an ALE-55 towed electronic-countermeasures array. As well as acting as a jamming antenna and decoy, the array could also act like an air target by making its radar cross-section larger and by sending out identification signals.

"Any chance he'll run out of gas before he catches up with the Megafortress?" Whitley asked.

"He hasn't caught it yet, Wildman," Luger said.

"Control, I have a weak radar return at my two o'clock position, sixty-four K," the MiG-29 pilot reported. "I initially saw the target heading east, but this one appears to be heading west. Can you verify my radar contact? He's at my two o'clock, sixty K meters, descending at two hundred and forty kilometers per hour. No infrared signature yet—he is either very stealthy or unpowered."

"Negative, Two-one," the ground controller reported. "We show negative radar contacts. Be advised, Tashnit Four-seven is engaging targets approximately in your vicinity. Recommend you return to— Stand by, Two-one." The MiG pilot cursed in frustration. It took several moments for the controller to come back up. "Two-one, we now have a pop-up radar contact, unidentified aircraft, altitude base plus sixteen, range one-one-five K, bearing one-zero-five degrees, heading east at four-eight-zero K. Vector ninety-five left to intercept."

The MiG pilot hated giving up the chase on a sure contact, but he had no choice except to comply. He plugged in min afterburner as he turned to the new vector heading. At min afterburner, flying just below the speed of sound, it would take him nearly ten minutes to catch up with the unidentified plane. "I'm going to need a relief chaser here in a few minutes, control," he advised.

"Tashnit Four-nine flight of two will be airborne in a few minutes," the controller reported. "They'll join you after they prosecute the westbound target. You are clear to engage your target, Two-one."

"Two-one understands, cleared to engage," the pilot acknowledged.

Since the ground-radar controller had radar contact now, he didn't need to activate his own radar. Moments later his infrared search-and-track sensor picked up the unidentified aircraft. With the IRSTS locked on, he could close to infrared-missile range and shoot him down without ever being detected. The target was still flying along, fat, dumb, and happy—no evasive maneuvers, just straight, slow, high-altitude flight, exactly like a training target.

"Range twenty K, Two-one."

"Acknowledged," the MiG pilot replied. The IRSTS gave him azimuth and elevation, not range, so he didn't know exactly when the R-73 heat-seeking missile would lock on, but all he had to do was—

There! He heard a loud *beepbeepbeep!* and saw a REYS indication on his heads-up display. He flipped open the safety cover on his fire button and—

At that moment the target dropped quickly in altitude—slowly at first, then faster and faster. In less than three seconds, it had completely disappeared! That didn't make sense! He searched in the darkness to see if he could spot it . . . nothing! "Control, Two-one, I have lost the target! It appears to have dropped straight down. Vector!"

"Two-one, target last seen at your twelve o'clock position, eighteen K. Negative contact at this time."

"Khuy na!" the MiG-29 pilot swore. How in hell could he be *right there* one second, as big as a fucking house, and then completely gone the next? He had no choice: He had to activate his pulse-Doppler radar to reacquire.

As soon as he flicked it on, *there it was,* right at the very right edge of his radarscope and lower, as big as day. But just as he flicked the switch on his control stick to switch from heat-seeking missiles to radar-guided missiles and take a shot, he received heavy jamming so persistent and agile that his counter-countermeasures equipment still couldn't burn through it. "Detskaya, this is Tashnit Two-one, be advised, as soon as I was able to lock on with my radar, I encountered very heavy jamming, all frequencies and modes."

But as soon as he let up on the mike button, he heard an unbelievably loud squealing noise. Comm jamming! This bastard had jammed his radio frequencies as well! He was hostile, no doubt about it now. But once the pilot turned toward the fleeing aircraft, his IRSTS sensor picked him up once again. Without the radar and without vectors, his only chance now was to close in to heat-seeking-missile range again. And he had better hurry—the bastard was flying farther and farther away from base, and his own bingo fuel level was fast approaching.

The enemy aircraft had sped up now, but it was still about half of the fighter's speed. Keeping the power up but being careful not to select a higher afterburner power setting, he zoomed in for the kill.

"Here he comes," Whitley said. He had cut loose the towed decoy array just as the MiG closed within twelve miles, the max range of the AA-11 "Archer" missile, and as soon as he did, he turned the EB-52 bomber hard right, started a rapid descent, and jammed the throttles to full military power. If the MiG had locked on to the towed decoy, once it was cut loose, he would disappear from sight—but not for long. Even a stealthy bird like the Megafortress couldn't hide its four huge, hot turbofans for long. "Sir?"

"Take him down," Dave Luger said simply.

"Roger that." Whitley entered instructions to his remote aircraft-control section, who designated the MiG-29 as an active target. The EB-52 aircraft that launched the Condor aircraft and StealthHawk unmanned attack aircraft couldn't carry its normal complement of weapons, but it did carry some defensive weapons: two AIM-120 Scorpion air-to-air radar-guided missiles on each wing pylon.

On Whitley's command, one missile was launched from the left pylon. The missile shot forward ahead of the bomber, then looped overhead in an "over the shoulder" missile-attack profile. The EB-52's laser-radar arrays datalinked steering information to the missile, aiming the missile to a point in space where the MiG would be on its projected flight path. When the targeting computer determined that the MiG would be in range, the Scorpion missile activated its own radar and locked on to the MiG.

That was the first indication the MiG-29 pilot had that he was under attack—and by then it was too late. The Russian activated his electronic countermeasures and ejected chaff and flares to try to decoy the oncoming missile, but he stubbornly stayed on the same flight path, hoping to catch up to his quarry in the next few seconds. Undeterred by the decoys, the Scorpion missile scored a direct hit on the MiG's left wing, sending the fighter into an uncontrollable spin into the Bering Sea.

"Splash one MiG-29, guys," Whitley announced.

"Roger that, Wildman," Luger said. "Let's bring that Megafortress around so it can refuel the StealthHawks coming back from the Kamchatka Peninsula, and then we'll bring it back to Shemya for refueling and rearming."

"Should we fly it back to help the guys in the Condor?" Whitley asked. "We still have three Scorpions on board, plenty of gas, and three towed arrays left."

"We'll need the Megafortress for the follow-on attacks," Luger said. "Everything is proceeding as the general planned so far. Besides, it looks like the StealthHawks are lining up a target of their own."

"At'yibis at min'a! Get the hell away from me!" the Russian MiG-29 pilot screamed in his oxygen mask. One second he was pursuing an unidentified pop-up target below him, heading south down the middle of the Kamchatka Peninsula just a hundred kilometers north of his home base, and the next he was surrounded by airborne threats. "Control, Four-seven, I'm being engaged! I've got a bandit on my tail! I need help!"

"Four-seven, Control, we are not picking up any more targets on radar," the ground radar controller at Petropavlovsk replied. "Four-nine flight of two will be airborne in three minutes. ETE five minutes." Silence. "Four-seven, do you copy? Acknowledge." Still no response. Suddenly the radar-data block representing the lone MiG-29 on patrol started to blink. The altitude readout from the fighter's encoding transponder showed it in a rapid descent . . . then it disappeared. "Tashnit Four-seven, do you copy?" Something was wrong. "Tashnit Four-nine, we've lost radar contact with Four-seven. Your initial vector is three-three-zero, base plus twelve. Radar is clear, but use extreme caution."

"Four-nine flight of two, acknowledged. We'll be airborne in two minutes." The two MiG-29 fighters taxied rapidly down the taxiway, their pilots quickly running alert-takeoff checklists as they made their way to the active runway. At the end of the runway, they lined up side by side, received a "cleared for takeoff" light-gun signal from the control tower, locked brakes, pushed the throttles to max afterburner, and screamed down the runway together. Both were off the runway in less than fifteen hundred meters. The pilots raised gear and flaps, accelerated to five hundred kilometers per hour, pulled the throttles back to full military power, and started a left-echelon formation turn to the northwest.

Almost at the same instant, both fighters exploded in midair. There was no time for either pilot to eject—the burning aircraft hit the ground almost immediately, still in formation.

"Splash two more," Matt Whitley reported. "StealthHawk One took out the MiG on the Condor's tail, and StealthHawk Two took care of the two MiGs launching from Petropavlovsk. Both are returning to Bobcat Two-three for refueling, and they'll all recover to Shemya for rearming. StealthHawks Three and Four are proceeding across the Sea of Okhotsk to the feet-dry point."

"Roger that, Wildman," Hal Briggs said. He felt naked now without the vaunted StealthHawks, a commando's best friend. The RAQ-15 StealthHawk was the improved version of Dreamland's FlightHawk remotely piloted attack vehicle. Small, stealthy, fast, and powerful, the StealthHawk could fly through the most heavily defended areas in the world at up to ten miles per minute and attack targets with pinpoint precision. The StealthHawks carried a mix of weapons in their ten-foot-long bomb bays; these birds were configured for both air defense and defense suppression, with AIM-9 Sidewinder heat-seeking anti-aircraft missiles and AGM-211 mini-Maverick guided missiles configured to home in on and destroy enemy radars. The best part: The StealthHawks could be retrieved by their unmanned EB-1C Vampire motherships, brought up inside the bomb bay, refueled and rearmed, and flown back into battle.

The same unmanned EB-52 Megafortress bomber that launched the Condor had launched two StealthHawks from wing pylons. That was the reason the plane was visible from so far away one moment, then invisible to radar the next: The StealthHawks riding on the wing pylons completely destroyed the Megafortress's stealth capabilities, which were fully restored once the StealthHawks were released. The EB-52 could refuel the StealthHawks in midair from a hose-and-drogue-type refueling system.

Meanwhile, an EB-1C Vampire bomber from Battle Mountain had launched two more StealthHawks over the Sea of Okhotsk between the southern tip of the Kamchatka Peninsula and Sakhalin Island; those two StealthHawks would escort the Condor in toward the Siberian coast. The Vampire bomber would then retrieve, refuel, rearm, and relaunch the EB-52's two StealthHawks and send them inland to rotate patrols with the other two StealthHawks. The rotations would continue until the Vampire had to return to Eareckson to refuel and reload.

Briggs's Condor infiltration aircraft had leveled off at ten thousand feet and proceeded west-northwest across the west side of the Kamchatka Peninsula toward the Sea of Okhotsk. The Condor's turbojet engine was running at 80 percent power, sending them smoothly on their way at a little over six miles per minute. The Condor descended slightly to five thousand feet above the sea, likely high enough to prevent any Russian naval patrols from hearing or seeing it but low enough to avoid the long-range surveillance radars and anti-aircraft missile batteries located along the shore and on patrol vessels on the Sea of Okhotsk.

The crossing was treacherous. The Russian patrol vessels were arrayed so tightly across the Sea of Okhotsk that Battle Mountain had to make the Condor do several heading changes to avoid detection—they were even forced to steer the Condor toward a slightly less capable weapon system in order to avoid another, deadlier missile system that suddenly appeared.

Soon the inevitable happened—they vectored themselves

right into the radar footprint of a Russian warship that had appeared as if out of nowhere. "Air-search radar!" Dave Luger shouted over the secure satellite link. "Echo-band air-search radar, close aboard, two o'clock, twenty-eight miles—probably a big-ass destroyer!"

"Get us out of here, Dave!" Hal Briggs shouted.

"Too late," Whitley said. "You're already inside his radar coverage. We're descending you to one hundred feet and turning you south. He's got another ship on his right— maybe he'll turn right into the bastard."

"Warning, missile-guidance radar, SA-N-17, two o'clock, twenty-six miles," the threat-warning receiver blared. *"Warning, fire-control radar, DP-130, ten o'clock, twenty-five miles."*

"The patrol boat at your nine o'clock position is turning northeast," Dave Luger said. "It's trying to either engage you or force you to fly north into that destroyer."

"Warning, air-search radar, nine o'clock, nine miles," the warning receiver intoned. *"Warning, fire-control radar, DP-76, nine o'clock, ten miles."*

"We gotta nail that patrol boat, Dave," Hal Briggs said. "We don't have any choice."

Luger hesitated—but not for long. He knew they had no choice as well. "Matt . . ."

"Roger that," Whitley said. He entered commands into his computer console. "Designating Sierra One-nine as a target. Commit one StealthHawk."

"Commit," Luger ordered.

The StealthHawk unmanned attack missile received position and velocity information moments later by satellite and activated its own millimeter-wave radar and imaging infrared sensors as it cruised at ten miles per minute toward the Russian *Molnya*-class patrol boat. Once it was within range, its bomb-bay doors slid open, and it fired both of its mini-Maverick missiles at the vessel. Configured to act as antiradar weapons, the missiles homed in on the

Hotel/India-band fire-control radar, which controlled the seventy-six-millimeter dual-purpose gun on the patrol boat. Although the patrol boat carried SA-N-5 anti-aircraft missiles, the dual-purpose gun had almost three times the range of the missiles and, coupled to the radar, had almost the same accuracy.

"Good hit . . . second missile missed," Luger reported. "India-band radar down. Echo-band radar still locked on in target-tracking mode, but I think he's locked on to the StealthHawk. We're changing your course to bring you closer to the patrol boat and keep you away from the destroyer."

"You're sure making this exciting, Dave," Hal Briggs deadpanned.

"The missiles on the patrol boat have a fairly short range and are only infrared-guided," Luger said. "We'll keep you out of range of those. We're just trying to stay away from that destroyer and keep you out of range of that seventy-six-millimeter job in case they have—" Suddenly Hal Briggs could see the horizon illuminate with several spectacular flashes of light. "Optronic guidance," he finished.

"Lost track of the StealthHawk," Whitley reported. "Looks like we lost her. The patrol boat is turning—man, that thing is *fast!* At this range they can keep us in front of them easily."

"Commit the second StealthHawk," Luger said.

"Roger . . . target designated." The sky lit up with more gun blasts for several seconds, but soon Hal could see two streaks of light from the sky down to the sea. A fraction of a second later, he saw a tremendous burst of light and a brief flicker of flame on the horizon. "Air-search radar is down," Whitley reported. "Looks like we slowed him up a bit."

"I'd say you started a little bonfire on his decks," Briggs said. Even from his range, he could see flickers of light rippling across the sea. "I love those StealthHawk things, guys. Every kid should own one."

Whitley managed to keep the Condor away from all other patrol boats; the destroyer stopped its pursuit to assist the smaller patrol boat fight its deck fire, so they avoided that threat as well. Fighters were vectored into the area to search for the unidentified attackers, but both the Condor and the StealthHawk were too small to be detected, and all it took was minor course corrections to keep them clear of the pursuing fighters.

Ninety minutes after passing the Kamchatka Peninsula, the tiny Condor jet crossed the coast of Siberia and headed inland. Twenty minutes later they crossed the Dzhugdzhur Mountains along the eastern coast of Siberia and finally left the warnings of the Magadan and Petropavlovsk surveillance radars behind—only to be replaced by warning messages for the Yakutsk surveillance radar. Unlike the rugged, volcanic terrain of the coastline and the Kamchatka Peninsula, the terrain here was rapidly smoothing out to flat, seemingly endless tundra, interspersed with sections of marshy swamps, gravelly kharst, and peat bogs—in short, there was no longer anywhere to hide. It seemed as if they could see forever—but if they could see forever, the enemy could certainly see *them*.

"Man, oh, man," Hal Briggs said after studying the terrain map on his multifunction displays, "if this ain't the end of the fuckin' world, you can sure as hell see it from here." But every twelve seconds—the time it took for a radar antenna to make one complete revolution—they were reminded of what lay ahead: the threat-warning receiver announcing, *"Caution, early-warning and fighter-intercept radar, twelve o'clock, three hundred miles . . . Caution, early warning and fighter-intercept radar, two hundred ninety-nine miles. . . ."*

"Shaddup already," Briggs said, flipping a switch to silence the threat-warning voice.

RYAZAN' ALTERNATE MILITARY COMMAND CENTER, RUSSIAN FEDERATION
A short time later

From his decades as an air forces commander, from lowly lieutenant to general, Anatoliy Gryzlov could pick up on the slightest change in noise, tempo, or state of alert of the personnel in his command centers. The changes were incredibly subtle—but enough to awaken him with a start from a deep sleep and catapult him out of his seat. He had been catnapping in his small battle-staff meeting room, but even after less than an hour of sleep, he was wide-awake and on the move. He stormed through the office door and into the main battle-staff area. "What has happened, Stepashin?" he shouted.

"Several air-defense units engaging unidentified hostile aircraft, sir," Stepashin said. He stepped quickly over to the wall chart. "Fighter wings based at both Petropavlovsk and Anadyr report some losses, and one naval unit in the Sea of Okhotsk was attacked by antiradar weapons."

Gryzlov had grabbed a long measuring plotter and was running it across some lines drawn on the chart. He pointed gleefully at one of the time markers. "I told you, Nikolai—right dead on schedule," he said. "McLanahan is so punctual that you can set your watch by him."

"Sir, all of the fighters reported very small contacts," Stepashin said. "If McLanahan was coming with bombers . . . ?"

"No bombers—not yet," Gryzlov said confidently. "These are StealthHawks—unmanned attack aircraft. They can launch missiles, but their primary function is reconnaissance. I told you to pass the word along, Nikolai—*use no radars,* or they'll be destroyed by stealth aircraft. The StealthHawks are launched by Megafortresses and Vampires, but McLanahan is not ready to send in his heavy jets—not yet, but soon. They were probably launched by unmanned aircraft."

He pointed at the lines drawn to several bases in southern Siberia. "He is right on time, Nikolai, so get your men ready," he said, a sparkle in his eyes showing his excitement at the chase. "The next warning we get will be the main force of bombers trying to penetrate our air defenses. Petropavlovsk may pick up the first wave, but more likely it'll be the terminal defenses around Anadyr again, Blagoveshchensk, Vladivostok, Sakhalin Island, or Magadan that will get the first indication of an attack.

"You must swarm all over any sensor contact you have and launch every missile possible at it, and keep firing until it goes down or until your crews run out of missiles," Gryzlov said, stabbing at Stepashin with his cigarette. "We can achieve a stalemate or even a victory if we are successful in shooting down one transport or stealth aircraft—just one! Once the Americans realize they are not invulnerable to attack, they will quickly come back to the bargaining table."

YAKUTSK, SIBERIA, RUSSIAN FEDERATION
Several hours later

There was no sweeter sight in the entire world than when you broke out of a thick, angry overcast and saw the landing strip, especially through sheets of almost frozen rain pelting the windscreen. The pilot of the Russian Federation air force's Ilyushin-78 aerial-refueling tanker breathed a sigh of relief that he was sure could be heard throughout his large, noisy aircraft. *"Kalyosa, nizhniy,"* he ordered, and the co-pilot grasped the large landing-gear lever, squeezed the unlock trigger, and lowered the lever. "Flaps to thirty. Ignition switches on." He reduced power and aimed for the end of the runway as the copilot flipped his plastic-covered checklist pages to the "Aborted Landing" section, ready to read to the pilot in case a go-around was required. But it didn't look as if it would be needed. The winds were right down the runway, and although the rain was falling pretty hard, restricting visibility, he had this landing nailed. "Unit Three-four-four, field in sight."

"Unit Four-four, cleared to land, winds three-five-zero at eighteen gusting to twenty-two knots." The pilot looked through the whipping rain and saw the steady green light from the tower cab, a visual indication that he was cleared to land.

"Acknowledged, cleared to land," the pilot repeated. The young, easily excitable copilot looked immensely relieved—this had been one hell of a past couple days. It wasn't just the attack against the United States that made it so amazing—the pilot still wasn't convinced that that had been a wise move, but he had to give General Gryzlov credit for daring to twist the tiger's tail like that.

No, not just to twist the tiger's tail—to rip off the tiger's legs and beat him with them!

What was really astonishing was the rapid and generational transformation of the Russian military, especially its air forces. No longer would Russia's military strength rest with its ground and naval forces. The air forces had metamorphosed from a mere transportation-and-support group to a global, rapid-response, precision-striking force. Never before had the air forces been decisive in any battle—this was the first complete victory, and certainly not the last.

Yakutsk Air Base was the prototype of that incredible transformation. In the past, Russia had relied on enormous aircraft and many immense bases located throughout its vast territory to fuel its strike aircraft. Most of the bases east of the Urals had been abandoned, since most military leaders thought that the wastelands of Siberia represented more of an obstacle to be avoided or overflown rather than a target of conquest.

No longer. Aerial-refueling tankers ruled Siberia, and tankers led the way in this war against America and would lead the way for decades to come. With the fleet of late-model tankers Russia was developing, like this Ilyushin-78, the entire globe was truly within reach. There were a few bombers and fighters stationed at Yakutsk, as at every other Russian military base with enough concrete to park one, but here *tankers ruled*.

With Yakutsk's tankers opening an air bridge between the bases in the west and North America, Russia finally had a chance to regain its rightful status as a world superpower. General Gryzlov—most Russian military officers still did not refer to him as "President," believing strongly that it was more of an honor to be called by his military rank than by any political appellation—had to be one of the most visionary airpower leaders in history.

It appeared that the rest of the fleet had already returned from their missions—the ramp was choked with Il-78 and Tupolev-16 tankers, MiG-29 and MiG-23 fighter jets, and even several Tu-95 and Tu-22M bombers. There was a security vehicle parked right on the hold line at the approach end of the runway—rather unusual, but not unexpected with the heightened security. There didn't seem to be too much activity elsewhere, except for a few roving security patrols, mostly wheeled armored personnel carriers with a large cannon or machine gun mounted on top.

"Check the runway status, copilot," the pilot ordered.

"*Da.*" On the command radio, the copilot spoke, "Tower, braking action and runway visual-range report?"

"Runway visual range two thousand meters," the tower operator reported. Then, hesitantly, he continued, "Caution, runway braking action *khudshiy.* I repeat, runway braking action *khudshiy. Khudshiy!*"

The Il-78 copilot stared at his pilot with a look of absolute horror. The pilot was concentrating on nailing this landing with the weather conditions worsening outside, so it took a few seconds for the message and the copilot's stunned expression to register. *"Uyedi na huy!"* the pilot shouted. "Go around! Go around! *Full power!"* The copilot slowly but deliberately shoved the throttles up to full military power. The pilot pitched the nose to level, arresting their descent less than fifty meters aboveground. It seemed to take forever for the airspeed to come up, and for a moment the pilot was sure they'd stall and smack into the ground, well short of the runway.

But they were low on fuel, and gross weight was very low. Soon the airspeed started to increase as the engines spooled up to full power. Once they had reached best-angle climb speed, he carefully raised the nose, every nerve ending in his body alert to the possibility of an accelerated stall. When the vertical speed, airspeed, and altimeter needles all crept upward together, he ordered, "Gear up, flaps to twenty."

"Who should I call?" the copilot yelled frantically. He was looking out the windscreen in a panic, trying to see anything that might indicate what the emergency was. "Who should I talk to?"

"Wait until I get the plane cleaned up, damn it!" the pilot shouted. "Flaps full up! Check igniters on and inertial separators deployed!" The copilot checked the switch positions, then nervously scanned out the windscreens for any sign of trouble. As soon as the plane was safely climbing and the gear and flaps retracted, the pilot banked steeply away from the airfield, expecting any moment to feel or hear an explosion.

As relieved as he'd been just moments earlier to break out of the clouds and see the runway, he was even more relieved when he finally *reentered* the clouds a few moments later.

"Sorry about that, sir," Ted Merritt radioed. He was stationed up inside the control tower cab at Yakutsk Air Base, along with a Russian-speaking Marine. Another Marine was tightly binding the Russian noncom's hands behind him with plastic handcuffs—he was already facedown on the floor, gagged with a rag strapped around his mouth. "Looks like he used a 'scatter' code—first time I've heard one. I've got the tower operator secured now—we can't trust him on the radios any longer. My corporal will do the radios from now on."

"Roger that," Colonel Hal Briggs responded. "That tanker's not going far." "Stand by," he responded. "Break. Briggs to McLanahan. One got away at the last second. You got him, or do you want us to take him?"

"Stand by, Dave," Patrick McLanahan replied from aboard his EB-52 Megafortress, flying just southeast of Yakutsk. He briefly activated the Megafortress's laser radar, which used laser emitters mounted on all sides of the aircraft to instantly "draw" a detailed picture of every object within three hundred miles of the bomber. He immediately spotted the retreating Il-78 tanker. Although it was not yet out of range of the weapons he carried aboard his bomber, his guys on the ground could do this job much better, and he could save his munitions. "McLanahan to Wohl," he spoke, using his subcutaneous satellite transceiver to talk directly to his men at Yakutsk. "Sergeant Major, take it down."

"Roger, sir," Sergeant Major Chris Wohl responded. He, along with a four-man Marine fire team reinforced by a security team armed with M249 squad automatic weapons, had already set out sensors and mines around the base and were now guarding the main entrance, which was just a few kilometers from a major highway that led to the city of Yakutsk itself, just twenty klicks away. Two more fire teams were spread out around the perimeter of the base, accompanied by Bastian and Angel, while the last team was sent out to help secure the fuel depot and drive vehicles. "Angel, take it."

"Copy," Staff Sergeant Emily Angel responded simply. Like Wohl, she was wearing her Tin Man electronic battle armor, standing guard at the north side of the base. She already had her electromagnetic rail gun raised and, using her powered exoskeleton, effortlessly and precisely tracked the Russian aircraft. Moments after she responded, she squeezed the trigger. An eighteen-ounce titanium projectile sped out of the weapon with a muzzle velocity of over eighteen thousand feet per second, leaving a blue-orange trail of vaporized air behind it.

As usual, it appeared as if the projectile missed, and Angel took another shot a few seconds later. But the first shot did not miss. Instead of hitting the outboard engine on the left wing, the projectile pierced the engine's pylon, severing several fuel, pneumatic, hydraulic, and bleed air lines. The Il-78's pilot had no choice but to shut the engine down before it tore itself apart.

The second shot also did not miss. It traveled directly up the tailpipe of the inboard engine on the left wing, exactly where Angel had aimed. The projectile had already softened from friction as it traveled through the air, and flying through the nearly two-thousand-degree jet exhaust made it softer still—so when the practically molten titanium hit the engine's combustion chamber, it completely disintegrated into a fist-size slug of metal that sped through the compressor section of the engine and spattered, shredding the compressor blades and instantly tearing apart the Soloviev D-30KP engine.

The Ilyushin-78 could fly very well on just two engines, especially at its light gross weight, but the pilot had to lower the nose to regain his lost airspeed, and he was hit at just over four hundred meters aboveground—there was no time to try to coax it back to flying speed. The pilot made the decision to pull the right throttles to idle and do a controlled crash landing. The Il-78 flew much better with the right engines pulled back to more closely match the destroyed left engines, so the pilot was able to pancake his tanker into the boggy tundra in an almost perfectly wings-level attitude.

"Splash one big-ass plane," Angel reported.

"Good shooting, Angel," Wohl said. "Take your fire team

and check for survivors. Bring back the injured and nonre-sisters—deal with the others. We have enough captives here already."

"Copy," Angel said simply—she rarely said much more than that while wearing the Tin Man battle armor. She radioed her Marine fire team to pick her up in a Russian wheeled armored personnel carrier, and they drove quickly out to the crash site.

In thirty minutes she returned with all seven crew members, including one fatality and two injured in the crash. The conscious Russians were shocked to see the U.S. Marines at their air base in the middle of nowhere in Siberia, and even more amazed to see Angel in her Tin Man electronic battle armor.

But not as amazed as they were when they saw a weird-looking B-52 bomber on final approach to their runway. It *was* a B-52, but with a long pointed nose, angled downward like a supersonic transport's so the pilot could see the runway better, and with a strange, angled V-shaped tail that looked almost invisible.

The B-52 stopped in less than half the length of the runway and quickly taxied to a designated parking spot, where fuel trucks were waiting. With the engines still running, the belly hatch popped open, and Patrick McLanahan and twelve more men and women stepped out. This EB-52's crew compartment, which normally carried just two crew members, had been modified with bolt-in seats to accommodate six additional crew members on both the upper and lower decks. After stretching their cramped and aching muscles, the twelve maintenance technicians got to work refueling the Megafortress bomber.

"*Dobro pozhalovat* Yakutsk, General," Hal Briggs said to Patrick when they met up at the base-operations complex at the foot of the control tower. Even in his own Tin Man battle armor, he was able to salute the general as he entered the building, then shook hands with him. He had a broad smile on his face after he removed his helmet and ran a hand across his shaved head. "I've been learning a little Russian just in case. Welcome to Camp Vengeance, sir."

"Camp Vengeance? Excellent name."

"One of the Marines named it—I think it's damned appropriate."

"I agree," Patrick said. "Run down the situation here for me, Hal. We'll blast off again as soon as we're refueled, and we'll set up air-base defense from the air and help escort in the other planes."

"Roger that, sir," Hal said. He led Patrick over to a large map of Yakutsk hanging on the wall behind the flight-planning desk. "We're here in the base-ops buildings, which includes radar, communications, weather, and security forces. This west complex here is the main aircraft-parking area—eighteen hangars and a mass parking apron for about thirty heavies. We've moved all the Russian planes out of the hangars to make way for our guys, and we've got the captives housed in these two hangars, about two hundred or so."

"Two hundred? We expected a lot more than that, didn't we?"

"We made a decision and put all the troops we feel are noncombatant types in a separate hangar, under minimal guard," Briggs said. "It's a risk, but putting four or five hundred together is riskier. The hard-core security troops, fliers, senior officers, and noncoms are under close guard. Eventually the others will screw up enough courage to sneak out and try to free the others, and that's when we might have to waste a few. Until we get more guys in here, that's the best I can do."

"How long can you hold out?"

"Twelve Marines to guard two hundred captives—I'd say so far it's a fair fight, until the jarheads start getting real tired or the noncombatants start getting real stupid. So far it's quiet. Mark Bastian is supervising. The sight of us in Tin Man getups really freaks 'em out, but it won't take them long to get over their fear and start planning a breakout. Now that you brought some more aircraft techs, that'll leave more of the Marines available for perimeter security and guard duty.

"We parked a few planes here and there outside base ops to make it look busy. There were a few bombers getting some work done in the east hangar complex—shut that down, captured a Russian colonel.

"Across the runway is the industrial area—storage, fuel tanks, physical plant, et cetera. Back here is the housing area, squadron ready rooms, and other support buildings. We believe that most of the place was pretty much closed down for the night, but in about an hour or so, the regular folks will start showing up, and then the shit will hit the fan. We've got 'detour' and 'road closed' signs up to try to get folks turned around, but that won't fool 'em for long. Chris has set up mines and sensors around the perimeter, and the Marines are ready for a fight. They even brought a few unmanned recon planes to help themselves scan the perimeter. Those guys are damned good."

Patrick nodded. It wasn't much of a defense—their forces were stretched hair thin. But the Marines were accustomed to dropping into hot landing zones surrounded by bad guys and being asked to do the impossible with almost nothing. These twenty-first-century Marines had a lot more high-tech gadgets to help them, but it still came down to the basic task of sending a few brave fighters into the breach and hoping they utilized their skills, courage, and tenacity to the max. "Pass along my thanks to Lieutenant Merritt and the Tin Men for a job well done," Patrick said. "Again, I have no intention of staying here a second longer than I have to."

"Everyone else on time, sir?"

"So far," Patrick said. "The MC-17 transports should be penetrating Petropavlovsk's airspace any minute now, with Rebecca and Daren leading a three-ship Vampire escort team. By tonight, with some luck, we'll be ready to start attack operations."

OVER THE BERING SEA, EAST OF PETROPAVLOVSK
That same time

"Time to go night-night, tovarich," Daren Mace said. He touched his supercockpit display on the icon for Petropavlovsk's surveillance radar and spoke, "Attack target."

"Attack order received, stop attack," the computer responded, and moments later Mace's EB-1C Vampire bomber had fired two AGM-88 high-speed antiradar missiles at the ground radar. Soon the Russian long-range radar was off the air.

"The radar is down," Daren reported. "The fighters will have to start finding targets on their own." He entered a few more voice commands. "Jammers and countermeasures are active, and the MC-17 is going active as well." Daren briefly activated his laser radar, which instantly "painted" a picture of the airspace around him. "Two fighters in the vicinity, eleven o'clock, thirty-five miles. They're *mine*."

Rebecca Furness glanced over at Daren's supercockpit display on the right side of the Vampire's instrument panel, which clearly depicted the tactical situation: They were flying twenty miles ahead of their charges, two MC-17 special-operations transport planes. Modified by the aircraft and weapons experts at the High Technology Aerospace Weapons Center, the same unit that had designed and fielded the modified B-52s and B-1s, the MC-17s had sophisticated navigation and self-defense systems that allowed them to fly deep into enemy territory. Each was carrying seventy to eighty crew members, technicians, and security forces, plus a hundred fifty thousand pounds of ordnance, equipment, and supplies to support this mission.

Another EB-1C Vampire had launched two StealthHawks to attack Petropavlovsk; it was now standing by a couple hundred miles to the northeast, ready to recover and rearm them for follow-on attacks. Both StealthHawks were armed with a mix of antiradar and mine-dispensing standoff munitions that would destroy all of Petropavlovsk's air-defense missile sites and, with luck, shut down the airstrip as well. A third Vampire was standing by with Longhorn missiles, heavier mine-laying munitions, and defensive air-to-air missiles, ready to rush in to completely shut down the base and help escort the MC-17s through to the Siberian coastline once the StealthHawks finished their attack runs on Petropavlovsk.

"Attack fighters," Daren ordered.

"Attack order received, stop attack," the computer responded. Moments later: *"Forward bomb doors opening . . . Launcher rotating . . . Scorpion away."*

Suddenly the datalink from Petropavlovsk that was providing steering cues to the air-defense fighters was cut off. That happened frequently, especially if the enemy was jamming the radar. The antijam circuits would take over and change frequencies, and soon the datalink would be active again. The MiG-29's fire-control system kept the target's heading and speed in memory, providing an estimated position on the heads-up display, so if necessary the MiG pilot could simply—

"Zima flight, Zima flight!" the radio suddenly blared, startling the pilot. "The base is under attack! The airfield has been bombed, and the surveillance radar has been destroyed! Take over the—" And just then the transmission was cut off by loud squealing and popping on the UHF radio frequency.

The MiG pilot couldn't help but think of his alternate landing bases: Magadan, their primary alternate, was over a thousand kilometers away, and Kavaznya, their emergency landing base, was not that much closer. They were already close to bingo fuel, and they hadn't even launched any missiles yet! Almost time to activate his own radar and attack. He hoped his wingman was watching his fuel gauges. What in hell hit them? Was it a cruise missile?

The pilot's attention was focused on his abort base and not on his threat-warning receiver, so he hesitated just a second or two too long when the MISSILE LAUNCH warning flashed on his instrument panel and on his heads-up display. By the time he thought to react, it was too late—the AIM-120 Scorpion missile hit him squarely in the center of his jet, turning it instantly into a fireball and sending it crashing into the Bering Sea.

"Splash one," Daren Mace announced. "Stand by . . . second missile away."

But the wingman wasn't as distracted. He had just activated his radar and locked up the target at seventy kilometers when his warning receiver blared. He punched off two R-77s—seconds before another Scorpion missile slammed into him from the left rear quarter. He was able to put his hands on his ejection-seat handles but didn't have time to pull them before the fireball engulfed his plane as well.

"Missiles away! Missiles away! Shit, he launched!" Colonel Daren Mace shouted. He could hardly believe that the wingman could fire his own missiles so fast—usually wingmen were just set up to guard the leader, and rarely did they have the situational awareness to prosecute an attack so quickly after losing their leader. The Russians must have changed tactics, Daren decided—all fighters must be ordered to blaze away with every missile they had from maximum range as soon as they got a target locked up. "Two AA-12s. Time to impact . . . crap, *thirty-five seconds.*"

The Vampire's laser-radar arrays were tracking the AA-12s perfectly. They had just a few seconds to try to knock those missiles out of the sky—the MC-17 was sending jamming signals, but the AA-12s were still speeding dead on course, perhaps homing on the jamming. "Daren, get them!" Rebecca shouted.

"Attack AA-12s," Daren ordered the attack computer. But even as he did so, he knew that it was going to be a very, very close call. The AA-12s had accelerated to Mach 3. The AIM-120s had similar range and speed, but it was going to be a head-to-head intercept—that was the lowest-percentage shot there was. If even one AA-12 missed by less than a few dozen yards, the MC-17 was going down.

Before the attack computer could acknowledge Daren's order, he spoke, "Countermeasures to standby. Chaff, left and right. Chaff, left and right. Wings level, Rebecca. Electronic cloaking to standby."

"Daren, what are you doing?" Rebecca shouted. Part of the EB-1C's stealth enhancements was an electronic system nicknamed the "cloaking device" that absorbed a great deal of electromagnetic energy aimed at the bomber. At longer ranges it could make the bomber virtually invisible. "You can't shut off the cloaking—it'll quadruple our radar cross-section! What in hell do you think you're . . . ?"

But then she looked again at the supercockpit display, and she understood perfectly. Just for good measure, she pulled the throttles on her EB-1C Vampire bomber to idle—to make it easier for the AA-12 missiles to acquire and track them. The tactic worked. Seconds later both Russian AA-12 missiles diverted off course, locked on to the unguarded Vampire bomber, and slammed into it.

Rebecca and Daren were ready—they could see the missiles coming on the supercockpit display, and as soon as they felt the impact, they ejected. They were well clear of the stricken bomber long before it exploded into a huge fiery mass of metal and fuel and plunged straight down into the icy Bering Sea.

10

OVER YAKUTSK, RUSSIAN FEDERATION
Minutes later

"Patrick, you copy?"

Patrick simply sat back in his seat, suddenly unable to move or speak. His aircraft commander, Summer O'Dea, looked at her mission commander with a mixture of sorrow and apprehension. She had never seen the Air Battle Force commander frozen in shock like this before. "General? Target inbound, sir—looks like a helicopter gunship or surveillance aircraft." Still no response. "Sir, answer me."

"Roger," Patrick said somberly. He was airborne in the EB-52 Megafortress again, orbiting over Yakutsk and scanning for any threats or armed response. He had already launched one AGM-177 "Wolverine" autonomous-attack cruise missile, which had scattered over fifty bomblets in the path of a column of trucks and armored personnel carriers to keep them from approaching the base; the helicopter was the first aerial responder that morning. He touched the icon on the supercockpit display. "Attack target," he ordered, his voice little more than a ghostly echo. Neither of them noticed the computer's response, an AIM-120 missile firing from the left wing's weapon fairing, or the computer's report that the target had been struck. "Dave . . . ?"

"We launched the Pave Dasher from Shemya—it should be on station in about forty minutes," Luger said. "The MC-130P should be airborne in about thirty minutes to refuel the Dasher." They had received an MC-130P "Combat Shadow" aerial-refueling tanker from the Alaska Air National Guard at Kulis Air National Guard Base at Anchorage to refuel the turboprop and helicopter aircraft. "We'll find them, Muck."

It was difficult—no, almost impossible—to get his mind back in the game, but he knew he had to do it before his sorrow and shock spread to the others under his command. "Status of the MC-17s, Dave?"

"Safe, over the Sea of Okhotsk with the other two Vampires tagging along. ETE ninety minutes. Rebecca and Daren were flying cover for the transports when they got hit—looks like they used their own plane as a shield."

"We're going to need to divide up Rebecca's targets with the other planes."

"In the works, Muck," Luger said. "Shouldn't be a problem. We're receiving fresh updates on the SS-24s' and -25s' locations. They're dispersing more of them out of their garrisons, but they still have at least half of the -25s in garages, and we can hit them anytime. The SS-24s are all on the move. I wish I knew if they were decoys or not."

"We can't afford to ignore them," Patrick said. He knew they would not be—Dave Luger was on top of it. But they wouldn't be ready to strike for several more hours, and a whole lot of things could easily change by then.

RYAZAN' ALTERNATE MILITARY COMMAND CENTER, RUSSIAN FEDERATION
A short time later

Nikolai Stepashin came into the conference room almost at a dead run, a message form in his hand. The president was looking over reports from all over the world, shaking his head—none of it was good. "How in hell did the press get the news about the attack on Shemya so fast, and in so much detail?" Gryzlov asked when he heard Stepashin enter the room. "The Americans must have reporters embedded right on board their airborne military command post." He looked up and noticed the panicked expression on the chief of the general staff's face. "McLanahan . . . ?" Gryzlov asked, jumping to his feet.

"Unknown as yet, sir," Stepashin said. "It appears our air base at Petropavlovsk came under antiradar-missile attack again."

"What losses on our side?"

"Two MiG-29s from Petropavlovsk." Gryzlov grimaced in surprise and disappointment. The MiG-29s were among the world's best fighters, but they were taking heavy losses tonight. "The airfield itself is temporarily shut down—some bomblets were scattered on the runways and taxiways."

"Have we done *anything* to the enemy yet, Stepashin?"

"One fighter reported downing a large aircraft, type unknown, about sixty kilometers east of Petropavlovsk," Stepashin responded. "No more attacks occurred after it was taken out, even though Petropavlovsk's radar was down and there were no fighters on patrol for several minutes."

"That's good—that is very good," Gryzlov said. "Whatever was hit must have been very costly to them. If McLanahan used unmanned attack aircraft to attack Petropavlovsk, perhaps the aircraft we downed was their control mothership; or, even better, perhaps it was a manned Megafortress or Vampire. Destroying one of those planes is akin to shooting down an entire flight of our best fighter-bombers. Americans have no stomach for protracted battle. If they can't win in one night's worth of bombing, or if they lose more than a few troops, they'll go home.

"It hurt them, Nikolai, I know it did," the Russian president remarked, wearing a rare smile. "McLanahan's forces *must* be stretched to the limit. Every aircraft we shoot down means he has fewer and fewer resources to draw upon. If we can remove one of his tankers, he'll have to think twice before flying his bombers out to the far east."

He studied the wall chart of Siberia again. "He's a little bit behind schedule," Gryzlov said. "I would've expected attacks on Magadan or Vladivostok by now. I want ops-normal reports from every one of our Far East Military District bases every hour. Keep your men ready, General. In a very short time, McLanahan is going to attack. He knows now that he can be hurt. Let's just see what he is made out of."

YAKUTSK AIR BASE, RUSSIA
A short time later

Less than two hours after passing the Kamchatka Peninsula, sadly leaving their escort Vampire bomber behind, the two MC-17 cargo planes were safely inside hangars at Yakutsk, and the EB-52s and EB-1Cs were being loaded. The MC-17s brought in enough weaponry to completely load four EB-52s and two EB-1Cs, plus refuel the two deployed AL-52s. Patrick's armada at Yakutsk already included two manned EB-1Cs loaded and on defensive patrol, along with two unmanned EB-1Cs dedicated to refueling and rearming StealthHawk unmanned attack aircraft. In addition, Patrick had two EB-52 Megafortresses and one AL-52 Dragon battleship on patrol, plus two KC-10 Extender aerial-refueling tankers, with one continuously airborne to support the patrol planes.

At the end of the day, Patrick and "Shade" O'Dea landed their EB-52 for rearming and refueling, and so Patrick could attend the mass briefing. He assembled the men and women together in the base-operations building's conference room. The crews were beyond dog tired—they were zombies, guzzling hours-old coffee and trying to keep their drooping eyelids from closing completely. Patrick was stunned to realize how small his force was.

But he was even more surprised to see these hardworking professionals come to attention when he stepped into the room. Through the nearly seventy-two hours of almost continuous flying, mission planning, and preflighting, they still cared enough to practice military etiquette.

"As you were, ladies and gentlemen," Patrick said. The crews, already on their feet in an effort to stay awake, shuffled to more relaxed positions, stifling yawns and draining coffee cups. "First of all, I have no news on General Furness and Colonel Mace. The Pave Dasher and an MC-130 are out looking for them. I have asked Colonel Cheshire to task one Megafortress crew to head out there to provide air cover for the rescue effort.

"Here's the situation as we know it: Despite promising the president of the United States that they would disarm, the Russians attempted to attack Eareckson Air Base with nuclear weapons and have now deployed their mobile ICBMs and appear to be ready to launch them. Our mission tonight is to find and destroy numerous Russian intercontinental-ballistic-missile sites—a total of six SS-18 launch-control centers and seventy-two silos, plus one hundred and eighty road-mobile SS-25 units. If we are successful, we'll eliminate almost half of the Russians' land-based intercontinental-ballistic-missile fleet, which, after the attack on the U.S., will bring us to rough parity and may avert another nuclear exchange.

"The Russians have a very sophisticated and dense anti-aircraft network, and it is fully functional and on the highest state of alert. We have the advantage of stealth and precision firepower, but the Russians are fielding twenty fighters and at least fifty surface-to-air missiles *for every one* of our bombers. The National Command Authority made the decision not to use nuclear weapons of any kind, not even enhanced radiation, microyield, or electromagnetic-pulse weapons, for fear of precipitating an all-out nuclear exchange. This means we have to go after the ICBMs without any defensive laydowns whatsoever. It's a lousy hand we've been dealt. Normally, I would have done whatever I felt necessary to get the job done, even if it meant using special weapons, but I feel we can do the job without them. If I'm wrong"—he paused, looking each man and woman in the room straight in the eye—"I'll burn in hell along with Gryzlov and all the other nutcases who started this war.

"Here's the lineup for tonight: Bobcat Two-three has the longest drive—two SS-18 launch-control centers at Aleysk with Wolverine thermium-nitrate penetrator cruise missiles, plus Wolverine cruise missiles dropping thermium-nitrate bomblets on all twenty-four of their silos. We've modified the Wolverine missiles with delayed-action fuzes so the missiles will penetrate at least a hundred feet underground before the warheads detonate, which gives us a good chance of taking out the underground launch-control centers. We don't know if the bomblets will be strong enough to do any damage on the silo doors, but it's the best we have. All we need to do is try to dislodge the doors from their tracks or jam them closed, and we've done our jobs. Bobcat Two-four will do the same on the SS-18 wing at Uzhur, which has four LCCs and forty-eight silos.

"Bobcat One-two and One-three will locate and attack the SS-25 units at Novosibirsk and Barnaul, with StealthHawks and Longhorns. Right now we're targeting the garrison locations where a number of SS-25 launch units have been dispersed to. We're hoping to tag as much as fifty percent of their road units in their garages. You also have locations of known field-dispersal and launch points that we've seen the Russians use in the past, so your job will be to keep an eye on those locations in case any units show up. Bobcat One-four will attack the SS-25 wings at Irkutsk. Bobcat Two-five will attack the SS-25 wing at Kansk, and Bobcat Two-six will attack the SS-25 wing at Drovyanaya.

"Colonel O'Dea and I, in Bobcat One-one, along with Bobcat Two-seven, have a special task," Patrick went on.

"Our job is to seek out and destroy four SS-24 rail-mobile ICBM squadrons that our intelligence tells us have been dispersed north of Krasnoyarsk on the national rail lines. Each SS-24 squadron carries three missiles, each of those with a ten-thousand-mile range—long enough to decimate every American city and military base on planet Earth. They were supposed to be taken out of service years ago, but they're still out there, so we must assume that if they violated that provision of the START II Treaty, they violated more, and thus they still have their full complement of ten independently targetable warheads. Bobcats One-five and Two-eight will stay behind to guard Yakutsk until the MC-17s depart and to provide backup for all other sorties, and Bobcat One-eight will provide air cover for search-and-rescue forces out in the Bering Sea.

"The AL-52 Dragon aircraft, Bobcat Three-one and Three-two, will take up patrol orbits over two locations. They'll be in a position to cover our ingress and egress on our strikes, and in case the Russians fire any missiles, they'll be able to intercept them.

"After your assigned attacks, withhold any weapons you have left for follow-on attacks or any other pop-up targets you might encounter or that are datalinked to you," Patrick said. "Follow your egress routings to the Sea of Japan and the Pacific Ocean, and rendezvous with your assigned tankers. The planned recovery base is Battle Mountain, but we may be sending you directly to dispersal bases if Battle Mountain has come under attack. Questions or comments?" Patrick fielded a few, and then they received a weather briefing and current threat analysis.

Finally, when the last briefer finished, Patrick moved to the front of the room again. "Ladies and gentlemen, if we're successful tonight, we can seriously degrade between one-third and one-half of Russia's ICBM force," he said. "We call this base 'Camp Vengeance.' Taking this base marks the beginning of the American counteroffensive against Russia.

If we're successful, we might even the score and avert any more nuclear exchanges. That's not a certainty by any means, but at the very least it'll be exactly what this base was named for: vengeance."

Patrick paused for a moment, then said, "I want to let you all know, before we get airborne again, that it's been a privilege to serve with you. You have all proved that you truly are the best of the best. You've gotten this far with skill, determination, professionalism, and audacity. Now we need to put every ounce of that skill to the test. I know you can do it. We will prevail, and with God's help we'll all be on our way home very soon. Good luck, good hunting. I'll see you all airborne in about one hour."

RYAZAN' ALTERNATE MILITARY COMMAND CENTER
That same time

Anatoliy Gryzlov was on the phone to a member of the Duma when he looked up and saw something he very rarely saw—General Nikolai Stepashin chewing out some young officer, screaming at the top of his lungs at him—and then actually striking him in the face! Oh, shit, he thought, this looks very serious.

"Get a confirmation from the commanding general," Stepashin was saying when Gryzlov approached him. "I need to know exactly what he saw, as soon as possible!"

"What is it, Nikolai?"

"Sir, a report came in early this morning that said an Ilyushin-78 tanker aircraft was damaged at Yakutsk."

Gryzlov's blood turned ice cold, and his eyes bugged out in shock. *This morning!?* he shouted.

"Sir, the message came in saying an aircraft was 'damaged'—that's all," Stepashin said excitedly. "The lieutenant who took the report asked to speak with the commanding general at the base. He did not get to speak with him because the commander was at the crash scene, but then the lieutenant forgot to follow up, thinking it was just a minor accident. He finally followed up a short time ago and reported in his log that *yefreytor* radio operators at Yakutsk confirmed the accident but said that it was minor and that investigators and commanders were investigating, but gave no other details except to insist that it was not a result of hostile action. However, we also learned that the base has been closed off all day. Day-shift workers were turned away supposedly because of a hazardous chemical spill, believed to be weapons-related but unconfirmed. I ordered a security team from Magadan to fly out via the fastest way available to investigate and report back to me at once."

"Did *anyone* speak with the commanding general?"

"The operator said he was at the crash site, sir. That is highly unusual and not standard procedure, but—"

"It is not just unusual, Stepashin—*it is not the truth!*" Gryzlov shouted. "I don't know how, but McLanahan is there."

"McLanahan?" Stepashin had to consciously keep from rolling his eyes and snorting in disgust in front of the president of the Russian Federation and the Commonwealth of Independent States. "Sir, Yakutsk is a support base in the middle of Siberia. They have aerial-refueling tankers and a long runway, and that is all. Why would McLanahan shoot down a tanker over Siberia?"

"The answer is obvious, Stepashin—McLanahan knows that our bombers cannot strike America without tanker support, and Yakutsk was central to the plan," Gryzlov said. He shook his head, his mind frantically calculating and plotting. "I underestimated McLanahan again, Stepashin. I believed he would use his stealth bombers and high-tech weapons to destroy our bomber bases. Instead he attacked Yakutsk. He knows that without the tankers we cannot mount another attack on the American mainland."

Stepashin appeared relieved. "If it is true, sir, it was a daring attack," he said warily, "but he drove his planes a very long way for nothing. We can ascertain very quickly if Yakutsk has been destroyed or if he simply shot down a few tankers. But he bypassed several more viable targets just to attack a relatively unimportant support base. The air base at Petropavlovsk was attacked but is still operational; our sub bases at Rybachiy and Vladivostok, our naval base at Magadan, and our air bases at Kavaznya and Anadyr are still fully operational. It was a pinprick, an irritation, nothing more. Even if he managed to destroy a number of tankers, we can reconstitute those lost forces quickly."

"They may be just pinpricks to you, General, but McLanahan's attacks are targeted for a very specific purpose," Gryzlov said. "He attacks radar sites and fighter airfields because that allows him to fly larger, less stealthy aircraft such as tankers and transports through our airspace. Besides, this is not like the army, where the loss of a few tanks or artillery pieces means little, General. Aerial-refueling tankers are force multipliers. A long-range bomber needs several of them to be effective. McLanahan knows that if he can destroy even a few tankers at just one key base, he degrades dozens, perhaps hundreds of bombers, fighters, reconnaissance, intelligence, and transport planes." He paused, a thought still nagging at his head. "Get in contact immediately with the commanding general at Yakutsk, Nikolai. Something else is happening there, I know it."

"I have a call in already, sir." At that moment a phone rang, and Stepashin snatched it up. He listened for a moment.

And then Gryzlov saw the look of complete fear in Stepashin's face, and he knew that McLanahan's real plan was now finally going to reveal itself. "What happened, General?" Gryzlov growled.

"The security team I dispatched from Magadan Air Base overflew the tanker-crash site in a MiG-27, then overflew the base after receiving very confused and improper radio transmissions from the control tower at Yakutsk," Stepashin said. "He reports seeing several American B-52 and B-1 bombers *taxiing around* on the field!"

"Taxiing at Yakutsk Air Base?" Gryzlov shouted. His stunned expression quickly turned into one of disbelief, then to amazement and grudging respect. "Of course—it makes sense now," he said. "His last safe refueling for his bombers has to be at least two thousand kilometers away, back over the Aleutians. He would not risk taking a large, unstealthy tanker across Siberia with his stealthy bombers. And although his bombers can easily make it back out to Alaska with one refueling, having a landing base inside Russia greatly expands his . . . his . . ."

Gryzlov stopped in midsentence, his mouth agape, and then he walked over to the wall chart of Russia, studying the territory around Yakutsk, measuring off distances with his fingers used as a plotter. "My God . . . it's brilliant," he gasped. He paused, nodded, then said, "I want Yakutsk Air Base attacked at once," Gryzlov said.

"Sir?"

"Attacked—destroyed if necessary," Gryzlov said. "Every hangar, every meter of runway, every aircraft that doesn't look like a Russian aircraft must be destroyed at once. Use nuclear weapons if you have to."

"You cannot be serious, sir!" Stepashin exploded. "You are ordering the use of nuclear weapons *on Russian soil?*"

"Don't you see, Stepashin?" Gryzlov asked. "McLanahan knows exactly what we based our entire attack strategy on— building a tanker base in Siberia allowed us to fly our bombers halfway around the world with impunity. Now McLanahan occupies that base! From Yakutsk he has an almost unlimited supply of jet fuel, from our own Siberian oil fields, and he is within unrefueled heavy-bomber range of *every military base in Russia!*" He pointed to the chart. "He has to be stopped before he can launch his attacks. I want you to order a cruise-missile barrage into that base immediately. Do whatever it takes, but you must stop him from launching his bombers from Yakutsk! Give the order—*now!*"

YAKUTSK AIR BASE, RUSSIAN FEDERATION
A short time later

Patrick's chest couldn't help but swell with pride as he watched his little air armada taxi for takeoff. Five EB-1C Vampires and four EB-52 Megafortress flying battleships, plus one KC-10 Extender aerial-refueling tanker, all lined up and getting ready for launch.

This would be a very impressive display of American firepower anywhere in the United States—but to think that they were getting ready to launch *from a Russian air base,* getting ready to *attack Russian missile sites,* was even more incredible. This mission was possible only because he had professional, hard-charging troops willing to sacrifice to make his plan happen. These aviators were the hardest-working, most dedicated men and women he had ever served with. He couldn't believe how privileged he was to be leading them.

"Got some updates being transmitted to you, sir," Dave Luger radioed. "A few more SS-25s moved out of garrisoned positions in a real big hurry. We're thinking that maybe the Russians are starting to disperse more units."

"Think they're on to us?"

"That would be my guess, Muck," Luger said. "It may complicate targeting a bit more, but I think that the more they try to run and hide, they'll make it easier for us to find what they're hiding, because we already have several days' worth of comparison imagery—we'll see pretty quickly where they moved. We don't see any missiles being erected. Wish we had a better fix on the SS-24s. We're trying our best to pinpoint them, but no luck so far."

"Keep trying, Dave," Patrick responded. "We'll just plan on hitting the known garrisons and presurveyed launch points and hope we get lucky. Send a message to the load crews and get an update on when they'll be loaded up and ready to get out."

"Just did that, Muck," Dave responded. "By the time your guys start launching their first missiles, the MC-17s should be in the air."

"I want them off the ground right away," Patrick said. "Have them abandon all but the classified equipment—they can leave all the bomb jammers, test equipment, power carts, tools, and anything else that won't reveal important info on our bombers. I want them airborne right behind us."

"I'll pass the word, sir," Luger said.

Because they had the longest distance to fly, Bobcat Two-three and Two-four were the first in line to launch, followed by the first Dragon airborne-laser aircraft, Bobcat Three-one, which had to have repairs done on the ground; the other Dragon, Bobcat Three-two, was already airborne, flying cover over the base, along with one Megafortress and one Vampire. The KC-10 was next, to replace the other KC-10 already airborne to refuel the three planes guarding the base; once the second tanker was airborne, the first tanker would land, refuel, pick up the last of the crew chiefs and ground technicians, and fly out to a refueling track five hundred miles south of Yakutsk to await the returning bombers. Patrick was next, in Bobcat One-one, followed by the rest of the Megafortresses and finally the rest of the Vampires.

So far everything looked good. Every plane but one taxied out on schedule; the straggler, Bobcat One-four, began taxiing once all the others departed, after being swarmed by a dozen maintenance techs. If there were any more maintenance glitches, no one was reporting them. Everything was being done on a strict timetable, so there were no required radio calls unless—

"Bobcat, Bobcat, this is Three-two, missiles inbound, missiles inbound!" the mission commander of the AL-52

Dragon shouted on the command channel. "We're picking up numerous high-speed missiles coming in from three different directions, very high altitude. We count at least six flights so far. First missile impacts in *three minutes!*"

"All Bobcat forces, all Bobcat forces, launch without delay!" Patrick ordered. "Take ten-second spacing, fan out after liftoff. *Move! Move!*"

The first two EB-1C Vampire bombers were off within seconds—they had already lined up on the runway and were about to begin their takeoff roll. The AL-52 Dragon took much longer than expected, but soon it was rolling down the runway, with the KC-10 right behind it, almost obscured in the Dragon's dark engine exhaust.

"Go, Summer, *go!*" Patrick shouted to his aircraft commander. "Get right behind the tanker! Go!" When Summer actually pulled the throttles back to make the turn onto the runway, Patrick shoved the throttles to full military power himself. The tight turn made the wheels slip and skid on the ungrooved pavement, and it felt as if O'Dea might not be able to hold it, but she finally got it lined up on the runway by the time the engines spooled up to full power.

"Dave, Yakutsk is under attack!" Patrick said over his subcutaneous transceiver. "Get the MC-17s airborne *now!*"

"General . . ." Luger hesitated, then went on. "Sir, there's no way. They weren't even halfway from loading up all the personnel—they haven't even started engines. I directed them to get into shelters."

"Damn it, Dave, *no!*"

"It's the only chance they have, Patrick," Luger said, the anguish painfully evident in his voice. "I . . . I had to make a decision. There are plenty of underground shelters there—it's the only chance they have," he repeated.

Patrick cursed into his oxygen visor, but there was nothing he could do except watch his supercockpit display as the battle began to unfold.

The incoming missiles were all visible, and now, as

Patrick watched, the launch aircraft also became visible: The AL-52 Dragon already airborne over Yakutsk had locked on to one of them with the laser's adaptive optics, so he could see an image of a group of two flights, each with four Tupolev-160 Blackjack supersonic bombers, flying at very high altitude from the south, firing supersonic missiles; another group of three flights of four Blackjacks coming in from the southwest, launching more missiles; and a group of two flights of six Tupolev-22M Backfire bombers coming in supersonic from the west-southwest.

There were several hypersonic cruise missiles inbound as well; Patrick couldn't see on his display where they were launched from, but now it didn't matter—they were going to hit in just a few seconds, unless the anti-ballistic-missile weapons on board his Dragons and Vampires could stop them.

Gryzlov was launching everything he had at Yakutsk, in the final showdown between American and Russian bombers.

The Dragon engaged the oncoming missiles from maximum range. At first it engaged the hypersonic cruise missiles heading toward Yakutsk itself, shooting down several of them right away, but then it directed its firepower toward other supersonic missiles being fired by the Backfires—because their target was not Yakutsk, but the AL-52 Dragon itself. The Vampire crew guarding Yakutsk launched four long-range AIM-154 Anaconda missiles, two at Russian cruise missiles and finally two at the Backfire bombers. The Megafortress bomber on guard launched a stream of AIM-120 Scorpion missiles.

But they weren't fast enough to catch the mass of AS-17 Krypton missiles fired by the Backfire bombers. Three missiles simultaneously hit the Dragon, sending it crashing in flames to the Siberian tundra.

The two Vampires that had launched from Yakutsk engaged the Backfire bombers with Scorpion missiles, downing the remainder of the bombers from the first flight and two from the second flight. But the Megafortress bomber that was already airborne had quickly expended its supply of defensive missiles, and when it turned to escape the area, it was hit by two AS-17 missiles and exploded in a tremendous cloud of fire. The Vampires avenged it by downing the remaining four Backfire bombers from long range with Scorpion missiles.

The second Dragon aircraft turned south immediately after takeoff and began engaging the incoming bombers—but by then every Blackjack bomber had launched its missiles at Yakutsk: supersonic AS-16 "Kickback" missiles, one every ten seconds. Each Blackjack bomber pumped two dozen Mach-2 missiles into the sky.

"Missiles inbound, missiles inbound!" Patrick cried on the command channel. "Take off two at a time! *Hurry!*"

But time had run out. Three Megafortresses and two Vampires had launched, and two Vampires were turning onto the runway just seconds behind another, when the first AS-X-19 Koala missile exploded five thousand feet aboveground and less than a mile north of Yakutsk. Its small, one-kiloton nuclear warhead did not touch the ground, but it didn't need to—the overpressure caused by the explosion created a ripple of force that radiated outward like an erupting volcano, sweeping over the air base in the blink of an eye.

Three more missiles also exploded over Yakutsk, but by then the devastation had already been done. Every building, structure, aircraft, and human being aboveground within two miles of each detonation was tossed hundreds of yards across the flat plains of Siberia like dust in a windstorm, crushed beneath several thousand pounds per square inch of pure nuclear horror, or swatted out of the sky and squashed into the ground like a clay pigeon hit by a shotgun blast.

RYAZAN' ALTERNATE MILITARY COMMAND CENTER, RUSSIA
Several hours later

"This is President Thorn."

"Greetings, Mr. President," Anatoliy Gryzlov said, his voice light and cheerful. His interpreter quickly translated on the hot line. With him in the underground Ryazan' Alternate Military Command Center was the chief of the general staff, Nikolai Stepashin, and other members of the general staff.

"Called to gloat, Gryzlov?"

"I called to express my admiration and respect for General McLanahan and all the brave men and women under his command," Gryzlov said, lacing his tone with as much triumph as he could. He thought he could hear Thorn gritting his teeth in anger. "I must say, I tried my best to anticipate the general's actions, and he stayed one step ahead of me the entire time. He very nearly succeeded in attacking my missile bases and mobile-missile units. Very impressive."

"Attacking your what?"

"Did I not tell you, Thorn?" Gryzlov asked sarcastically. "We have sent rescuers in to Yakutsk. They may not stay on the ground for very long, they must wear many layers of protective clothing, and we will allow a man to go in only once, for no more than thirty minutes, but we have communicated with many American survivors."

"*Survivors?* There are Americans still there, in Yakutsk?"

"Apparently the general wisely decided to get the ones into shelters that could not make it off the ground in time," Gryzlov said. "We count one hundred and four Americans, men and women, in our underground shelters, safe and sound. The officer in charge is Air Force Colonel Harold Briggs. He has given us only his name, rank, and date of birth."

"I want those men and women released immediately, Gryzlov," Thorn said.

"Don't be stupid, Thorn," Gryzlov said. "I would not release them even if I could. They are prisoners of war and will be treated as such. But we have not learned a safe way to get them out without exposing ourselves to radiation. They are quite safe where they are, and we believe they have enough food and water to last until the radiation levels subside. They have sealed themselves inside a prison, and there is where they shall stay until we can take them out and place them in custody."

"You are obligated to keep them safe, provide them with medical attention, food, and water, let them communicate with the International Red Cross, and abide by all the other provisions of the Geneva Conventions," President Thorn said. "I don't care under what conditions they are imprisoned—conditions *you* are responsible for creating!"

"And I warn you, Thorn, if those men and women harm any of my soldiers, all of them will be *shot dead!*" Gryzlov shouted. "I am not in the mood for listening to your whining and bleating. Your troops are responsible for imprisoning several hundred of my soldiers based at Yakutsk—all of whom perished in the attack. Undoubtedly in your troops' rush to protect themselves, they conveniently forgot to release their captives. I know you have Tin Man commandos among the survivors. They had better think twice before harming any Russian soldiers."

"Gryzlov, let's leave the negotiations for our foreign-affairs officers—"

"Quite so, Thorn," Gryzlov said. "As I was saying, however, we have interrogated other survivors, ones that were unfortunate enough not to make it to the shelters in time. They sustained very serious injuries, I'm afraid—"

"Thanks to you, you *son of a bitch!*"

"—despite our best efforts to help them, and they told me before they died many details of McLanahan's attack plan: about our missile silos at Aleysk and Uzhur, our mobile-missile units, even stories about going out and hunting Russian heavy mobile missiles with multiple warheads. Your General McLanahan is certainly an imaginative fellow."

"If he said you still have illegal weapons in the field, Gryzlov, I'm sure it's true," Thorn said.

"We must put an end to this, Thorn," Gryzlov said. "My analysts suggest that many of McLanahan's bombers escaped from Yakutsk. Since they have not attacked any of their planned targets yet, and it is just a few hours until daybreak, I think perhaps my analysts are wrong. But if you could verify the whereabouts of all of McLanahan's forces, I'm sure my commanders will see to it that our nuclear forces and air-defense units stand down, which will obviously relieve the stress on them and will undoubtedly help prevent an accidental launch of—"

"More threats, Gryzlov?" Thomas Thorn asked. "You threaten me with more nuclear attacks unless I give you the exact location and number of our bomber forces? You can go to hell, Gryzlov!"

"If you remain uncooperative, Thorn, I must give my strategic commanders full authority to respond to any threat against the Russian Federation with every weapon at their disposal," Gryzlov said. "You do not seem to realize how serious this is, Thorn! McLanahan landed *an entire bomber wing* on a Russian airfield! He killed dozens of troops, captured and imprisoned nearly a thousand men and women, stole millions of rubles' worth of fuel and weapons, and was responsible for the deaths of all his captives by keeping them in a battle zone—in essence attempting to use them as human shields!—instead of evacuating them to a safer area, as required by the Geneva Conventions. You must do more, *much* more to assure the Russian people, the Duma, myself, and the chiefs of the general staff that you want peace, not war."

"I don't have to give you anything, Gryzlov," President Thorn said.

"Where is McLanahan?" Gryzlov asked angrily. "Have you had any contact with him?"

"Go to hell."

"Don't be stupid, Thorn. Tell me if he is on his way back to the United States. Do something smart for a change, Thorn! At least tell me if you have had contact with him."

"I promise you, Gryzlov, the United States will be on guard against any other sneak attacks by Russia, and we will deal with them. The next call I get from you had better be an unconditional stand-down of all your military forces." And Thorn terminated the call.

Gryzlov hung up the receiver and sat back in his seat, a smile spreading across his face. "What a fool," he muttered. "If the American people are even a tenth as soft as he is, this war will be over very shortly."

"Sir," Stepashin said, his voice and visage tense and irritable, "you must address the general staff, the Duma, and the press regarding your actions in Yakutsk."

"That can wait, Stepashin."

"There are reports of hundreds of casualties coming in from the city of Yakutsk," Stepashin said. "The nuclear bursts have damaged or destroyed billions of rubles in oil-distribution and pumping facilities. All communications in and out of the city and the civil airfield have been disrupted by the electromagnetic-pulse effects."

"Stepashin, I did what I had to do," Gryzlov said dismissively. "The Americans landed a dozen long-range bombers and over a hundred troops in Yakutsk and were in the process of launching attacks against us. What was I supposed to do—ask Thorn or McLanahan to sit tight *on our homeland* while we negotiate a cease-fire?"

Stepashin fell silent for a few moments, glancing over at his general-staff officers and receiving concerned, angry glances in return. There was no doubt that the Americans' staging air raids from Yakutsk was a serious development—but Gryzlov's using *nuclear weapons* on Russian soil, killing hundreds or perhaps even thousands of his own people and troops, did not sit well with them at all. Finally he said, "Why did you tell Thorn that we had interrogated American survivors? We have not sent in any troops or medical personnel yet to Yakutsk to see how bad the radiation levels are."

"Thorn doesn't know that," Gryzlov said. "I wanted to hear his reaction when I mentioned the ballistic-missile bases—and he all but confirmed that those were indeed McLanahan's intended targets."

"Aren't we obligated to search for survivors and help anyone that might really be in the shelters?" Stepashin asked.

"And risk the health of our own men by exposing them to radioactivity? Don't be crazy, General," Gryzlov said. "Have everyone stay away from Yakutsk and have combat engineers test the air and soil every day or so for radioactivity levels. If any Americans are there, they deserve to die—and if there are any Russian survivors, we will simply tell the world they were executed by the Americans."

Stepashin looked down at the floor to hide his expression of disgust at the idea that they were simply going to abandon any Russians who might still be alive at Yakutsk.

"Now," Gryzlov went on, "what more can we expect from the United States in the wake of this episode?"

"Thomas Thorn did not have much of a stomach to fight before—I see no reason to expect he'd be more willing to do so now," Stepashin replied. "McLanahan was his Doberman pinscher—with him out of the picture, I think he will wait, size up his forces, and then open negotiations or decide how to respond. But he does not have the conventional forces available anymore to hold any strategic targets in Russia at risk. He can certainly hurt us with his sea-launched ballistic missiles, but I do not think he will respond with nuclear weapons, even in an extremely limited manner."

"I am not concerned about Thorn, but I *am* worried about

McLanahan and what remains of his forces—and with any other Patrick Shane McLanahans out there," Gryzlov said. He thought for a moment, then said, "And there is still the question of the targets we failed to destroy, especially Cheyenne Mountain, Barksdale, Battle Mountain—and Sacramento, California.

"In case McLanahan surfaces again, Stepashin, he will be naming his own poison," Gryzlov said. "Just in case one of McLanahan's bombers does attack any of our ballistic-missile sites, I want Battle Mountain and Sacramento destroyed. Be sure one warhead hits Beale Air Force Base, just so everyone understands that it was the real target—but I want McLanahan's home town destroyed in punishment. Hopefully, Thorn has the brains to recall him, if he is still alive, but in case he feels like acting the hero again, he and his family will suffer for it."

At that moment the conference room's phone rang. Nikolai Stepashin picked it up. Gryzlov was busy tamping down the tobacco on a cigarette and didn't notice Stepashin's confused, worried expression until he said in a loud voice, "I authorized no such thing! Get an identification on that aircraft immediately!"

Gryzlov threw the unlit cigarette to the floor. "What is it, General?"

"A large transport plane is circling Yakutsk Air Base," Stepashin said. "It made a low approach and appeared to try to land but pulled up at the last moment."

"Is it a combat-engineering team, checking radiation levels?"

"They use helicopters, not large transport planes, sir," Stepashin said. "Whoever it is, he is not authorized to go anywhere near that base."

Gryzlov's shoulders drooped, and he felt his face drain of life. Once again, right when he felt like celebrating, something else had begun to happen. . . .

YAKUTSK AIR BASE
That same time

"Not enough room—you'll have to move that debris," said the loadmaster of the MC-17 special-operations transport plane. He pointed out the open rear cargo doors. "That fuel truck and whatever that pile of stuff is there has got to go."

"Got it," said Air Force Technical Sergeant James "JD" Daniels, his voice electronically amplified by the communications suite built into his Tin Man battle armor. He and his partner, U.S. Marine Corps Lance Corporal Johnny "Hulk" Morris, stood at the edge of the cargo ramp, one hand on a handhold, the other gripping their electromagnetic rail guns. Both men were stunned to see the carnage below them—buildings flattened, trucks and aircraft tossed around like toys in a young child's room, and large craters of eerie gray gravel, like cremated remains. There was absolutely nothing left standing aboveground for miles. Daniels nodded to Morris. "Radiation levels are moderate, Hulk—not as bad as we thought."

"You're shitting me, right, Sarge?" Morris asked. The MC-17 started a steep right bank over the base, lining up on the downwind side for another pass. "This place got hit by four or five nukes, and you're saying it's not as bad as we thought?"

"I'm picking up less than twenty rads per hour," Brigadier General David Luger radioed from Battle Mountain Air Reserve Base. "That's good for about six hours—and safe endurance will be much longer in the Tin Man armor. Should be more than enough time."

"The young sergeant is a little skittish because he hasn't had any kids yet, and he's afraid his family jewels might get zapped, sir."

"You're just jealous because no woman would have *you,* Sarge."

"Save it for when you're back home, boys," Luger said. "Get ready."

It took a few minutes, but soon the MC-17 was making another low approach over the devastated runway. The big transport swooped in, descending to just over forty feet above the runway. As soon as the plane leveled off, at the approach end of the runway, Daniels stepped off the edge of the cargo ramp, holding the rail gun in his hands at port arms.

Morris had practiced these jumps back at Battle Mountain a few times, but he was relatively new to the unit and didn't quite fully trust all this high-tech gear. He had made many parachute jumps of all kinds in his Marine Corps career—free-fall, static-line, HALO—and he'd even jumped from moving helicopters without a parachute before in thirty-thirty jumps—thirty feet above water, traveling thirty knots. But he had never jumped from a moving transport plane going three hundred knots—*onto solid ground*.

But now was not the time to question the wisdom of doing it. He briefly wondered which job was stupider—jumping off a cargo plane like this or riding in that crazy Condor insertion aircraft, like the commander and the sergeant major did: a plastic turd with wings, dropped from inside a B-52 flying at thirty-six thousand feet, then riding in it for over three hours right over the bad guys' heads! Now, *that* was crazy. He gripped his rail gun tighter, took a last deep breath, and stepped off the cargo ramp just seconds after Daniels.

As they fell to Earth, gyros and accelerometers in their electronic battle-armor suits told them which way they needed to lean into the fall and at the same time measured their speed and the distance to the ground and adjusted the thrusters on their boots to compensate for being pushed by the jet blast from the MC-17. As they neared the ground, their boot thrusters fired at full power, slowing their fall—but even so, Daniels hit the ground hard and clattered to the concrete in a heap.

"You okay, Sarge?" Morris radioed.

"Affirmative," Daniels responded. He was unhurt, but the rail gun's data and power cable had broken. He cursed to himself and set the rifle near a distance-remaining sign on the edge of the runway so he could find it again. "Broke my damned rail gun, though. Let's move, Hulk."

The two Tin Man commandos in microhydraulically powered exoskeletons, working together, had the runway completely cleared of debris in minutes, including a partially crushed fuel truck. By the time they finished and stepped clear of the runway, the MC-17 had come around once again, smoothly touched down, and quickly powered to a stop using thrust reversers.

Daniels, Morris, and the others on board the MC-17 worked fast. After the transport plane lowered its cargo ramp, they unloaded what it carried: two forty-six-foot-long self-contained nuclear-biological-chemical—(NBC)—weapon-decontamination trailers, pulled by diesel tugs; two rubber water bladders on flatbed trailers, each holding three thousand gallons of fresh water and pulled alongside the decontamination trailers; and twenty NBC technicians.

Led by Daniels and Morris, the group headed toward the central west side of the runway. Beside where the west cluster of aircraft hangars used to be located were two low structures, less than four feet aboveground and, amazingly, still intact—they were each little more than a roof composed of eighteen inches of solid reinforced concrete, with a single steel door facing the aircraft parking ramp. One decontamination trailer backed up to each steel door, and the Tin Man commandos attached protective plastic tunnels to each shelter entrance and to the trailer entry door.

"Knock knock, Sergeant Major," Daniels radioed.

"Door's coming open," Marine Corps Sergeant Major Chris Wohl responded. A few moments later, the steel doors swung open, and six individuals ran out of the underground shelters and directly into each door marked ENTER on both decontamination trailers. After the first group entered the trailers, Chris Wohl and Colonel Hal Briggs both emerged from the shelters, wearing Tin Man battle armor.

The two knocked fists with Daniels and Morris in greeting. "Good to see you guys," Hal Briggs said. "What's the situation?"

"No opposition, aircraft is code one, all personnel good to go, sir," Daniels responded.

"What are the radiation levels?"

"We're reading about forty rads per hour here. That's good for about four hours' exposure time. It's a bit higher out on the parking ramp, but the isolation chamber inside the MC-17 and in the cockpit is about ten to fifteen rads. The max we detected inside our suits has been five rads per hour."

"We gotta hand it to the Russkies—they know how to build bomb shelters," Hal said. "We picked up just five rads during the attack and less than two rads per hour since then. Pretty damned good."

"How many made it inside, sir?"

It was obvious, even concealed by his battle armor, that Briggs was sorrowful. "We have fifty-one in our shelter and forty-two in the other," Hal said. "We were shoulder to shoulder in there. We managed to grab about thirty Russians and take them in with us."

"My God," Daniels breathed. He knew that the Air Battle Force had flown about a hundred fifty personnel into Yakutsk with them on the MC-17s, plus several more on the Megafortresses. That meant that about ninety American technicians had died in the attack, plus the aircrew members who were caught on the ground when the nukes hit.

The decontamination trailers had four separate stations, each of which could accommodate six people at once. Each person removed excess contaminated equipment in the first room, which was ventilated with filtered air to remove any radioactive fallout. Next each person scrubbed and showered in warm water and detergent in the second compartment, with clothes still on. In the third compartment, clothing was stripped off under water-and-detergent showers and discarded; and in the fourth compartment, each person again showered and scrubbed in warm water and detergent, then dried with warm-air blowers that exhausted to the outside. The person then dressed in clean clothes, underwent a quick medical scan to be sure as many radioactive particles as possible were removed, then was transported back to the MC-17. A positive-pressure plastic tunnel led from the decontamination trailer to a shielded waiting area set up in the forward part of the cargo compartment, with a positive-pressure filtered-air ventilation system activated to keep radioactive particles out.

"Twenty minutes to do six people per trailer, about thirty-six people per hour—we should be done in less than three hours," Hal Briggs radioed. "I'm not sure how we'll decontaminate the Tin Man battle armor—we might end up leaving it behind and blowing it in place."

"Decontaminate the armor if you can," Dave Luger said, "but don't waste time with it. If you can't safely decontaminate it or keep it separate from the personnel, go ahead and blow the gear, and then get the hell out. We'll be leaving the decontamination trailers behind, unfortunately."

"Any activity around the base?" Briggs asked.

"Lots of it, but even the aircraft are staying at least ten miles away," Luger said. "They know you're there, but it looks like they're leaving you alone—at least for now."

RYAZAN' ALTERNATE MILITARY COMMAND CENTER, RUSSIA
Minutes later

"That's correct, sir," General Nikolai Stepashin said. "Our reconnaissance aircraft observers believe that the aircraft is an American C-17 'Globemaster' transport plane. It was carrying what they believe to be decontamination vehicles. They are attaching the vehicles to the base's bomb shelters, waiting there a period of time, then driving over to the transport. It is apparent that the Americans are decontaminating their personnel and are preparing to airlift the survivors out of Yakutsk."

"This is unbelievable!" President Anatoliy Gryzlov shouted. "I cannot believe the sheer audacity of these Americans! They have flown another military aircraft right past our air defenses and landed at a Russian air base *again*, completely disregarding the sovereignty of our airspace!"

Stepashin had to bite a lip to keep from grimacing—after what they had done to the United States of America, they had no cause to criticize anyone else's breach of air sovereignty!

"Do they think they own that airfield now? Do they expect us to just look the other way while they load up their transport and fly away again? We should hit that transport immediately with another air strike—blow the Americans to hell, where they belong!"

"Sir, I strongly suggest we let that transport load up and leave Yakutsk unharmed," Stepashin said measuredly, not risking angering the already frantic-looking president but trying to be firm at the same time. "They undoubtedly have Russians in those shelters with them—they could be helping our soldiers. It is a humanitarian airlift, not an offensive strike. We should not interfere with it, especially since we did nothing similar ourselves to help survivors at Yakutsk."

"Are you saying I am a coward, Stepashin?" Gryzlov shouted. "You will be silent, Stepashin, or you will be dismissed! I will not tolerate insubordination in my own command center!"

"With all due respect, sir, I was making a recommendation," Stepashin said, his rising anger barely restrained. "We should not attack an unarmed humanitarian rescue mission."

"I do not care if they flew in a children's choir carrying

daisies and magic pixie dust, General—I want that plane destroyed!" Gryzlov shouted. Stepashin noted the large, dark bags under his eyes, the drooping shoulders, the shaking hands, and the pale complexion—the man probably hadn't had any sleep for the past two days and was subsisting mostly on cigarettes and coffee. "See to it immediately! I want—"

At that moment the conference room's telephone rang again. Gryzlov jumped, then stared at it as if it were a gigantic hairy spider. He's losing it, Stepashin thought as he picked up the phone. "Stepashin . . . Yes, I copy. Alert all air-defense sectors. Keep all other air-defense radar systems in standby, and use optronic sensors to locate it. Repeat, do not use radar—they will only be destroyed as well."

"What the hell happened, General?" Gryzlov gasped.

"Air-defense alert issued by Novgorod air-defense region," Stepashin said. "Small, subsonic aircraft detected east-northeast of the capital. Intermittent and very weak return, too small to be a stealth aircraft. Possibly an unmanned aircraft or reconnaissance drone."

"My God . . . he's *here*," Gryzlov murmured, eyes bulging in fear. "McLanahan's here! He's decided not to attack our Siberian bases but is going to attack Moscow itself!"

"McLanahan is not the only threat out there, sir," Stepashin said. "Our air defenses are much more capable around Moscow than anywhere else in the world. Perhaps this is just—"

"Order an attack, Stepashin," Gryzlov said. "I want a full retaliatory strike launched on the United States."

"Sir?" Stepashin retorted. "You want to order a *nuclear attack* on the United States? You cannot do this!"

"They are attacking my capital—I will retaliate with everything I've got and make them pay for their actions!" Gryzlov shouted. He stepped quickly over to the Strategic Forces officer carrying the special briefcase and snatched it out of his hands—he had to drag the officer to the conference table, because the briefcase was still handcuffed to him. Gryzlov unlocked the briefcase, withdrew a circular slide-rule-like decoder device from under his shirt, dialed in the current Greenwich Mean Time, wrote down a series of numbers, then selected a card from a row of red cards in the briefcase. He punched the series of numbers into a keypad in the bottom of the briefcase, then inserted the card in a slot and pressed a green button. He then turned to Stepashin and said, "Enter the authentication instructions, General."

"Are you absolutely sure, Mr. President?" the chief of the general staff asked. He took the card but held it up to the president, using it to focus Gryzlov's attention. The president couldn't seem to keep his eyes steady on any target for more than a second or two, and it appeared as if he was having trouble keeping his eyelids open. "This will certainly start a world war, Mr. President. Millions of lives could be lost in the next hour if you proceed."

"Our lives will be lost and millions of our people's lives will be held hostage if we do not do this," Gryzlov said. "Give the authentication code, General."

Stepashin sighed. He looked around the room, hoping to find someone who might be sympathetic or help him try to talk Gryzlov out of this, but there was no one. He withdrew his own decoder from inside his tunic, glanced at the clock, dialed in the time, inserted the red card in the slot, and entered the resultant code and his own personal passcode into the briefcase device. Moments later a strip of paper printed out of the briefcase. Stepashin tore it out, read it over to be sure it had printed correctly, then nodded.

"Do it, General," Gryzlov said through clenched teeth. "Let us get this war over with. I want McLanahan to pay, not with his own life but with the lives of his fellow Americans."

Stepashin walked over to the telephone on the conference table, picked up the receiver, dialed some numbers, and waited. After a short wait, he spoke. "This is Chief of the

General Staff of the Armed Forces of the Russian Federation General Nikolai Stepashin. I am with President Gryzlov in the Alternate Military Command Center at Oksky Reserve, Lybedskaya Street, Ryazan'. I am prepared to authenticate." He waited another few moments, dialed in the date and time again on his decoder, and said, "I authenticate *iyul' pyatnadtsat'*. Authenticate *noyabr' shyest'*." He waited again, checked his decoder, then said, "That authentication is correct. I have a priority emergency-action message from the commander in chief. Advise when ready to copy." He waited once more, then read the characters from the printout twice. "Go ahead with your readback." Again he was silent for several long moments as he checked off each character. "The readback was correct," he said finally. "You may hand over the phone to your deputy, who will reread the message back to me. . . . Yes, I hear you clearly, Captain. Go ahead with the readback."

The second authentication readback seemed to be taking longer than the first one. Gryzlov had been through many exercises simulating this procedure—he had in fact devised most of these very same procedures himself, when he was chief of the general staff—but for some reason this seemed to be taking longer than usual.

Gryzlov lit up a cigarette and was halfway through it when all of a sudden he saw two officers running toward the conference room, with two armed security men behind them. Stepashin turned toward them, the phone still to his ear, then held up a hand, silently ordering the men not to enter. The officers hesitated, conversed between themselves for a moment, then decided to enter anyway.

"What is the meaning of this!" Gryzlov shouted. "Get out of here! Go back to your posts!"

"Sir!" the senior officer said, snapping to attention momentarily. "I am Captain Federov, the communications-section commander of this facility."

"Get out of here, Captain," Stepashin said. "We are busy here. That is an order!"

"Sir . . ." He saw the phone in Stepashin's hand, his eyes bulging in surprise, then turned to Gryzlov and said excitedly, "Mr. President, we have detected an unauthorized overseas call being placed from this room!"

"A . . . *what?*" Gryzlov shouted.

"Someone . . ." The captain turned to Stepashin, swallowed, and said, "Sir, the chief of the general staff is making an unauthorized telephone call—to the United States of America."

Gryzlov turned to Stepashin, his mouth dropping open in surprise. "*The United States?* I thought he was talking to the communications center! He is relaying an emergency-action message—"

"He called the United States, sir—specifically, the general exchange at Battle Mountain Air Reserve Base in Nevada." Gryzlov looked as if he were going to pass out in shock. "He has been connected to the Battle Management Center and is speaking with the facility commander, Brigadier General David Luger. They have been connected for the past several—"

"*No!*" Gryzlov shouted. Ignoring the phone and the open connection, he threw himself at Stepashin, grasping him by the throat and wrestling him to the floor. Stepashin put the phone under his body and held on to Gryzlov's wrists, not allowing the president to choke him but keeping his body atop his so the security guards couldn't grab the phone. Ultimately, he heard the phone clatter to the floor, so he assumed that Federov had pulled its cord from the wall.

"*Pizda tyebya rodila!*" Gryzlov was shouting. "You fucking traitor!" Stepashin barely noticed the muzzle of the semiautomatic pistol pushed up under his left cheek before he heard a loud bang, felt a brief sting in his left eye, and then felt nothing at all.

It seemed like a long time later when Gryzlov finally got up from on top of Stepashin's nearly headless corpse. "*Mandavoshka,*" he swore. "Shit-ass bastard. You turned out to be a coward after all." The echo of the gunshot and the stench of gunpowder and blood still hung in the air.

Just then the sound of an air-raid siren started wailing throughout the facility—but it could not drown out the sound of explosions overhead that slowly but relentlessly drove closer and closer, until the lights flickered and went out, the ceiling of the underground facility caved in, and there was nothing but waves of fire, shock, smoke, and flying debris all around him . . . and then nothingness.

"I've got secondaries already, One-one," radioed the mission commander aboard Bobcat Two-four, the second EB-1C Vampire bomber on the attack run. "Two-three opened something up right under those coordinates we received. I think we found it."

"Roger," Patrick McLanahan responded. "Launch all of your Wolverines on those coordinates. I'll withhold mine in case we get any more tips from the Russian chief of the general staff." Patrick's EB-52 Megafortress was thirty minutes behind the two Vampire bombers. The two Vampires had sped on ahead of the lone surviving Megafortress bomber, launching antiradar weapons at Novgorod to plow a way through Russia's air defenses. Although Patrick had targeted the Ryazan' alternate military command center as soon as he escaped the devastation at Yakutsk seven hours earlier, he didn't really know exactly where to launch his weapons.

Until the call came from Ryazan' itself, from a man calling himself General Stepashin, the chief of the general staff, reading off the exact geographic coordinates of the underground facility and even describing its location so it could be found by reading a street map! The first Vampire bomber launched two Wolverine cruise missiles with penetrating thermium-nitrate warheads on the coordinates, still not prepared to believe that the information was factual—but when the secondary explosions revealed the underground complex below, they knew they had the right spot.

"It looks like a volcano down there, sir. We hit either that command center or some huge underground weapons-storage area, or both," the mission commander said. "What next, boss?"

Patrick plotted a course that would take them through southwest Russia, the shortest path to the Kazakhstan border—near Engels Air Base, it so happened, the base Patrick's bombers had attacked the year before, the attack that apparently drove Anatoliy Gryzlov crazy enough to first engineer a coup in Russia and then wage nuclear war with the United States. Patrick then deconflicted the course with all available intelligence data, then beamed the flight plan to the two Vampires.

"Next we get the hell out of here," Patrick said. "Let's go home."

EPILOGUE

BELLEVUE, NEBRASKA
January 2005

"So help me God."

The chief justice of the Supreme Court shook hands with the newly inaugurated president, but unlike in past years when the new president of the United States completed his swearing-in, there was now no applause, no "Hail to the Chief" playing in the background, and no cheering. The crowd was just a fraction of its normal size, just a few hundred people—vastly outnumbered by troops, law enforcement, and Secret Service agents surrounding the venue, a large tent set up in what remained of a farmer's home, just a few miles outside what once was Offutt Air Force Base.

The chill January winds sent icy bits of frozen rain swirling through the tent, which made everyone inside skittish. They were assured that there was no longer any danger of radioactive fallout, but even so, many attendees took the opportunity of the cold to cover their faces tightly with scarves to avoid directly breathing the air.

"Good luck, and may God watch over you, Mr. President," the chief justice said.

"Thank you, Mr. Chief Justice," President Kevin Martindale said. The fifty-two-year-old Republican had just repeated history: He was only the second president in U.S. history, after Grover Cleveland, to be elected president after being previously voted out of office. Like Cleveland, Martindale was a bachelor, so rather than having one of his Hollywood-actress girlfriends hold the Bible for his swearing-in, his vice president, former secretary of state under Thomas Thorn, Maureen Hershel, held it for him.

Hershel was likewise unmarried; for her swearing-in, Maureen had asked Lieutenant General Patrick McLanahan to do the honors. When President Martindale stepped up to the podium, Maureen stepped back beside Patrick on the dais, and her hand slipped into his. He looked at her and smiled—and then she saw him glance over her shoulder toward the empty, snow-covered fields and beyond toward the devastated Air Force base. She had grown accustomed to the "ten-thousand-yard stare," as many called it—instantaneous and jarring remembrances of death and near-death, destruction, and horrifying events.

But Patrick was not the only one she saw with that look—many others in America had it these days, men and women in the military especially, but many others whose lives were forever and utterly devastated by the nuclear attacks on the United States.

"My fellow Americans," President Martindale began, "I want to thank you, and especially thank President Thomas Thorn, for allowing me the privilege of changing the venue for my inauguration from Washington to Nebraska. The security difficulties in granting this request were enormous, but President Thorn accepted responsibility for all the logistics necessary to honor my request, and for that I thank him.

"Normally, inaugurations are supposed to be joyous occasions: joyous because we as Americans celebrate the pride, the respect, and the gift of another peaceful transition of power. Events have overshadowed the joy. It may have been in the best interest of the nation for us to celebrate, but this nation has been deeply scarred, and wounds so deep take a long time and much personal reflection and community strength to heal.

"I know that the attacks of last year hurt us, emotionally as well as personally. I was saddened by President Thorn's decision not to run for reelection, and I was equally saddened when no other candidates chose to run and the voter turnout was so low. But I also understand that America needed time to heal, and healing means drawing and lending strength and support from family and community. Politics means little to a country that has suffered so greatly as America has suffered.

"But as I stand here before you today, on an American's property that was leveled by the attack on Offutt Air Force Base just a few miles away, I call upon my fellow Americans to join me to begin to put America back as leader of the free world. It is time, my friends, to stand tall again. America is still strong. Although its military has suffered incredible losses, we are still safe from any enemy that threatens us, and I promise you we will become stronger still.

"We have been forced by circumstances and evil intentions to rebuild our military forces. I promise you, with the shades of the men and women of Offutt Air Force Base and the other bases destroyed and damaged by nuclear attack as my witnesses, that I will build the most modern, the most effective, and the most powerful Air Force the world has ever seen. I once challenged our military leaders and planners to 'skip a generation' in developing our military forces, to discard the remnants of past wars, ineffective strategies, and outdated thinking. Unfortunately, the events of last year force us now to do exactly that. The structures and weaponry that served us so well for decades have been ripped from us. Now is the time to rebuild them, better and smarter than ever. With God's help and your support, I will do just that.

"I once chided President Thorn when he didn't show up for his own inauguration, choosing instead to march directly into the White House one minute after his term of office began and getting immediately to work. I thought, how can any man be so uncaring, so ignorant of what had just transpired? Here there was taking place a peaceful transition of power of the most powerful nation on Earth, and the new president was completely failing to acknowledge that event in history.

"Some may well be ridiculing me after this, but I'm going to continue President Thorn's example today: I'm going back to Washington, and I'm going to get to work rebuilding our nation and our military forces. I know that few Americans feel like celebrating anyway. But I want all Americans to celebrate, each in your own way. Celebrate by hugging your children, by raising your voices in song, by lowering your heads in prayer, and by offering your strength and your help whenever you can. Celebrate the continuity of the greatest nation on Earth, and do everything you can to make sure our flag still flies and our nation still stands strong and proud.

"I assure you, America still has heroes we can look to for the strength, leadership, and wisdom we need to rebuild." He paused, turned, looked directly at Patrick, and nodded before turning back to the microphone. "We lost many good men and women in the American Holocaust of 2004, but I can tell you, my fellow Americans, that the soldiers who served us so well trained an entire new generation of capable men and women to take their places. Thanks to them, America is in worthy hands.

"As the new commander in chief, I'm telling you this: Mourning time is over. It's time to start the rebuilding. The wounds are well on their way to being healed—now it's time to start exercising the muscles, retraining the mind for the challenges that lie ahead, and getting back into the race— the race to ensure and defend peace, democracy, and freedom here in America and around the world."

And with that, the inauguration of the forty-fourth president of the United States was over. Again there was no applause, no music, no marches, no parades, no cannon salutes. The officials on the dais were quickly led to waiting armored, stretch Suburbans and whisked away, and the crowd was left to depart the ceremony in cold, stony silence, ushered off by troops in full combat gear.

Maureen Hershel and Patrick McLanahan sat in the back of their armored car, holding hands, staring silently out the thick smoked-glass windows. A television broadcast was replaying the swearing-in and address, but they had the sound turned off. No one spoke. The only sound came from Maureen, a quiet gasp of surprise as they passed the skeleton of a billboard on the main highway, blackened and crumpled from the effects of one of the four nuclear blasts that had devastated this area. A single tear rolled down her cheek; she did not have the will to wipe it away.

It felt as if she were on a state visit to some Middle Eastern or African nation that had been embroiled in a long and bloody civil war, like Lebanon or Sudan. But this was America, and she was the new vice president of the United States. And that damage hadn't been caused by rioting, vandalism, or civil war—it had been caused by several thermonuclear explosions, right here in the heartland. It was her problem now.

"It's okay, Maureen," Patrick said. "It will be rebuilt. All of it."

She turned and saw him looking at her carefully, and she smiled contentedly. They hadn't seen very much of each other since he'd returned from combat operations in Siberia and she'd gone on the campaign trail, understated as the campaign had been. But since the election, they'd seen quite a bit of each other. She was with him and his son, Bradley, when he received his third star from former president Thomas Thorn at a Pentagon ceremony, and today he'd been with her at her swearing-in as vice president.

But now she was on her way to Washington, and . . . well,

she might be the vice president, but she had no idea where Patrick was going. She and most of the world had fully expected McLanahan, the hero who'd ended the American Holocaust by leading a sneak attack on Anatoliy Gryzlov's underground bunker and killing the Russian president before he could launch another nuclear strike on the United States, to be chosen as Kevin Martindale's running mate. But Patrick was a military airman, not a politician. Besides, he and Martindale had too much of a history of doing things by circumventing established procedures, if not outright law-breaking. America didn't need that kind of worry now.

"Billboards—or air bases?" she asked.

"Maybe neither," Patrick said. "It's like the president said, Maureen—we've been forced to rebuild. The question becomes, do we rebuild the same things all over again, or do we build something new and different? If there's a better billboard or a better air base, now is the time to make it a reality."

"Martindale got that from you, you know."

"I think I got it from him and Brad Elliott a long time ago," Patrick said. "Brad never looked at a system or attacked a problem like others did, even if it hurt his reputation and his career. Kevin Martindale was smart enough to let him do his thing, even if he was hurt politically. I was content to be a bomber jockey until I met Brad Elliott and Kevin Martindale."

Maureen took a deep breath, and Patrick could hear the little catch of apprehension in her throat. "Jesus, I'm scared," she said. "I have no idea what I'm doing. I'm the vice president of the United States, and I have no idea what that means."

"Yes you do," Patrick said. "You might not know it now, sitting in this cold limo driving past farms and homes leveled by a nuclear bomb, but when you sit down at your desk in the White House and assemble your staff around you and the president asks for your advice, you'll have an answer. You'll know what to do."

She looked at him and smiled, thankful for the reassurance. "Will you come to Washington with me?" she asked.

"If you'd like me to, I will."

"I couldn't do it without you."

"Yes you could," Patrick said. "I'd be happy to be with you, in Washington or anywhere." He turned and stared blankly out the window. "I think the third star was a retirement present from Thorn. He knew I was on my way out before I did."

"You're not out unless you want to be," Maureen said.

"I've led crews and units and commands long enough—I think it's time to support some important people for a while," Patrick said. He turned back and looked at the vice president seated beside him, clasping her hand tightly. "Could you stand to have Bradley and me hanging around, Maureen?"

"Of course I could," she said, a little laugh of joy escaping from her lips as she spoke. But then she averted her eyes, and when she raised them back to his, they were deeply probing, careful to look for any sign of hesitation or equivocation. "The question is, Lieutenant General Patrick Shane McLanahan—could *you* stand to be hanging around *anywhere,* for *any* length of time?"

And her heart, which was moments ago filled with such happiness and love, broke—because he hesitated, and he looked away, and he stared that damnable ten-thousand-yard stare. She held on to his hand tightly, and he did likewise—but she knew he was gone.

The car phone rang in the distinctive two-ring style. An aide reached for it, but Maureen, still unaccustomed to others answering her phone for her, picked it up immediately. "Yes, Mr. President?" she said.

"Call me Kevin in private, Maureen," Martindale said. "Our first order of business once we get back to Washington is to start lining up the Cabinet and senior-adviser posts. We meet with the congressional leadership first thing in the morning, and I want our names and talking points nailed down tight. Too bad we can't fly back together, but that's the rules."

"I'll be ready when I get back, Kevin. You've got my list and my bullets; send over your changes, and we'll merge them together."

"Hope you don't mind, but I'm going to steal Patrick away from you on the trip back. We've got a lot of things to discuss."

Maureen hesitated, looked at Patrick's faraway expression, then said in a sharp but pleasant voice, "In fact, I do mind, Kevin." Patrick glanced at her with surprise through narrowed, quizzical eyes. "When we get back to Washington, you can have him. He's mine until then."

Martindale chuckled. "You crazy kids," he said. "Put him on."

Maureen handed the phone to Patrick. "Yes, Mr. President?" he said.

"I'll tell you the same thing I told Maureen, Patrick: If we're going to work together, I want you to call me Kevin. Save the formalities for the public. I may be the senior partner, but I consider you my partner. Clear?"

"Not exactly, Kevin."

"Feel like wearing a business suit instead of a flight suit for a while?"

"Doing what, sir?"

"Special assistant to the president," Martindale said. "I'm going to ask for an emergency two-hundred-fifty-billion-dollar budget to quickly rebuild strategic offensive and defensive forces. You know there's going to be a huge food fight on Capitol Hill and the Pentagon on what the new force should look like once those kinds of budget numbers are introduced. I want you to help me sort through the noise and help me pick the right programs to support."

"I'm a bomber guy, Kevin," Patrick said. "You know that. Folks think I'm already too biased."

"Can you be honest with me and everyone you deal with, Patrick?" Martindale asked. "I think you can. You saw first-hand what we faced. You need to find the right systems that will help prevent a repeat of those attacks. What do you say?"

Patrick looked at Maureen, took a deep breath, and said, "I'll do it, Mr. President."

"I knew you would. Meeting tomorrow at ten-thirty in the Oval Office—you know the way. Be ready with your plan of action. I want to hit the press with the plan in time for tomorrow's prime-time news. Thanks, my friend. Good to be working with you again." And he hung up.

Patrick replaced the phone on its hook. Maureen looked at him closely—and her heart leaped again. He had that far-away gaze once more—but this time there was fire in those blue eyes. He was no longer looking back into the dead eyes of his friends or scenes of blackened devastation; he was staring into the future, and she could see the excitement lighting up his face.

Maybe someday, she thought, I'll light up his face like that. It was too soon to know if she would ever get that chance, but at least perhaps he was going to be around long enough for her to try.

"Got some phone calls to make, General?" she asked.

"Yes," Patrick replied. He reached over to her face, pulled her gently to him, and kissed her lips. "Just take a minute." He then spoke, "McLanahan to Luger."

BATTLE MOUNTAIN AIR RESERVE BASE, NEVADA
That same time

"Go ahead, Muck," David Luger responded. He was sitting in the superviser of flying's radio truck, out at the approach end of Battle Mountain's twelve-thousand-foot-long runway. His driver's-side window was open slightly, enough for the interior not to fog up and so he could raise a pair of binoculars to his eyes occasionally.

The parking apron and taxiways on the isolated base in north-central Nevada were beehives of activity. Along with the few surviving EB-52 Megafortresses, EB-1C Vampires, and the one remaining AL-52 Dragon aircraft, the two surviving B-2A Spirit stealth bombers had been relocated to the 111th Bombardment Wing at Battle Mountain to undergo modification as QB-2 unmanned bombers. In addition, the first QA-45C "Hunter" unmanned combat air vehicles—slightly smaller versions of the B-2 stealth bomber, capable of carrying ten thousand pounds of ordnance or sensors and attacking targets with pinpoint precision—had been deployed to Battle Mountain for operational tests. The surviving E-4B National Airborne Operations Center command posts, RC-135 reconnaissance planes, KC-135R tankers, C-21 transports, and EC-135 intelligence-gathering aircraft that had been based at Offutt Air Force Base had also been reassigned to Battle Mountain. The Battle Management Center had been redesignated the new U.S. Strategic Command battle-staff area.

"I need you in Washington tonight," Patrick said. "I need the strategic-transformation report we've been working on updated with the latest intelligence and industrial-research data." He paused, then added, "And pack for an extended stay."

"I'll be there," Dave said. He raised the binoculars and focused them on an aircraft preparing to turn base leg in the visual pattern. "Break. Luger to Furness."

"Go ahead."

"You guys just about done playing around? I've got a flight to catch to Washington."

Aboard the EB-1C Vampire bomber in the visual pattern, Major General Rebecca Furness shook her head. "I figured as much," she said. "I'm glad we got our flying in early. You need me to watch the store for a few days?"

"Might be for a lot longer than that, Rebecca."

"Roger that," she said. She turned to her mission commander and remarked on intercom, "Sixth or seventh time the boss has been called away. I have a feeling he's not coming back this time."

"I agree," her mission commander, Brigadier General Daren Mace, replied. He still bore some of the scars on his face and extremities from frostbite after spending almost three days in a life raft in the Bering Sea, but he was now back on full flying status after his rehabilitation.

"I think we're ready to take charge of this place, don't you, General? I'll run the Air Battle Force, and you take over the One-eleventh Bomb Wing. How does that sound?"

"I hate to admit it, Rebecca," Daren said, "but I think I'm ready for a desk job. I love flying, but I think these high-tech birds are getting smarter than me. And I can't keep up with these young sticks. They're trying to tell me I'm too old for this shit, I think."

"They're trying to tell you to stay here, with me. We'll run this place the way *we* think it should be run, and we'll show these hot-shot young techie nerds how the war is supposed to be fought," Rebecca said. "Then, in a few years, when they put us out to pasture, let's build a ranch out here so we can raise a few head of cattle and some horses, take long dips in the hot tub together, and keep an eye on this place—from a distance. How does that sound to you?"

"Perfect," Daren said, patting Rebecca's gloved hand on the center-console control stick of their Vampire bomber, his eyes dancing. "Just perfect."

Books by Dale Brown